MW00852581

PRAIS
THE WEISER BOOK OF OCCULT DETECTIVES

"Timely and elegant; spooky and intriguing; and highly recommended for both readers and writers interested in the great beyond, *The Weiser Book of Occult Detectives* is an amazing collection of stories, sure to delight any reader interested in mysteries, in general, and the supernatural and occult, in particular. But writers of such fiction have much to learn here as well. This compilation will be your go-to read for excellence in occult mysteries for years to come."

—J. T. ELLISON, *New York Times* bestselling author of *Field of Graves* and *Lie to Me.*

"With an excellent introduction by Judika Illes, *The Weiser Book of Occult Detectives* combines well-recognized supernatural sleuths with their colleagues who ought to be well-recognized. For decades, scholars treated the occult detective cross-genre as developing after Sherlock Holmes appeared in 1887—only one or two prototypes glimmering before then. This book continues the new push to show that these characters rose much earlier and, in fact, can be traced to the very start of modern detective fiction. Carefully and creatively chosen works of occult detective fiction follow a smart introduction by Illes."

—TIM PRASIL, author of *Help for the Haunted: A Decade of Vera Van Slyke Ghostly Mysteries* and editor of *Those Who Haunt Ghosts: A Century of Ghost Hunter Fiction* and *Giving Up the Ghosts: Short-Lived Occult Detective Series by Six Renowned Authors*

Edgar Allan Poe is credited with writing the first detective stories and the incredible skills of *ur*-detective C. Auguste Dupin seem at times to be supernatural. The sleuths in *The Weiser Book of Occult Detectives* embrace the uncanny when approaching a mystery and include experts in the esoteric arts, paranormal investigators, and detectives with psychic powers. Judika Illes' informative introduction and notes on each author explain how the thirteen ground-breaking tales in the collection, which date from 1855–1922, helped establish conventions of this fascinating sub-genre and laid the groundwork for today's popular occult detective novels, comics, television series, films, and video games. An entertaining, engaging book providing mystery and otherworldly chills that will have the reader searching out further works by the authors included."

—KAREN LEE STREET, author of *Edgar Allan Poe and the London Monster* and *Writing and Selling Crime Film Screenplays*

"*The Weiser Book of Occult Detectives* is an outstanding collection of classic thrillers that celebrate occult detective work—a genre more appropriate than ever in the current age of paranormal investigations and interests. Settle in for a riveting read!"

—ROSEMARY ELLEN GUILEY, author of *The Encyclopedia of Ghosts and Spirits*

"Dark forces, supernatural powers, and sinister villains: even the most serious occultist has a soft spot in their heart for these tales of what the magical world should be. Containing classics from authors such as Blackwood, Blavatsky, Dion Fortune, and Conan Doyle, among others, these extraordinary tales of the uncanny will delight, fascinate . . . and perhaps terrify."

—LIZ WILLIAMS, author of the Detective Inspector Chen novels and *Diary of a Witchcraft Shop*

"Read *The Weiser Book of Occult Detectives* when you find yourself slumped over your own desk, your typewriter teeth glaring at you, and your lamplight flickering in disgust at your writer's block. Not only will you find inspiration, you will get so lost in the pages that you will forget all about your own dying novel and instead try your hand at solving a mystery by any means possible. Any. Means. Necessary."

—VARLA VENTURA, author of *Fairies, Pookas & Changelings*

"I proudly parade my near lifelong obsession for the occult detective genre in all its forms and guises. That obsession led me to not only pursue a writing career entrenched in the conceits of the genre, but to explore the preternatural outside the realm of fiction as a paranormal investigator. Judika Illes has compiled an amazing collection of occult detective stories, mining some of the best paranormal mysteries the early twentieth century had to offer, written by such legendary authors as Algernon Blackwood, William Hope Hodgson, Sax Rohmer, Dion Fortune, Helena Petrovna Blavatsky, and Sir Arthur Conan Doyle.

"As one devoted to the genre, both as a fan and an author, I understand the awesome task Illes has undertaken. To pore over the sheer volume of early occult detective tales and select the very best and defining tales for a collection such as this would be a maddening endeavor for any scholar, but Judika Illes has done an admirable job of putting together a brilliant and impressive table of contents here. As well read in the genre as I am, Judika Illes has managed to unearth no less than four spectacular tales that had escaped my attention: 'The Dead Hand' by L. T. Meade and Robert Eustace, 'The Vampire' by Alice and Claude Askew, 'The Witness in the Wood' by Rose Champion de Crespigny, and 'The Eyes of Doom' by Ella M. Scrymsour. Whether you are new to the genre or a lifelong fan, *The Weiser Book of Occult Detectives: 13 Stories of Supernatural Sleuthing* is a collection you absolutely cannot do without."

—BOB FREEMAN, the Occult Detective, author of *Shadows Over Somerset*, *Keepers of the Dead,* and The Liber Monstrorum series

The Weiser Book of

OCCULT DETECTIVES

The Weiser Book of

OCCULT DETECTIVES

13 Stories of Supernatural Sleuthing

Edited and Introduced by Judika Illes

WEISER BOOKS

This edition first published in 2017 by Weiser Books, an imprint of
Red Wheel/Weiser, LLC
With offices at:
65 Parker Street, Suite 7
Newburyport, MA 01950
www.redwheelweiser.com

ISBN 978-1-57863-624-2
Library of Congress Cataloging-in-Publication Data available upon request

Cover design by Jim Warner
Cover Imagery: © Symonenko Viktoriia / Shutterstock
Interior by Maureen Forys, Happenstance Type-O-Rama
Typeset in Mrs. Eaves and Futura

Printed in Canada
MAR
10 9 8 7 6 5 4 3 2 1

In memory of my mother, Herta Illes, lover of fine mysteries and juicy stories

CONTENTS

Heartfelt thanks to everyone at Red Wheel/Weiser Books, as well as to Rachel and Jordan Nagengast for their love, support, and especially their patience.

INTRODUCTION

A wise man once told me that mystery is the most essential ingredient of life, for the following reason: mystery creates wonder, which leads to curiosity, which in turn provides the ground for our desire to understand who and what we truly are.

—FROM *THE SECRET HISTORY OF TWIN PEAKS*, by Mark Frost

Angel Heart, Anita Blake, Constantine, Dr. Spektor, Dr. Occult, Death Note, The Dresden Files, Dirk Gently's Holistic Detective Agency, Foucault's Pendulum, Hellblazer, Hellboy, Buffy the Vampire Slayer and its spin-off *Angel, Kolchak: The Night Stalker, Nightwalker: The Midnight Detective, Tokyo Babylon, Penny Dreadful, Supernatural, The X-Files, YuYu Hakusho, Witchblade, Zatanna*

That list above features titles of a small selection of popular entertainment in various genres. They do share something in common: all feature occult detectives. I've let the genres be jumbled, not separating films from comics from television shows from books, because so much overlap exists. For example, occult detective John Constantine first appeared in comics but can now be found in movies and television. *The X-Files,* whose FBI agents Fox Mulder and Dana Scully investigate the paranormal, premiered on television but is now featured in movies, comic books, novels, and a video game.

Occult detectives have evolved into a mainstay of popular entertainment, appearing in books, comics, manga, anime, television shows, movies, and video games. They are sometimes also known as psychic detectives or occasionally as psychic physicians, as many of them, like Dana Scully, are doctors.

What is an occult detective?

Regular detectives solve crimes or mysteries. Occult detectives explore paranormal mysteries or use their own supernatural gifts to solve crimes. To qualify as an occult detective, some sort of supernatural or occult element must exist; although what appears to be supernatural *sometimes* turns out to have rational, mundane, or conventional causes.

Various kinds of occult detectives exist:

✹ Some are detectives who investigate what appear, at least, to be supernatural or paranormal crimes and mysteries. They rely on evidence, as well as their powers of deduction and observation to discover a solution.

✹ Others are well versed in occult lore—they are themselves occultists. This knowledge is used to solve mysteries, both supernatural and mundane.

✹ Still others possess psychic powers of some kind with which they solve crimes, both supernatural and mundane. For example, Norton Vyse uses his powers of psychometry—the ability to gain information by touching an object—whereas Shiela Crerar is clairvoyant.

It is a fluid genre, and how one categorizes some of these detectives will likely depend on the opinions and perceptions of the beholder: Diana Marburg solves crimes through her ability to read palms—does this make her innately psychic, or is she just exceptionally well versed in palmistry?

The examples I gave at the beginning of this introduction are modern, but this genre has long roots. *The Weiser Book of Occult Detectives: 13 Stories of Supernatural Sleuthing* presents some of its foundational material, the original authors and stories that were the genre's inspiration. The stories in *The Weiser Book of Occult Detectives* star both female and male sleuths. The mysteries they tackle include murder, missing funds, demons, ghosts, vampires, and more.

Occult detectives featured include beloved favorites, such as Dr. Hesselius, Thomas Carnacki, and John Silence, but also the unjustly forgotten and obscure, such as Shiela Crerar and Diana Marburg. Techniques utilized by the various detectives include palmistry, clairvoyance, psychometry, mesmerism, dreams, and, of course, good old deductive reasoning.

In the 21st century, *The X-Files* and *Supernatural* are hugely popular. Books on the occult are easy to find and purchase. Television features ghost hunters and mediums. Within that context, the literary genre of the occult detective has been reappraised and is now given scholarly attention. Its lovers have come out from the shadows. This, however, was not always the case. For a very long time, English-language occult detective fiction was considered disreputable, even amongst fans of general detective fiction. To put it plainly, it was widely considered to be the bottom of the bin.

"The Murders in the Rue Morgue," by Edgar Allan Poe, published in 1841, is widely considered to be the first detective story, predating by a year the very word "detective."[1] The story features C. Auguste Dupin, who investigates a mysterious crime. The story is narrated by Dupin's sidekick. In this manner, Poe established a prototype that has been followed in much, although not all, detective fiction and is exemplified by the relationship of the phenomenally more famous Sherlock Holmes and Dr. Watson. Dupin served as the template for Holmes, Monsieur LeCoq, Hercule Poirot, and so many other fictional detectives, including the occult detectives, many of whom have their own sidekick narrators, as you will see in these pages.

Because what we now call paranormal phenomena was—and remains—widely considered to be fraudulent or not *real,* the

---

1 Victor A. Berch, "A Note on the Word 'Detective,'" *Mystery File,* November 8, 2010, *www.mysteryfile.com.*

fictional use of metaphysical solutions or skills within detective fiction was perceived as cheating. Authors of such fiction were scornfully believed to be taking shortcuts, of being lazy, or of not taking the time to create a genuine mystery with a clever, satisfying, and hard-to-guess solution. Sherlock Holmes, who, with his keen powers of observation, noticed clues and caught what others missed, was the ideal.

In 1928, author Willard Huntington Wright, creator of popular detective Philo Vance and writing under his pen name S. S. Van Dine, published "Twenty Rules for Writing Detective Fiction." Rule number eight states, "The problem of the crime must be solved by strictly naturalistic means. Such methods for learning the truth as slate-writing, ouija-boards, mind-reading, spiritualistic séances, crystal-gazing, and the like, are taboo. A reader has a chance when matching his wits with a rationalistic detective, but if he must compete with the world of spirits and go chasing about the fourth dimension of metaphysics, he is defeated *ab initio*."

Of course, that assumes that readers are completely unfamiliar with the world of spirits and metaphysics. That may have been widely true in 1928, but now in the 21st century, perhaps not so much.

Despite its disreputable reputation, however, over the decades, two frequently distinct groups of readers steadfastly carried a torch for occult detectives—fans of pulp fiction and the occultists themselves.

Let's look at each individually.

Pulp fiction and its subset, weird fiction, now often classified as speculative fiction, are literary genres that have historically been treated with as little respect as occult fiction (sometimes considered a subgenre of weird fiction). This type of popular literature was widely considered disposable, even sometimes by their authors and publishers. Typically printed on cheap paper ("pulp"), it was anticipated that they would be read, enjoyed, then thrown away, in the manner of comic books or a daily newspaper. Just as with comic books, however, some readers became passionate fans of the genre, collecting and preserving this literature and debating its merits with one another. It was readers like this who preserved and cataloged the occult detectives, essentially rescuing many of them.

However, among them are many who simultaneously mock the genre, even as they love it, because it seems ridiculous that the supernatural might be real. They may enjoy the literary value of the stories or their history, or they may enjoy the genre, especially because they perceive it as goofy or as truly weird—the weirdest of weird fiction. Alternatively, many favor tales where ghosts or psychic phenomena are ultimately proved to derive from mundane causes—one can simultaneously enjoy the suspense of a ghost story *and* the victory of rationality.

On the other hand, there is another group of devoted readers of occult detective fiction, but these fans have no problem with supernatural elements and solutions. These are the occultists themselves, a growing breed in the 21st century. For those who consider supernatural themes and powers to be plausible and at least in the realm of reality, not merely literary devices or shortcuts, then occult detective stories may be appraised and appreciated in a different light.

This book that you read is not just *any* compilation of occult detective stories. It's the *Weiser* book of occult detectives. "Weiser" refers to Weiser Books, the venerable and highly respected publisher of esoteric books, whose sixtieth year of publishing coincides with the publication of this book. Weiser Books is an outgrowth of the Samuel Weiser Bookshop in New York City, one of the first stores to specialize exclusively in the esoteric. It's easy to imagine that some of the fictional occult detectives in this book—Dr. Taverner, for instance, or Moris Klaw—might have had accounts at this shop.

I write fiction and am a passionate fan of detective stories and mysteries, but, as a modern occultist, I am also the author of non-fiction books devoted to witchcraft, magic spells, the paranormal, and esoteric spirituality. What this means in plain English is that this book was prepared by those who acknowledge that the mysteries of the universe might just possibly be more complex than merely establishing "who done it?"

Occult detective fiction can be considered in the context of regular detective fiction (Dupin, Holmes, and their successors), but it can also be appraised in the context of the occult renaissance of the 19th century. "The Pot of Tulips," the oldest story in *The Weiser Book of Occult Detectives,* was first published in 1855; while the most recent, "The Return of the Ritual," first appeared in 1922. All other stories in this book fall in between those dates.

Let's put this in context:

- ✳ Many metaphysical societies and organizations emerged during this period, most famously the Hermetic Order of the Golden Dawn, the magical organization devoted to the study and practice of metaphysics, the occult, and what would now be called paranormal activity.

- ✳ March 31, 1848 is widely considered the birthdate of modern Spiritualism, as it is the day that the young Fox Sisters ("the Rochester rappers") first made contact with the noisy spirit haunting their upstate New York home.

- ✳ The Ghost Club, believed to be the oldest society dedicated to paranormal research and investigation, was founded in London in 1862. (At least a couple of the fictional detectives in our book appear to be members of this or similar organizations.)

✴ The extreme death toll of the Civil War brought Spiritualism and mediums to the forefront in the United States. People sought confirmation of continued existence after death, in addition to communication with lost loved ones. Previously, divination and communication with the deceased would have been categorized as witchcraft or necromancy and severely punished; this was no longer the case, at least in many places and among the educated, wealthy, and prominent. During Abraham Lincoln's presidency, at least eight séances were held in the White House. It's believed that Lincoln attended at least one.[2] Among the fervent devotees of Spiritualism was Sir Arthur Conan Doyle, creator of Sherlock Holmes and author of the occult detective story, "The Leather Funnel," contained in this volume.

✴ The Theosophical Society was founded in New York City in 1875. Among its cofounders was Helena Blavatsky, the Russian occultist and medium, whose short story, "The Cave of the Echoes," appears in this book.

✴ The spirit board made its American debut in 1880. Although the earliest were homemade, by 1890, manufacturers were mass producing these divination and spirit-communication devices. The most famous example of a spirit board, also known as a witch board, is the Ouija board. The device made it possible for séances to be held privately in one's home without the need to consult professional mediums.

Although some creators of occult detective fiction were simply authors who enjoyed the trope or wished to sell a story, others were genuine occultists. Blavatsky and Dion Fortune, for example,

---

2 Judith Joyce, *The Weiser Field Guide to the Paranormal* (Newburyport, MA: Weiser Books, 2011).

whose fiction is represented in *The Weiser Book of Occult Detectives,* are ranked among the greatest occultists, not only of their time but also of our own. Their influence continues to resonate.

Blavatsky and Fortune are renowned for their occult nonfiction. Few are aware that Blavatsky wrote occult and horror stories. Although they may have been written to earn some much-needed cash, Blavatsky's occult knowledge still features. Fortune and Rose Champion de Crespigny, another author of a story in this book, might not have written occult fiction if only it had been easier to publish metaphysical nonfiction in their day. When these stories were written, it was only possible to publish occult information as fiction—it could only be offered as entertainment.

Prior to the 1951 repeal of the Witchcraft Act of 1604, books that might be interpreted as advocating the practice of witchcraft could not be published in the United Kingdom, where so many occult detective stories originate. (Meanwhile, in the United States, those who mailed occult-related material risked prosecution for using the post office for fraudulent purposes.) Thus, while some of the stories in our collection were written purely for entertaining readers, others contain hidden messages and teachings that their authors could not otherwise publish.

———————⟫●⟪———————

Abraham Van Helsing, the occult physician of Bram Stoker's epistolary novel, *Dracula,* is widely described as the first occult detective. However, *Dracula* was first published in 1897, which is after the publication date of the first three stories in this book. Stoker was familiar with at least one of them, "Green Tea," by his fellow Irishman, J. Sheridan Le Fanu.

However, the concept of someone with superior metaphysical knowledge and skills, who investigates mysteries and solves crimes, existed much earlier, albeit in different cultures and languages. Here are two examples.

Detective rabbis who solve mysteries, supernatural or otherwise, through spiritual and magical means, are a frequent trope in Jewish folklore. Sometimes, like modern occult detectives, they solve supernatural mysteries; in other instances, they themselves must resort to magical means, drawing magical circles and utilizing practical Kabbalah. Whether or not the stories themselves are fictional, they frequently feature historical rabbis, who were held in high esteem by their communities. The stories were told to entertain, as well as to preserve legends.

- ✻ Rabbi Jannai, the 3rd-century sage, uses conventional and magical detecting techniques to solve a missing persons case in the story of "The Rabbi and the Witch," first found in the Babylonian Talmud, tractate Sanhedrin, 67b. AT 430.

- ✻ Judah Loew (c.1513–1609) was the first documented chief rabbi of Moravia before he moved to Prague, where a statue of him now stands and where you can visit his grave. Rabbi Loew, renowned for creating the world's most famous golem, the Golem of Prague, is the hero of many legends. For example, by using magical means, he discovers the root cause of a plague afflicting his community and is empowered to stop it. This legend, retold in the story "The Cause of the Plague" can be found, along with "The Rabbi and the Witch" and other tales of occult detective rabbis, in the anthology *Lilith's Cave: Jewish Tales of the Supernatural* by Howard Schwartz (Oxford University Press, 1988), as well as in other books containing Jewish folktales.

Likewise, the heroes of Chinese *Gong'an* fiction are respected judges and magistrates who solve mysteries that often, although not always, feature supernatural themes. The word *Gong'an* originally referred to a magistrate's bench, desk, or table—the place where he does his work and may be consulted—but it is now translated into English as "crime-case fiction." This genre of literature first appeared during the Song dynasty (960–1279). As with the Jewish tales, whether or not the stories themselves are entirely fictional, the most famous protagonists of these tales are based on actual people who once lived; for example, Judge Bao and Judge Dee.

* Judge Bao is based on Bao Zheng (999–1062), often called Bao Gong ("Lord Bao"), who was a government official during the reign of Emperor Renzong during the Song dynasty. Even now, he is perceived as the epitome of justice. Stories retelling his exploits first appeared in the form of performance art, such as public storytelling and opera. By the Yuan dynasty (1271–1368), written forms of his legends had appeared. His popularity continues unabated, and he appears in modern novels, television series, films, comics, manga, and video games.

* Judge Dee is based on Die Renjie (c.630–700), an official of the Tang and Zhou dynasties. He is featured in numerous novels; the earliest, *Di Gong An* or *Dee Goong An,* was published in the 18th century by an anonymous author.

English-language readers were first introduced to Judge Dee and the *Gong'an* genre by R. H. van Gulik, the Dutch diplomat and sinologist, who translated the stories and used them as the basis for his own versions, first published in English in 1949 as *Celebrated Cases of Judge Dee*. Fictional portrayals of Judge Dee remain immensely popular, both inside and outside China. He appears in comics, novels, television series, and movies, such as *Detective Dee and the Mysteries of the Phantom Flame,* a 2010 Chinese/Hong Kong production, directed by Tsui Hark.

The stories in this book are arranged chronologically by publication date, from the oldest to the most recent. Each story is preceded by a brief introduction with information about its author and its detective. The authors of the stories are a dissimilar lot: Sir

Arthur Conan Doyle, for example, ranks among the most famous of *all* authors, while others are now barely remembered. Considering the era in which these stories were written, women writers are well represented. Of the thirteen tales in our collection, four are written exclusively by women, while another three were coauthored by female and male authors.

The literary genre featuring occult detectives is vast. The stories in this book are just the tip of the iceberg. Other early occult detectives include, in no particular order, Aleister Crowley's Simon Iff, F. Tennyson Jesse's Solange Fontaine, Margery Lawrence's Miles Pennoyer, Arthur Machen's Dyson, Seabury Quinn's Jules de Grandin, and Manly Wade Wellman's Judge Pursuivant.

Be forewarned, these stories are a product of their time. This compilation is intended to provide enjoyment. I hope you love them and occult detectives as much as I do. I've attempted to avoid those stories featuring the prejudices and bias that was so prevalent in the literature of the era in which these stories were first published. Engaging in stereotypes was perceived as acceptable and was so endemic to that era's popular literature that I'm not entirely sure that I've succeeded.

Every effort has been made to maintain the original flavor of the stories as much as possible and so the sharp-eyed among you may see inconsistencies in language and spelling that you may be unaccustomed to seeing in one book. Some stories were written in British English; others in American English. As much as possible, we have left the idiosyncrasies as they were. Language adjusts with time and so you may observe some now anachronistic spelling.

Whatever your orientation and opinions on the occult, may these stories bring you hours of pleasure and enjoyable food for thought.

JUDIKA ILLES, author of *Encyclopedia of Witchcraft,
Encyclopedia of 5,000 Spells, Encyclopedia of Spirits,* and
other books devoted to the magical arts

THE STORIES

THE POT OF TULIPS

Fitz-James O'Brien

Known as the "Celtic Poe," author, playwright, and soldier, Fitz-James O'Brien is now considered among the most significant forerunners of modern science fiction. "The Diamond Lens"—his most famous short story, first published in 1858—ranks among H. P. Lovecraft's favorite tales. O'Brien is also considered among the pioneers of occult detective fiction. Tim Prasil, editor of Giving Up the Ghosts: Short-Lived Occult Detective Series by Six Renowned Authors, *suggests that O'Brien's creation, Harry Escott, might be considered "modern horror literature's first full-fledged occult detective."[3] It is tempting to consider what O'Brien's literary output might have been, if only he had lived longer.*

Michael Fitz-James O'Brien was born in County Cork, Ireland, on December 31, 1828. Little is known of his early life. After graduating from the University of Dublin, O'Brien moved to London, where he became a journalist and blew through an £8,000 inheritance in four years. He immigrated to the United States in approximately 1852. Within a year, he was writing for Harper's Magazine. *In the ten years O'Brien lived in New York City, he wrote almost three hundred magazine and newspaper pieces while maintaining a lively social life. He was considered a member of the Bohemians, a loosely organized group of artists, writers, and creative people that included Walt Whitman as one of its members.*

A social activist, O'Brien volunteered for the Union Army in January 1861, joining the Seventh Regiment of the New York National Guard with the rank of captain. One year later, O'Brien was appointed to the staff of General Frederick W. Lander. Wounded in a skirmish on February 26, 1862, O'Brien never recovered. The wound itself was not serious, but treatment was delayed and initially inadequate. He developed tetanus and died, aged thirty-three, on April 6, 1862, in Cumberland, Maryland.

---

3 Tim Prasil, ed., *Giving Up the Ghosts: Short-Lived Occult Detective Series by Six Renowned Authors* (Greenville, OH: Coachwhip Publications, 2015), 16.

A lavish funeral was held at Green-Wood Cemetery in Brooklyn, New York, where his coffin was placed in a receiving vault. The plan may originally have been to return his body to Ireland, where his mother survived him, but this did not occur. After twelve years in Green-Wood's receiving vault, Fitz-James O'Brien was buried in Public Lot 17263, Section 15, Grave 1183.

Harry Escott, O'Brien's occult detective, appears in only two stories: "A Pot of Tulips" and "What Was It? A Mystery." The latter story, published in 1859, is the more famous of the two. Among the earliest known depictions of invisibility in fiction, "What Was It? A Mystery" predates "The Horla," by Guy de Maupassant, and "The Damned Thing," by Ambrose Bierce, as well as H. G. Wells's novella, The Invisible Man.

"A Pot of Tulips," first published in the November 1855 issue of Harper's New Monthly Magazine, shows the young detective first learning his craft. It's also one of my own personal favorite stories because of its depictions of country life in 19th-century midtown Manhattan, an area extremely familiar to me in its modern and less bucolic incarnation.

Harry Escott displays no supernatural aptitude of his own, although he describes himself as sufficiently "sensitive" to apprehend occult phenomena. He earned the steel nerves required of an occult detective via his extensive esoteric studies.

A Pot of Tulips

TWENTY-EIGHT years ago I went to spend the summer at an old Dutch villa which then lifted its head from the wild country that, in present days, has been tamed down into a site for a Crystal Palace. Madison Square was then a wilderness of fields and scrub oak, here and there diversified with tall and stately elms. Worthy citizens who could afford two establishments rusticated in the groves that then flourished where ranks of brown-stone porticos now form the landscape; and the locality of Fortieth Street, where my summer palace stood, was justly looked upon as at an enterprising distance from the city.

I had an imperious desire to live in this house ever since I can remember. I had often seen it when a boy, and its cool verandas

and quaint garden seemed, whenever I passed, to attract me irre-
sistibly. In after years, when I grew up to man's estate, I was not
sorry, therefore, when one summer, fatigued with the labors of my
business, I beheld a notice in the papers intimating that it was to
be let furnished. I hastened to my dear friend, Jasper Joye, painted
the delights of this rural retreat in the most glowing colors, easily
obtained his assent to share the enjoyments and the expense with
me, and a month afterward we were taking our ease in this new
paradise.

Independent of early associations, other interests attached me
to this house. It was somewhat historical, and had given shelter to
George Washington on the occasion of one of his visits to the city.
Furthermore, I knew the descendants of the family to whom it had
originally belonged. Their history was strange and mournful, and
it seemed to me as if their individuality was somehow shared by
the edifice. It had been built by a Mr. Van Koeren, a gentleman of
Holland, the younger son of a rich mercantile firm at the Hague,
who had emigrated to this country in order to establish a branch of
his father's business in New York, which even then gave indications
of the prosperity it has since reached with such marvellous rapidity.
He had brought with him a fair young Belgian wife; a loving girl, if
I may believe her portrait, with soft brown eyes, chestnut hair, and
a deep, placid contentment spreading over her fresh and innocent
features. Her son, Alain Van Koeren, had her picture an old miniature in a red gold frame as well as that of his father, and in truth,
when looking on the two, one could not conceive a greater contrast
than must have existed between husband and wife. Mr. Van Koeren
must have been a man of terrible will and gloomy temperament.
His face in the picture is dark and austere, his eyes deep-sunken,
and burning as if with a slow, inward fire. The lips are thin and
compressed, with much determination of purpose; and his chin,
boldly salient, is brimful of power and resolution. When first I saw
those two pictures I sighed inwardly and thought, "Poor child! you

must often have sighed for the sunny meadows of Brussels, in the long, gloomy nights spent in the company of that terrible man!"

I was not far wrong, as I afterward discovered. Mr. and Mrs. Van Koeren were very unhappy. Jealousy was his monomania, and he had scarcely been married before his girl-wife began to feel the oppression of a gloomy and ceaseless tyranny. Every man under fifty, whose hair was not white and whose form was erect, was an object of suspicion to this Dutch Bluebeard. Not that he was vulgarly jealous. He did not frown at his wife before strangers, or attack her with reproaches in the midst of her festivities. He was too well-bred a man to bare his private woes to the world. But at night, when the guests had departed and the dull light of the quaint old Flemish lamps but half illuminated the nuptial chamber, then it was that with monotonous invective Mr. Van Koeren crushed his wife. And Marie, weeping and silent, would sit on the edge of the bed listening to the cold, trenchant irony of her husband, who, pacing up and down the room, would now and then stop in his walk to gaze with his burning eyes upon the pallid face of his victim. Even the evidences that Marie gave of becoming a mother did not check him. He saw in that coming event, which most husbands anticipate with mingled joy and fear, only an approaching incarnation of his dishonor. He watched with a horrible refinement of suspicion for the arrival of that being in whose features he madly believed he should but too surely trace the evidences of his wife's crime.

Whether it was that these ceaseless attacks wore out her strength, or that Providence wished to add another chastening misery to her burden of woe, I dare not speculate; but it is certain that one luckless night Mr. Van Koeren learned with fury that he had become a father two months before the allotted time. During his first paroxysm of rage, on the receipt of intelligence which seemed to confirm all his previous suspicions, it was, I believe, with difficulty that he was prevented from slaying both the innocent causes of his resentment. The caution of his race and the presence of the physicians induced him, however, to put a curb upon his furious will until reflection suggested quite as criminal, if not as dangerous, a vengeance. As soon as his poor wife had recovered from her illness, unnaturally prolonged by the delicacy of constitution induced by previous mental suffering, she was astonished to find, instead of increasing his persecutions, that her husband had changed his tactics and treated her with studied neglect. He rarely spoke to her except on occasions when the decencies of society demanded that he should address her. He avoided her presence, and no longer inhabited the same apartments. He seemed, in short, to strive as much as possible to forget her existence. But if she did not suffer from personal ill-treatment it was because a punishment more acute was in store for her. If Mr. Van Koeren had chosen to affect to consider her beneath his vengeance, it was because his hate had taken another direction, and seemed to have derived increased intensity from the alteration.

It was upon the unhappy boy, the cause of all this misery, that the father lavished a terrible hatred. Mr. Van Koeren seemed determined, that, if this child sprang from other loins than his, the mournful destiny which he forced upon him should amply avenge his own existence and the infidelity of his mother. While the child was an infant his plan seemed to have been formed. Ignorance and neglect were the two deadly influences with which he sought to assassinate the moral nature of this boy; and his terrible campaign against the virtue of his own son was, as he grew up, carried into execution with the most consummate generalship. He gave him money, but debarred him from education. He allowed him liberty of action, but withheld advice.

It was in vain that his mother, who foresaw the frightful consequences of such a training, sought in secret by every means in her power to nullify her husband's attempts. She strove in vain to seduce her son into an ambition to be educated. She beheld with horror all her agonized efforts frustrated, and saw her son and only child becoming, even in his youth, a drunkard and a libertine. In the end it proved too much for her strength; she sickened, and went home to her sunny Belgian plains. There she lingered for a few months in a calm but rapid decay, whose calmness was broken but by the one grief; until one autumn day, when the leaves were falling from the limes, she made a little prayer for her son to the good God—and died.

Vain orison! Spendthrift, gamester, libertine, and drunkard by turns, Alain Van Koeren's earthly destiny was unchangeable. The father, who should have been his guide, looked on each fresh depravity of his son's with a species of grim delight. Even the death of his wronged wife had no effect upon his fatal purpose. He still permitted the young man to run blindly to destruction by the course into which he himself had led him.

As years rolled by, and Mr. Van Koeren himself approached to that time of life when he might soon expect to follow his persecuted wife, he relieved himself of the hateful presence of his son altogether. Even the link of a systematic vengeance, which had hitherto united them, was severed, and Alain was cast adrift without either money or principle. The occasion of this final separation between father and son was the marriage of the latter with a girl of humble, though honest extraction. This was a good excuse for the remorseless Van Koeren, so he availed himself of it by turning his son out of doors.

From that time forth they never met. Alain lived a life of meagre dissipation, and soon died, leaving behind him one child, a daughter. By a coincidence natural enough, Mr. Van Koeren's death followed his son's almost immediately. He died as he had lived, sternly. But those who were around his couch in his last moments mentioned some singular facts connected with the manner of his death. A few moments before he expired, he raised himself in the bed, and seemed as if conversing with some person invisible to the spectators. His lips moved as if in speech, and immediately afterward he sank back, bathed in a flood of tears. "Wrong! wrong!" he was heard to mutter, feebly; then he implored passionately the forgiveness of some one who, he said, was present. The death struggle ensued almost immediately, and in the midst of his agony he seemed wrestling for speech. All that could be heard, however, were a few broken words. "I was wrong. My—unfounded—For God's sake, look in—You will find—" Having uttered these fragmentary sentences, he seemed to feel that the power of speech had passed away forever. He fixed his eyes piteously on those around him, and, with a great sigh of grief, expired. I gathered these facts from his granddaughter and Alain's daughter, Alice Van Koeren, who had been summoned by some friend to her grandfather's dying couch when it was too late. It was the first time she had seen him, and then she saw him die.

The results of Mr. Van Koeren's death were a nine days' wonder to all the merchants in New York. Beyond a small sum in the bank, and the house in which he lived, which was mortgaged for its full value, Mr. Van Koeren had died a pauper! To those who knew him and knew his affairs, this seemed inexplicable. Five or six years before his death he had retired from business with a fortune of over a hundred thousand dollars. He had lived quietly since then, was known not to have speculated, and could not have gambled. The question then was, where had his wealth vanished to. Search was made in every secretary, in every bureau, for some document which might throw a light on the mysterious disposition that he had made of his property. None was found. Neither will, nor certificates of stock, nor title deeds, nor bank accounts, were anywhere discernible. Inquiries were made at the offices of companies in which Mr. Van Koeren was known to be largely interested; he had sold out his stock years ago. Real estate that had been believed to be his was found on investigation to have passed into other hands. There could be no doubt that for some years past Mr. Van Koeren had been steadily converting all his property into money, and what he had done with that money no one knew. Alice Van Koeren and her mother, who at the old gentleman's death were at first looked on as millionnaires, discovered, when all was over, that they were no better off than before. It was evident that the old man had made away with his fortune before his death, determined that one who, though bearing his name, he believed not to be of his blood should never inherit his wealth or any share of it—a posthumous vengeance, which was the only one by which the laws of the State of New York relative to inheritance could be successfully extracted.

I took a peculiar interest in the case, and even helped to make some researches after the lost property, not so much, I confess, from a spirit of general philanthropy, as from certain feelings which I experienced toward Alice Van Koeren, the heir to this invisible estate. I had long known both her and her mother, when they were living in honest poverty and earning a scanty subsistence by their own labor; Mrs. Van Koeren worked as an embroideress, and Alice turned to account, as a preparatory governess, the education which her good mother, spite of her limited means, had bestowed on her.

In a few words, then, I loved Alice Van Koeren, and was determined to make her my wife as soon as my means would allow me to support a fitting establishment. My passion had never been declared. I was content for the time with the secret consciousness of my own love, and the no less grateful certainty that Alice returned it, all unuttered as it was. I had, therefore, a double interest in passing the summer at the old Dutch villa, for I felt it to be connected somehow with Alice, and I could not forget the singular desire to inhabit it which I had so often experienced as a boy.

It was a lovely day in June when Jasper Joye and myself took up our abode in our new residence; and as we smoked our cigars on the piazza in the evening we felt for the first time the unalloyed pleasure with which a townsman breathes the pure air of the country.

The house and grounds had a quaint sort of beauty that to me was eminently pleasing. Landscape gardening, in the modern acceptation of the term, was then almost unknown in this country, and the "laying out" of the garden that surrounded our new home would doubtless have shocked Mr. London, the late Mr. Downing, or Sir Thomas Dick Lauder. It was formal and artificial to the last degree. The beds were cut into long parallelograms, rigid and severe of aspect, and edged with prim rows of stiff dwarf box. The walks, of course, crossed always at right angles, and the laurel and cypress trees that grew here and there were clipped into cones, and spheres, and rhomboids. It is true that, at the time my friend and I hired the house, years of neglect had restored to this formal garden somewhat of the raggedness of nature. The box edgings were rank and wild. The clipped trees, forgetful of geometric propriety, flourished into unauthorized boughs and rebel offshoots. The walks were green with moss, and the beds of Dutch tulips, which had been planted in the shape of certain gorgeous birds, whose colors were represented by masses of blossoms, each of a single hue, had transgressed their limits, and the purple of a parrot's wings might have been seen running recklessly into the crimson of his head. As bulbs, however well-bred, *will* create other bulbs, the flower-birds of this queer old Dutch garden became in time abominably distorted in shape; flamingoes with humps, golden pheasants with legs preternaturally elongated, macaws afflicted with an attack of hydrocephalus. Each species of deformity was proportioned to the rapidity with which the roots had spread in some particular direction. Still, this strange mixture of raggedness and formality, this conglomerate of nature and art, had its charms. It was pleasant to watch the struggle, as it were, between the opposing elements, and to see nature triumphing by degrees in every direction.

Then the house itself was pleasant and commodious. Rooms that, though not lofty, were spacious; wide windows, and cool piazzas extending over the four sides of the building; and a collection of antique carved furniture, some of which, from its elaborateness, might well have come from the chisel of Master Grinling Gibbons. There was a mantel-piece in the dining-room, with which I remember being very much struck when first I came to take possession. It was a singular and fantastical piece of carving. It was a perfect tropical garden, menagerie, and aviary, in one. Birds, beasts, and flowers were sculptured on the wood with exquisite correctness of detail, and painted with the hues of nature. The Dutch taste for color was here fully gratified. Parrots, love-birds, scarlet lories, blue-faced baboons, crocodiles, passion-flowers, tigers, Egyptian lilies, and Brazilian butterflies, were all mixed in gorgeous confusion. The artist, whoever he was, must have been an admirable naturalist, for the ease and freedom of his carving were only equalled by the wonderful accuracy with which the different animals were represented. Altogether it was one of those oddities of Dutch conception, whose strangeness was in this instance redeemed by the excellence of the execution.

Such was the establishment that Jasper Joye and myself were to inhabit for the summer months.

"What a strange thing it was," said Jasper, as we lounged on the piazza together the night of our arrival, "that old Van Koeren's property should never have turned up!"

"It is a question with some people whether he had any at his death," I answered.

"Pshaw! every one knows that he did not or could not have lost that with which he retired from business."

"It is strange," said I, thoughtfully, "yet every possible search has been made for documents that might throw light on the mystery. I have myself sought in every quarter for traces of this lost wealth—but in vain."

"Perhaps he buried it," suggested Jasper, laughing; "if so, we may find it here in a hole one fine morning."

"I think it much more likely that he destroyed it," I replied. "You know he never could be got to believe that Alain Van Koeren was his son, and I believe him quite capable of having flung all his money into the sea in order to prevent those whom he considered not of his blood inheriting it, which they must have done under our laws."

"I am sorry that Alice did not become an heiress, both for your sake and hers. She is a charming girl."

Jasper, from whom I concealed nothing, knew of my love.

"As to that," I answered, "it is little matter. I shall in a year or two be independent enough to marry, and can afford to let Mr. Van Koeren's cherished gold sleep wherever he has concealed it."

"Well, I'm off to bed," said Jasper, yawning. "This country air makes one sleepy early. Be on the lookout for trap-doors and all that sort of thing, old fellow. Who knows but the old chap's dollars will turn up. Good night!"

"Good night, Jasper!"

So we parted for the night. He to his room, which lay on the west side of the building; I to mine on the east, situated at the end of a long corridor and exactly opposite to Jasper's.

The night was very still and warm. The clearness with which I heard the song of the katydid and the croak of the bull-frog seemed to make the silence more distinct. The air was dense and breathless, and, although longing to throw wide my windows, I dared not; for, outside, the ominous trumpetings of an army of mosquitoes sounded threateningly.

I tossed on my bed oppressed with the heat; kicked the sheets into every spot where they ought not to be; turned my pillow every two minutes in the hope of finding a cool side; in short, did everything that a man does when he lies awake on a very hot night and cannot open his window.

Suddenly, in the midst of my miseries, and when I had made up my mind to fling open the casement in spite of the legion of mosquitoes that I knew were hungrily waiting outside, I felt a continuous stream of cold air blowing upon my face. Luxurious as the sensation was, I could not help starting as I felt it. Where could this draught come from? The door was closed; so were the windows. It did not come from the direction of the fireplace, and, even if it did, the air without was too still to produce so strong a current. I rose in my bed and gazed round the room, the whole of which, though only lit by a dim twilight, was still sufficiently visible. I thought at first it was a trick of Jasper's, who might have provided himself with a bellows or a long tube; but a careful investigation of the apartment convinced me that no one was present. Besides, I had locked the door, and it was not likely that any one had been concealed in the room before I entered it. It was exceedingly strange; but still the draught of cool wind blew on my face and chest, every now and then changing its direction, sometimes on one side, sometimes on the other. I am not constitutionally nervous, and had been too long accustomed to reflect on philosophical subjects to become the prey of fear in the presence of mysterious phenomena. I had devoted much time to the investigation of what are popularly called supernatural matters, by those who have not reflected or examined sufficiently to discover that none of these apparent miracles are super-natural, but all, however singular, directly dependent on certain natural laws. I became speedily convinced, therefore, as I sat up in my bed peering into the dim recesses of my chamber, that this mysterious wind was the effect or forerunner of a supernatural visitation, and I mentally determined to investigate it, as it developed itself, with a philosophical calmness.

"Is any one in this room?" I asked, as distinctly as I could. No reply; while the cool wind still swept over my cheek. I knew, in the case of Elizabeth Eslinger, who was visited by an apparition while in the Weinsberg jail,[4] and whose singular and apparently authentic experiences were made the subject of a book by Dr. Kerner, that the manifestation of the spirit was invariably accompanied by such a breezy sensation as I now experienced. I therefore gathered my will, as it were, into a focus, and endeavored, as much as lay in my power, to put myself in accord with the disembodied spirit, if such there were, knowing that on such conditions alone would it be enabled to manifest itself to me.

Presently it seemed as if a luminous cloud was gathering in one corner of the room, a sort of dim phosphoric vapor, shadowy and ill-defined. It changed its position frequently, sometimes coming nearer and at others retreating to the furthest end of the room. As it grew intenser and more radiant, I observed a sickening and corpse-like odor diffuse itself through the chamber, and, despite my anxiety to witness this phenomenon undisturbed, I could with difficulty conquer a feeling of faintness which oppressed me.

The luminous cloud now began to grow brighter and brighter as I gazed. The horrible odor of which I have spoken did not cease to oppress me, and gradually I could discover certain lines making themselves visible in the midst of this lambent radiance. These lines took the form of a human figure, a tall man, clothed in a long dressing-robe, with a pale countenance, burning eyes, and a very bold and prominent chin. At a glance I recognized the original of the picture of old Van Koeren that I had seen with Alice. My interest was now aroused to the highest point; I felt that I stood face

---

4 The case of Elizabeth Eslinger, a ghost seer who was troubled by a ghostly apparition while incarcerated in the Weinsberg jail, is discussed in Catherine Crowe's 1848 book, *The Night Side of Nature: Or, Ghosts and Ghost Seers.* Presumably, O'Brien read it—the book is mentioned in O'Brien's story "What Was It? A Mystery."

to face with a spirit, and doubted not that I should learn the fate of the old man's mysteriously concealed wealth.

The spirit presented a very strange appearance. He himself was not luminous, except some tongues of fire that seemed to proceed from the tips of his fingers, but was completely surrounded by a thin gauze of light, so to speak, through which his outlines were visible. His head was bare, and his white hair fell in huge masses around his stern, saturnine face. As he moved on the floor, I distinctly heard a strange crackling sound, such as one hears when a substance has been overcharged with electricity. But the circumstance that seemed to me most incomprehensible connected with the apparition was that Yan Koeren held in both hands a curiously painted flower-pot, out of which sprang a number of the most beautiful tulips in full blossom. He seemed very uneasy and agitated, and moved about the room as if in pain, frequently bending over the pot of tulips as if to inhale their odor, then holding it out to me, seemingly in the hope of attracting my attention to it. I was, I confess, very much puzzled. I knew that Mr. Van Koeren had in his lifetime devoted much of his leisure to the cultivation of flowers, importing from Holland the most expensive and rarest bulbs; but how this innocent fancy could trouble him after death I could not imagine. I felt assured, however, that some important reason lay at the bottom of this spectral eccentricity, and determined to fathom it if I could.

"What brings you here?" I asked audibly, at the same time directing mentally the question to the spirit with all the power of my will. He did not seem to hear me, but still kept moving uneasily about, with the crackling noise I have mentioned, and holding the pot of tulips toward me.

"It is evident," I said to myself, "that I am not sufficiently en rapport with this spirit for him to make himself understood by speech. He has, therefore, recourse to symbols. The pot of tulips is a symbol. But of what?"

Thus reflecting on these things I continued to gaze upon the spirit. While observing him attentively, he approached my bedside by a rapid movement, and laid one hand on my arm. The touch was icy cold, and pained me at the moment. Next morning my arm was swollen, and marked with a round blue spot. Then, passing to my bedroom-door, the spirit opened it and went out, shutting it behind him. Catching for a moment at the idea that I was the dupe of a trick, I jumped out of bed and ran to the door. It was locked with the key on the inside, and a brass safety-bolt, which lay above the lock, shot safely home. All was as I had left it on going to bed. Yet I declare most solemnly, that, as the ghost made his exit, I not only saw the door open, but I saw the corridor outside, and distinctly observed a large picture of William of Orange that hung just opposite to my room. This to me was the most curious portion of the phenomena I had witnessed. Either the door had been opened by the ghost, and the resistance of physical obstacles overcome in some amazing manner, because in this case the bolts must have been replaced when the ghost was outside the door, or he must have had a sufficient magnetic rapport with my mind to impress upon it the belief that the door was opened, and also to conjure up in my brain the vision of the corridor and the picture, features that I should have seen if the door had been opened by any ordinary physical agency.

The next morning at breakfast I suppose my manner must have betrayed me, for Jasper said to me, after staring at me for some time, "Why, Harry Escott, what's the matter with you? You look as if you had seen a ghost!"

"So I have, Jasper."

Jasper, of course, burst into a loud fit of laughter, and said he'd shave my head and give me a shower-bath.

"Well, you may laugh," I answered, "but you shall see it to-night, Jasper."

He became serious in a moment, I suppose there was something earnest in my manner that convinced him that my words were not idle, and asked me to explain. I described my interview as accurately as I could.

"How did you know that it was old Van Koeren?" he asked.

"Because I have seen his picture a hundred times with Alice," I answered, "and this apparition was as like it as it was possible for a ghost to be like a miniature."

"You must not think I'm laughing at you, Harry," he continued, "but I wish you would answer this. We have all heard of ghosts, ghosts of men, women, children, dogs, horses, in fact every living animal; but hang me if ever I heard of the ghost of a flower-pot before."

"My dear Jasper, you would have heard of such things if you had studied such branches of learning. All the phenomena I witnessed last night are supportable by well-authenticated facts. The cool wind has attended the appearance of more than one ghost, and Baron Reichenbach asserts that his patients, who you know are for the most part sensitive to apparitions, invariably feel this wind when a magnet is brought close to their bodies. With regard to the flower-pot about which you make so merry, it is to me the least wonderful portion of the apparition. When a ghost is unable to find a person of sufficient receptivity, in order to communicate with him by speech it is obliged to have recourse to symbols to express its wishes. These it either creates by some mysterious power out of the surrounding atmosphere, or it impresses, by magnetic force on the mind of the person it visits, the form of the symbol it is anxious to have represented. There is an instance mentioned by Jung Stilling of a student at Brunswick, who appeared to a professor of his college, with a picture in his hands, which picture had a hole in it that the ghost thrust his head through. For a long time this symbol was a mystery; but the student was persevering, and appeared every night with his head through the picture, until at last it was discovered that, before he died, he had got some painted slides for a magic lantern from a shopkeeper in the town, which had not been paid for at his death; and when the debt had been discharged, he and his picture vanished forevermore. Now here was a symbol distinctly bearing on the question at issue. This poor student could find no better way of expressing his uneasiness at the debt for the painted slides than by thrusting his head through a picture. How he conjured up the picture I cannot pretend to explain, but that it was used as a symbol is evident."

"Then you think the flower-pot of old Van Koeren is a symbol?"

"Most assuredly, the pot of tulips he held was intended to express that which he could not speak. I think it must have had some reference to his missing property, and it is our business to discover in what manner."

"Let us go and dig up all the tulip beds," said Jasper, "who knows but he may have buried his money in one of them?"

I grieve to say that I assented to Jasper's proposition, and on that eventful day every tulip in that quaint old garden was ruthlessly uprooted. The gorgeous macaws, and ragged parrots, and long-legged pheasants, so cunningly formed by those brilliant flowers, were that day exterminated. Jasper and I had a regular battue amidst this floral preserve, and many a splendid bird fell before our unerring spades. We, however, dug in vain. No secret coffer turned up out of the deep mould of the flower-beds. We evidently were not on the right scent. Our researches for that day terminated, and Jasper and myself waited impatiently for the night.

It was arranged that Jasper should sleep in my room. I had a bed rigged up for him near my own, and I was to have the additional assistance of his senses in the investigation of the phenomena that we so confidently expected to appear.

The night came. We retired to our respective couches, after carefully bolting the doors, and subjecting the entire apartment to the strictest scrutiny, rendering it totally impossible that a secret entrance should exist unknown to us. We then put out the lights, and awaited the apparition.

We did not remain in suspense long. About twenty minutes after we retired to bed, Jasper called out, "Harry, I feel the cool wind!"

"So do I," I answered, for at that moment a light breeze seemed to play across my temples.

"Look, look, Harry!" continued Jasper in a tone of painful eagerness, "I see a light there in the corner!"

It was the phantom. As before, the luminous cloud appeared to gather in the room, growing more and more intense each minute. Presently the dark lines mapped themselves out, as it were, in the midst of this pale, radiant vapor, and there stood Mr. Van Koeren, ghastly and mournful as ever, with the pot of tulips in his hands.

"Do you see it?" I asked Jasper.

"My God! yes," said Jasper, in a low voice. "How terrible he looks!"

"Can you speak to me, to-night?" I said, addressing the apparition, and again concentrating my will upon my question. "If so, unburden yourself. We will assist you, if we can."

There was no reply. The ghost preserved the same sad, impassive countenance; he had heard me not. He seemed in great distress on this occasion, moving up and down, and holding out the pot of tulips imploringly toward me, each motion of his being accompanied by the crackling noise and the corpse-like odor. I felt sorely troubled myself to see this poor spirit torn by an endless grief, so anxious to communicate to me what lay on his soul, and yet debarred by some occult power from the privilege.

"Why, Harry," cried Jasper after a silence, during which we both watched the motions of the ghost intently, "why, Harry, my boy, there are two of them!"

Astonished by his words, I looked around, and became immediately aware of the presence of a second luminous cloud, in the midst of which I could distinctly trace the figure of a pale but lovely woman. I needed no second glance to assure me that it was the unfortunate wife of Van Koeren.

"It is his wife, Jasper," I replied; "I recognize her, as I have recognized her husband, by the portrait."

"How sad she looks!" exclaimed Jasper in a low voice.

She did indeed look sad. Her face, pale and mournful, did not, however, seem convulsed with sorrow, as was her husband's. She seemed to be oppressed with a calm grief, and gazed with a look of interest that was painful in its intensity, on Van Koeren. It struck me, from his air, that, though she saw him, he did not see her. His whole attention was concentrated on the pot of tulips, while Mrs. Van Koeren, who floated at an elevation of about three feet from the floor, and thus overtopped her husband, seemed equally absorbed in the contemplation of his slightest movement. Occasionally she would turn her eyes on me, as if to call my attention to her companion, and then, returning, gaze on him with a sad, womanly, half-eager smile, that to me was inexpressibly mournful.

There was something exceedingly touching in this strange sight; these two spirits so near, yet so distant. The sinful husband torn with grief and weighed down with some terrible secret, and so blinded by the grossness of his being as to be unable to see the wife-angel who was watching over him; while she, forgetting all her wrongs, and attracted to earth by perhaps the same human sympathies, watched from a greater spiritual height, and with a tender interest, the struggles of her suffering spouse.

"By Jove!" exclaimed Jasper, jumping from his bed, "I know what it means now."

"What does it mean?" I asked, as eager to know as he was to communicate.

"Well, that flower-pot that the old chap is holding." Jasper, I grieve to say, was rather profane.

"Well, what of that flower-pot?"

"Observe the pattern. It has two handles made of red snakes, whose tails twist round the top and form a rim. It contains tulips of three colors, yellow, red, and purple."

"I see all that as well as you do. Let us have the solution."

"Well, Harry, my boy! don't you remember that there is just such a flower-pot, tulips, snakes and all, carved on the queer old painted mantel-piece in the dining-room."

"So there is!" and a gleam of hope shot across my brain, and my heart beat quicker.

"Now as sure as you are alive, Harry, the old fellow has concealed something important behind that mantel-piece."

"Jasper, if ever I am Emperor of France, I will make you chief of police; your inductive reasoning is magnificent."

Actuated by the same impulse, and without another word, we both sprang out of bed and lit a candle. The apparitions, if they remained, were no longer visible in the light. Hastily throwing on some clothes, we rushed down stairs to the dining-room, determined to have the old mantel-piece down without loss of time. We had scarce entered the room when we felt the cool wind blowing on our faces.

"Jasper," said I, "they are here!"

"Well," answered Jasper, "that only confirms my suspicions that we are on the right track this time. Let us go to work. See! here's the pot of tulips."

This pot of tulips occupied the centre of the mantelpiece, and served as a nucleus round which all the fantastic animals sculptured elsewhere might be said to gather. It was carved on a species of raised shield, or boss, of wood, that projected some inches beyond the plane of the remainder of the mantel-piece. The pot itself was painted a brick color. The snakes were of bronze color, gilt, and the tulips yellow, red, and purple were painted after nature with the most exquisite accuracy.

For some time Jasper and myself tugged away at this projection without any avail. We were convinced that it was a movable panel of some kind, but yet were totally unable to move it. Suddenly it struck me that we had not yet twisted it. I immediately proceeded to apply all my strength, and after a few seconds of vigorous exertion I had the satisfaction of finding it move slowly round. After giving it half a dozen turns, to my astonishment the long upper panel of the mantel-piece fell out toward us, apparently on concealed hinges, after the manner of the portion of *escritoires* that is used as a writing-table. Within were several square cavities sunk in the wall, and lined with wood. In one of these was a bundle of papers.

We seized these papers with avidity, and hastily glanced over them. They proved to be documents vouching for property to the amount of several hundred thousand dollars, invested in the name of Mr. Van Koeren in a certain firm at Bremen, who, no doubt, thought by this time that the money would remain unclaimed forever. The desires of these poor troubled spirits were accomplished. Justice to the child had been given through the instrumentality of the erring father.

The formulas necessary to prove Alice and her mother sole heirs to Mr. Van Koeren's estate were briefly gone through, and the poor governess passed suddenly from the task of teaching stupid children to the envied position of a great heiress. I had ample reason afterward for thinking that her heart did not change with her fortunes.

That Mr. Van Koeren became aware of his wife's innocence, just before he died, I have no doubt. How this was manifested I cannot of course say, but I think it highly probably that his poor wife herself was enabled at the critical moment of dissolution, when the link that binds body and soul together is attenuated to the last thread, to put herself in accord with her unhappy husband.

Hence his sudden starting up in his bed, his apparent conversation with some invisible being, and his fragmentary disclosures, too broken, however, to be comprehended.

The question of apparitions has been so often discussed that I feel no inclination to enter here upon the truth or fallacy of the ghostly theory. I myself believe in ghosts. Alice, my wife—for we are married, dear reader—believes in them firmly. If it suited me to do so, I could overwhelm you with a scientific theory of my own on the subject, reconciling ghosts and natural phenomena. I will spare you, however, for I intend to deliver a lecture on the subject at Hope Chapel this winter, and if I disclosed my theory now, some one of our "gifted lecturers" would perhaps forestall me and make "his arrangements for the season" on the strength of my ideas. Anyone, however, who wishes to investigate this subject will find an opportunity by addressing a note to Mr. Harry Escott, care of the publishers of this Magazine.

GREEN TEA

J. Sheridan Le Fanu

Many consider Dr. Martin Hesselius, who makes his debut in "Green Tea"—albeit posthumously—to be Western literature's first occult detective, and he was the first famous one. The character served as inspiration for Abraham Van Helsing, whose name is almost an anagram of Hesselius—possibly Bram Stoker's sly little tribute to his fellow Irishman, Le Fanu, and to "Carmilla," a vampire story from the casebooks of Dr. Hesselius in which anagrams play a major role.

A specialist in metaphysical medicine, Hesselius claims no magic powers or supernatural gifts. Instead, his detecting arsenal consists of a vast accumulation of information, knowledge, and intuition, deriving from his incessant studies and travels. He appears in In a Glass Darkly, *a collection of five tales by Le Fanu— two the length of novellas, including "Carmilla"—first published in 1872. These tales derive from the casebooks of the deceased doctor about whom very little is actually known. Narrative is provided—and filtered—by Dr. Hesselius's unnamed medical secretary and executor. The title of the collection,* In a Glass Darkly, *is an intentional garbling of 1 Corinthians 13:12, rendered in the King James Bible as, "For now we see through a glass, darkly, but then face to face."*

In this story, Le Fanu, like so many other authors of occult detective fiction, allows readers to decide for themselves whether a mystery is truly supernatural or mundane. Is the situation that Jennings describes to Dr. Hesselius really occurring, or is Jennings delusional or suffering from stress or mental illness? Has green tea really opened Jennings's spiritual inner eye, enabling him to see what others cannot?

For those quick to dismiss Hesselius's diagnosis, it may be worth noting that at least one National Health website suggests that when more than eight to ten cups of green tea are drunk per day, symptoms of anxiety, delirium, agitation, and psychosis may occur." [5] *And for those like me, who are enthusiastic fans of green tea, don't worry: Dr. Hesselius points out that, while green tea may have stimulated Jennings's troubles, his final course of action was predicated by other factors, as well.*

Irish author Joseph Thomas Sheridan Le Fanu (1814—1873), a pioneer of the ghost story and the supernatural tale, was born into a literary family in Dublin. His father was a stern Church of Ireland clergyman. Le Fanu studied law at Trinity College but preferred literature. He is acclaimed as a master of the supernatural tale.

Green Tea

PROLOGUE

MARTIN HESSELIUS,
THE GERMAN PHYSICIAN

THOUGH CAREFULLY EDUCATED in medicine and surgery, I have never practised either. The study of each continues, nevertheless, to interest me profoundly. Neither idleness nor caprice caused my secession from the honourable calling which I had just entered. The cause was a very trifling scratch inflicted by a dissecting knife. This trifle cost me the loss of two fingers, amputated promptly, and the more painful loss of my health, for I have never been quite well since, and have seldom been twelve months together in the same place.

In my wanderings I became acquainted with Dr Martin Hesselius, a wanderer like myself, like me a physician, and like me an enthusiast in his profession. Unlike me in this, that his wanderings were voluntary, and he a man, if not of fortune, as we estimate fortune in England, at least in what our forefathers used to term "easy circumstances." He was an old man when I first saw him; nearly five-and-thirty years my senior.

---

5 Theodore Dalrymple, "Green Tea and Monkey Business," The *BMJ,* May 5, 2007, *www.ncbi.nlm.nih.gov.*

In Dr. Martin Hesselius I found my master. His knowledge was immense, his grasp of a case was an intuition. He was the very man to inspire a young enthusiast like me with awe and delight. My admiration has stood the test of time and survived the separation of death. I am sure it was well-founded.

For nearly twenty years I acted as his medical secretary. His immense collection of papers he has left in my care, to be arranged, indexed and bound. His treatment of some of these cases is curious. He writes in two distinct characters. He describes what he saw and heard as an intelligent layman might; and when in this style of narrative he had seen the patient either through his own hall-door to the light of day, or through the gates of darkness to the caverns of the dead, he returns upon the narrative, and in the terms of his art, and with all the force and originality of genius, proceeds to the work of analysis, diagnosis and illustration.

Here and there a case strikes me as of a kind to amuse or horrify a lay reader with an interest quite different from the peculiar one which it may possess for an expert. With slight modifications, chiefly of language, and of course a change of names, I copy the following. The narrator is Dr Martin Hesselius. I find it among the voluminous notes of cases which we made during a tour in England about sixty-four years ago.

It is related to a series of letters to his friend Professor Van Loo of Leyden. The professor was not a physician, but a chemist, and a man who read history and metaphysics and medicine, and had, in his day, written a play.

The narrative is therefore, if somewhat less valuable as a medical record, necessarily written in a manner more likely to interest an unlearned reader.

These letters, from a memorandum attached, appear to have been returned, on the death of the professor in 1819, to Dr Hesselius. They are written, some in English, some in French, but the greater part in German. I am a faithful, though I am conscious by no means a graceful translator, and although here and there I omit some passages, and shorten others, and disguise names, I have interpolated nothing.

CHAPTER I

DR HESSELIUS RELATES HOW
HE MET THE REV. MR JENNINGS

The Rev. Mr Jennings is tall and thin. He is middle-aged, and dresses with a natty, old-fashioned high-church precision. He is naturally a little stately, but not at all stiff. His features, without being handsome, are well formed, and their expression extremely kind, but also shy.

I met him one evening at Lady Mary Heyduke's. The modesty and benevolence of his countenance are extremely prepossessing.

We were but a small party, and he joined agreeably enough in the conversation. He seems to enjoy listening very much more than contributing to the talk; but what he says is always to the purpose and well said. He is a great favourite of Lady Mary's, who it seems, consults him upon many things, and thinks him the most happy and blessed person on earth. Little knows she about him.

The Rev. Mr Jennings is a bachelor, and has, they say, sixty thousand pounds in the funds. He is a charitable man. He is most anxious to be actively employed in his sacred profession, and yet, though always tolerably well elsewhere, when he goes down to his vicarage in Warwickshire, to engage in the actual duties of his sacred calling, his health soon fails him, and in a very strange way. So says Lady Mary.

There is no doubt that Mr Jennings' health does break down in generally a sudden and mysterious way, sometimes in the very act of officiating in his old and pretty church at Kenlis. It may be his heart, it may be his brain. But so it has happened, three or four times or oftener, that after proceeding a certain way in the service, he has on a sudden stopped short; and after a silence, apparently quite unable to resume, he has fallen into solitary, inaudible prayer, his hands and his eyes uplifted, and then pale as death, and in the agitation of a strange shame and horror, descended trembling, and got into the vestry-room, leaving his congregation, without explanation, to themselves. This occurred when his curate was absent. When he goes down to Kenlis now, he always takes care to provide a clergyman to share his duty, and to supply his place on the instant should he become thus suddenly incapacitated.

When Mr Jennings breaks down quite, and beats a retreat from the vicarage, and returns to London—where, in a dark street off Piccadilly, he inhabits a very narrow house—Lady Mary says that he is always perfectly well. I have my own opinion about that. There are degrees, of course. We shall see.

Mr Jennings is a perfectly gentlemanlike man. People, however, remark something odd. There is an impression a little ambiguous. One thing which certainly contributes to it, people I think don't remember or, perhaps, distinctly remark. But I did, almost immediately. Mr Jennings has a way of looking sidelong upon the carpet, as if his eye followed the movements of something there. This, of course, is not always. It occurs only now and then. But often enough to give a certain oddity, as I have said, to his manner, and in this glance travelling along the floor there is something both shy and anxious.

A medical philosopher, as you are good enough to call me, elaborating theories by the aid of cases sought out by himself and by him watched and scrutinized with more time at command, and consequently infinitely more minuteness than the ordinary practitioner can afford, falls insensibly into habits of observation, which accompany him everywhere, and are exercised, as some people would say, impertinently, upon every subject that presents itself with the least likelihood of rewarding inquiry.

There was a promise of this kind in the slight, timid, kindly, but reserved gentleman, whom I met for the first time at this agreeable little evening gathering. I observed, of course, more than I here set down; but I reserve all that borders on the technical for a strictly scientific paper.

I may remark, that when I here speak of medical science, I do so, as I hope some day to see it more generally understood, in a much more comprehensive sense than its generally material treatment would warrant. I believe the entire natural world is but the ultimate expression of that spiritual world from which, and in which alone, it has its life. I believe that the essential man is a spirit, that the spirit is an organized substance, but as different in point of material from what we ordinarily understand by matter, as light or electricity is; that the material body is, in the most literal sense, a vesture, and death consequently no interruption of the living man's existence, but simply his extrication from the natural body—a process which commences at the moment of what we term death, and the completion of which, at furthest a few days later, is the resurrection "in power."

The person who weighs the consequences of these positions will probably see their practical bearing upon medical science. This is, however, by no means the proper place for displaying the proofs and discussing the consequences of this too generally unrecognized state of facts.

In pursuance of my habit, I was covertly observing Mr Jennings with all my caution—I think he perceived it—and I saw plainly that he was as cautiously observing me. Lady Mary happening to address me by name, as Dr Hesselius, I saw that he glanced at me more sharply, and then became thoughtful for a few minutes.

After this, as I conversed with a gentleman at the other end of the room, I saw him look at me more steadily, and with an interest which I thought I understood. I then saw him take an opportunity of chatting with Lady Mary, and was, as one always is, perfectly aware of being the subject of a distant inquiry and answer.

This tall clergyman approached me by-and-by; and in a little time we had got into conversation. When two people who like reading, and know books and places, having travelled, wish to discourse, it is very strange if they can't find topics. It was not accident that brought him near me, and led him into conversation. He knew German, and had read my *Essays on Metaphysical Medicine*, which suggest more than they actually say.

This courteous man, gentle, shy, plainly a man of thought and reading, who, moving and talking among us, was not altogether of us, and whom I already suspected of leading a life whose transactions and alarms were carefully concealed, with an impenetrable reserve from, not only the world, but his best beloved friends—was cautiously weighing in his own mind the idea of taking a certain step with regard to me.

I penetrated his thoughts without his being aware of it, and was careful to say nothing which could betray to his sensitive vigilance my suspicions respecting his position, or my surmises about his plans respecting myself.

We chatted upon different subjects for a time, but at last he said:

"I was very much interested by some papers of yours, Dr Hesselius, upon what you term Metaphysical Medicine—I read them in German, ten or twelve years ago—have they been translated?"

"No, I'm sure they have not—I should have heard. They would have asked my leave, I think."

"I asked the publishers here, a few months ago, to get the book for me in the original German; but they tell me it is out of print."

"So it is, and has been for some years; but it flatters me as an author to find that you have not forgotten my little book, although," I added laughing, "ten or twelve years is a considerable time to have managed without it; but I suppose you have been turning the subject over again in your mind, or something has happened lately to revive your interest in it."

At this remark, accompanied by a glance of inquiry, a sudden embarrassment disturbed Mr Jennings, analogous to that which makes a young lady blush and look foolish. He dropped his eyes, and folded his hands together uneasily, and looked oddly, and you would have said guiltily, for a moment.

I helped him out of his awkwardness in the best way, by appearing not to observe it; and going straight on, I said: "Those revivals of interest in a subject happen to me often; one book suggests another, and often sends me back a wild-goose chase over an interval of twenty years. But if you still care to possess a copy, I shall be only too happy to provide you; I have still got two or three by me— and if you allow me to present one I shall be very much honoured."

"You are very good indeed," he said, quite at his ease again, in a moment: "I almost despaired—I don't know how to thank you."

"Pray don't say a word; the thing is really so little worth that I am only ashamed of having offered it, and if you thank me any more I shall throw it into the fire in a fit of modesty."

Mr Jennings laughed. He inquired where I was staying in London, and after a little more conversation on a variety of subjects, he took his departure.

CHAPTER II

THE DOCTOR QUESTIONS LADY MARY AND SHE ANSWERS

"I like your vicar so much, Lady Mary," said I, as soon as he was gone. "He has read, travelled, and thought, and having also suffered, he ought to be an accomplished companion."

"So he is, and, better still, he is a really good man," said she. "His advice is invaluable about my schools, and all my little undertakings at Dawlbridge, and he's so painstaking, he takes so much trouble—you have no idea—wherever he thinks he can be of use; he's so good-natured and so sensible."

"It is pleasant to hear so good an account of his neighbourly virtues. I can only testify to his being an agreeable and gentle companion, and in addition to what you have told me, I think I can tell you two or three things about him," said I.

"Really!"

"Yes, to begin with, he's unmarried."

"Yes, that's right—go on."

"He has been writing, that is he *was*; but for two or three years, perhaps, he has not gone on with his work, and the book was upon some rather abstract subject—perhaps theology."

"Well, he was writing a book, as you say; I'm not quite sure what it was about, but only that it was nothing that I cared for; very likely you are right, and he certainly did stop—yes."

"And although he only drank a little coffee here to-night, he likes tea, at least, did like it, extravagantly."

"Yes, that's *quite* true."

"He drank green tea, a good deal, didn't he?" I pursued.

"Well, that's very odd! Green tea was a subject on which we used almost to quarrel."

"But he has quite given that up," said I.

"So he has."

"And, now, one more fact. His mother or his father, did you know them?"

"Yes, both; his father is only ten years dead, and their place is near Dawlbridge. We knew them very well," she answered.

"Well, either his mother or his father—I should rather think his father, saw a ghost," said I.

"Well, you really are a conjurer, Dr Hesselius."

"Conjurer or no, haven't I said right?" I answered merrily.

"You certainly have, and it *was* his father: he was a silent, whimsical man, and he used to bore my father about his dreams, and at last he told him a story about a ghost he had seen and talked with; and a very odd story it was. I remember it particularly, because I was so afraid of him. This story was long before he died—when I was quite a child—and his ways were so silent and moping, and he used to drop in sometimes, in the dusk, when I was alone in the drawing-room, and I used to fancy there were ghosts about him."

I smiled and nodded.

"And now, having established my character as a conjurer, I think I must say good-night," said I.

"But how *did* you find it out?"

"By the planets, of course, as the gipsies do," I answered, and so, gaily we said good-night.

Next morning I sent the little book he had been inquiring after, and a note, to Mr Jennings, and on returning late that evening, I found that he had called at my lodgings and left his card. He asked whether I was at home, and asked at what hour he would be most likely to find me.

Does he intend opening his case, and consulting me "professionally," as they say? I hope so. I have already conceived a theory about him. It is supported by Lady Mary's answers to my parting questions. I should like much to ascertain from his own lips. But what can I do consistently with good breeding to invite a confession? Nothing. I rather think he meditates one. At all events, my dear Van L., I shan't make myself difficult of access; I mean to return his visit to-morrow. It will be only civil, in return for his politeness, to ask to see him. Perhaps something may come of it. Whether much, little, or nothing, my dear Van L., you shall hear.

CHAPTER III

DR HESSELIUS PICKS UP
SOMETHING IN LATIN BOOKS

Well, I have called at Blank Street.

On inquiring at the door, the servant told me that Mr Jennings was engaged very particularly with a gentleman, a clergyman from Kenlis, his parish in the country. Intending to reserve my privilege, and to call again, I merely intimated that I should try another time, and had turned to go, when the servant begged my pardon, and asked me, looking at me a little more attentively than well-bred persons of his order usually do, whether I was Dr Hesselius; and, on learning that I was, he said, "Perhaps then, sir, you would allow me to mention it to Mr Jennings, for I am sure he wishes to see you."

The servant returned in a moment, with a message from Mr Jennings asking me to go into his study, which was in effect his back drawing-room, promising to be with me in a very few minutes.

This was really a study—almost a library. The room was lofty, with two tall slender windows, and rich dark curtains. It was much larger than I had expected, and stored with books on every side, from the floor to the ceiling. The upper carpet—for to my tread it felt that there were two or three—was a Turkey carpet. My steps fell noiselessly. The book-cases standing out, placed the windows, particularly narrow ones, in deep recesses. The effect of the room was, although extremely comfortable, and even luxurious, decidedly gloomy and, aided by the silence, almost oppressive. Perhaps, however, I ought to have allowed something for association. My mind had connected peculiar ideas with Mr Jennings. I stepped into this perfectly silent room, of a very silent house, with a peculiar foreboding; and its darkness and solemn clothing of books—for except where two narrow looking-glasses were set in the wall they were everywhere—helped this sombre feeling.

While awaiting Mr Jennings' arrival, I amused myself by looking into some of the books with which his shelves were laden. Not among these, but immediately under them, with their backs upward, on the floor, I lighted upon a complete set of Swedenborg's *Arcana Caelestia*, in the original Latin, a very fine folio set, bound in the natty livery which theology affects, pure vellum namely, gold letters, and carmine edges. There were paper markers in several of these volumes; I raised and placed them, one after another, upon the table, and opening where these papers were placed, I read in the solemn Latin phraseology a series of sentences indicated by a pencilled line at the margin. Of these I copy here a few, translating them into English.

"When man's interior sight is opened, which is that of his spirit, then there appear the things of another life, which cannot possibly be made visible to the bodily sight.". . .

"By the internal sight it has been granted to me to see the things that are in the other life, more clearly than I see those that are in the world. From these considerations, it is evident that external vision exists from interior vision, and this from a vision still more interior, and so on.". . .

"There are with every man at least two evil spirits.". . .

"With wicked genii there is also a fluent speech, but harsh and grating. There is also among them a speech which is not fluent, wherein the dissent of the thoughts is perceived as something secretly creeping along within it.". . .

"The evil spirits associated with man are, indeed, from the hells, but when with man they are not then in hell, but are taken out thence. The place where they then are, is in the midst between heaven and hell, and is called the world of spirits—when the evil spirits who are with man, are in that world, they are not in any infernal torment, but in every thought and affection of the man, and so, in all that the man himself enjoys. But when they are remitted into their hell, they return to their former state.". . .

"If evil spirits could perceive that they were associated with man, and yet that they were spirits separate from him, and if they could flow in into the things of his body, they would attempt by a thousand means to destroy him; for they hate man with a deadly hatred.". . .

"Knowing, therefore, that I was a man in the body, they were continually striving to destroy me, not as to the body only, but especially as to the soul; for to destroy any man or spirit is the very delight of life of all who are in hell; but I have been continually protected by the Lord.

Hence it appears how dangerous it is for man to be in a living consort with spirits, unless he be in the good of faith.". . .

"Nothing is more carefully guarded from the knowledge of associate spirits than their being thus conjoint with a man, for if they knew it they would speak to him, with the intention to destroy him."

"The delight of hell is to do evil to man, and to hasten his eternal ruin."

A long note, written with a very sharp and fine pencil, in Mr Jennings' neat hand, at the foot of the page, caught my eye. Expecting his criticism upon the text, I read a word or two, and stopped; for it was something quite different, and began with these words, *Deus misereatur mei*—"May God compassionate me." Thus warned of its private nature, I averted my eyes, and shut the book, replacing all the volumes as I had found them, except one which interested me, and in which, as men studious and solitary in their habits will do, I grew so absorbed as to take no cognizance of the outer world, nor to remember where I was.

I was reading some pages which refer to "representatives" and "correspondents," in the technical language of Swedenborg, and had arrived at a passage, the substance of which is that evil spirits, when seen by other eyes than those of their infernal associates, present themselves, by "correspondence," in the shape of the beast (*fera*) which represents their particular lust and life, in aspect direful and atrocious. This is a long passage, and particularizes a number of those bestial forms.

CHAPTER IV

FOUR EYES WERE READING THE PASSAGE

I was running the head of my pencil-case along the line as I read it, and something caused me to raise my eyes.

Directly before me was one of the mirrors I have mentioned, in which I saw reflected the tall shape of my friend Mr Jennings, leaning over my shoulder, and reading the page at which I was busy, and with a face so dark and wild that I should hardly have known him.

I turned and rose. He stood erect also, and with an effort laughed a little, saying:

"I came in and asked you how you did, but without succeeding in awaking you from your book; so I could not restrain my curiosity, and very impertinently, I'm afraid, peeped over your shoulder. This is not your first time of looking into those pages. You have looked into Swedenborg, no doubt, long ago?"

"Oh dear, yes! I owe Swedenborg a great deal; you will discover traces of him in the little book on Metaphysical Medicine, which you were so good to remember."

Although my friend affected a gaiety of manner, there was a slight flush in his face, and I could perceive that he was inwardly much perturbed.

"I'm scarcely yet qualified, I know so little of Swedenborg. I've only had them a fortnight," he answered, "and I think they are rather likely to make a solitary man nervous—that is, judging from the very little I have read—I don't say that they have made me so," he laughed; "and I'm so very much obliged for the book. I hope you got my note?"

I made all proper acknowledgements and modest disclaimers.

"I never read a book that I go with, so entirely, as that of yours," he continued. "I saw at once there is more in it than is quite unfolded. Do you know Dr Harley?" he asked, rather abruptly.

[In passing, the editor remarks that the physician here named was one of the most eminent who had ever practised in England.]

I did, having had letters to him, and had experienced from him great courtesy and considerable assistance during my visit to England.

"I think that man one of the very greatest fools I ever met in my life," said Mr Jennings.

This was the first time I had ever heard him say a sharp thing of anybody, and such a term applied to so high a name a little startled me.

"Really! and in what way?" I asked.

"In his profession," he answered.

I smiled.

"I mean this," he said: "he seems to me, one half, blind—I mean one half of all he looks at is dark—preternaturally bright and vivid all the rest; and the worst of it is, it seems *wilful*. I can't get him—I mean he won't—I've had some experience of him as a physician, but I look on him as, in that sense, no better than a paralytic mind, an intellect half dead. I'll tell you—I know I shall some time—all about it," he said, with a little agitation. "You stay some months longer in England. If I should be out of town during your stay for a little time, would you allow me to trouble you with a letter?"

"I should be only too happy," I assured him.

"Very good of you. I am so utterly dissatisfied with Harley."

"A little leaning to the materialistic school," I said.

"A *mere* materialist," he corrected me; "you can't think how that sort of thing worries one who knows better. You won't tell anyone—any of my friends you know—that I am hippish; now, for instance, no one knows—not even Lady Mary—that I have seen Dr Harley, or any other doctor. So pray don't mention it; and, if I should have any threatening of an attack, you'll kindly let me write, or, should I be in town, have a little talk with you."

I was full of conjecture, and unconsciously I found I had fixed my eyes gravely on him, for he lowered his for a moment, and he said:

"I see you think I might as well tell you now, or else you are forming a conjecture; but you may as well give it up. If you were guessing all the rest of your life, you will never hit on it."

He shook his head smiling, and over that wintry sunshine a black cloud suddenly came down, and he drew his breath in, through his teeth, as men do in pain.

"Sorry, of course, to learn that you apprehend occasion to consult any of us; but command me when and how you like, and I need not assure you that your confidence is sacred."

He then talked of quite other things, and in a comparatively cheerful way, and after a little time I took my leave.

CHAPTER V

DR HESSELIUS IS SUMMONED TO RICHMOND

We parted cheerfully, but he was not cheerful, nor was I. There are certain expressions of that powerful organ of spirit—the human face—which, although I have seen them often, and possess a doctor's nerve, yet disturb me profoundly. One look of Mr Jennings haunted me. It had seized my imagination with so dismal a power that I changed my plans for the evening, and went to the opera, feeling that I wanted a change of ideas.

I heard nothing of or from him for two or three days, when a note in his hand reached me. It was cheerful, and full of hope. He said that he had been for some little time so much better—quite well, in fact—that he was going to make a little experiment, and run down for a month or so to his parish, to try whether a little work might not quite set him up. There was in it a fervent religious expression of gratitude for his restoration, as he now almost hoped he might call it.

A day or two later I saw Lady Mary, who repeated what his note had announced, and told me that he was actually in Warwickshire, having resumed his clerical duties at Kenlis; and she added, "I begin to think that he is really perfectly well, and that there never was anything the matter, more than nerves and fancy; we are all nervous, but I fancy there is nothing like a little hard work for that kind of weakness, and he has made up his mind to try it. I should not be surprised if he did not come back for a year."

Notwithstanding all this confidence, only two days later I had this note, dated from his house off Piccadilly:

Dear Sir—

I have returned disappointed. If I should feel at all able to see you, I shall write to ask you kindly to call. At present I am too low and, in fact, simply unable to say all I wish to say. Pray don't mention my name to my friends. I can see no one. By-and-by, please God, you shall hear from me. I mean to take a run into Shropshire, where some of my people are. God bless you! May we, on my return, meet more happily than I can now write.

About a week after this I saw Lady Mary at her own house, the last person, she said, left in town, and just on the wing for Brighton, for the London season was quite over. She told me that she had heard from Mr Jennings' niece, Martha, in Shropshire. There was nothing to be gathered from her letter, more than that he was low and nervous. In those words, of which health people think so lightly, what a world of suffering is sometimes hidden!

Nearly five weeks had passed without any further news of Mr Jennings. At the end of that time I received a note from him. He wrote:

"I have been in the country, and have had change of air, change of scene, change of faces, change of everything—and in everything—but *myself*. I have made up my mind, so far as the most irresolute creature on earth can do it, to tell my case fully to you. If your engagements will permit, pray come to me to-day, to-morrow, or the next day; but, pray defer as little as possible. You know not how much I need help. I have a quiet house at Richmond, where I now am. Perhaps you can manage to come to dinner, or to luncheon, or even to tea. You shall have no trouble in finding me out. The servant at Blank Street, who takes this note, will have a carriage at your door at any hour you please; and I am always to be found. You will say that I ought not to be alone. I have tried everything. Come and see."

I called up the servant, and decided on going out the same evening, which accordingly I did.

He would have been much better in a lodging-house, or hotel, I thought, as I drove up through a short double row of sombre elms to a very old-fashioned brick house, darkened by the foliage of these trees, which overtopped and nearly surrounded it. It was a perverse choice, for nothing could be imagined more triste and silent. The house, I found, belonged to him. He had stayed for a day or two in town, and, finding it for some cause insupportable, had come out here, probably because, being furnished and his own, he was relieved of the thought and delay of selection, by coming here.

The sun had already set, and the red reflected light of the western sky illuminated the scene with the peculiar effect with which we are all familiar. The hall seemed very dark, but, getting to the back drawing-room, whose windows command the west, I was again in the same dusky light.

I sat down, looking out upon the richly-wooded landscape that glowed in the grand and melancholy light which was every moment fading. The corners of the room were already dark; all was growing dim, and the gloom was insensibly toning my mind, already prepared for what was sinister. I was waiting alone for his arrival, which soon took place. The door communicating with the front room opened, and the tall figure of Mr Jennings, faintly seen in the ruddy twilight, came, with quiet stealthy steps, into the room.

We shook hands, and, taking a chair to the window, where there was still light enough to enable us to see each other's faces, he sat down beside me, and, placing his hand upon my arm, with scarcely a word of preface began his narrative.

CHAPTER VI

HOW MR JENNINGS MET HIS COMPANION

The faint glow of the west, the pomp of the then lonely woods of Richmond, were before us, behind and about us the darkening room, and on the stony face of the sufferer—for the character of his face, though still gentle and sweet, was changed—rested that dim, odd glow which seems to descend and produce, where it touches, lights, sudden though faint, which are lost, almost without gradation, in darkness. The silence, too, was utter; not a distant wheel, or bark, or whistle from without; and within the depressing stillness of an invalid bachelor's house.

I guessed well the nature, though not even vaguely the particulars of the revelations I was about to receive, from that fixed face of suffering that, so oddly flushed, stood out, like a portrait of Schalken's, before its background of darkness.

"It began," he said, "on the 15th of October, three years and eleven weeks ago, and two days—I keep very accurate count, for every day is torment. If I leave anywhere a chasm in my narrative tell me.

"About four years ago I began a work which had cost me very much thought and reading. It was upon the religious metaphysics of the ancients."

"I know," said I; "the actual religion of educated and thinking paganism, quite apart from symbolic worship? A wide and very interesting field."

"Yes; but not good for the mind—the Christian mind, I mean. Paganism is all bound together in essential unity, and, with evil sympathy, their religion involves their art, and both their manners, and the subject is a degrading fascination and the Nemesis sure. God forgive me!

"I wrote a great deal; I wrote late at night. I was always thinking on the subject, walking about, wherever I was, everywhere. It thoroughly infected me. You are to remember that all the material ideas connected with it were more or less of the beautiful, the subject itself delightfully interesting, and I, then, without a care."

He sighed heavily.

"I believe, that every one who sets about writing in earnest does his work, as a friend of mine phrased it, *on* something—tea, or coffee, or tobacco. I suppose there is a material waste that must be hourly supplied in such occupations, or that we should grow too abstracted, and the mind, as it were, pass out of the body, unless it were reminded often of the connection by actual sensation. At all events, I felt the want, and I supplied it. Tea was my companion—at first the ordinary black tea, made in the usual way, not too strong: but I drank a good deal, and increased its strength as I went on. I never experienced an uncomfortable symptom from it. I began to take a little green tea. I found the effect pleasanter, it cleared and intensified the power of thought so. I had come to take it frequently, but not stronger than one might take it for pleasure. I wrote a great deal out here, it was so quiet, and in this room. I used to sit up very late, and it became a habit with me to sip my tea—green tea—every now and then as my work proceeded. I had a little kettle on my table, that swung over a lamp, and made tea two or three times between eleven o'clock and two or three in the morning, my hours of going to bed. I used to go into town every day. I was not a monk, and, although I spent an hour or two in a library hunting up authorities and looking out lights upon my theme, I was in no morbid state as far as I can judge. I met my friends pretty much as usual and enjoyed their society, and, on the whole, existence had never been, I think, so pleasant before.

"I had met with a man who had some odd old books, German editions in mediaeval Latin, and I was only too happy to be permitted access to them. This obliging person's books were in the City, a very out-of-the-way part of it. I had rather out-stayed my intended hour, and, on coming out, seeing no cab near, I was tempted to get into the omnibus which used to drive past this house. It was darker than this by the time the 'bus had reached an old house you may have remarked, with four poplars at each side of the door, and there the last passenger but myself got out. We drove along rather faster. It was twilight now. I leaned back in my corner next the door, ruminating pleasantly.

"The interior of the omnibus was nearly dark. I had observed in the corner opposite to me at the other side, and at the end next the horses, two small circular reflections, as it seemed to me of a reddish light. They were about two inches apart, and about the size of those small brass buttons that yachting men used to put upon their jackets. I began to speculate, as listless men will, upon this trifle, as it seemed. From what centre did that faint but deep red light come, and from what—glass beads, buttons, toy decorations—was it reflected? We were lumbering along gently, having nearly a mile still to go. I had not solved the puzzle, and it became in another minute more odd, for these two luminous points, with a sudden jerk, descended nearer the floor, keeping still their relative distance and horizontal position, and then, as suddenly, they rose to the level of the seat on which I was sitting, and I saw them no more.

"My curiosity was now really excited, and, before I had time to think, I saw again these two dull lamps, again together near the floor; again they disappeared, and again in their old corner I saw them.

"So, keeping my eyes upon them, I edged quietly up to my own side, towards the end at which I still saw these tiny discs of red.

"There was very little light in the 'bus. It was nearly dark. I leaned forward to aid my endeavour to discover what these little circles really were. They shifted their position a little as I did so. I began now to perceive an outline of something black, and I soon saw, with tolerable distinctness, the outline of a small black monkey, pushing its face forward in mimicry to meet mine; those were its eyes, and I now dimly saw its teeth grinning at me.

"I drew back, not knowing whether it might not meditate a spring. I fancied that one of the passengers had forgot this ugly pet, and wishing to ascertain something of its temper, though not caring to trust my fingers to it, I poked my umbrella softly towards it. It remained unmovable—up to it—*through* it. For through it, and back and forward it passed, without the slightest resistance.

"I can't, in the least, convey to you the kind of horror that I felt. When I had ascertained that the thing was an illusion, as I then supposed, there came a misgiving about myself and a terror that fascinated me in impotence to remove my gaze from the eyes of the brute for some moments. As I looked it made a little skip back, quite into the corner, and I, in a panic, found myself at the door, having put my head out, drawing deep breaths of the outer air, and staring at the lights and trees we were passing, too glad to reassure myself of reality.

"I stopped the 'bus and got out. I perceived the man look oddly at me as I paid him. I daresay there was something unusual in my looks and manner, for I had never felt so strangely before."

CHAPTER VII

THE JOURNEY: FIRST STAGE

"When the omnibus drove on, and I was alone on the road, I looked carefully round to ascertain whether the monkey had followed me. To my indescribable relief I saw it nowhere. I can't describe easily what a shock I had received, and my sense of genuine gratitude on finding myself, as I supposed, quite rid of it.

"I had got out a little before we reached this house, two or three hundred steps. A brick wall runs along the footpath, and inside the wall is a hedge of yew, or some dark evergreen of that kind, and within that again the row of fine trees which you may have remarked as you came.

"This brick wall is about as high as my shoulder, and happening to raise my eyes I saw the monkey, with that stooping gait, on all fours, walking or creeping, close beside me on top of the wall. I stopped, looking at it with a feeling of loathing and horror. As I stopped so did it. It sat up on the wall with its long hands on its knees looking at me. There was not light enough to see it much more than in outline, nor was it dark enough to bring the peculiar light of its eye into strong relief. I still saw, however, that red foggy light plainly enough. It did not show its teeth, nor exhibit any sign of irritation, but seemed jaded and sulky, and was observing me steadily.

"I drew back into the middle of the road. It was an unconscious recoil, and there I stood, still looking at it. It did not move.

"With an instinctive determination to try something—anything, I turned about and walked briskly toward town, with askance look, all the time watching the movements of the beast. It crept swiftly along the wall, at exactly my pace.

"Where the wall ends, near the turn of the road, it came down, and with a wiry spring or two brought itself close to my feet, and continued to keep up with me as I quickened my pace. It was at my left side, so close to my leg that I felt every moment as if I should tread upon it.

"The road was quite deserted and silent, and it was darker every moment. I stopped dismayed and bewildered, turning, as I did so, the other way—I mean towards this house, away from which I had been walking. When I stood still, the monkey drew back to a distance of, I suppose, about five or six yards, and remained stationary, watching me.

"I had been more agitated than I have said. I had read, of course, as everyone has, something about 'spectral illusions,' as you physicians term the phenomena of such cases. I considered my situation, and looked my misfortune in the face.

"These affections, I had read, are sometimes transitory and sometimes obstinate. I had read of cases in which the appearance, at first harmless, had, step by step, degenerated into something direful and insupportable, and ended by wearing its victim out. Still, as I stood there, but for my bestial companion, quite alone, I tried to comfort myself by repeating again and again the assurance, 'the thing is purely disease, a well-known physical affection, as distinctly as small-pox or neuralgia. Doctors are all agreed on that, philosophy demonstrates it. I must not be a fool. I've been sitting up too late, and I daresay my digestion is quite wrong, and, with God's help, I shall be all right, and this is but a symptom of nervous dyspepsia.' Did I believe all this? Not one word of it, no more than any other miserable being ever did who is once seized and riveted in this satanic captivity. Against my convictions, I might say my knowledge, I was simply bullying myself into a false courage.

"I now walked homeward. I had only a few hundred yards to go. I had forced myself into a sort of resignation, but I had not got over the sickening shock and the flurry of the first certainty of my misfortune.

"I made up my mind to pass the night at home. The brute moved close beside me, and I fancied there was the sort of anxious drawing toward the house, which one sees in tired horses or dogs, sometimes as they come toward home.

"I was afraid to go into town, I was afraid of any one's seeing and recognizing me. I was conscious of an irrepressible agitation to my manner. Also, I was afraid of any violent change in my habits, such as going to a place of amusement, or walking from home in order to fatigue myself. At the hall door it waited till I mounted the steps, and when the door was opened entered with me.

"I drank no tea that night. I got cigars and some brandy and water. My idea was that I should act upon my material system, and by living for a while in sensation apart from thought, send myself forcibly, as it were, into a new groove. I came up here to this drawing-room. I sat just here. The monkey then got upon a small table that then stood *there*. It looked dazed and languid. An irrepressible uneasiness as to its movements kept my eyes always upon it. Its eyes were half closed, but I could see them glow. It was looking steadily at me. In all situations, at all hours, it is awake and looking at me. That never changes.

"I shall not continue in detail my narrative of this particular night. I shall describe, rather, the phenomena of the first year, which never varied essentially. I shall describe the monkey as it appeared in daylight. In the dark, as you shall presently hear, there are peculiarities. It is a small monkey, perfectly black. It had only one peculiarity—a character of malignity—unfathomable malignity. During the first year it looked sullen and sick. But this character of intense malice and vigilance was always underlying that surly languor. During all that time it acted as if on a plan of giving me as little trouble as was consistent with watching me. Its eyes were never off me. I have never lost sight of it, except in my sleep, light or dark, day or night, since it came here, excepting when it withdraws for some weeks at a time, unaccountably.

"In total dark it is visible as in daylight. I do not merely its eyes. It is *all* visible distinctly in a halo that resembles a glow of red embers, and which accompanies it in all its movements.

"When it leaves me for a time it is always at night, in the dark, and in the same way. It grows at first uneasy, and then furious, and then advances towards me, grinning and shaking, its paws clenched, and, at the same time, there comes the appearance of fire in the grate. I never have any fire. I can't sleep in the room where there is any, and it draws nearer and nearer to the chimney, quivering, it seems, with rage, and when its fury rises to the highest pitch it springs into the grate, and up the chimney, and I see it no more.

"When first this happened I thought I was released. I was now a new man. A day passed—a night—and no return, and a blessed week—a week—another week. I was always on my knees, Dr Hesselius, always, thanking God and praying. A whole month passed of liberty; but, on a sudden, it was with me again."

CHAPTER VIII

THE SECOND STAGE

"It was with me, and the malice which before was torpid under a sullen exterior was now active. It was perfectly unchanged in every other respect. This new energy was apparent in its activity and its looks, and soon in other ways.

"For a time, you will understand, the change was shown only in an increased vivacity, and an air of menace, as if it was always brooding over some atrocious plan. Its eyes, as before, were never off me."

"Is it here now?" I asked.

"No," he replied, "it has been absent exactly a fortnight and a day—fifteen days. It has sometimes been away so long as nearly two months, once for three. Its absence always exceeds a fortnight, although it may be but by a single day. Fifteen days having past since I saw it last, it may return now at any moment."

"Is its return," I asked, "accompanied by any peculiar manifestation?"

"Nothing—no," he said. "It is simply with me again. On lifting my eyes from a book, or turning my head, I see it, as usual, looking at me, and then it remains, as before, for its appointed time. I have never told so much and so minutely before to anyone."

I perceived that he was agitated, and looking like death, and he repeatedly applied his handkerchief to his forehead; I suggested that he might be tired, and told him that I would call, with pleasure, in the morning, but he said:

"No, if you don't mind hearing it all now. I have got so far, and I should prefer making one effort of it. When I spoke to Dr Harley, I had nothing like so much to tell. You are a philosophic physician. You give spirit its proper rank. If this thing is real—"

He paused, looking at me with agitated inquiry.

"We can discuss it by-and-by, and very fully. I will give you all I think," I answered, after an interval.

"Well—very well. If it is anything real, I say, it is prevailing, little by little, and drawing me more interiorly into hell. Optic nerves, he talked of. Ah! well—there are other nerves of communication. May God Almighty help me! You shall hear.

"Its power of action, I tell you, has increased. Its malice became, in a way, aggressive. About two years ago, some questions that were pending between me and the bishop having been settled, I went down to my parish in Warwickshire, anxious to find occupation in my profession. I was not prepared for what happened, although I have since thought I might have apprehended something like it. The reason for my saying so is this—"

He was beginning to speak with a great deal more effort and reluctance, and sighed often, and seemed at times nearly overcome.

But at this time his manner was not agitated. It was more like that of a sinking patient, who has given himself up.

"Yes, but I will first tell you about Kenlis, my parish.

"It was with me when I left this place for Dawlbridge. It was my silent travelling companion, and it remained with me at the vicarage. When I entered on the discharge of my duties, another change took place. The thing exhibited an atrocious determination to thwart me. It was with me in the church—in the reading-desk—in the pulpit—within the communion rails. At last it reached this extremity, that while I was reading to the congregation it would spring upon the open book and squat there, so that I was unable to see the page. This happened more than once.

"I left Dawlbridge for a time. I placed myself in Dr Harley's hands. I did everything he told me. He gave my case a great deal of thought. It interested him, I think. He seemed successful. For nearly three months I was perfectly free from a return. I began to think I was safe. With his full assent I returned to Dawlbridge.

"I travelled in a chaise. I was in good spirits. I was more—I was happy and grateful. I was returning, as I thought, delivered from a dreadful hallucination, to the scene of duties which I longed to enter upon. It was a beautiful sunny evening, everything looked serene and cheerful, and I was delighted. I remember looking out of the window to see the spire of my church at Kenlis among the trees, at the point where one has the earliest view of it. It is exactly where the little stream that bounds the parish passes under the road by a culvert; and where it emerges at the road-side a stone with an old inscription is placed. As we passed this point I drew my head in and sat down, and in the corner of the chaise was the monkey.

"For a moment I felt faint, and then quite wild with despair and horror. I called to the driver, and got out, and sat down at the road-side, and prayed to God silently for mercy. A despairing resignation supervened. My companion was with me as I re-entered the vicarage. The same persecution followed. After a short struggle I submitted, and soon I left the place.

"I told you," he said, "that the beast has before this become in certain ways aggressive. I will explain a little. It seemed to be actuated by intense and increasing fury whenever I said my prayers, or even meditated prayer. It amounted at last to a dreadful interruption. You will ask, how could a silent immaterial phantom effect that? It was thus, whenever I meditated praying; it was always before me, and nearer and nearer.

"It used to spring on a table, on the back of a chair, on the chimney piece, and slowly to swing itself from side to side, looking at me all the time. There is in its motion an indefinable power to dissipate thought, and to contract one's attention to that monotony, till the ideas shrink, as it were, to a point, and at last to nothing—and unless I had started up, and shook off the catalepsy, I have felt as if my mind were on the point of losing itself. There are other ways," he sighed heavily; "thus, for instance, while I pray with my eyes closed, it comes closer and closer, and I see it. I know it is not to be accounted for physically, but I do actually see it, though my lids are closed, and so it rocks my mind, as it were, and overpowers me, and I am obliged to rise from my knees. If you had ever yourself known this, you would be acquainted with desperation."

CHAPTER IX

THE THIRD STAGE

"I see, Dr Hesselius, that you don't lose one word of my statement. I need not ask you to listen specially to what I am now going to tell you. They talk of optic nerves, and of spectral illusions, as if the organ of sight was the only point assailable by the influences that have fastened upon me—I know better. For two years in my direful case that limitation prevailed. But as food is taken in softly at the lips, and then brought under the teeth, as the tip of the little finger caught in a mill crank will draw in the hand, and the arm, and the whole body, so the miserable mortal who has been once caught firmly by the end of the finest fibre of his nerve is drawn in and in, by the enormous machinery of hell, until he is as I am. Yes, Doctor, as *I* am, for while I talk to you, and implore relief, I feel that my prayer is for the impossible, and my pleading with the inexorable."

I endeavoured to calm his visibly increasing agitation, and told him that he must not despair.

While we talked the night had overtaken us. The filmy moonlight was wide over the scene which the window commanded, and I said:

"Perhaps you would prefer having candles. This light, you know, is odd. I should wish you, as much as possible, under your usual conditions, while I make my diagnosis, shall I call it—otherwise I don't care."

"All lights are the same to me," he said. "Except when I read or write, I care not if night were perpetual. I am going to tell you what happened about a year ago. The thing began to speak to me."

"Speak! How do you mean—speak as a man does, do you mean?"

"Yes; speak in words and consecutive sentences, with perfect coherence and articulation; but there is a peculiarity. It is not like the tone of a human voice. It is not by my ears it reaches me—it comes like a singing through my head.

"This faculty, the power of speaking to me, will be my undoing. It won't let me pray, it interrupts me with dreadful blasphemies. I dare not go on, I could not. Oh! Doctor, can the skill, and thought, and prayers of man avail me nothing!"

"You must promise me, my dear sir, not to trouble yourself with unnecessarily exciting thoughts; confine yourself strictly to the narrative of *facts;* and recollect, above all, that even if the thing that infests you be, as you seem to suppose, a reality with an actual independent life and will, yet it can have no power to hurt you, unless it be given from above: its access to your senses depends mainly upon your physical conditions—this is, under God, your comfort and reliance: we are all alike environed. It is only that in your case, the '*paries*,' the veil of the flesh, the screen, is a little out of repair, and sights and sounds are transmitted. We must enter on a new course, sir,—be encouraged. I'll give to-night to the careful consideration of the whole case."

"You are very good, sir; you think it worth trying, you don't give me quite up; but, sir, you don't know, it is gaining such an influence over me: it orders me about, it is such a tyrant, and I'm growing so helpless. May God deliver me!"

"It orders you about—of course you mean by speech?"

"Yes, yes; it is always urging me to crimes, to injure others, or myself. You see, Doctor, the situation is urgent, it is indeed. When I was in Shropshire, a few weeks ago" (Mr Jennings was speaking rapidly and trembling now, holding my arm with one hand, and looking in my face), "I went out one day with a party of friends for a walk: my persecutor, I tell you, was with me at the time. I lagged behind the rest: the country near the Dee, you know, is beautiful. Our path happened to lie near a coal mine, and at the verge of the wood is a perpendicular shaft, they say, a hundred and fifty feet deep. My niece had remained behind with me—she knows, of course, nothing of the nature of my sufferings. She knew, however, that I had been ill, and was low, and she remained to prevent my being quite alone. As we loitered slowly on together, the brute that accompanied me was urging me to throw myself down the shaft. I tell you now—oh, sir, think of it!—the one consideration that saved me from that hideous death was the fear lest the shock of witnessing the occurrence should be too much for the poor girl. I asked her to go on and take her walk with her friends, saying that I could go no further. She made excuses, and the more I urged her the firmer she became. She looked doubtful and frightened. I suppose there was something in my looks or manner that alarmed her; but she would not go, and that literally saved me. You had no idea, sir, that a living man could be made so abject a slave of Satan," he said, with a ghastly groan and a shudder.

There was a pause here, and I said, "You *were* preserved nevertheless. It was the act of God. You are in His hands and in the power of no other being: be therefore confident for the future."

CHAPTER X

HOME

I made him have candles lighted, and saw the room looking cheery and inhabited before I left him. I told him that he must regard his illness strictly as one dependent on physical, though *subtle* physical causes. I told him that he had evidence of God's care and love in the deliverance which he had just described, and that I had perceived with pain that he seemed to regard its peculiar features as indicating that he had been delivered over to spiritual reprobation. Than such a conclusion nothing could be, I insisted, less warranted; and not only so, but more contrary to facts, as disclosed in his mysterious deliverance from that murderous influence during his Shropshire excursion. First, his niece had been retained by his side without his intending to keep her near him; and, secondly, there had been infused into his mind an irresistible repugnance to execute the dreadful suggestion in her presence.

As I reasoned this point with him, Mr Jennings wept. He seemed comforted. One promise I exacted, which was that should the monkey at any time return, I should be sent for immediately; and, repeating my assurance that I would give neither time nor thought to any other subject until I had thoroughly investigated his case, and that to-morrow he should hear the result, I took my leave.

Before getting into the carriage I told the servant that his master was far from well, and that he should make a point of frequently looking into his room. My own arrangements I made with a view to being quite secure from interruption.

I merely called at my lodgings, and with a travelling-desk and carpet-bag set off in a hackney carriage for an inn, about two miles out of town, called "The Horns," a very quiet and comfortable house with good thick walls. And there I resolved, without the possibility of intrusion or distraction, to devote some hours of the night, in my comfortable sitting-room, to Mr Jennings' case, and so much of the morning as it might require.

[There occurs here a careful note of Dr Hesselius' opinion upon the case, and of the habits, dietary, and medicines which he prescribed. It is curious—some persons would say mystical. But, on the whole, I doubt whether it would sufficiently interest a reader of the kind I am likely to meet with, to warrant its being here reprinted. The whole letter was plainly written at the inn where he had hid himself for the occasion. The next letter is dated from his town lodgings.]

I left town for the inn where I slept last night at half-past nine, and did not arrive at my room in town until one o'clock this afternoon. I found a letter in Mr Jennings' hand upon my table. It had not come by post, and, on inquiry, I learned that Mr Jennings' servant had brought it, and, on learning that I was not to return until to-day and that no one could tell him my address, he seemed very uncomfortable, and said that his orders from his master were that he was not to return without an answer.

I opened the letter and read:

DEAR DOCTOR HESSELIUS.—It is here. You had not been an hour gone when it returned. It is speaking. It knows all that has happened. It knows everything—it knows you, and is frantic and atrocious. It reviles. I send you this. It knows every word I have written—I write. This I promised, and I therefore write, but I fear very confused, very incoherently. I am so interrupted, disturbed.

Ever yours, sincerely yours,
Robert Lynder Jennings."

"When did this come?" I asked.

"About eleven last night: the man was here again, and has been here three times to-day. The last time is about an hour since."

Thus answered, and with the notes I had made upon his case in my pocket, I was in a few minutes driving towards Richmond to see Mr Jennings.

I by no means, as you perceive, despaired of Mr Jennings' case. He had himself remembered and applied, though quite in a mistaken way, the principle which I lay down in my Metaphysical Medicine, and which governs all such cases. I was about to apply it in earnest. I was profoundly interested, and very anxious to see and examine him while the "enemy" was actually present.

I drove up to the somber house, and ran up the steps and knocked. The door, in a little time, was opened by a tall woman in black silk. She looked ill, and as if she had been crying. She curtseyed, and heard my question, but she did not answer. She turned her face away, extending her hand towards two men who were coming down-stairs; and thus having, as it were, tacitly made me over to them, she passed through a side-door hastily and shut it.

The man who was nearest the hall, I at once accosted, but being now close to him I was shocked to see that both his hands were covered with blood.

I drew back a little, and the man, passing downstairs, merely said in a low tone, "Here's the servant, sir."

The servant had stopped on the stairs, confounded and dumb at seeing me. He was rubbing his hands in a handkerchief, and it was steeped in blood.

"Jones, what is it? what has happened?" I asked, while a sickening suspicion overpowered me.

The man asked me to come up to the lobby. I was beside him in a moment, and, frowning and pallid, with contracted eyes, he told me the horror which I already half guessed.

His master had made away with himself.

I went upstairs with him to the room—what I saw there I won't tell you. He had cut his throat with his razor. It was a frightful gash. The two men had laid him on the bed, and composed his limbs. It had happened, as the immense pool of blood on the floor declared, at some distance between the bed and the window. There was carpet round his bed, and a carpet under his dressing-table, but none on the rest of the floor, for the man said he did not like a carpet in his bedroom. In this sombre and now terrible room, one of the great elms that darkened the house was slowly moving the shadow of one of its great boughs upon this dreadful floor.

I beckoned to the servant, and we went downstairs together. I turned off the hall into an old-fashioned panelled room, and there standing, I heard all the servant had to tell. It was not a great deal.

"I concluded, sir, from your words, and looks, sir, as you left last night, that you thought my master seriously ill. I thought it might be that you were afraid of a fit, or something. So I attended very close to your directions. He sat up late, till past three o'clock. He was not writing or reading. He was talking a great deal to himself, but that was nothing unusual. At about that hour I assisted him to undress, and left him in his slippers and dressing-gown. I went back softly in about half-an-hour. He was in his bed, quite undressed, and a pair of candles lighted on the table beside his bed. He was leaning on his elbow, and looking out at the other side of the bed when I came in. I asked him if he wanted anything, and he said No.

"I don't know whether it was what you said to me, sir, or something a little unusual about him, but I was uneasy, uncommon uneasy about him last night.

"In another half hour, or it might be a little more, I went up again. I did not hear him talking as before. I opened the door a little. The candles were both out, which was not usual. I had a bedroom candle, and I let the light in, a little bit, looking softly round. I saw him sitting in that chair beside the dressing-table with his clothes on again. He turned round and looked at me. I thought it strange he should get up and dress, and put out the candles to sit in the dark, that way. But I only asked him again if I could do anything for him. He said, No, rather sharp, I thought. I asked if I might light the candles, and he said, 'Do as you like, Jones.' So I lighted them, and I lingered about the room, and he said, 'Tell me truth, Jones; why did you come again—you did not hear anyone cursing?' 'No, sir,' I said, wondering what he could mean.

"'No,' said he, after me, 'of course, no'; and I said to him, 'Wouldn't it be well, sir, you went to bed? It's just five o'clock'; and he said nothing but, 'Very likely; good-night, Jones.' So I went, sir, but in less than an hour I came again. The door was fast, and he heard me, and called as I thought from the bed to know what I wanted, and he desired me not to disturb him again. I lay down and slept for a little. It must have been between six and seven when I went up again. The door was still fast, and he made no answer, so I did not like to disturb him, and thinking he was asleep I left him till nine. It was his custom to ring when he wished me to come, and I had no particular hour for calling him. I tapped very gently, and getting no answer I stayed away a good while, supposing he was getting some rest then. It was not till eleven o'clock I grew really uncomfortable about him—for at the latest he was never, that I could remember, later than half-past ten. I got no answer. I knocked and called, and still no answer. So not being able to force the door, I called Thomas from the stables, and together we forced it, and found him in the shocking way you saw."

Jones had no more to tell. Poor Mr Jennings was very gentle and very kind. All his people were fond of him. I could see that the servant was very much moved.

So, dejected and agitated, I passed from that terrible house, and its dark canopy of elms, and I hope I shall never see it more. While I write to you I feel like a man who has but half waked from a frightful and monotonous dream. My memory rejects the picture with incredulity and horror. Yet I know it is true. It is the story of the process of a poison, a poison which excites the reciprocal action of spirit and nerve, and paralyses the tissue that separates those cognate functions of the senses, the external and the interior. Thus we find strange bed-fellows, and the mortal and immortal prematurely make acquaintance.

CONCLUSION

A WORD FOR THOSE WHO SUFFER

My dear Van L—, you have suffered from an affection similar to that which I have just described. You twice complained of a return of it.

Who, under God, cured you? Your humble servant, Martin Hesselius. Let me rather adopt the more emphasised piety of a certain good old French surgeon of three hundred years ago: "I treated, and God cured you."

Come, my friend, you are not to be hippish. Let me tell you a fact.

I have met with, and treated, as my book shows, fifty-seven cases of this kind of vision, which I term indifferently "sublimated," "precocious," and "interior."

There is another class of affections which are truly termed— though commonly confounded with those which I describe— spectral illusions. These latter I look upon as being no less simply curable than a cold in the head or a trifling dyspepsia.

It is those which rank in the first category that test our promptitude of thought. Fifty-seven such cases have I encountered, neither more nor less. And in how many of these have I failed? In no one single instance.

There is no one affliction of mortality more easily and certainly reducible, with a little patience and a rational confidence in the physician. With these simple conditions I look upon the cure as absolutely certain.

You are to remember that I had not even commenced to treat Mr Jennings' case. I have not any doubt that I should have cured him perfectly in eighteen months, or possibly it might have extended to two years. Some cases are very rapidly curable, others extremely tedious. Every intelligent physician who will give thought and diligence to the task will effect a cure.

You know my tract on "The Cardinal Functions of the Brain." I there, by the evidence of innumerable facts, prove, as I think, the high probability of a circulation, arterial and venous in its mechanism, through the nerves. Of this system, thus considered, the brain is the heart. The fluid, which is propagated hence through one class of nerves, returns in an altered state through another, and the nature of that fluid is spiritual, though not immaterial, any more than, as I before remarked, light or electricity are so.

By various abuses, among which the habitual use of such agents as green tea is one, this fluid may be affected as to its quality, but it is more frequently disturbed as to equilibrium. This fluid being that which we have in common with spirits, a congestion found upon the masses of brain or nerve, connected with the interior sense, forms a surface unduly exposed, on which disembodied spirits may operate: communication is thus more or less effectually established. Between this brain circulation and the heart circulation there is an intimate sympathy. The seat, or rather the instrument of exterior vision, is the eye. The seat of interior vision is the nervous tissue and brain, immediately about and above the eyebrow. You remember how effectually I dissipated your pictures by the simple application of iced eau-de-cologne. Few cases, however, can be treated exactly alike with anything like rapid success. Cold acts powerfully as a repellant of the nervous fluid. Long enough continued it will even produce that permanent insensibility which we call numbness, and a little longer, muscular as well as sensational paralysis.

I have not, I repeat, the slightest doubt that I should have first dimmed and ultimately sealed that inner eye which Mr Jennings had inadvertently opened. The same senses are opened in delirium tremens, and entirely shut up again when the overaction of the cerebral heart, and the prodigious nervous congestions that attend it, are terminated by a decided change in the state of the body. It is by acting steadily upon the body, by a simple process, that this result is produced—and inevitably produced—I have never yet failed.

Poor Mr Jennings made away with himself. But that catastrophe was the result of a totally different malady, which, as it were, projected itself upon that disease which was established. His case was in the distinctive manner a complication, and the complaint under which he really succumbed, was hereditary suicidal mania. Poor Mr Jennings I cannot call a patient of mine, for I had not even begun to treat his case, and he had not yet given me, I am convinced, his full and unreserved confidence. If the patient do not array himself on the side of the disease, his cure is certain.

THE CAVE OF
THE ECHOES

Helena Petrovna Blavatsky

Helena Petrovna Blavatsky (1831–1891)—the Russian-born author; occultist; intrepid world traveler; philosopher; visionary; and cofounder of Theosophy, the hugely influential esoteric, spiritual, and philosophical tradition—is responsible for introducing Eastern concepts of karma and reincarnation to the West. Her groundbreaking best seller, Isis Unveiled, *published in 1877, serves as Theosophy's manifesto. Among those claiming to be influenced by the book were Mohandas Gandhi and Thomas Edison.* The Secret Doctrine, *considered by many to be her masterwork, was published in 1888.*

Blavatsky traveled the world in the manner that one envisions fictional occult detective Dr. Hesselius traveling—except that she did it in real life, as a woman alone, and further afield. She was among the first Europeans to enter Tibet. During her travels, Blavatsky worked as a bareback rider, a lady's companion, and a spirit medium, among other occupations. Blavatsky demonstrated clairvoyant abilities from childhood. Wherever she traveled, she studied occult philosophy and practices. Arriving in New York City flat broke in 1873, having spent all her money paying for her passage, Blavatsky initially supported herself by laboring in a sweatshop, where she sewed purses and pen wipers.

According to Blavatsky, the incident described in "The Cave of the Echoes" is based on a true story. The dénouement had been witnessed by one of her relatives. She wrote several slightly different versions, which were published in both English and Russian. The earliest version seems to have appeared in the spiritualist journal, Banner of Light *in the March 30, 1873 edition.* [6]

The Theosophical Publishing Society in London published an anthology of Blavatsky's occult-themed stories in 1892 under the title Nightmare Tales. *"The Cave of the*

---

6 Katinka Hesselink.Net, *http://www.katinkahesselink.net/blavatsky/articles/v1/y1878_017.htm*

Echoes" is among them. The Weiser Book of Occult Detectives *features that 1892 version. The occult detective featured in "The Cave of the Echoes" is a mysterious and unnamed Hungarian traveler, whose arrival is "preceded by a great reputation for eccentricity, wealth and mysterious powers."*

The word "shaman" derives from Siberia, and in this story, Blavatsky carefully reserves that title for the Hungarian's also unnamed Siberian traveling companion. A shaman's traditional functions include locating missing people and objects, as well as solving otherwise unsolvable mysteries and restoring balance to a community—all these are accomplished in the tale by shamanic means. By 21st-century conventions, the Hungarian might also be described as a shaman, and it's tempting to think that Blavatsky was aware of linguistic similarities between Hungarian and certain indigenous Siberian languages. He utilizes mesmerism, "native magic," the sending of a double or fetch, and shamanic drumming to solve a crime.

The Cave of the Echoes

A Strange but True Story

(This story is given from the narrative of an eye-witness, a Russian gentleman, very pious, and fully trustworthy. Moreover, the facts are copied from the police records of P—. The eye-witness in question attributes it, of course, partly to divine interference and partly to the Evil One.   —H. P. B.)*

IN ONE OF THE DISTANT governments of the Russian empire, in a small town on the borders of Siberia, a mysterious tragedy occurred more than thirty years ago. About six versts from the little town of P—, famous for the wild beauty of its scenery, and for the wealth of its inhabitants—generally proprietors of mines and of iron foundries—stood an aristocratic mansion. Its household consisted of the master, a rich old bachelor and his brother, who was a widower and the father of two sons and three daughters.

It was known that the proprietor, Mr. Izvertzoff, had adopted his brother's children, and, having formed an especial attachment for his eldest nephew, Nicolas, he made him the sole heir of his numerous estates.

Time rolled on. The uncle was getting old, the nephew was coming of age. Days and years had passed in monotonous serenity, when, on the hitherto clear horizon of the quiet family, appeared a cloud. On an unlucky day one of the nieces took it into her head to study the zither. The instrument being of purely Teutonic origin, and no teacher of it residing in the neighbourhood, the indulgent uncle sent to St. Petersburg for both. After diligent search only one Professor could be found willing to trust himself in such close proximity to Siberia. It was an old German artist, who, sharing his affections equally between his instrument and a pretty blonde daughter, would part with neither. And thus it came to pass that, one fine morning, the old Professor arrived at the mansion, with his music box under one arm and his fair Munchen leaning on the other.

From that day the little cloud began growing rapidly; for every vibration of the melodious instrument found a responsive echo in the old bachelor's heart. Music awakens love, they say, and the work begun by the zither was completed by Munchen's blue eyes. At the expiration of six months the niece had become an expert zither player, and the uncle was desperately in love.

One morning, gathering his adopted family around him, he embraced them all very tenderly, promised to remember them in his will, and wound up by declaring his unalterable resolution to marry the blue-eyed Munchen. After this he fell upon their necks, and wept in silent rapture. The family, understanding that they were cheated out of the inheritance, also wept; but it was for another cause. Having thus wept, they consoled themselves and tried to rejoice, for the old gentleman was sincerely beloved by all. Not all of them rejoiced, though. Nicolas, who had himself been smitten to the heart by the pretty German, and who found himself defrauded at once of his belle and of his uncle's money, neither rejoiced nor consoled himself, but disappeared for a whole day.

Meanwhile, Mr. Izvertzoff had given orders to prepare his traveling carriage on the following day, and it was whispered that he was going to the chief town of the district, at some distance from his home, with the intention of altering his will. Though very wealthy, he had no superintendent on his estate, but kept his books himself. The same evening after supper, he was heard in his room, angrily scolding his servant, who had been in his service for over thirty years. This man, Ivan, was a native of northern Asia, from Kamschatka; he had been brought up by the family in the Christian religion, and was thought to be very much attached to his master. A few days later, when the first tragic circumstance I am about to relate had brought all the police force to the spot, it was remembered that on that night Ivan was drunk; that his master, who had a horror of this vice, had paternally thrashed him, and turned him out of his room, and that Ivan had been seen reeling out of the door, and had been heard to mutter threats.

On the vast domain of Mr. Izvertzoff there was a curious cavern, which excited the curiosity of all who visited it. It exists to this day, and is well known to every inhabitant of P—. A pine forest, commencing a few feet from the garden gate, climbs in steep terraces up a long range of rocky hills, which it covers with a broad belt of impenetrable vegetation. The grotto leading into the cavern, which is known as the "Cave of the Echoes," is situated about half a mile from the site of the mansion, from which it appears as a small excavation in the hillside, almost hidden by luxuriant plants, but not so completely as to prevent any person entering it from being readily seen from the terrace in front of the house. Entering the grotto, the explorer finds at the rear a narrow cleft; having passed through which he emerges into a lofty cavern, feebly lighted through fissures in the vaulted roof, fifty feet from the ground. The cavern itself is immense, and would easily hold between two and three thousand people. A part of it, in the days of Mr. Izvertzoff, was paved with flagstones, and was often used in the summer as a ball-room by picnic parties. Of an irregular oval, it gradually narrows into a broad corridor, which runs for several miles underground, opening here and there into other chambers, as large and lofty as the ball-room, but, unlike this, impassable otherwise than in a boat, as they are always full of water. These natural basins have the reputation of being unfathomable.

On the margin of the first of these is a small platform, with several mossy rustic seats arranged on it, and it is from this spot that the phenomenal echoes, which give the cavern its name, are heard in all their weirdness. A word pronounced in a whisper, or even a sigh, is caught up by endless mocking voices, and instead of diminishing in volume, as honest echoes do, the sound grows louder and louder at every successive repetition, until at last it bursts forth like the repercussion of a pistol shot, and recedes in a plaintive wail down the corridor.

On the day in question, Mr. Izvertzoff had mentioned his intention of having a dancing party in this cave on his wedding day, which he had fixed for an early date. On the following morning, while preparing for his drive, he was seen by his family entering the grotto, accompanied only by his Siberian servant. Half-an-hour later, Ivan returned to the mansion for a snuff-box which his master had forgotten in his room, and went back with it to the cave. An hour later the whole house was startled by his loud cries. Pale and dripping with water, Ivan rushed in like a madman, and declared that Mr. Izvertzoff was nowhere to be found in the cave. Thinking he had fallen into the lake, he had dived into the first basin in search of him and was nearly drowned himself.

The day passed in vain attempts to find the body. The police filled the house, and louder than the rest in his despair was Nicolas, the nephew, who had returned home only to meet the sad tidings.

A dark suspicion fell upon Ivan, the Siberian. He had been struck by his master the night before, and had been heard to swear revenge. He had accompanied him alone to the cave, and when his room was searched a box full of rich family jewellery, known to have been carefully kept in Mr. Izvertzoff's apartment, was found under Ivan's bedding. Vainly did the serf call God to witness that the box had been given to him in charge by his master himself, just before they proceeded to the cave; that it was the latter's purpose to have the jewellery reset, as he intended it for a wedding present to his bride; and that he, Ivan, would willingly give his own life to recall that of his master, if he knew him to be dead. No heed was paid to him, however, and he was arrested and thrown into prison, upon a charge of murder. There he was left, for under the Russian law a criminal cannot—at any rate, he could not in those days—be sentenced for a crime, however conclusive the circumstantial evidence, unless he confessed his guilt.

After a week had passed in useless search, the family arrayed themselves in deep mourning; and as the will as originally drawn remained without a codicil, the whole of the property passed into the hands of the nephew. The old teacher and his daughter bore this sudden reverse of fortune with true Germanic phlegm, and prepared to depart. Taking again his zither under one arm, the old man was about to lead away his Munchen by the other, when the nephew stopped him by offering himself as the fair damsel's husband in the place of his departed uncle. The change was found to be an agreeable one, and, without much ado, the young people were married.

Ten years rolled away, and we meet the happy family once more at the beginning of 1859. The fair Munchen had grown fat and vulgar. From the day of the old man's disappearance, Nicolas had become morose and retired in his habits, and many wondered at the change in him, for now he was never seen to smile. It seemed as if his only aim in life were to find out his uncle's murderer, or rather to bring Ivan to confess his guilt. But the man still persisted that he was innocent.

An only son had been born to the young couple, and a strange child it was. Small, delicate, and ever ailing, his frail life seemed to hang by a thread. When his features were in repose, his resemblance to his uncle was so striking that the members of the family often shrank from him in terror. It was the pale shrivelled face of a man of sixty upon the shoulders of a child nine years old. He was never seen either to laugh or to play, but, perched in his high chair, would gravely sit there, folding his arms in a way peculiar to the late Mr. Izvertzoff; and thus he would remain for hours, drowsy and motionless. His nurses were often seen furtively crossing themselves at night, upon approaching him, and not one of them would consent to sleep alone with him in the nursery. His father's behaviour towards him was still more strange. He seemed to love him passionately, and at the same time to hate him bitterly. He seldom embraced or caressed the child, but with livid cheek and staring eye, he would pass long hours watching him, as the child sat quietly in his corner, in his goblin-like, old-fashioned way.

The child had never left the estate, and few outside the family knew of his existence.

About the middle of July, a tall Hungarian traveller, preceded by a great reputation for eccentricity, wealth and mysterious powers, arrived at the town of P— from the North, where, it was said, he had resided for many years. He settled in the little town, in company with a Shaman or South Siberian magician, on whom he was said to make mesmeric experiments. He gave dinners and parties, and invariably exhibited his Shaman, of whom he felt very proud, for the amusement of his guests. One day the notables of P— made an unexpected invasion of the domains of Nicolas Izvertzoff, and requested the loan of his cave for an evening entertainment. Nicolas consented with great reluctance, and only after still greater hesitancy was he prevailed upon to join the party.

The first cavern and the platform beside the bottomless lake glittered with lights. Hundreds of flickering candles and torches, stuck in the clefts of the rocks, illuminated the place and drove the shadows from the mossy nooks and corners, where they had crouched undisturbed for many years. The stalactites on the walls sparkled brightly, and the sleeping echoes were suddenly awakened by a joyous confusion of laughter and conversation. The Shaman, who was never lost sight of by his friend and patron, sat in a corner, entranced as usual. Crouched on a projecting rock, about midway between the entrance and the water, with his lemon-yellow, wrinkled face, flat nose, and thin beard, he looked more like an ugly stone idol than a human being. Many of the company pressed around him and received correct answers to their questions, the Hungarian cheerfully submitting his mesmerized "subject" to cross-examination.

Suddenly one of the party, a lady, remarked that it was in that very cave that old Mr. Izvertzoff had so unaccountably disappeared ten years before. The foreigner appeared interested, and desired to learn more of the circumstances, so Nicolas was sought amid the crowd and led before the eager group. He was the host and he found it impossible to refuse the demanded narrative. He repeated the sad tale in a trembling voice, with a pallid cheek, and tears were seen glittering in his feverish eyes. The company were greatly affected, and encomiums upon the behaviour of the loving nephew in honouring the memory of his uncle and benefactor were freely circulating in whispers, when suddenly the voice of Nicolas became choked, his eyes started from their sockets, and, with a suppressed groan, he staggered back. Every eye in the crowd followed with curiosity his haggard look, as it fell and remained riveted upon a weazened little face, that peeped from behind the back of the Hungarian.

"Where do you come from? Who brought you here, child?" gasped out Nicolas, as pale as death.

"I was in bed, papa; this man came to me, and brought me here in his arms," answered the boy simply, pointing to the Shaman, beside whom he stood upon the rock, and who, with his eyes closed, kept swaying himself to and fro like a living pendulum.

"That is very strange," remarked one of the guests, "for the man has never moved from his place."

"Good God! what an extraordinary resemblance!" muttered an old resident of the town, a friend of the lost man.

"You lie, child!" fiercely exclaimed the father. "Go to bed; this is no place for you."

"Come, come," interposed the Hungarian, with a strange expression on his face, and encircling with his arm the slender childish figure; "the little fellow has seen the double of my Shaman, which roams sometimes far away from his body, and has mistaken the phantom for the man himself. Let him remain with us for a while."

At these strange words the guests stared at each other in mute surprise, while some piously made the sign of the cross, spitting aside, presumably at the devil and all his works.

"By-the-bye," continued the Hungarian with a peculiar firmness of accent, and addressing the company rather than any one in particular; "why should we not try, with the help of my Shaman, to unravel the mystery hanging over the tragedy? Is the suspected party still lying in prison? What? he has not confessed up to now? This is surely very strange. But now we will learn the truth in a few minutes! Let all keep silent!"

He then approached the Tehuktchene, and immediately began his performance without so much as asking the consent of the master of the place. The latter stood rooted to the spot, as if petrified with horror, and unable to articulate a word. The suggestion met with general approbation, save from him; and the police inspector, Col. S—, especially approved of the idea.

"Ladies and gentlemen," said the mesmerizer in soft tones, "allow me for this once to proceed otherwise than in my general fashion. I will employ the method of native magic. It is more appropriate to this wild place, and far more effective as you will find, than our European method of mesmerization."

Without waiting for an answer, he drew from a bag that never left his person, first a small drum, and then two little phials—one full of fluid, the other empty. With the contents of the former he sprinkled the Shaman, who fell to trembling and nodding more violently than ever. The air was filled with the perfume of spicy odours, and the atmosphere itself seemed to become clearer. Then, to the horror of those present, he approached the Tibetan, and taking a miniature stiletto from his pocket, he plunged the sharp steel into the man's forearm, and drew blood from it, which he caught in the empty phial. When it was half filled, he pressed the orifice of the wound with his thumb, and stopped the flow of blood as easily as if he had corked a bottle, after which he sprinkled the blood over the little boy's head. He then suspended the drum from his neck, and, with two ivory drum-sticks, which were covered with magic signs and letters, he began beating a sort of *reveille*, to drum up the spirits, as he said.

The bystanders, half-shocked and half-terrified by these extraordinary proceedings, eagerly crowded round him, and for a few moments a dead silence reigned throughout the lofty cavern. Nicolas, with his face livid and corpse-like, stood speechless as before. The mesmerizer had placed himself between the Shaman and the platform, when he began slowly drumming. The first notes were muffled, and vibrated so softly in the air that they awakened no echo, but the Shaman quickened his pendulum-like motion and the child became restless. The drummer then began a slow chant, low, impressive and solemn.

As the unknown words issued from his lips, the flames of the candles and torches wavered and flickered, until they began dancing in rhythm with the chant. A cold wind came wheezing from the dark corridors beyond the water, leaving a plaintive echo in its trail. Then a sort of nebulous vapour, seeming to ooze from the rocky ground and walls, gathered about the Shaman and the boy. Around the latter the aura was silvery and transparent, but the cloud which enveloped the former was red and sinister.

Approaching nearer to the platform the magician beat a louder roll upon the drum, and this time the echo caught it up with terrific effect! It reverberated near and far in incessant peals; one wail followed another louder and louder, until the thundering roar seemed the chorus of a thousand demon voices rising from the fathomless depths of the lake. The water itself, whose surface, illuminated by many lights, had previously been smooth as a sheet of glass, became suddenly agitated, as if a powerful gust of wind had swept over its unruffled face.

Another chant, and a roll of the drum, and the mountain trembled to its foundation with the cannon-like peals which rolled through the dark and distant corridors. The Shaman's body rose two yards in the air, and nodding and swaying, sat, self-suspended like an apparition. But the transformation which now occurred in the boy chilled everyone, as they speechlessly watched the scene. The silvery cloud about the boy now seemed to lift him, too, into the air; but, unlike the Shaman, his feet never left the ground. The child began to grow, as though the work of years was miraculously accomplished in a few seconds. He became tall and large, and his senile features grew older with the ageing of his body.

A few more seconds, and the youthful form had entirely disappeared. It was totally absorbed in another individuality, and, to the horror of those present who had been familiar with his appearance, this individuality was that of old Mr. Izvertzoff, and on his temple was a large gaping wound, from which trickled great drops of blood.

This phantom moved towards Nicolas, till it stood directly in front of him, while he, with his hair standing erect, with the look of a madman gazed at his own son, transformed into his uncle. The sepulchral silence was broken by the Hungarian, who, addressing the child phantom, asked him, in solemn voice:

"In the name of the great Master, of Him who has all power, answer the truth, and nothing but the truth. Restless spirit, hast thou been lost by accident, or foully murdered?"

The spectre's lips moved, but it was the echo which answered for them in lugubrious shouts: "Murdered! mur-der-ed!! murdered!!!"

"Where? How? By whom?" asked the conjuror.

The apparition pointed a finger at Nicolas and, without removing its gaze or lowering its arms, retreated backwards slowly towards the lake. At every step it took, the younger Izvertzoff, as if compelled by some irresistible fascination, advanced a step towards it, until the phantom reached the lake, and the next moment was seen gliding on its surface. It was a fearful, ghostly scene!

When he had come within two steps of the brink of the watery abyss, a violent convulsion ran through the frame of the guilty man. Flinging himself upon his knees, he clung to one of the rustic seats with a desperate clutch, and staring wildly, uttered a long piercing cry of agony. The phantom now remained motionless on the water, and bending his extended finger, slowly beckoned him to come. Crouched in abject terror, the wretched man shrieked until the cavern rang again and again: "I did not . . . No, I did not murder you!"

Then came a splash, and now it was the boy who was in the dark water, struggling for his life, in the middle of the lake, with the same motionless stern apparition brooding over him.

"Papa! papa! Save me . . . I am drowning!" . . . cried a piteous little voice amid the uproar of the mocking echoes.

"My boy!" shrieked Nicolas, in the accents of a maniac, springing to his feet. "My boy! Save him! Oh, save him! . . . Yes I confess . . . I am the murderer . . . It is I who killed him!"

Another splash, and the phantom disappeared. With a cry of horror the company rushed towards the platform; but their feet were suddenly rooted to the ground, as they saw amid the swirling eddies a whitish shapeless mass holding the murderer and the boy in tight embrace, and slowly sinking into the bottomless lake . . .

On the morning after these occurrences, when, after a sleepless night, some of the party visited the residence of the Hungarian gentleman, they found it closed and deserted. He and the Shaman had disappeared. Many are among the old inhabitants of P— who remember him; the Police Inspector, Col. S—, dying a few years ago in the full assurance that the noble traveller was the devil. To add to the general consternation the Izvertzoff mansion took fire on that same night and was completely destroyed. The Archbishop performed the ceremony of exorcism, but the locality is considered accursed to this day. The Government investigated the facts, and—ordered silence.

THE STORY OF
YAND MANOR HOUSE

Kate and Hesketh Prichard
(H. Heron and E. Heron)

*Flaxman Low, the occult psychologist who solves the mystery at Yand Manor House,
has been described as the first "true occult detective" or, at least, the first occult detective
to appear in a series of stories. An argument could be made that* In a Glass Darkly
*introduces Dr. Hesselius and predates Low; but Hesselius is not always an active partic-
ipant in his stories, unlike Low, who is an athlete as well as a scientist and author.*

Flaxman first appeared in a series of stories published in Pearson's Magazine
*in 1898 and 1899, which were credited to authors E. and H. Heron. These were then
collected and published in book form in 1899 under the title* Ghosts: Being the
Experiences of Flaxman Low, *but the authors' true names were revealed:
mother-and-son writing team, Kate and Hesketh Prichard.*

*Major Hesketh Vernon Hesketh-Prichard (1876–1922)—called Hex by his
friends—was born in Jhansi, India, where his father, an officer in the King's Own Scottish Borderers, had died from typhoid six weeks before his son's birth. Kate O'Brien Ryall
Prichard (1851–1935) soon returned to Britain with her infant son. They would remain
close for the rest of Hesketh's life. The Flaxman Low stories were not their only literary
collaboration, and Hesketh also had an extensive independent literary career.*

*Hesketh–Prichard was a larger–than–life character—in addition to being an author,
athlete, scholar, and soldier, he was an adventurer, a lauded marksman, and a big game
hunter, who, like Teddy Roosevelt, was simultaneously a conservationist. By contrast,
little is known of Kate, beyond her role as Hesketh's mother and collaborator.*

*Many early readers did not understand that Flaxman Low and his stories were fic-
tional and assumed otherwise. Just as E. and H. Heron are pseudonyms for Kate and*

Hesketh Prichard, so many believed that Flaxman Low was a pseudonym for an actual occult psychologist, whose real name remained undisclosed. This is not so far-fetched when one considers Dion Fortune's later occult physician, Dr. Taverner. (See "The Return of the Ritual" on page 269.)

Flaxman, unlike so many occult detectives, lacks a Watson-style sidekick, although he does travel with a friend in "The Story of Yand Manor House." It's unclear who narrates his tales—the impression is given that the authors themselves are narrating and that the stories are based on Flaxman's papers and case studies.

Low, calm and detached, is among the most Holmesian of the occult detectives: he solves crimes based on his extensive occult and scientific knowledge, as well as his powers of observation. The psychic phenomena he encounters tend toward the unusual. Although he is described as having "devoted his life to the study of psychical phenomena," Flaxman discourages others who "feel inclined to dabble in spiritualism, without any serious motive for doing so."

The Story of Yand Manor House

Looking through the notes of Mr. Flaxman Low, one sometimes catches through the steel-blue hardness of facts, the pink flush of romance, or more often the black corner of a horror unnameable. The following story may serve as an instance of the latter. Mr. Low not only unravelled the mystery at Yand, but at the same time justified his life-work to M. Thierry, the well-known French critic and philosopher.

At the end of a long conversation, M. Thierry, arguing from his own standpoint as a materialist, had said:

"The factor in the human economy which you call 'soul' cannot be placed."

"I admit that," replied Low. "Yet, when a man dies, is there not one factor unaccounted for in the change that comes upon him? Yes! For though his body still exists, it rapidly falls to pieces, which proves that that has gone which held it together."

The Frenchman laughed, and shifted his ground.

"Well, for my part, I don't believe in ghosts! Spirit manifestations, occult phenomena—is not this the ashbin into which a certain clique shoot everything they cannot understand, or for which they fail to account?"

"Then what should you say to me, Monsieur, if I told you that I have passed a good portion of my life in investigating this particular ashbin, and have been lucky enough to sort a small part of its contents with tolerable success?" replied Flaxman Low.

"The subject is doubtless interesting—but I should like to have some personal experience in the matter," said Thierry dubiously.

"I am at present investigating a most singular case," said Low. "Have you a day or two to spare?"

Thierry thought for a minute or more.

"I am grateful," he replied. "But, forgive me, is it a convincing ghost?"

"Come with me to Yand and see. I have been there once already, and came away for the purpose of procuring information from MSS. to which I have the privilege of access, for I confess that the phenomena at Yand lie altogether outside any former experience of mine."

Low sank back into his chair with his hands clasped behind his head—a favourite position of his—and the smoke of his long pipe curled up lazily into the golden face of an Isis, which stood behind him on a bracket. Thierry, glancing across, was struck by the strange likeness between the faces of the Egyptian goddess and this scientist of the nineteenth century. On both rested the calm, mysterious abstraction of some unfathomable thought. As he looked, he decided.

"I have three days to place at your disposal."

"I thank you heartily," replied Low. "To be associated with so brilliant a logician as yourself in an inquiry of this nature is more than I could have hoped for! The material with which I have to deal is so elusive, the whole subject is wrapped in such obscurity and hampered by so much prejudice, that I can find few really qualified persons who care to approach these investigations seriously. I go down to Yand this evening, and hope not to leave without clearing up the mystery. You will accompany me?"

"Most certainly. Meanwhile pray tell me something of the affair."

"Briefly the story is as follows. Some weeks ago I went to Yand Manor House at the request of the owner, Sir George Blackburton, to see what I could make of the events which took place there. All they complain of is the impossibility of remaining in one room— the dining-room."

"What then is he like, this M. le Spook?" asked the Frenchman, laughing.

"No one has ever seen him, or for that matter heard him."

"Then how—"

"You can't see him, nor hear him, nor smell him," went on Low, "but you can feel him and—taste him!"

"*Mon Dieu!* But this is singular! Is he then of so bad a flavour?"

"You shall taste for yourself," answered Flaxman Low smiling. "After a certain hour no one can remain in the room, they are simply crowded out."

"But who crowds them out?" asked Thierry.

"That is just what I hope we may discover to-night or tomorrow."

The last train that night dropped Mr. Flaxman Low and his companion at a little station near Yand. It was late, but a trap in waiting soon carried them to the Manor House. The big bulk of the building stood up in absolute blackness before them.

"Blackburton was to have met us, but I suppose he has not yet arrived," said Low. "Hullo! the door is open," he added as he stepped into the hall.

Beyond a dividing curtain they now perceived a light. Passing behind this curtain they found themselves at the end of the long hall, the wide staircase opening up in front of them.

"But who is this?" exclaimed Thierry.

Swaying and stumbling at every step, there tottered slowly down the stairs the figure of a man. He looked as if he had been drinking, his face was livid, and his eyes sunk into his head.

"Thank Heaven you've come! I heard you outside," he said in a weak voice.

"It's Sir George Blackburton," said Low, as the man lurched forward and pitched into his arms.

They laid him down on the rugs and tried to restore consciousness.

"He has the air of being drunk, but it is not so," remarked Thierry. "Monsieur has had a bad shock of the nerves. See the pulses drumming in his throat."

In a few minutes Blackburton opened his eyes and staggered to his feet.

"Come. I could not remain there alone. Come quickly."

They went rapidly across the hall, Blackburton leading the way down a wide passage to a double-leaved door, which, after a perceptible pause, he threw open, and they all entered together.

On the great table in the centre stood an extinguished lamp, some scattered food, and a big, lighted candle. But the eyes of all three men passed at once to a dark recess beside the heavy, carved chimneypiece, where a rigid shape sat perched on the back of a huge, oak chair.

Flaxman Low snatched up the candle and crossed the room towards it.

On the top of the chair, with his feet upon the arms, sat a powerfully-built young man huddled up. His mouth was open, and his eyes twisted upwards. Nothing further could be seen from below but the ghastly pallor of cheek and throat.

"Who is this?" cried Low. Then he laid his hand gently on the man's knee.

At the touch the figure collapsed in a heap upon the floor, the gaping, set, terrified face turned up to theirs.

"He's dead!" said Low after a hasty examination. "I should say he's been dead some hours."

"Oh, Lord! Poor Batty!" groaned Sir George, who was entirely unnerved. "I'm glad you've come."

"Who is he?" said Thierry, "and what was he doing here?"

"He's a gamekeeper of mine. He was always anxious to try conclusions with the ghost, and last night he begged me to lock him in here with food for twenty-four hours. I refused at first, but then I thought if anything happened while he was in here alone, it would interest you. Who could imagine it would end like this?"

"When did you find him?" asked Low.

"I only got here from my mother's half an hour ago. I turned on the light in the hall and came in here with a candle. As I entered the room, the candle went out, and—and—I think I must be going mad."

"Tell us everything you saw," urged Low.

"You will think I am beside myself; but as the light went out and I sank almost paralysed into an armchair, I saw two barred eyes looking at me!"

"Barred eyes? What do you mean?"

"Eyes that looked at me through thin vertical bars, like the bars of a cage. What's that?"

With a smothered yell Sir George sprang back. He had approached the dead man and declared something had brushed his face.

"You were standing on this spot under the overmantel. I will remain here. Meantime, my dear Thierry, I feel sure you will help Sir George to carry this poor fellow to some more suitable place," said Flaxman Low.

When the dead body of the young gamekeeper had been carried out, Low passed slowly round and about the room. At length he stood under the old carved overmantel, which reached to the ceiling and projected bodily forward in quaint heads of satyrs and animals.

One of these on the side nearest the recess represented a griffin with a flanged mouth. Sir George had been standing directly below this at the moment when he felt the touch on his face. Now alone in the dim, wide room, Flaxman Low stood on the same spot and waited. The candle threw its dull yellow rays on the shadows, which seemed to gather closer and wait also. Presently a distant door banged, and Low, leaning forward to listen, distinctly felt something on the back of his neck!

He swung round. There was nothing! He searched carefully on all sides, then put his hand up to the griffin's head. Again came the same soft touch, this time upon his hand, as if something had floated past on the air.

This was definite. The griffin's head located it. Taking the candle to examine more closely, Low found four long black hairs depending from the jagged fangs. He was detaching them when Thierry reappeared.

"We must get Sir George away as soon as possible," he said.

"Yes, we must take him away, I fear," agreed Low. "Our investigation must be put off till to-morrow."

On the following day they returned to Yand. It was a large country house, pretty and old-fashioned, with lattice windows and deep gables, that looked out between tall shrubs and across lawns set with beaupots, where peacocks sunned themselves on the velvet turf. The church spire peered over the trees on one side; and an old wall covered with ivy and creeping plants, and pierced at intervals with arches, alone separated the gardens from the churchyard.

The haunted room lay at the back of the house. It was square and handsome, and furnished in the style of the last century. The oak overmantel reached to the ceiling, and a wide window, which almost filled one side of the room, gave a view of the west door of the church.

Low stood for a moment at the open window looking out at the level sunlight which flooded the lawns and parterres.

"See that door sunk in the church wall to the left?" said Sir George's voice at his elbow. "That is the door of the family vault. Cheerful outlook, isn't it?"

"I should like to walk across there presently," remarked Low.

"What! Into the vault?" asked Sir George, with a harsh laugh. "I'll take you if you like. Anything else I can show you or tell you?"

"Yes. Last night I found this hanging from the griffin's head," said Low, producing the thin wisp of black hair. "It must have touched your cheek as you stood below. Do you know to whom it can belong?"

"It's a woman's hair! No, the only woman who has been in this room to my knowledge for months is an old servant with grey hair, who cleans it," returned Blackburton. "I'm sure it was not here when I locked Batty in."

"It is human hair, exceedingly coarse and long uncut," said Low; "but it is not necessarily a woman's."

"It is not mine at any rate, for I'm sandy; and poor Batty was fair. Good-night; I'll come round for you in the morning."

Presently, when the night closed in, Thierry and Low settled down in the haunted room to await developments. They smoked and talked deep into the night. A big lamp burned brightly on the table, and the surroundings looked homely and desirable.

Thierry made a remark to that effect, adding that perhaps the ghost might see fit to omit his usual visit.

"Experience goes to prove that ghosts have a cunning habit of choosing persons either credulous or excitable to experiment upon," he added.

To M. Thierry's surprise, Flaxman Low agreed with him.

"They certainly choose suitable persons," he said, "that is, not credulous persons, but those whose senses are sufficiently keen to detect the presence of a spirit. In my own investigations, I try to eliminate what you would call the supernatural element. I deal with these mysterious affairs as far as possible on material lines."

"Then what do you say of Batty's death? He died of fright—simply."

"I hardly think so. The manner of his death agrees in a peculiar manner with what we know of the terrible history of this room. He died of fright and pressure combined. Did you hear the doctor's remark? It was significant. He said: 'The indications are precisely those I have observed in persons who have been crushed and killed in a crowd!'"

"That is sufficiently curious, I allow. I see that it is already past two o'clock. I am thirsty; I will have a little seltzer." Thierry rose from his chair, and, going to the side-board, drew a tumblerful from the syphon. "Pah! What an abominable taste!"

"What? The seltzer?"

"Not at all?" returned the Frenchman irritably. "I have not touched it yet. Some horrible fly has flown into my mouth, I suppose. Pah! Disgusting!"

"What is it like?" asked Flaxman Low, who was at the moment wiping his own mouth with his handkerchief.

"Like? As if some repulsive fungus had burst in the mouth."

"Exactly. I perceive it also. I hope you are about to be convinced."

"What?" exclaimed Thierry, turning his big figure round and staring at Low. "You don't mean—."

As he spoke the lamp suddenly went out.

"Why, then, have you put the lamp out at such a moment?" cried Thierry.

"I have not put it out. Light the candle beside you on the table."

Low heard the Frenchman's grunt of satisfaction as he found the candle, then the scratch of a match. It sputtered and went out. Another match and another behaved in the same manner, while Thierry swore freely under his breath.

"Let me have your matches, Monsieur Flaxman; mine are, no doubt damp," he said at last.

Low rose to feel his way across the room. The darkness was dense.

"It is the darkness of Egypt—it may be felt. Where then are you, my dear friend?" he heard Thierry saying, but the voice seemed a long way off.

"I am coming," he answered, "but it's so hard to get along."

After Low had spoken the words, their meaning struck him. He paused and tried to realise in what part of the room he was. The silence was profound, and the growing sense of oppression seemed like a nightmare. Thierry's voice sounded again, faint and receding.

"I am suffocating, Monsieur Flaxman, where are you? I am near the door. Ach!"

A strangling bellow of pain and fear followed, that scarcely reached Low through the thickening atmosphere.

"Thierry, what is the matter with you?" he shouted. "Open the door."

But there was no answer. What had become of Thierry in that hideous, clogging gloom! Was he also dead, crushed in some ghastly fashion against the wall? What was this?

The air had become palpable to the touch, heavy, repulsive, with the sensation of cold humid flesh!

Low pushed out his hands with a mad longing to touch a table, a chair, anything but this clammy, swelling softness that thrust itself upon him from every side, baffling him and filling his grasp.

He knew now that he was absolutely alone—struggling against what?

His feet were slipping in his wild efforts to feel the floor—the dank flesh was creeping upon his neck, his cheek—his breath came short and labouring as the pressure swung him gently to and fro, helpless, nauseated!

The clammy flesh crowded upon him like the bulk of some fat, horrible creature; then came a stinging pain on the cheek. Low clutched at something—there was a crash and a rush of air—

The next sensation of which Mr. Flaxman Low was conscious was one of deathly sickness. He was lying on wet grass, the wind blowing over him, and all the clean, wholesome smells of the open air in his nostrils.

He sat up and looked about him. Dawn was breaking windily in the east, and by its light he saw that he was on the lawn of Yand Manor House. The latticed window of the haunted room above him was open. He tried to remember what had happened. He took stock of himself, in fact, and slowly felt that he still held something clutched in his right hand—something dark-coloured, slender, and twisted. It might have been a long shred of bark or the cast skin of an adder—it was impossible to see in the dim light.

After an interval the recollection of Thierry recurred to him. Scrambling to his feet, he raised himself to the window-sill and looked in. Contrary to his expectation, there was no upsetting of furniture; everything remained in position as when the lamp went out. His own chair and the one Thierry had occupied were just as when they had arisen from them. But there was no sign of Thierry.

Low jumped in by the window. There was the tumbler full of seltzer, and the litter of matches about it. He took up Thierry's box of matches and struck a light. It flared, and he lit the candle with ease. In fact, everything about the room was perfectly normal; all the horrible conditions prevailing but a couple of hours ago had disappeared.

But where was Thierry? Carrying the lighted candle, he passed out of the door, and searched in the adjoining rooms. In one of them, to his relief, he found the Frenchman sleeping profoundly in an armchair.

Low touched his arm. Thierry leapt to his feet, fending off an imaginary blow with his arm. Then he turned his scared face on Low.

"What! You, Monsieur Flaxman! How have you escaped?"

"I should rather ask you how you escaped," said Low, smiling at the havoc the night's experiences had worked on his friend's looks and spirits.

"I was crowded out of the room against the door. That infernal thing—what was it?—with its damp, swelling flesh, inclosed me!" A shudder of disgust stopped him. "I was a fly in an aspic. I could not move. I sank into the stifling pulp. The air grew thick. I called to you, but your answers became inaudible. Then I was suddenly thrust against the door by a huge hand—it felt like one, at least. I had a struggle for my life, I was all but crushed, and then, I do not know how, I found myself outside the door. I shouted to you in vain. Therefore, as I could not help you, I came here, and—I will confess it, my dear friend—I locked and bolted the door. After some time I went again into the hall and listened; but, as I heard nothing, I resolved to wait until daylight and the return of Sir George."

"That's all right," said Low. "It was an experience worth having."

"But, no! Not for me! I do not envy you your researches into mysteries of this abominable description. I now comprehend perfectly that Sir George has lost his nerve if he has had to do with this horror. Besides, it is entirely impossible to explain these things."

At this moment they heard Sir George's arrival, and went out to meet him.

"I could not sleep all night for thinking of you!" exclaimed Blackburton on seeing them; "and I came along as soon as it was light. Something has happened?"

"But certainly something has happened," cried M. Thierry shaking his head solemnly; "something of the most bizarre, of the most horrible! Monsieur Flaxman, you shall tell Sir George this story. You have been in that accursed room all night, and remain alive to tell the tale!"

As Low came to the conclusion of the story Sir George suddenly exclaimed:

"You have met with some injury to your face, Mr. Low."

Low turned to the mirror. In the now strong light three parallel weals from eye to mouth could be seen.

"I remember a stinging pain like a lash on my cheek. What would you say these marks were caused by, Thierry?" asked Low.

Thierry looked at them and shook his head.

"No one in their senses would venture to offer any explanation of the occurrences of last night," he replied.

"Something of this sort, do you think?" asked Low again, putting down the object he held in his hand on the table.

Thierry took it up and described it aloud.

"A long and thin object of a brown and yellow colour and twisted like a sabre-bladed corkscrew," then he started slightly and glanced at Low.

"It's a human nail, I imagine," suggested Low.

"But no human being has talons of this kind—except, perhaps, a Chinaman of high rank."

"There are no Chinamen about here, nor ever have been, to my knowledge," said Blackburton shortly. "I'm very much afraid that, in spite of all you have so bravely faced, we are no nearer to any rational explanation."

"On the contrary, I fancy I begin to see my way. I believe, after all, that I may be able to convert you, Thierry," said Flaxman Low.

"Convert me?"

"To a belief in the definite aim of my work. But you shall judge for yourself. What do you make of it so far? I claim that you know as much of the matter as I do."

"My dear good friend, I make nothing of it," returned Thierry, shrugging his shoulders and spreading out his hands. "Here we have a tissue of unprecedented incidents that can be explained on no theory whatever."

"But this is definite," and Flaxman Low held up the blackened nail.

"And how do you propose to connect that nail with the black hairs—with the eyes that looked through the bars of a cage—the fate of Batty, with its symptoms of death by pressure and suffocation—our experience of swelling flesh, that something which filled and filled the room to the exclusion of all else? How are you going to account for these things by any kind of connected hypothesis?" asked Thierry, with a shade of irony.

"I mean to try," replied Low.

At lunch time Thierry inquired how the theory was getting on. "It progresses," answered Low. "By the way, Sir George, who lived in this house for some time prior to, say, 1840? He was a man—it may have been a woman, but, from the nature of his studies, I am inclined to think it was a man—who was deeply read in ancient necromancy, Eastern magic, mesmerism, and subjects of a kindred nature. And was he not buried in the vault you pointed out?"

"Do you know anything more about him?" asked Sir George in surprise.

"He was I imagine," went on Flaxman Low reflectively, "hirsute and swarthy, probably a recluse, and suffered from a morbid and extravagant fear of death."

"How do you know all this?"

"I only asked about it. Am I right?"

"You have described my cousin, Sir Gilbert Blackburton, in every particular. I can show you his portrait in another room."

As they stood looking at the painting of Sir Gilbert Blackburton, with his long, melancholy, olive face and thick, black beard, Sir George went on. "My grandfather succeeded him at Yand. I have often heard my father speak of Sir Gilbert, and his strange studies and extraordinary fear of death. Oddly enough, in the end he died rather suddenly, while he was still hale and strong. He predicted his own approaching death, and had a doctor in attendance for a week or two before he died. He was placed in a coffin he had had made on some plan of his own and buried in the vault. His death occurred in 1842 or 1843. If you care to see them I can show you some of his papers, which may interest you."

Mr. Flaxman Low spent the afternoon over the papers. When evening came, he rose from his work with a sigh of content, stretched himself, and joined Thierry and Sir George in the garden.

They dined at Lady Blackburton's, and it was late before Sir George found himself alone with Mr. Flaxman Low and his friend.

"Have you formed any opinion about the thing which haunts the Manor House?" he asked anxiously.

Thierry elaborated a cigarette, crossed his legs, and added: "If you have in truth come to any definite conclusion, pray let us hear it, my dear Monsieur Flaxman."

"I have reached a very definite and satisfactory conclusion," replied Low. "The Manor House is haunted by Sir Gilbert Black-burton, who died, or, rather, who seemed to die, on the 15th of August, 1842."

"Nonsense! The nail fifteen inches long at the least—how do you connect it with Sir Gilbert?" asked Blackburton testily.

"I am convinced that it belonged to Sir Gilbert," Low answered.

"But the long black hair like a woman's?"

"Dissolution in the case of Sir Gilbert was not complete—not consummated, so to speak—as I hope to show you later. Even in the case of dead persons the hair and nails have been known to grow. By a rough calculation as to the growth of nails in such cases, I was enabled to indicate approximately the date of Sir Gilbert's death. The hair too grew on his head."

"But the barred eyes? I saw them myself!" exclaimed the young man.

"The eyelashes grow also. You follow me?"

"You have, I presume, some theory in connection with this?" observed Thierry. "It must be a very curious one."

"Sir Gilbert in his fear of death appears to have mastered and elaborated a strange and ancient formula by which the grosser factors of the body being eliminated, the more ethereal portions continue to retain the spirit, and the body is thus preserved from absolute disintegration. In this manner true death may be indefinitely deferred. Secure from the ordinary chances and changes of existence, this spiritualised body could retain a modified life practically for ever."

"This is a most extraordinary idea, my dear fellow," remarked Thierry.

"But why should Sir Gilbert haunt the Manor House, and one special room?"

"The tendency of spirits to return to the old haunts of bodily life is almost universal. We cannot yet explain the reason of this attraction of environment."

"But the expansion—the crowding substance which we ourselves felt? You cannot meet that difficulty," said Thierry persistently.

"Not as fully as I could wish, perhaps. But the power of expanding and contracting to a degree far beyond our comprehension is a well-known attribute of spiritualised matter."

"Wait one little moment, my dear Monsieur Flaxman," broke in Thierry's voice after an interval; "this is very clever and ingenious indeed. As a theory I give it my sincere admiration. But proof—proof is what we now demand."

Flaxman Low looked steadily at the two incredulous faces.

"This," he said slowly, "is the hair of Sir Gilbert Blackburton, and this nail is from the little finger of his left hand. You can prove my assertion by opening the coffin."

Sir George, who was pacing up and down the room impatiently, drew up.

"I don't like it at all, Mr. Low, I tell you frankly. I don't like it at all. I see no object in violating the coffin. I am not concerned to verify this unpleasant theory of yours. I have only one desire; I want to get rid of this haunting presence, whatever it is."

"If I am right," replied Low, "the opening of the coffin and exposure of the remains to strong sunshine for a short time will free you for ever from this presence."

In the early morning, when the summer sun struck warmly on the lawns of Yand, the three men carried the coffin from the vault to a quiet spot among the shrubs where, secure from observation, they raised the lid.

Within the coffin lay the semblance of Gilbert Blackburton, maned to the ears with long and coarse black hair. Matted eyelashes swept the fallen cheeks, and beside the body stretched the bony hands, each with its dependent sheaf of switch-like nails. Low bent over and raised the left hand gingerly.

The little finger was without a nail!

Two hours later they came back and looked again. The sun had in the meantime done its work; nothing remained but a fleshless skeleton and a few half-rotten shreds of clothing.

The ghost of Yand Manor House has never since been heard of.

When Thiery bade Flaxman Low good-bye, he said:

"In time, my dear Monsieur Flaxman, you will add another to our sciences. You establish your facts too well for my peace of mind."

THE LEATHER FUNNEL

Sir Arthur Conan Doyle

Sir Arthur Conan Doyle is, of course, renowned as the creator of the world's most famous and influential detective, Sherlock Holmes. His influence can be felt in many of the stories by other authors in The Weiser Book of Occult Detectives. *Ironically, Doyle himself was ambivalent toward his literary creation, killing off the character at one point, only to eventually resurrect him in response to public demand—and to his own personal financial demands.*

Many readers identified Doyle with the resolutely rationalist Holmes. However, Doyle was a spiritual seeker with a deep commitment to Spiritualism. He authored several books devoted to Spiritualism, including nonfiction works such as The History of Spiritualism *and* Wanderings of a Spiritualist. *He also wrote fiction with supernatural themes. Doyle created other detectives, in addition to Holmes, although never with any comparable success. In "The Leather Funnel," Lionel Dacre, an occultist residing in Paris, investigates the provenance of antiquities. Although he is an educated, book-learned authority on the occult, Dacre also relies on dreams and psychometry to solve his mystery.*

SPOILER ALERT: Although this story is fictional, it's based on history. Marie-Madeleine-Marguerite D'Aubray, the Marquise de Brinvilliers, was arrested and charged with murder and witchcraft in 1676. Although the story presupposes her guilt, her confession was obtained under duress—she was brutally tortured—and there's no way to determine whether or not she was, indeed, guilty. Her trial sparked a massive witch-hunt that eventually reached into the household of Louis XIV. "The Leather Funnel" follows aspects of her story faithfully. Those seeking more information about the case will find information in Encyclopedia of Witchcraft *by Judika Illes (HarperOne, 2014).*

The Leather Funnel

MY FRIEND, LIONEL DACRE, lived in the Avenue de Wagram, Paris. His house was that small one, with the iron railings and grass plot in front of it, on the left-hand side as you pass down from the Arc de Triomphe. I fancy that it had been there long before the avenue was constructed, for the grey tiles were stained with lichens, and the walls were mildewed and discoloured with age. It looked a small house from the street, five windows in front, if I remember right, but it deepened into a single long chamber at the back. It was here that Dacre had that singular library of occult literature, and the fantastic curiosities which served as a hobby for himself, and an amusement for his friends. A wealthy man of refined and eccentric tastes, he had spent much of his life and fortune in gathering together what was said to be a unique private collection of Talmudic, cabalistic, and magical works, many of them of great rarity and value. His tastes leaned toward the marvellous and the monstrous, and I have heard that his experiments in the direction of the unknown have passed all the bounds of civilization and of decorum. To his English friends he never alluded to such matters, and took the tone of the student and virtuoso; but a Frenchman whose tastes were of the same nature has assured me that the worst excesses of the black mass have been perpetrated in that large and lofty hall, which is lined with the shelves of his books, and the cases of his museum.

Dacre's appearance was enough to show that his deep interest in these psychic matters was intellectual rather than spiritual. There was no trace of asceticism upon his heavy face, but there was much mental force in his huge, dome-like skull, which curved upward from amongst his thinning locks, like a snowpeak above its fringe of fir trees. His knowledge was greater than his wisdom, and his powers were far superior to his character. The small bright eyes, buried deeply in his fleshy face, twinkled with intelligence and an unabated curiosity of life, but they were the eyes of a sensualist and an egotist. Enough of the man, for he is dead now, poor devil, dead at the very time that he had made sure that he had at last discovered the elixir of life. It is not with his complex character that I have to deal, but with the very strange and inexplicable incident which had its rise in my visit to him in the early spring of the year '82.

I had known Dacre in England, for my researches in the Assyrian Room of the British Museum had been conducted at the time when he was endeavouring to establish a mystic and esoteric meaning in the Babylonian tablets, and this community of interests had brought us together. Chance remarks had led to daily conversation, and that to something verging upon friendship. I had promised him that on my next visit to Paris I would call upon him. At the time when I was able to fulfil my compact I was living in a cottage at Fontainebleau, and as the evening trains were inconvenient, he asked me to spend the night in his house.

"I have only that one spare couch," said he, pointing to a broad sofa in his large salon; "I hope that you will manage to be comfortable there."

It was a singular bedroom, with its high walls of brown volumes, but there could be no more agreeable furniture to a bookworm like myself, and there is no scent so pleasant to my nostrils as that faint, subtle reek which comes from an ancient book. I assured him that I could desire no more charming chamber, and no more congenial surroundings.

"If the fittings are neither convenient nor conventional, they are at least costly," said he, looking round at his shelves. "I have expended nearly a quarter of a million of money upon these objects which surround you. Books, weapons, gems, carvings, tapestries, images—there is hardly a thing here which has not its history, and it is generally one worth telling."

He was seated as he spoke at one side of the open fire-place, and I at the other. His reading-table was on his right, and the strong lamp above it ringed it with a very vivid circle of golden light. A half-rolled palimpsest lay in the centre, and around it were many quaint articles of bric-a-brac. One of these was a large funnel, such as is used for filling wine casks. It appeared to be made of black wood, and to be rimmed with discoloured brass.

"That is a curious thing," I remarked. "What is the history of that?"

"Ah!" said he, "it is the very question which I have had occasion to ask myself. I would give a good deal to know. Take it in your hands and examine it."

I did so, and found that what I had imagined to be wood was in reality leather, though age had dried it into an extreme hardness. It was a large funnel, and might hold a quart when full. The brass rim encircled the wide end, but the narrow was also tipped with metal.

"What do you make of it?" asked Dacre.

"I should imagine that it belonged to some vintner or malt-ster in the Middle Ages," said I. "I have seen in England leathern drinking flagons of the seventeenth century—'black jacks' as they were called—which were of the same colour and hardness as this filler."

"I dare say the date would be about the same," said Dacre, "and, no doubt, also, it was used for filling a vessel with liquid. If my suspicions are correct, however, it was a queer vintner who used it, and a very singular cask which was filled. Do you observe nothing strange at the spout end of the funnel."

As I held it to the light I observed that at a spot some five inches above the brass tip the narrow neck of the leather funnel was all haggled and scored, as if someone had notched it round with a blunt knife. Only at that point was there any roughening of the dead black surface.

"Someone has tried to cut off the neck."

"Would you call it a cut?"

"It is torn and lacerated. It must have taken some strength to leave these marks on such tough material, whatever the instrument may have been. But what do you think of it? I can tell that you know more than you say."

Dacre smiled, and his little eyes twinkled with knowledge.

"Have you included the psychology of dreams among your learned studies?" he asked.

"I did not even know that there was such a psychology."

"My dear sir, that shelf above the gem case is filled with volumes, from Albertus Magnus onward, which deal with no other subject. It is a science in itself."

"A science of charlatans."

"The charlatan is always the pioneer. From the astrologer came the astronomer, from the alchemist the chemist, from the mesmerist the experimental psychologist. The quack of yesterday is the professor of tomorrow. Even such subtle and elusive things as dreams will in time be reduced to system and order. When that time comes the researches of our friends on the bookshelf yonder will no longer be the amusement of the mystic, but the foundations of a science."

"Supposing that is so, what has the science of dreams to do with a large, black, brass-rimmed funnel?"

"I will tell you. You know that I have an agent who is always on the look-out for rarities and curiosities for my collection. Some days ago he heard of a dealer upon one of the Quais who had acquired some old rubbish found in a cupboard in an ancient house at the back of the Rue Mathurin, in the Quartier Latin. The dining-room of this old house is decorated with a coat of arms, chevrons, and bars rouge upon a field argent, which prove, upon inquiry, to be the shield of Nicholas de la Reynie, a high official of King Louis XIV. There can be no doubt that the other articles in the cupboard date back to the early days of that king. The inference is, therefore, that they were all the property of this Nicholas de la Reynie, who was, as I understand, the gentleman specially concerned with the maintenance and execution of the Draconic laws of that epoch."

"What then?"

"I would ask you now to take the funnel into your hands once more and to examine the upper brass rim. Can you make out any lettering upon it?"

There were certainly some scratches upon it, almost obliterated by time. The general effect was of several letters, the last of which bore some resemblance to a B.

"You make it a B?"

"Yes, I do."

"So do I. In fact, I have no doubt whatever that it is a B."

"But the nobleman you mentioned would have had R for his initial."

"Exactly! That's the beauty of it. He owned this curious object, and yet he had someone else's initials upon it. Why did he do this?"

"I can't imagine; can you?"

"Well, I might, perhaps, guess. Do you observe something drawn a little farther along the rim?"

"I should say it was a crown."

"It is undoubtedly a crown; but if you examine it in a good light, you will convince yourself that it is not an ordinary crown. It is a heraldic crown—a badge of rank, and it consists of an alternation of four pearls and strawberry leaves, the proper badge of a marquis. We may infer, therefore, that the person whose initials end in B was entitled to wear that coronet."

"Then this common leather filler belonged to a marquis?"

Dacre gave a peculiar smile.

"Or to some member of the family of a marquis," said he. "So much we have clearly gathered from this engraved rim."

"But what has all this to do with dreams?" I do not know whether it was from a look upon Dacre's face, or from some subtle suggestion in his manner, but a feeling of repulsion, of unreasoning horror, came upon me as I looked at the gnarled old lump of leather.

"I have more than once received important information through my dreams," said my companion in the didactic manner which he loved to affect. "I make it a rule now when I am in doubt upon any material point to place the article in question beside me as I sleep, and to hope for some enlightenment. The process does not appear to me to be very obscure, though it has not yet received the blessing of orthodox science. According to my theory, any object which has been intimately associated with any supreme paroxysm of human emotion, whether it be joy or pain, will retain a certain atmosphere or association which it is capable of communicating to a sensitive mind. By a sensitive mind I do not mean an abnormal one, but such a trained and educated mind as you or I possess."

"You mean, for example, that if I slept beside that old sword upon the wall, I might dream of some bloody incident in which that very sword took part?"

"An excellent example, for, as a matter of fact, that sword was used in that fashion by me, and I saw in my sleep the death of its owner, who perished in a brisk skirmish, which I have been unable to identify, but which occurred at the time of the wars of the Frondists. If you think of it, some of our popular observances show that the fact has already been recognized by our ancestors, although we, in our wisdom, have classed it among superstitions."

"For example?"

"Well, the placing of the bride's cake beneath the pillow in order that the sleeper may have pleasant dreams. That is one of several instances which you will find set forth in a small brochure which I am myself writing upon the subject. But to come back to the point, I slept one night with this funnel beside me, and I had a dream which certainly throws a curious light upon its use and origin."

"What did you dream?"

"I dreamed—" He paused, and an intent look of interest came over his massive face. "By Jove, that's well thought of," said he. "This really will be an exceedingly interesting experiment. You are yourself a psychic subject—with nerves which respond readily to any impression."

"I have never tested myself in that direction."

"Then we shall test you tonight. Might I ask you as a very great favour, when you occupy that couch tonight, to sleep with this old funnel placed by the side of your pillow?"

The request seemed to me a grotesque one; but I have myself, in my complex nature, a hunger after all which is bizarre and fantastic. I had not the faintest belief in Dacre's theory, nor any hopes for success in such an experiment; yet it amused me that the experiment should be made. Dacre, with great gravity, drew a small stand to the head of my settee, and placed the funnel upon it. Then, after a short conversation, he wished me good night and left me.

I sat for some little time smoking by the smouldering fire, and turning over in my mind the curious incident which had occurred, and the strange experience which might lie before me. Sceptical as I was, there was something impressive in the assurance of Dacre's manner, and my extraordinary surroundings, the huge room with the strange and often sinister objects which were hung round it, struck solemnity into my soul. Finally I undressed, and turning out the lamp, I lay down. After long tossing I fell asleep. Let me try to describe as accurately as I can the scene which came to me in my dreams. It stands out now in my memory more clearly than anything which I have seen with my waking eyes. There was a room which bore the appearance of a vault. Four spandrels from the corners ran up to join a sharp, cup-shaped roof. The architecture was rough, but very strong. It was evidently part of a great building.

Three men in black, with curious, top-heavy, black velvet hats, sat in a line upon a red-carpeted dais. Their faces were very solemn and sad. On the left stood two long-gowned men with port-folios in their hands, which seemed to be stuffed with papers. Upon the right, looking toward me, was a small woman with blonde hair and singular, light-blue eyes—the eyes of a child. She was past her first youth, but could not yet be called middle-aged. Her figure was inclined to stoutness and her bearing was proud and confident. Her face was pale, but serene. It was a curious face, comely and yet feline, with a subtle suggestion of cruelty about the straight, strong little mouth and chubby jaw. She was draped in some sort of loose, white gown. Beside her stood a thin, eager priest, who whispered in her ear, and continually raised a crucifix before her eyes. She turned her head and looked fixedly past the crucifix at the three men in black, who were, I felt, her judges.

As I gazed the three men stood up and said something, but I could distinguish no words, though I was aware that it was the central one who was speaking. They then swept out of the room, followed by the two men with the papers. At the same instant several rough-looking fellows in stout jerkins came bustling in and removed first the red carpet, and then the boards which formed the dais, so as to entirely clear the room. When this screen was removed I saw some singular articles of furniture behind it. One looked like a bed with wooden rollers at each end, and a winch handle to regulate its length. Another was a wooden horse. There were several other curious objects, and a number of swinging cords which played over pulleys. It was not unlike a modern gymnasium.

When the room had been cleared there appeared a new figure upon the scene. This was a tall, thin person clad in black, with a gaunt and austere face. The aspect of the man made me shudder. His clothes were all shining with grease and mottled with stains. He bore himself with a slow and impressive dignity, as if he took command of all things from the instant of his entrance. In spite of his rude appearance and sordid dress, it was now his business, his room, his to command. He carried a coil of light ropes over his left forearm. The lady looked him up and down with a searching glance, but her expression was unchanged. It was confident—even defiant. But it was very different with the priest. His face was ghastly white, and I saw the moisture glisten and run on his high, sloping forehead. He threw up his hands in prayer and he stooped continually to mutter frantic words in the lady's ear.

The man in black now advanced, and taking one of the cords from his left arm, he bound the woman's hands together. She held them meekly toward him as he did so. Then he took her arm with a rough grip and led her toward the wooden horse, which was little higher than her waist. On to this she was lifted and laid, with her back upon it, and her face to the ceiling, while the priest, quivering with horror, had rushed out of the room. The woman's lips were moving rapidly, and though I could hear nothing I knew that she was praying. Her feet hung down on either side of the horse, and I saw that the rough varlets in attendance had fastened cords to her ankles and secured the other ends to iron rings in the stone floor.

My heart sank within me as I saw these ominous preparations, and yet I was held by the fascination of horror, and I could not take my eyes from the strange spectacle. A man had entered the room with a bucket of water in either hand. Another followed with a third bucket. They were laid beside the wooden horse. The second man had a wooden dipper—a bowl with a straight handle—in his other hand. This he gave to the man in black. At the same moment one of the varlets approached with a dark object in his hand, which even in my dream filled me with a vague feeling of familiarity. It was a leathern filler. With horrible energy he thrust it—but I could stand no more. My hair stood on end with horror. I writhed, I struggled, I broke through the bonds of sleep, and I burst with a shriek into my own life, and found myself lying shivering with terror in the huge library, with the moonlight flooding through the window and throwing strange silver and black traceries upon the opposite wall. Oh, what a blessed relief to feel that I was back in the nineteenth century—back out of that mediaeval vault into a world where men had human hearts within their bosoms. I sat up on my couch, trembling in every limb, my mind divided between thankfulness and horror. To think that such things were ever done—that they could be done without God striking the villains dead. Was it all a fantasy, or did it really stand for something which had happened in the black, cruel days of the world's history? I sank my throbbing head upon my shaking hands. And then, suddenly, my heart seemed to stand still in my bosom, and I could not even scream, so great was my terror. Something was advancing toward me through the darkness of the room.

It is a horror coming upon a horror which breaks a man's spirit. I could not reason, I could not pray; I could only sit like a frozen image, and glare at the dark figure which was coming down the great room. And then it moved out into the white lane of moonlight, and I breathed once more. It was Dacre, and his face showed that he was as frightened as myself.

"Was that you? For God's sake what's the matter?" he asked in a husky voice.

"Oh, Dacre, I am glad to see you! I have been down into hell. It was dreadful."

"Then it was you who screamed?"

"I dare say it was."

"It rang through the house. The servants are all terrified." He struck a match and lit the lamp. "I think we may get the fire to burn up again," he added, throwing some logs upon the embers. "Good God, my dear chap, how white you are! You look as if you had seen a ghost."

"So I have—several ghosts."

"The leather funnel has acted, then?"

"I wouldn't sleep near the infernal thing again for all the money you could offer me."

Dacre chuckled.

"I expected that you would have a lively night of it," said he. "You took it out of me in return, for that scream of yours wasn't a very pleasant sound at two in the morning. I suppose from what you say that you have seen the whole dreadful business."

"What dreadful business?"

"The torture of the water—the 'Extraordinary Question,' as it was called in the genial days of 'Le Roi Soleil.' Did you stand it out to the end?"

"No, thank God, I awoke before it really began."

"Ah! it is just as well for you. I held out till the third bucket. Well, it is an old story, and they are all in their graves now, anyhow, so what does it matter how they got there? I suppose that you have no idea what it was that you have seen?"

"The torture of some criminal. She must have been a terrible malefactor indeed if her crimes are in proportion to her penalty."

"Well, we have that small consolation," said Dacre, wrapping his dressing-gown round him and crouching closer to the fire. "They WERE in proportion to her penalty. That is to say, if I am correct in the lady's identity."

"How could you possibly know her identity?"

For answer Dacre took down an old vellum-covered volume from the shelf.

"Just listen to this," said he; "it is in the French of the seventeenth century, but I will give a rough translation as I go. You will judge for yourself whether I have solved the riddle or not.

"'The prisoner was brought before the Grand Chambers and Tournelles of Parliament, sitting as a court of justice, charged with the murder of Master Dreux d'Aubray, her father, and of her two brothers, MM. d'Aubray, one being civil lieutenant, and the other a counsellor of Parliament. In person it seemed hard to believe that she had really done such wicked deeds, for she was of a mild appearance, and of short stature, with a fair skin and blue eyes. Yet the Court, having found her guilty, condemned her to the ordinary and to the extraordinary question in order that she might be forced to name her accomplices, after which she should be carried in a cart to the Place de Greve, there to have her head cut off, her body being afterwards burned and her ashes scattered to the winds.'

"The date of this entry is July 16, 1676."

"It is interesting," said I, "but not convincing. How do you prove the two women to be the same?"

"I am coming to that. The narrative goes on to tell of the woman's behaviour when questioned. 'When the executioner approached her she recognized him by the cords which he held in his hands, and she at once held out her own hands to him, looking at him from head to foot without uttering a word.' How's that?"

"Yes, it was so."

"'She gazed without wincing upon the wooden horse and rings which had twisted so many limbs and caused so many shrieks of agony. When her eyes fell upon the three pails of water, which were all ready for her, she said with a smile, "All that water must have been brought here for the purpose of drowning me, Monsieur. You have no idea, I trust, of making a person of my small stature swallow it all."' Shall I read the details of the torture?"

"No, for Heaven's sake, don't."

"Here is a sentence which must surely show you that what is here recorded is the very scene which you have gazed upon tonight: 'The good Abbe Pirot, unable to contemplate the agonies which were suffered by his penitent, had hurried from the room.' Does that convince you?"

"It does entirely. There can be no question that it is indeed the same event. But who, then, is this lady whose appearance was so attractive and whose end was so horrible?"

For answer Dacre came across to me, and placed the small lamp upon the table which stood by my bed. Lifting up the ill-omened filler, he turned the brass rim so that the light fell full upon it. Seen in this way the engraving seemed clearer than on the night before.

"We have already agreed that this is the badge of a marquis or of a marquise," said he. "We have also settled that the last letter is B."

"It is undoubtedly so."

"I now suggest to you that the other letters from left to right are, M, M, a small d, A, a small d, and then the final B."

"Yes, I am sure that you are right. I can make out the two small d's quite plainly."

"What I have read to you tonight," said Dacre, "is the official record of the trial of Marie Madeleine d'Aubray, Marquise de Brinvilliers, one of the most famous poisoners and murderers of all time."

I sat in silence, overwhelmed at the extraordinary nature of the incident, and at the completeness of the proof with which Dacre had exposed its real meaning. In a vague way I remembered some details of the woman's career, her unbridled debauchery, the cold-blooded and protracted torture of her sick father, the murder of her brothers for motives of petty gain. I recollected also that the bravery of her end had done something to atone for the horror of her life, and that all Paris had sympathized with her last moments, and blessed her as a martyr within a few days of the time when they had cursed her as a murderess. One objection, and one only, occurred to my mind.

"How came her initials and her badge of rank upon the filler? Surely they did not carry their mediaeval homage to the nobility to the point of decorating instruments of torture with their titles?"

"I was puzzled with the same point," said Dacre, "but it admits of a simple explanation. The case excited extraordinary interest at the time, and nothing could be more natural than that La Reynie, the head of the police, should retain this filler as a grim souvenir. It was not often that a marchioness of France underwent the extraordinary question. That he should engrave her initials upon it for the information of others was surely a very ordinary proceeding upon his part."

"And this?" I asked, pointing to the marks upon the leathern neck.

"She was a cruel tigress," said Dacre, as he turned away. "I think it is evident that like other tigresses her teeth were both strong and sharp."

THE DEAD HAND:
Being the First of the Experiences of the Oracle of Maddox Street

L. T. Meade and Robert Eustace

L. T. Meade was the nom de plume of Elizabeth Thomasina Meade Smith (1844–1914), prolific writer of girls' stories. In addition to children's books, Meade wrote historical novels, adventure tales, romance novels, and mysteries. She was the editor of the popular girls' magazine, Atalanta. *A feminist, Meade's fiction featured female protagonists and villains. Meade wrote both independently and with collaborators.*

Born in County Cork, Ireland, Meade began writing at age seventeen. Over the course of her lifetime, she published at least 280 books in addition to innumerable short stories and articles. The Irish Times *described Meade as "the JK Rowling of her day."* [7]

Robert Eustace, her frequent collaborator, was the pen name of English physician Eustace Robert Barton (1854–1943), also a prolific author, both independently and in collaboration. He may be most famous for coauthoring the 1930 novel The Documents in the Case *with Dorothy L. Sayers.*

Diana Marburg, Meade and Eustace's occult detective, is a professional palmist. Unlike Flaxman Low, who solves supernatural mysteries using his powers of deduction and observation, Marburg uses her psychic powers to solve crime. The character first appeared in 1902 in the US version of Pearson's Magazine.

---

7 Beth Rodgers, "LT Meade, the JK Rowling of Her Day, Remembered 100 Years On," *Irish Times*, October 24, 2014, *www.irishtimes.com.*

The Dead Hand:
Being the First of the Experiences
of the Oracle of Maddox Street

MY NAME IS DIANA MARBURG. I am a palmist by profession. Occult phenomena, spiritualism, clairvoyance, and many other strange mysteries of the unseen world, have, from my earliest years, excited my keen interest.

Being blessed with abundant means, I attended in my youth many foreign schools of thought. I was a pupil of Lewis, Darling, Braid and others. I studied Reichenbach and Mesmer, and, finally, started my career as a thought reader and palmist in Maddox Street.

Now I live with a brother, five years my senior. My brother Rupert is an athletic Englishman, and also a barrister, with a rapidly growing practice. He loves and pities me—he casts over me the respectability of his presence, and wonders at what he calls my lapses from sanity. He is patient, however, and when he saw that in spite of all expostulation I meant to go my own way, he ceased to try to persuade me against my inclinations.

Gradually the success of my reading of the lines of the human hand brought me fame—my prophecies turned out correct, my intuition led me to right conclusions, and I was sought after very largely by that fashionable world which always follows anything new. I became a favourite in society, and was accounted both curious and bizarre.

On a certain evening in late July, I attended Lady Fortescue's reception in Curzon Street. I was ushered into a small ante-room which was furnished with the view of adding to the weird effect of my own appearance and words. I wore an Oriental costume, rich in colour and bespangled with sparkling gems. On my head I had twisted a Spanish scarf, my arms were bare to the elbows, and my dress open at the throat. Being tall, dark, and, I believe, graceful, my quaint dress suited me well.

Lady Fortescue saw me for a moment on my arrival, and inquired if I had everything I was likely to want. As she stood by the door she turned.

"I expect, Miss Marburg, that you will have a few strange clients to-night. My guests come from a varied and ever widening circle, and to-night all sorts and conditions of men will be present at my reception."

She left me, and soon afterwards those who wished to inquire of Fate appeared before me one by one.

Towards the close of the evening a tall, dark man was ushered into my presence. The room was shadowy, and I do not think he could see me at once, although I observed him quite distinctly. To the ordinary observer he doubtless appeared as a well set up man of the world, but to me he wore quite a different appearance. I read fear in his eyes, and irresolution, and at the same time cruelty round his lips. He glanced at me as if he meant to defy any message I might have for him, and yet at the same time was obliged to yield to an over-powering curiosity. I asked him his name, which he gave me at once.

"Philip Harman," he said; "have you ever heard of me before?"

"Never," I answered.

"I have come here because you are the fashion, Miss Marburg, and because many of Lady Fortescue's guests are flocking to this room to learn something of their future. Of course, you cannot expect me to believe in your strange art, nevertheless, I shall be glad if you will look at my hand and tell me what you see there."

As he spoke he held out his hand. I noticed that it trembled. Before touching it I looked full at him.

"If you have no faith in me, why do you trouble to come here?" I asked.

"Curiosity brings me to you," he answered. "Will you grant my request or not?"

"I will look at your hand first if I may." I took it in mine. It was a long, thin hand, with a certain hardness about it. I turned the palm upward and examined it through a powerful lens. As I did so I felt my heart beat wildly and something of the fear in Philip Harman's eyes was communicated to me. I dropped the hand, shuddering inwardly as I did so.

"Well," he asked in astonishment, "what is the matter, what is my fate? Tell me at once. Why do you hesitate?"

"I would rather not tell you, Mr. Harman. You don't believe in me, go away and forget all about me."

"I cannot do that now. Your look says that you have seen something which you are afraid to speak about. Is that so?"

I nodded my head. I placed my hand on the little round table, which contained a shaded lamp, to steady myself.

"Come," he said rudely, "out with this horror—I am quite prepared."

"I have no good news for you," I answered. "I saw something very terrible in your hand."

"Speak."

"You are a ruined man," I said, taking his hand again in mine, and examining it carefully. "Yes, the marks are unmistakable. You will perpetrate a crime which will be discovered. You are about to commit a murder, and will suffer a shameful death on the scaffold!"

He snatched his hand away with a violent movement and started back. His whole face was quivering with passion.

"How dare you say such infamous things!" he cried. "You go very far in your efforts to amuse, Miss Marburg."

"You asked me to tell you," was my reply.

He gave a harsh laugh, bowed low and went out of the room. I noticed his face as he did so; it was white as death.

I rang my little hand-bell to summon the next guest, and a tall and very beautiful woman between forty and fifty years of age entered. Her dress was ablaze with diamonds, and she wore a diamond star of peculiar brilliancy just above her forehead. Her hair white as snow, and the glistening diamond star in the midst of the white hair, gave to her whole appearance a curious effect.

"My name is Mrs. Kenyon," she said; "you have just interviewed my nephew, Philip Harman. But what is the matter, my dear," she said suddenly, "you look ill."

"I have had a shock," was my vague reply, then I pulled myself together.

"What can I do for you?" I asked.

"I want you to tell me my future."

"Will you show me your hand?"

Mrs. Kenyon held it out, I took it in mine. The moment I glanced at it a feeling of relief passed over me. It was full of good qualities—the Mount of Jupiter well developed, the heart-line clear and unchained, a deep, long life-line, and a fate-line ascending clear upon the Mount of Saturn. I began to speak easily and rapidly, and with that fluency which often made me feel that my words were prompted by an unseen presence.

"What you tell me sounds very pleasant," said Mrs. Kenyon, "and I only hope my character is as good as you paint it. I fear it is not so, however; your words are too flattering, and you think too well of me. But you have not yet touched upon the most important point of all—the future. What is in store for me?"

I looked again very earnestly at the hand. My heart sank a trifle as I did so.

"I am sorry," I said, "I have to tell you bad news—I did not notice this at first but I see it plainly now. You are about to undergo a severe shock, a very great grief."

"Strange," answered Mrs. Kenyon. She paused for a moment, then she said suddenly, "You gave my nephew a bad report, did you not?"

I was silent. It was one of my invariable rules never to speak of one client to another.

"You need not speak," she continued, "I saw it in his face."

"I hope he will take the warning," I could not help murmuring faintly. Mrs. Kenyon overheard the words.

"And now you tell me that I am to undergo severe trouble. Will it come soon?"

"Yes," was my answer. "You will need all your strength to withstand it," and then, as if prompted by some strange impulse, I added. "I cannot tell you what that trouble may be, but I like you. If in the time of your trouble I can help you I will gladly do so."

"Thank you," answered Mrs. Kenyon, "you are kind. I do not profess to believe in you; that you should be able to foretell the future is, of course, impossible, but I also like you. I hope some day we may meet again."

She held out her hand; I clasped it. A moment later she had passed outside the thick curtain which shut away the anteroom from the gay throng in the drawing-rooms.

I went home late that night. Rupert was in and waiting for me.

"Why, what is the matter, Diana?" he said the moment I appeared. "You look shockingly ill; this terrible life will kill you."

"I have seen strange things to-night," was my answer. I flung myself on the sofa, and for just a moment covered my tired eyes with my hand.

"Have some supper," said Rupert gently. He led me to the table, and helped me to wine and food.

"I have had a tiring and exciting evening at Lady Fortescue's," I said. "I shall be better when I have eaten. But where have you been this evening?"

"At the Appollo—there was plenty of gossip circulating there— two society scandals, and Philip Harman's crash. That is a big affair and likely to keep things pretty lively. But, my dear Di, what is the matter?"

I had half risen from my seat; I was gazing at my brother with fear in my eyes, my heart once again beat wildly.

"Did you say Philip Harman?" I asked.

"Yes, why? Do you know him?"

"Tell me about him at once, Rupert, I must know. What do you mean by his crash?"

"Oh, he is one of the plungers, you know. He has run through the Harman property and cannot touch the Kenyon."

"The Kenyon!" I exclaimed.

"Yes. His uncle, Walter Kenyon, was a very rich man, and has left all his estates to his young grandson, a lad of about thirteen. That boy stands between Harman and a quarter of a million. But why do you want to know?"

"Only that I saw Philip Harman to-night," was my answer.

"You did? That is curious. He asked you to prophesy with regard to his fate?"

"He did, Rupert."

"And you told him?"

"What I cannot tell you. You know I never divulge what I see in my clients' hands."

"Of course you cannot tell me, but it is easy to guess that you gave him bad news. They say he wants to marry the heiress and beauty of the season, Lady Maud Greville. If he succeeds in this he will be on his feet once more, but I doubt if she will have anything to say to him. He is an attractive man in some ways and good-looking, but the Countess of Cheddsleigh keeps a sharp look out on the future of her only daughter."

"Philip Harman must on no account marry an innocent girl," was my next impulsive remark. "Rupert, your news troubles me very much, it confirms—" I could not finish the sentence. I was overcome by what Rupert chose to consider intense nervousness.

"You must have your quinine and go to bed," he said; "come, I insist, I won't listen to another word."

A moment later I had left him, but try-hard as I would I could not sleep that night. I felt that I myself was on the brink of a great catastrophe, that I personally, was mixed up in this affair. In all my experience I had never seen a hand like Philip Harman's before. There was no redeeming trait in it. The lines which denoted crime and disaster were too indelibly marked to be soon forgotten. When at last I did drop asleep that hand accompanied me into the world of dreams.

The London season came to an end. I heard nothing more about Philip Harman and his affairs, and in the excitement and interest of leaving town, was beginning more or less to forget him, when on the 25th of July, nearly a month after Lady Fortescue's party, a servant entered my consulting-room with a card. The man told me that a lady was waiting to see me, she begged for an interview at once on most urgent business. I glanced at the card. It bore the name of Mrs. Kenyon.

The moment I saw it that nervousness which had troubled me on the night when I saw Philip Harman and read his future in the ghastly lines of his hand returned. I could not speak at all for a moment; then I said, turning to the man who stood motionless waiting for my answer:

"Show the lady up immediately."

Mrs. Kenyon entered. She came hurriedly forward. When last I saw her she was a beautiful woman with great dignity of bearing and a kindly, sunshiny face. Now as she came into the room she was so changed that I should scarcely have known her. Her dress bore marks of disorder and hasty arrangement, her eyes were red with weeping.

"Pardon my coming so early, Miss Marburg," she said at once; then, without waiting for me to speak, she dropped into a chair.

"I am overcome," she gasped, "but you promised, if necessary, to help me. Do you remember my showing you my hand at Lady Fortescue's party?"

"I remember you perfectly, Mrs. Kenyon. What can I do for you?"

"You told me then that something terrible was about to happen. I did not believe it. I visited you out of curiosity and had no faith in you, but your predictions have come true, horribly true. I have come to you now for the help which you promised to give me if I needed it, for I believe it lies in your power to tell me something I wish to discover."

"I remember everything," I replied gravely; "what is it you wish me to do?"

"I want you to read a hand for me and to tell me what you see in it."

"Certainly, but will you make an appointment?"

"Can you come with me immediately to Godalming? My nephew Philip Harman has a place there."

"Philip Harman!" I muttered.

"Yes," she answered, scarcely noticing my words, "my only son and I have been staying with him. I want to take you there; can you come immediately?"

"You have not mentioned the name of the person whose hand you want me to read?"

"I would rather not do so—not yet, I mean."

"But can you not bring him or her here? I am very busy just now."

"That is impossible," replied Mrs. Kenyon. "I am afraid I must ask you to postpone all your other engagements, this thing is most imperative. I cannot bring the person whose hand I want you to read here, nor can there be any delay. You must see him if possible to-day. I implore you to come. I will give you any fee you like to demand."

"It is not a question of money," I replied, "I am interested in you. I will do what you require." I rose as I spoke. "By the way," I added, "I presume that the person whose hand you wish me to see has no objection to my doing so, otherwise my journey may be thrown away."

"There is no question about that," replied Mrs. Kenyon, "I thank you more than I can say for agreeing to come."

A few moments later we were on our way to the railway station. We caught our train, and between twelve and one o'clock arrived at Godalming. A carriage was waiting for us at the station, we drove for nearly two miles and presently found ourselves in a place with large shady grounds. We drew up beside a heavy portico, a man servant came gravely forward to help us to alight and we entered a large hall.

I noticed a curious hush about the place, and I observed that the man who admitted us did not speak, but glanced inquiringly at Mrs. Kenyon, as if for directions.

"Show Miss Marburg into the library," was her order. "I will be back again in a moment or two," she added, glancing at me.

I was ushered into a well-furnished library; there was a writing-table at one end of it on which papers of different sorts were scattered. I went forward mechanically and took up an envelope. It was addressed to Philip Harman, Esq., The Priory, Godalming. I dropped it as though I could not bear to touch it. Once again that queer nervousness seized me, and I was obliged to sit down weak and trembling. The next moment the room door was opened.

"Will you please come now, Miss Marburg?" said Mrs. Kenyon. "I will not keep you long."

We went upstairs together, and paused before a door on the first landing.

"We must enter softly," said the lady turning to me. There was something in her words and the look on her face which seemed to prepare me, but for what I could not tell. We found ourselves in a large room luxuriously furnished—the window blinds were all down, but the windows themselves were open and the blinds were gently moving to and fro in the soft summer air. In the centre of the room and drawn quite away from the wall was a small iron bedstead. I glanced towards it and a sudden irrepressible cry burst from my lips. On the bed lay a figure covered with a sheet beneath which its outline was indistinctly defined.

"What do you mean by bringing me here?" I said, turning to the elder woman and grasping her by the arm.

"You must not be frightened," she said gently, "come up to the bed. Hush, try to restrain yourself. Think of my most terrible grief; this is the hand I want you to read." As she spoke she drew aside the sheet and I found myself gazing down at the beautiful dead face of a child, a boy of about thirteen years of age.

"Dead! my only son!" said Mrs. Kenyon, "he was drowned this morning. Here is his hand; yesterday it was warm and full of life, now it is cold as marble. Will you take it, will you look at the lines? I want you to tell me if he met his death by accident or by design?"

"You say that you are living in Philip Harman's house?" I said.

"He asked us here on a visit."

"And this boy, this dead boy stood between him and the Kenyon property?" was my next inquiry.

"How can you tell? How do you know?"

"But answer me, is it true?"

"It is true."

I now went on *my* knees and took one of the child's small white hands in mine. I began to examine it.

"It is very strange," I said slowly, "this child has died a violent death, and it was caused by design."

"It was?" cried the mother. "Can you swear it?" She clutched me by the arm.

"I see it, but I cannot quite understand it," I answered, "there is a strong indication here that the child was murdered, and yet had I seen this hand in life I should have warned the boy against lightning, but a death by lightning would be accidental. Tell me how did the boy die?"

"By drowning. Early this morning he was bathing in the pool which adjoins a wide stream in the grounds. He did not return. We hastened to seek for him and found his body floating on the surface of the water. He was quite dead."

"Was the pool deep?"

"In one part it was ten feet deep, the rest of the pool was shallow. The doctor has been, and said that the child must have had a severe attack of cramp, but even then the pool is small, and he was a good swimmer for his age."

"Was no one with him?"

"No. His cousin, Philip Harman, often accompanied him, but he bathed alone this morning."

"Where was Mr. Harman this morning?"

"He went to town by an early train, and does not know yet. You say you think it was murder. How do you account for it?"

"The boy may have been drowned by accident, but I see something more in his hand than mere drowning, something that baffles me, yet it is plain—Lightning. Is there no mark on the body?"

"Yes, there is a small blue mark just below the inner ankle of the right foot, but I think that was a bruise he must have got yesterday. The doctor said it must have been done previously and not in the pool as it would not have turned blue so quickly."

"May I see it?"

Mrs. Kenyon raised the end of the sheet and showed the mark. I looked at it long and earnestly.

"You are sure there was no thunder-storm this morning?" I asked.

"No, it was quite fine."

I rose slowly to my feet.

"I have looked at the boy's hand as you asked me," I said, "I must repeat my words—there are indications that he came by his death not by accident but design."

Mrs. Kenyon's face underwent a queer change as I spoke. She came suddenly forward, seized me by the arms and cried:

"I believe you, I believe you. I believe that my boy has been murdered in some fiendish and inexplicable way. The police have been here already, and of course there will be an inquest, but no one is suspected. Who are we to suspect?"

"Philip Harman," I could not help answering.

"Why? Why do you say that?"

"I am not at liberty to tell you. I make the suggestion."

"But it cannot be the case. The boy went to bathe alone in perfect health. Philip went to town by an earlier train than usual. I saw him off myself, I walked with him as far as the end of the avenue. It was soon afterwards that I missed my little Paul, and began to wonder why he had not returned to the house. I went with a servant to the pool and I saw, oh, I saw that which will haunt me to my dying day. He was my only son, Miss Marburg, my one great treasure. What you have suggested, what I myself, alas, believe, drives me nearly mad. But you must tell me why you suspect Philip Harman."

"Under the circumstances it may not be wrong to tell you," I said slowly. "The night I read your hand I also as you know read his. I saw in his hand that he was about to be a murderer. I told him so in as many words."

"You saw that! You told him! Oh, this is too awful! Philip has wanted money of late and has been in the strangest state. He has always been somewhat wild and given to speculation, and lately I know lost heavily with different ventures. He proposed to a young girl, a great friend of mine last week, but she would have nothing to do with him. Yes, it all seems possible. My little Paul stood between him and a great property. But how did he do it? There is not a particle of evidence against him. Your word goes for nothing, law and justice would only scout you. But we must act, Miss Marburg, and you must help me to prove the murder of my boy, to discover the murderer. I shall never rest until I have avenged him."

"Yes, I will help you," I answered.

As I descended the stairs accompanied by Mrs. Kenyon a strange thought struck me.

"I have promised to help you, and we must act at once," I said. "Will you leave this matter for the present in my hands, and will you let me send a telegram immediately to my brother? I shall need his assistance. He is a barrister and has chambers in town, but he will come to me at once. He is very clever and practical."

"Is he entirely in your confidence?"

"Absolutely. But pray tell me when do you expect Mr. Harman back?"

"He does not know anything at present, as he was going into the country for the day; he will be back as usual to-night."

"That is so much the better. May I send for my brother?"

"Do anything you please. You will find some telegraph forms in the hall and the groom can take your message at once."

I crossed the hall, found the telegraph forms on a table, sat down and filled one in as follows:

"Come at once—I need your help most urgently. Diana."

I handed the telegram to a servant, who took it away at once.

"And now," I said turning to Mrs. Kenyon, "will you show me the pool? I shall go there and stay till my brother arrives."

"You will stay there, why?"

"I have my own reasons for wishing to do so. I cannot say more now. Please show me the way."

We went across the garden and into a meadow beyond. At the bottom of this meadow ran a swift-flowing stream. In the middle of the stream was the pool evidently made artificially. Beside it on the bank stood a small tent for dressing. The pool itself was a deep basin in the rock about seven yards across, surrounded by drooping willows which hung over it. At the upper end the stream fell into it in a miniature cascade—at the lower end a wire fence crossed it. This was doubtless done in order to prevent the cattle stirring the water.

I walked slowly round the pool, looking down into its silent depths without speaking. When I came back to where Mrs. Kenyon was standing I said slowly:

"I shall remain here until my brother comes. Will you send me down a few sandwiches, and bring him or send him to me directly he arrives?"

"But he cannot be with you for some hours," said Mrs. Kenyon. "I fail to understand your reason."

"I scarcely know that yet myself," was my reply, "but I am certain I am acting wisely. Will you leave me here? I wish to be alone in order to think out a problem."

Mrs. Kenyon slowly turned and went back to the house.

"I must unravel this mystery." I said to myself, "I must sift from the apparent facts of the case the awful truth which lies beneath. That sixth sense which has helped me up to the present shall help me to the end. Beyond doubt foul play has taken place. The boy met his death in this pool, but how? Beyond doubt this is the only spot where a solution can be found. I will stay here and think the matter through. If anything dangerous or fatal was put into the pool the murderer shall not remove his awful weapon without my knowledge."

So I thought and the moments flew. My head ached with the intensity of my thought, and as the afternoon advanced I was no nearer a solution than ever.

It was between four and five o'clock when to my infinite relief I saw Rupert hurrying across the meadow.

"What is the meaning of this, Diana?" he said. "Have you lost your senses? When I got your extraordinary wire I thought you must be ill."

I stood up, clasped his hands and looked into his face.

"Listen," I said. "A child has been murdered, and I want to discover the murderer. You must help me."

"Are you mad?" was his remark.

"No, I am sane," I answered; "little Paul Kenyon has been murdered. Do you remember telling me that he stood between Philip Harman and the Kenyon property? He was drowned this morning in this pool, the supposition being that the death occurred through accident. Now listen, Rupert, we have got to discover how the boy really met his death. The child was in perfect health when he entered the pool, his dead body was found floating on the water half-an-hour afterwards. The doctor said he died from drowning due to cramp. What caused such sudden and awful cramp as would drown a boy of his age within a few paces of the bank?"

"But what do you expect to find here?" said Rupert. He looked inclined to laugh at me when first he arrived, but his face was grave now, and even pale.

"Come here," I said suddenly, "I have already noticed one strange thing; it is this. Look!"

As I spoke I took his hand and approached the wire fence which protected the water from the cattle. Leaning over I said:

"Look down. Whoever designed this pool, for it was, of course, made artificially, took more precaution than is usual to prevent the water being contaminated. Do you see that fine wire netting which goes down to the bottom of the pool? That wire has been put there for some other reason than to keep cattle out. Rupert, do you think by any possibility it has been placed there to keep something in the pool?"

Rupert bent down and examined the wire carefully.

"It is curious," he said. "I see what you mean." A frown had settled on his face. Suddenly he turned to me.

"Your suggestion is too horrible. Diana. What can be in the pool? Do you mean something alive, something—" he stopped speaking, his eyes were fixed on my face with a dawning horror.

"Were there any marks on the boy?" was his next question.

"One small blue mark on the ankle. Ah! look, what is that?" At the further end and in the deep part of the pool I suddenly saw the surface move and a slight eddying swirl appear on the water. It increased into ever widening circles and vanished. Rupert's bronzed face was now almost as white as mine.

"We must drag the pool immediately," he said. "Harman cannot prevent us; we have seen enough to warrant what we do; I cannot let this pass. Stay here, Diana, and watch. I will bring Mrs. Kenyon with me and get her consent."

Rupert hurriedly left me and went back to the house across the meadow. It was fully an hour before he returned. The water was once more perfectly still. There was not the faintest movement of any living thing beneath its surface. At the end of the hour I saw Mrs. Kenyon, my brother, a gardener, and another man coming across the meadow. One of the men was dragging a large net, one side of which was loaded with leaden sinkers—the other held an old-fashioned single-barrelled gun.

Rupert was now all activity. Mrs. Kenyon came and stood by my side without speaking. Rupert gave quick orders to the men. Under his directions one of them waded through the shallows just below the pool, and reaching the opposite bank, threw the net across, then the bottom of the net with the sinkers was let down into the pool.

When this was done Rupert possessed himself of the gun and stood at the upper end of the pool beside the little waterfall. He then gave the word to the men to begin to drag. Slowly and gradually they advanced, drawing the net forward, while all our eyes were fixed upon the water. Not a word was spoken; the men had not taken many steps when again was seen the swirl in the water, and a few little eddies were sucked down. A sharp cry broke from Mrs. Kenyon's lips. Rupert kept the gun in readiness.

"What is it?" cried Mrs. Kenyon, but the words had scarcely died on her lips before a dark body lashed the surface of the water and disappeared. What it was we none of us had the slightest idea; we all watched spell-bound.

Still the net moved slowly on, and now the agitation of the water became great. The creature, whatever it was, lashed and lunged to and fro, now breaking back against the net, and now attempting to spring up the smooth rock and so escape into the stream.

The next instant Rupert raised the gun, and fired.

As we caught a glimpse and yet another glimpse of the long coiling body I wondered if there was a snake in the pool.

"Come on, quicker now," shouted Rupert to the men, and they pressed forward, holding the creature in the net, and, drawing it every moment nearer the rock. The next instant Rupert raised the gun, and leaning over the water, fired down. There was a burst of spray, and as the smoke cleared we saw that the water was stained with red blood.

Seizing the lower end of the net and exercising all their strength the men now drew the net up. In its meshes, struggling in death agony, was an enormous eel. The next moment it was on the grass coiling to and fro. The men quickly dispatched it with a stick, and then we all bent over it. It was an extraordinary looking creature, six feet in length, yet it had none of the ordinary appearance of the eel. I had never seen anything like it before. Rupert went down on his knees to examine it carefully. He suddenly looked up. A terrible truth had struck him—his face was white.

"What is it?" gasped poor Mrs. Kenyon.

"You were right, Diana," said Rupert. "Look, Mrs. Kenyon. My sister was absolutely right. Call her power what you will, she was guided by something too wonderful for explanation. This is an electric eel, no native of these waters—it was put here by someone. This is murder. One stroke from the tail of such an eel would give a child such a dreadful shock that he would be paralysed, and would drown to a certainty."

"Then that explains the mark by lightning on the dead child's hand," I said.

"Yes," answered my brother. "The police must take the matter up."

Before that evening Mr. Harman was arrested. The sensational case which followed was in all the papers. Against my will, I was forced to attend the trial in order to give the necessary evidence. It was all too damning and conclusive. The crime was brought home to the murderer, who suffered the full penalty of the law.

THE HORSE OF
THE INVISIBLE

William Hope Hodgson

William Hope Hodgson (1877–1918) was a bodybuilder, photographer, and prolific author who wrote novels and short stories in multiple genres, including weird tales, horror, and science fiction. Born in Blackmore End, Essex, England, the son of an Anglican priest, Hodgson ran away from boarding school at age thirteen, intending to become a sailor. He was caught and sent home, but eventually his father permitted him to fulfill his dream. Hodgson was apprenticed as a cabin boy in 1891, the start of years at sea.

Small and at the mercy of his fellow seamen, Hodgson began a program of personal training, initially for the purpose of self-defense. This led to a career in bodybuilding. In 1899, at age twenty-two, he opened W. H. Hodgson's School of Physical Culture in Blackburn, England. Students included members of the local police force. In 1902, Hodgson appeared on stage to restrain Harry Houdini, the escape artist, using handcuffs and other restraints supplied by the Blackburn police department. Houdini later complained that Hodgson had jammed the locks of the handcuffs and deliberately injured him. Hodgson died at the Fourth Battle of Ypres during World War I.

Hodgson began writing his occult detective stories because he was hard up for cash. Thomas Carnacki, his athletic, inventive detective, first appeared in stories published in the magazine The Idler, *beginning in January 1910. "The Horse of the Invisible" appeared in the April 1910 issue. The Carnacki stories were collected and published in the 1913 book* Carnacki: The Ghost-Finder *(London, Eveleigh Nash).*

The stories have a format and a consistent framework: Carnacki invites several friends to dine at his home at 472 Cheyne Walk, London. After dinner—and only after dinner—Carnacki regales them with highly anticipated tales of his sleuthing. The stories are narrated by Dodgson, Carnacki's friend and dinner guest. Carnacki, an occultist, relies on knowledge, his powers of observation, and his own occult inventions, such as the electric pentacle, to solve his cases.

Actor Donald Pleasence plays Carnacki in the BBC television adaptation of "The Horse of the Invisible," which was part of the 1970s series The Rivals of Sherlock Holmes. *Carnacki has continued to live on after the death of Hodgson, his creator. He appears in stories written by other authors and is among the protagonists of The League of Extraordinary Gentlemen, the comic book series written by Alan Moore and illustrated by Kevin O'Neill.*

Queen's Quorum: A History of the Detective-Crime Short Story as Revealed by the 106 Most Important Books Published in this Field since 1845 *by Ellery Queen (1951) identifies Carnacki as the "first psychic sleuth," although Flaxman Low and Harry Escott, among others, had appeared in print years earlier. In those days before the Internet and easy access to information, earlier and more obscure occult detectives had been forgotten.*

The Horse of the Invisible

I HAD THAT AFTERNOON received an invitation from Carnacki. When I reached his place I found him sitting alone. As I came into the room he rose with a perceptibly stiff movement and extended his left hand. His face seemed to be badly scarred and bruised and his right hand was bandaged. He shook hands and offered me his paper, which I refused. Then he passed me a handful of photographs and returned to his reading.

Now, that is just Carnacki. Not a word had come from him and not a question from me. He would tell us all about it later. I spent about half an hour looking at the photographs which were chiefly 'snaps' (some by flashlight) of an extraordinarily pretty girl; though in some of the photographs it was wonderful that her prettiness was so evident for so frightened and startled was her expression that it was difficult not to believe that she had been photographed in the presence of some imminent and overwhelming danger.

The bulk of the photographs were of interiors of different rooms and passages and in every one the girl might be seen, either full length in the distance or closer, with perhaps little more than a hand or arm or portion of the head or dress included in the photograph. All of these had evidently been taken with some definite aim that did not have for its first purpose the picturing of the girl, but obviously of her surroundings and they made me very curious, as you can imagine.

Near the bottom of the pile, however, I came upon something DEFINITELY extraordinary. It was a photograph of the girl standing abrupt and clear in the great blaze of a flashlight, as was plain to be seen. Her face was turned a little upward as if she had been frightened suddenly by some noise. Directly above her, as though half-formed and coming down out of the shadows, was the shape of a single enormous hoof.

I examined this photograph for a long time without understanding it more than that it had probably to do with some queer case in which Carnacki was interested. When Jessop, Arkright and Taylor came in Carnacki quietly held out his hand for the photographs which I returned in the same spirit and afterwards we all went in to dinner. When we had spent a quiet hour at the table we pulled our chairs round and made ourselves snug and Carnacki began:

'I've been North,' he said, speaking slowly and painfully between puffs at his pipe. 'Up to Hisgins of East Lancashire. It has been a pretty strange business all round, as I fancy you chaps will think, when I have finished. I knew before I went, something about the "horse story", as I have heard it called; but I never thought of it coming my way, somehow. Also I know NOW that I never considered it seriously—in spite of my rule always to keep an open mind. Funny creatures, we humans!

'Well, I got a wire asking for an appointment, which of course told me that there was some trouble. On the date I fixed old Captain Hisgins himself came up to see me. He told me a great many new details about the horse story; though naturally I had always known the main points and understood that if the first child were a girl, that girl would be haunted by the Horse during her courtship.

'It is, as you can see already, an extraordinary story and though I have always known about it, I have never thought it to be anything more than an old-time legend, as I have already hinted. You see, for seven generations the Hisgins family have had men children for their first-born and even the Hisgins themselves have long considered the tale to be little more than a myth.

'To come to the present, the eldest child of the reigning family is a girl and she has been often teased and warned in jest by her friends and relations that she is the first girl to be the eldest for seven generations and that she would have to keep her men friends at arm's length or go into a nunnery if she hoped to escape the haunting. And this, I think, shows us how thoroughly the tale had grown to be considered as nothing worthy of the least serious thought. Don't you think so?

'Two months ago Miss Hisgins became engaged to Beaumont, a young Naval Officer, and on the evening of the very day of the engagement, before it was even formally announced, a most extraordinary thing happened which resulted in Captain Hisgins making the appointment and my ultimately going down to their place to look into the thing.

'From the old family records and papers that were entrusted to me I found that there could be no possible doubt that prior to something like a hundred and fifty years ago there were some very extraordinary and disagreeable coincidences, to put the thing in the least emotional way. In the whole of the two centuries prior to that date there were five first-born girls out of a total of seven generations of the family. Each of these girls grew up to maidenhood and each became engaged, and each one died during the period of engagement, two by suicide, one by falling from a window, one from a "broken heart" (presumably heart failure, owing to sudden shock through fright). The fifth girl was killed one evening in the park round the house; but just how, there seemed to be no EXACT knowledge; only that there was an impression that she had been kicked by a horse. She was dead when found. 'Now, you see, all of these deaths might be attributed in a way—even the suicides—to natural causes, I mean as distinct from supernatural. You see? Yet, in every case the maidens had undoubtedly suffered some extraordinary and terrifying experiences during their various courtships for in all of the records there was mention either of the neighing of an unseen horse or of the sounds of an invisible horse galloping, as well as many other peculiar and quite inexplicable manifestations. You begin to understand now, I think, just how extraordinary a business it was that I was asked to look into.

'I gathered from one account that the haunting of the girls was so constant and horrible that two of the girls' lovers fairly ran away from their lady-loves. And I think it was this, more than anything else that made me feel that there had been something more in it than a mere succession of uncomfortable coincidences.

'I got hold of these facts before I had been many hours in the house and after this I went pretty carefully into the details of the thing that happened on the night of Miss Hisgins' engagement to Beaumont. It seems that as the two of them were going through the big lower corridor, just after dusk and before the lamps had been lighted, there had been a sudden, horrible neighing in the corridor, close to them. Immediately afterward Beaumont received a tremendous blow or kick which broke his right forearm. Then the rest of the family and the servants came running to know what was wrong. Lights were brought and the corridor and, afterwards, the whole house searched, but nothing unusual was found.

'You can imagine the excitement in the house and the half incredulous, half believing talk about the old legend. Then, later, in the middle of the night the old Captain was waked by the sound of a great horse galloping round and round the house.

'Several times after this both Beaumont and the girl said that they had heard the sounds of hoofs near to them after dusk, in several of the rooms and corridors.

'Three nights later Beaumont was waked by a strange neighing in the night-time seeming to come from the direction of his sweet-heart's bedroom. He ran hurriedly for her father and the two of them raced to her room. They found her awake and ill with sheer terror, having been awakened by the neighing, seemingly close to her bed.

'The night before I arrived, there had been a fresh happening and they were all in a frightfully nervy state, as you can imagine.

'I spent most of the first day, as I have hinted, in getting hold of details; but after dinner I slacked off and played billiards all the evening with Beaumont and Miss Hisgins. We stopped about ten o'clock and had coffee and I got Beaumont to give me full particulars about the thing that had happened the evening before.

'He and Miss Hisgins had been sitting quietly in her aunt's boudoir whilst the old lady chaperoned them, behind a book. It was growing dusk and the lamp was at her end of the table. The rest of the house was not yet lit as the evening had come earlier than usual. 'Well, it seems that the door into the hall was open and suddenly the girl said: "H'sh! what's that?" 'They both listened and then Beaumont heard it—the sound of a horse outside of the front door. '"Your father?" he suggested, but she reminded him that her father was not riding. 'Of course they were both ready to feel queer, as you can suppose, but Beaumont made an effort to shake this off and went into the hall to see whether anyone was at the entrance. It was pretty dark in the hall and he could see the glass panels of the inner draught-door, clear-cut in the darkness of the hall. He walked over to the glass and looked through into the drive beyond, but there nothing in sight. 'He felt nervous and puzzled and opened the inner door and went out on to the carriage-circle. Almost directly afterward the great hall door swung to with a crash behind him. He told me that he had a sudden awful feeling of having been trapped in some way—that is how he put it. He whirled round and gripped the door handle, but something seemed to be holding it with a vast grip on the other side. Then, before he could be fixed in his mind that this was so, he was able to turn the handle and open the door. 'He paused a moment in the doorway and peered into the hall, for he had hardly steadied his mind sufficiently to know whether he was really frightened or not. Then he heard his sweetheart blow him a kiss out of the greyness of the big, unlit hall and he knew that she had followed him from the boudoir. He blew her a kiss back and stepped inside the doorway, meaning to go to her. And then, suddenly, in a flash of sickening knowledge he knew that it was not his sweetheart who had blown him that kiss. He knew that something was trying to tempt him alone into the darkness and that the girl had never left the boudoir. He jumped back and in the same instant of time he heard the kiss again, nearer to him. He called out at the top of his voice: "Mary, stay in the boudoir. Don't move out of the boudoir until I come to you." He heard her call something in reply from the boudoir and then he had struck a clump of a dozen or so matches and was holding them above his head and looking round the hall. There was no one in it, but even as the matches burned out there came the sounds of a great horse galloping down the empty drive.

'Now you see, both he and the girl had heard the sounds of the horse galloping; but when I questioned more closely I found that the aunt had heard nothing, though it is true she is a bit deaf, and she was further back in the room. Of course, both he and Miss Hisgins had been in an extremely nervous state and ready to hear anything. The door might have been slammed by a sudden puff of wind owing to some inner door being opened; and as for the grip on the handle, that may have been nothing more than the sneck catching.

'With regard to the kisses and the sounds of the horse galloping, I pointed out that these might have seemed ordinary enough sounds, if they had been only cool enough to reason. As I told him, and as he knew, the sounds of a horse galloping carry a long way on the wind so that what he had heard might have been nothing more than a horse being ridden some distance away. And as for the kiss, plenty of quiet noises—the rustle of a paper or a leaf—have a somewhat similar sound, especially if one is in an overstrung condition and imagining things.

'I finished preaching this little sermon on common-sense versus hysteria as we put out the lights and left the billiard room. But neither Beaumont nor Miss Hisgins would agree that there had been any fancy on their parts.

'We had come out of the billiard room by this time and were going along the passage and I was still doing my best to make both of them see the ordinary, commonplace possibilities of the happening, when what killed my pig, as the saying goes, was the sound of a hoof in the dark billiard room we had just left.

'I felt the "creep" come on me in a flash, up my spine and over the back of my head. Miss Hisgins whooped like a child with the whooping-cough and ran up the passage, giving little gasping screams. Beaumont, however, ripped round on his heels and jumped back a couple of yards. I gave back too, a bit, as you can understand.

'"There it is," he said in a low, breathless voice. "Perhaps you'll believe now."

'"There's certainly something," I whispered, never taking my gaze off the closed door of the billiard room.

'"H'sh!" he muttered. "There it is again."

'There was a sound like a great horse pacing round and round the billiard room with slow, deliberate steps. A horrible cold fright took me so that it seemed impossible to take a full breath, you know the feeling, and then I saw we must have been walking backwards for we found ourselves suddenly at the opening of the long passage.

'We stopped there and listened. The sounds went on steadily with a horrible sort of deliberateness, as if the brute were taking a sort of malicious gusto in walking about all over the room which we had just occupied. Do you understand just what I mean?

'Then there was a pause and a long time of absolute quiet except for an excited whispering from some of the people down in the big hall. The sound came plainly up the wide stairway. I fancy they were gathered round Miss Hisgins, with some notion of protecting her.

'I should think Beaumont and I stood there, at the end of the passage for about five minutes, listening for any noise in the billiard room. Then I realized what a horrible funk I was in and I said to him: "I'm going to see what's there."

'"So'm I," he answered. He was pretty white, but he had heaps of pluck. I told him to wait one instant and I made a dash into my bedroom and got my camera and flashlight. I slipped my revolver into my right-hand pocket and a knuckle-duster over my left fist, where it was ready and yet would not stop me from being able to work my flashlight.

'Then I ran back to Beaumont. He held out his hand to show me that he had his pistol and I nodded, but whispered to him not to be too quick to shoot, as there might be some silly practical joking at work, after all. He had got a lamp from a bracket in the upper hall which he was holding in the crook of his damaged arm, so that we had a good light. Then we went down the passage towards the billiard room and you can imagine that we were a pretty nervous couple.

'All this time there had not been a sound, but abruptly when we were within perhaps a couple of yards of the door we heard the sudden clumping of a hoof on the solid parquet floor of the billiard room. In the instant afterward it seemed to me that the whole place shook beneath the ponderous hoof falls of some huge thing, coming towards the door. Both Beaumont and I gave back a pace or two, and then realized and hung on to our courage, as you might say, and waited. The great tread came right up to the door and then stopped and there was an instant of absolute silence, except that so far as I was concerned, the pulsing in my throat and temples almost deafened me.

'I dare say we waited quite half a minute and then came the further restless clumping of a great hoof. Immediately afterward the sounds came right on as if some invisible thing passed through the closed door and the ponderous tread was upon us. We jumped, each of us, to our side of the passage and I know that I spread myself stiff against the wall. The clungk clunck, clungk clunck, of the great hoof falls passed right between us and slowly and with deadly deliberateness, down the passage. I heard them through a haze of blood-beats in my ears and temples and my body was extraordinarily rigid and pringling and I was horribly breathless. I stood for a little time like this, my head turned so that I could see up the passage. I was conscious only that there was a hideous danger abroad. Do you understand?

'And then, suddenly, my pluck came back to me. I was aware that the noise of the hoof-beats sounded near the other end of the passage. I twisted quickly and got my camera to bear and snapped off the flashlight. Immediately afterward, Beaumont let fly a storm of shots down the passage and began to run, shouting: "It's after Mary. Run! Run!"

'He rushed down the passage and I after him. We came out on the main landing and heard the sound of a hoof on the stairs and after that, nothing. And from thence onward, nothing.

'Down below us in the big hall I could see a number of the household round Miss Hisgins, who seemed to have fainted and there were several of the servants clumped together a little way off, staring up at the main landing and no one saying a single word. And about some twenty steps up the stairs was the old Captain Hisgins with a drawn sword in his hand where he had halted, just below the last hoof-sound. I think I never saw anything finer than the old man standing there between his daughter and that infernal thing.

'I daresay you can understand the queer feeling of horror I had at passing that place on the stairs where the sounds had ceased. It was as if the monster were still standing there, invisible. And the peculiar thing was that we never heard another sound of the hoof, either up or down the stairs.

'After they had taken Miss Hisgins to her room I sent word that I should follow, so soon as they were ready for me. And presently, when a message came to tell me that I could come any time, I asked her father to give me a hand with my instrument box and between us we carried it into the girl's bedroom. I had the bed pulled well out into the middle of the room, after which I erected the electric pentacle round the bed.

'Then I directed that lamps should be placed round the room, but that on no account must any light be made within the pentacle; neither must anyone pass in or out. The girl's mother I had placed within the pentacle and directed that her maid should sit without, ready to carry any message so as to make sure that Mrs. Hisgins did not have to leave the pentacle. I suggested also that the girl's father should stay the night in the room and that he had better be armed.

'When I left the bedroom I found Beaumont waiting outside the door in a miserable state of anxiety. I told him what I had done and explained to him that Miss Hisgins was probably perfectly safe within the "protection"; but that in addition to her father remaining the night in the room, I intended to stand guard at the door. I told him that I should like him to keep me company, for I knew that he could never sleep, feeling as he did, and I should not be sorry to have a companion. Also, I wanted to have him under my own observation, for there was no doubt but that he was actually in greater danger in some ways than the girl. At least, that was my opinion and is still, as I think you will agree later.

'I asked him whether he would object to my drawing a pentacle round him for the night and got him to agree, but I saw that he did not know whether to be superstitious about it or to regard it more as a piece of foolish mumming; but he took it seriously enough when I gave him some particulars about the Black Veil case, when young Aster died. You remember, he said it was a piece of silly superstition and stayed outside. Poor devil!

'The night passed quietly enough until a little while before dawn when we both heard the sounds of a great horse galloping round and round the house just as old Captain Hisgins had described it. You can imagine how queer it made me feel and directly afterward, I heard someone stir within the bedroom. I knocked at the door, for I was uneasy, and the Captain came. I asked whether every-thing was right; to which he replied yes, and immediately asked me whether I had heard the galloping, so that I knew he had heard them also. I suggested that it might be well to leave the bedroom door open a little until the dawn came in, as there was certainly something abroad. This was done and he went back into the room, to be near his wife and daughter.

'I had better say here that I was doubtful whether there was any value in the "Defense" about Miss Hisgins, for what I term the "personal-sounds" of the manifestation were so extraordinarily material that I was inclined to parallel the case with that one of Harford's where the hand of the child kept materialising within the pentacle and patting the floor. As you will remember, that was a hideous business.

'Yet, as it chanced, nothing further happened and so soon as daylight had fully come we all went off to bed.

'Beaumont knocked me up about midday and I went down and made breakfast into lunch. Miss Hisgins was there and seemed in very fair spirits, considering. She told me that I had made her feel almost safe for the first time for days. She told me also that her cousin, Harry Parsket, was coming down from London and she knew that he would do anything to help fight the ghost. And after that she and Beaumont went out into the grounds to have a little time together.

'I had a walk in the grounds myself and went round the house, but saw no traces of hoof-marks and after that I spent the rest of the day making an examination of the house, but found nothing.

'I made an end of my search before dark and went to my room to dress for dinner. When I got down the cousin had just arrived and I found him one of the nicest men I have met for a long time. A chap with a tremendous amount of pluck, and the particular kind of man I like to have with me in a bad case like the one I was on. 'I could see that what puzzled him most was our belief in the genuineness of the haunting and I found myself almost wanting something to happen, just to show him how true it was. As it chanced, something did happen, with a vengeance.

'Beaumont and Miss Hisgins had gone out for a stroll just before the dusk and Captain Hisgins asked me to come into his study for a short chat whilst Parsket went upstairs with his traps, for he had no man with him.

'I had a long conversation with the old Captain in which I pointed out that the "haunting" had evidently no particular connection with the house, but only with the girl herself and that the sooner she was married, the better as it would give Beaumont a right to be with her at all times and further than this, it might be that the manifestations would cease if the marriage were actually performed.

'The old man nodded agreement to this, especially to the first part and reminded me that three of the girls who were said to have been "haunted" had been sent away from home and met their deaths whilst away. And then in the midst of our talk there came a pretty frightening interruption, for all at once the old butler rushed into the room, most extraordinarily pale:

'"Miss Mary, sir! Miss Mary, sir!" he gasped. "She's screaming... out in the Park, sir! And they say they can hear the Horse—"

'The Captain made one dive for a rack of arms and snatched down his old sword and ran out, drawing it as he ran. I dashed out and up the stairs, snatched my camera-flashlight and a heavy revolver, gave one yell at Parset's door: "The Horse!" and was down and into the grounds.

'Away in the darkness there was a confused shouting and I caught the sounds of shooting, out among the scattered trees. And then, from a patch of blackness to my left, there burst suddenly an infernal gobbling sort of neighing. Instantly I whipped round and snapped off the flashlight. The great light blazed out momentarily, showing me the leaves of a big tree close at hand, quivering in the night breeze, but I saw nothing else and then the ten-fold blackness came down upon me and I heard Parset shouting a little way back to know whether I had seen anything.

'The next instant he was beside me and I felt safer for his company, for there was some incredible thing near to us and I was momentarily blind because of the brightness of the flashlight. "What was it? What was it?" he kept repeating in an excited voice. And all the time I was staring into the darkness and answering, mechanically, "I don't know. I don't know."

'There was a burst of shouting somewhere ahead and then a shot. We ran towards the sounds, yelling to the people not to shoot; for in the darkness and panic there was this danger also. Then there came two of the game-keepers racing hard up the drive with their lanterns and guns; and immediately afterward a row of lights dancing towards us from the house, carried by some of the men-servants.

'As the lights came up I saw we had come close to Beaumont. He was standing over Miss Hisgins and he had his revolver in his hand. Then I saw his face and there was a great wound across his forehead. By him was the Captain, turning his naked sword this way and that, and peering into the darkness; a little behind him stood the old butler, a battle-axe from one of the arm-stands in the hall in his hands. Yet there was nothing strange to be seen anywhere.

'We got the girl into the house and left her with her mother and Beaumont, whilst a groom rode for a doctor. And then the rest of us, with four other keepers, all armed with guns and carrying lanterns, searched round the homepark. But we found nothing.

'When we got back we found that the doctor had been. He had bound up Beaumont's wound, which luckily was not deep, and ordered Miss Hisgins straight to bed. I went upstairs with the Captain and found Beaumont on guard outside of the girl's door. I asked him how he felt and then, so soon as the girl and her mother were ready for us, Captain Hisgins and I went into the bedroom and fixed the pentacle again round the bed. They had already got lamps about the room and after I had set the same order of watching as on the previous night, I joined Beaumont outside of the door.

'Parsket had come up while I had been in the bedroom and between us we got some idea from Beaumont as to what had happened out in the Park. It seems that they were coming home after their stroll from the direction of the West Lodge. It had got quite dark and suddenly Miss Hisgins said: "Hush!" and came to a standstill. He stopped and listened, but heard nothing for a little. Then he caught it—the sound of a horse, seemingly a long way off, galloping towards them over the grass. He told the girl that it was nothing and started to hurry her towards the house, but she was not deceived, of course. In less than a minute they heard it quite close to them in the darkness and they started running. Then Miss

Hisgins caught her foot and fell. She began to scream and that is what the butler heard. As Beaumont lifted the girl he heard the hoofs come thudding right at him. He stood over her and fired all five chambers of his revolver right at the sounds. He told us that he was sure he saw something that looked like an enormous horse's head, right upon him in the light of the last flash of his pistol. Immediately afterwards he was struck a tremendous blow which knocked him down and then the Captain and the butler came running up, shouting. The rest, of course, we knew.

'About ten o'clock the butler brought us up a tray, for which I was very glad, as the night before I had got rather hungry. I warned Beaumont, however, to be very particular not to drink any spirits and I also made him give me his pipe and matches. At midnight I drew a pentacle round him and Parsket and I sat one on each side of him, outside the pentacle, for I had no fear that there would be any manifestation made against anyone except Beaumont or Miss Hisgins.

'After that we kept pretty quiet. The passage was lit by a big lamp at each end so that we had plenty of light and we were all armed, Beaumont and I with revolvers and Parsket with a shot-gun. In addition to my weapon I had my camera and flashlight.

'Now and again we talked in whispers and twice the Captain came out of the bedroom to have a word with us. About half past one we had all grown very silent and suddenly, about twenty minutes later, I held up my hand, silently, for there seemed to be a sound of galloping out in the night. I knocked on the bedroom door for the Captain to open it and when he came I whispered to him that we thought we heard the Horse. For some time we stayed listening, and both Parsket and the Captain thought they heard it; but now I was not so sure, neither was Beaumont. Yet afterwards, I thought I heard it again.

'I told Captain Hisgins I thought he had better go into the bedroom and leave the door a little open and this he did. But from that time onward we heard nothing and presently the dawn came in and we all went very thankfully to bed.

'When I was called at lunch-time I had a little surprise, for Captain Hisgins told me that they had held a family council and had decided to take my advice and have the marriage without a day's more delay than possible. Beaumont was already on his way to London to get a special License and they hoped to have the wedding next day.

'This pleased me, for it seemed the sanest thing to be done in the extraordinary circumstances and meanwhile I should continue my investigations; but until the marriage was accomplished, my chief thought was to keep Miss Hisgins near to me.

'After lunch I thought I would take a few experimental photographs of Miss Hisgins and her SURROUNDINGS. Sometimes the camera sees things that would seem very strange to normal human eyesight.

'With this intention and partly to make an excuse to keep her in my company as much as possible, I asked Miss Hisgins to join me in my experiments. She seemed glad to do this and I spent several hours with her, wandering all over the house, from room to room and whenever the impulse came I took a flashlight of her and the room or corridor in which we chanced to be at the moment.

'After we had gone right through the house in this fashion, I asked her whether she felt sufficiently brave to repeat the experiments in the cellars. She said yes, and so I rooted out Captain Hisgins and Parsket, for I was not going to take her even into what you might call artificial darkness without help and companionship at hand.

'When we were ready we went down into the wine cellar, Captain Hisgins carrying a shot-gun and Parsket a specially prepared background and a lantern. I got the girl to stand in the middle of the cellar whilst Parsket and the Captain held out the background behind her. Then I fired off the flashlight, and we went into the next cellar where we repeated the experiment.

'Then in the third cellar, a tremendous, pitch-dark place, something extraordinary and horrible manifested itself. I had stationed Miss Hisgins in the centre of the place, with her father and Parsket holding the background as before. When all was ready and just as I pressed the trigger of the "flash", there came in the cellar that dreadful, gobbling neighing that I had heard out in the Park. It seemed to come from somewhere above the girl and in the glare of the sudden light I saw that she was staring tensely upward, but at no visible thing. And then in the succeeding comparative darkness, I was shouting to the Captain and Parsket to run Miss Hisgins out into the daylight.

'This was done instantly and I shut and locked the door afterwards making the First and Eighth signs of the Saaamaaa Ritual opposite to each post and connecting them across the threshold with a triple line.

'In the meanwhile Parsket and Captain Hisgins carried the girl to her mother and left her there, in a half-fainting condition whilst I stayed on guard outside of the cellar door, feeling pretty horrible for I knew that there was some disgusting thing inside, and along with this feeling there was a sense of half-ashamedness, rather miserable, you know, because I had exposed Miss Hisgins to the danger.

'I had got the Captain's shot-gun and when he and Parsket came down again they were each carrying guns and lanterns. I could not possibly tell you the utter relief of spirit and body that came to me when I heard them coming, but just try to imagine what it was like, standing outside of that cellar. Can you?

'I remember noticing, just before I went to unlock the door, how white and ghastly Parsket looked and the old Captain was grey-looking and I wondered whether my face was like theirs. And this, you know, had its own distinct effect upon my nerves, for it seemed to bring the beastliness of the thing bash down on to me in a fresh way. I know it was only sheer will power that carried me up to the door and made me turn the key.

'I paused one little moment and then with a nervy jerk sent the door wide open and held my lantern over my head. Parsket and the Captain came one on each side of me and held up their lanterns, but the place was absolutely empty. Of course, I did not trust to a casual look of this kind, but spent several hours with the help of the two others in sounding every square foot of the floor, ceiling and walls.

'Yet, in the end I had to admit that the place itself was absolutely normal and so we came away. But I sealed the door and outside, opposite each door-post I made the First and Last signs of the Saaamaaa Ritual, joined them as before, with a triple line. Can you imagine what it was like, searching that cellar?

'When we got upstairs I inquired very anxiously how Miss Hisgins was and the girl came out herself to tell me that she was all right and that I was not to trouble about her, or blame myself, as I told her I had been doing.

'I felt happier then and went off to dress for dinner and after that was done, Parsket and I took one of the bathrooms to develop the negatives that I had been taking. Yet none of the plates had anything to tell us until we came to the one that was taken in the cellar. Parsket was developing and I had taken a batch of the fixed plates out into the lamplight to examine them.

'I had just gone carefully through the lot when I heard a shout from Parsket and when I ran to him he was looking at a partly-developed negative which he was holding up to the red lamp. It showed the girl plainly, looking upward as I had seen her, but the thing that astonished me was the shadow of an enormous hoof, right above her, as if it were coming down upon her out of the shadows. And you know, I had run her bang into that danger. That was the thought that was chief in my mind.

'As soon as the developing was complete I fixed the plate and examined it carefully in a good light. There was no doubt about it at all, the thing above Miss Hisgins was an enormous, shadowy hoof. Yet I was no nearer to coming to any definite knowledge and the only thing I could do was to warn Parsket to say nothing about it to the girl for it would only increase her fright, but I showed the thing to her father for I considered it right that he should know.

'That night we took the same precaution for Miss Hisgins' safety as on the two previous nights and Parsket kept me company; yet the dawn came in without anything unusual having happened and I went off to bed.

'When I got down to lunch I learnt that Beaumont had wired to say that he would be in soon after four; also that a message had been sent to the Rector. And it was generally plain that the ladies of the house were in a tremendous fluster.

'Beaumont's train was late and he did not get home until five, but even then the Rector had not put in an appearance and the butler came in to say that the coachman had returned without him as he had been called away unexpectedly. Twice more during the evening the carriage was sent down, but the clergyman had not returned and we had to delay the marriage until the next day.

'That night I arranged the "Defense" round the girl's bed and the Captain and his wife sat up with her as before. Beaumont, as I expected, insisted on keeping watch with me and he seemed in a curiously frightened mood; not for himself, you know, but for Miss Hisgins. He had a horrible feeling he told me, that there would be a final, dreadful attempt on his sweetheart that night.

'This, of course, I told him was nothing but nerves; yet really, it made me feel very anxious; for I have seen too much not to know that under such circumstances a premonitory conviction of impending danger is not necessarily to be put down entirely to nerves. In fact, Beaumont was so simply and earnestly convinced that the night would bring some extraordinary manifestation that

I got Parsket to rig up a long cord from the wire of the butler's bell, to come along the passage handy.

'To the butler himself I gave directions not to undress and to give the same order to two of the footmen. If I rang he was to come instantly, with the footmen, carrying lanterns and the lanterns were to be kept ready lit all night. If for any reason the bell did not ring and I blew my whistle, he was to take that as a signal in the place of the bell.

'After I had arranged all these minor details I drew a pentacle about Beaumont and warned him very particularly to stay within it, whatever happened. And when this was done, there was nothing to do but wait and pray that the night would go as quietly as the night before.

'We scarcely talked at all and by about one a.m. we were all very tense and nervous so that at last Parsket got up and began to walk up and down the corridor to steady himself a bit. Presently I slipped off my pumps and joined him and we walked up and down, whispering occasionally for something over an hour, until in turning I caught my foot in the bell-cord and went down on my face; but without hurting myself or making a noise.

'When I got up Parsket nudged me.

'"Did you notice that the bell never rang?" he whispered.

'"Jove!" I said, "you're right."

'"Wait a minute," he answered. "I'll bet it's only a kink somewhere in the cord." He left his gun and slipped along the passage and taking the top lamp, tiptoed away into the house, carrying Beaumont's revolver ready in his right hand. He was a plucky chap, I remember thinking then, and again, later.

'Just then Beaumont motioned to me for absolute quiet. Directly afterwards I heard the thing for which he listened—the sound of a horse galloping, out in the night. I think that I may say I fairly shivered. The sound died away and left a horrible, desolate, eerie feeling in the air, you know. I put my hand out to the bell-cord, hoping Parsket had got it clear. Then I waited, glancing before and behind.

'Perhaps two minutes passed, full of what seemed like an almost unearthly quiet. And then, suddenly, down the corridor at the lighted end there sounded the clumping of a great hoof and instantly the lamp was thrown with a tremendous crash and we were in the dark. I tugged hard on the cord and blew the whistle; then I raised my snapshot and fired the flashlight. The corridor blazed into brilliant light, but there was nothing, and then the darkness fell like thunder. I heard the Captain at the bedroom-door and shouted to him to bring out a lamp, quick; but instead something started to kick the door and I heard the Captain shouting within the bedroom and then the screaming of the women. I had a sudden horrible fear that the monster had got into the bedroom, but in the same instant from up the corridor there came abruptly the vile, gobbling neighing that we had heard in the park and the cellar. I blew the whistle again and groped blindly for the bell-cord, shouting to Beaumont to stay in the Pentacle, whatever happened. I yelled again to the Captain to bring out a lamp and there came a smashing sound against the bedroom door. Then I had my matches in my hand, to get some light before that incredible, unseen Monster was upon us.

'The match scraped on the box and flared up dully and in the same instant I heard a faint sound behind me. I whipped round in a kind of mad terror and saw something in the light of the match—a monstrous horse-head close to Beaumont.

'"Look out, Beaumont!" I shouted in a sort of scream. "It's behind you!"

'The match went out abruptly and instantly there came the huge bang of Parsket's double-barrel (both barrels at once), fired evidently single-handed by Beaumont close to my ear, as it seemed. I caught a momentary glimpse of the great head in the flash and of an enormous hoof amid the belch of fire and smoke seeming to be descending upon Beaumont. In the same instant I fired three chambers of my revolver. There was the sound of a dull blow and then that horrible, gobbling neigh broke out close to me. I fired twice at the sound. Immediately afterward something struck me and I was knocked backwards. I got on to my knees and shouted for help at the top of my voice. I heard the women screaming behind the closed door of the bedroom and was dully aware that the door was being smashed from the inside, and directly afterwards I knew that Beaumont was struggling with some hideous thing near to me. For an instant I held back, stupidly, paralysed with funk and then, blindly and in a sort of rigid chill of goose-flesh I went to help him, shouting his name. I can tell you, I was nearly sick with the naked fear I had on me. There came a little, choking scream out of the darkness, and at that I jumped forward into the dark. I gripped a vast, furry ear. Then something struck me another great blow knocking me sick. I hit back, weak and blind and gripped with my other hand at the incredible thing. Abruptly I was dimly aware of a tremendous crash behind me and a great burst of light. There were other lights in the passage and a noise of feet and shouting. My hand-grips were torn from the thing they held; I shut my eyes stupidly and heard a loud yell above me and then a heavy blow, like a butcher chopping meat and then something fell upon me.

'I was helped to my knees by the Captain and the butler. On the floor lay an enormous horse-head out of which protruded a man's trunk and legs. On the wrists were fixed great hoofs. It was the monster. The Captain cut something with the sword that he held in his hand and stooped and lifted off the mask, for that is what it was. I saw the face then of the man who had worn it. It was Parsket. He had a bad wound across the forehead where the Captain's sword had bit through the mask. I looked bewilderedly from him to Beaumont, who was sitting up, leaning against the wall of the corridor. Then I stared at Parsket again.

'"By Jove!" I said at last, and then I was quiet for I was so ashamed for the man. You can understand, can't you? And he was opening his eyes. And you know, I had grown so to like him.

'And then, you know, just as Parsket was getting back his wits and looking from one to the other of us and beginning to remember, there happened a strange and incredible thing. For from the end of the corridor there sounded suddenly, the clumping of a great hoof. I looked that way and then instantly at Parsket and saw a horrible fear in his face and eyes. He wrenched himself round, weakly, and stared in mad terror up the corridor to where the sound had been, and the rest of us stared, in a frozen group. I remember vaguely half sobs and whispers from Miss Hisgins' bedroom, all the while that I stared frightenedly up the corridor.

'The silence lasted several seconds and then, abruptly there came again the clumping of the great hoof, away at the end of the corridor. And immediately afterward the clungk, clunk—clungk, clunk of mighty hoofs coming down the passage towards us.

'Even then, you know, most of us thought it was some mechanism of Parsket's still at work and we were in the queerest mixture of fright and doubt. I think everyone looked at Parsket. And suddenly the Captain shouted out:

'"Stop this damned fooling at once. Haven't you done enough?"

'For my part, I was now frightened for I had a sense that there was something horrible and wrong. And then Parsket managed to gasp out:

'"It's not me! My God! It's not me! My God! It's not me."

'And then, you know, it seemed to come home to everyone in an instant that there was really some dreadful thing coming down the passage. There was a mad rush to get away and even old Captain Hisgins gave back with the butler and the footmen. Beaumont fainted outright, as I found afterwards, for he had been badly mauled. I just flattened back against the wall, kneeling as I was, too stupid and dazed even to run. And almost in the same instant the ponderous hoof-falls sounded close to me and seeming to shake the solid floor as they passed. Abruptly the great sounds ceased and I knew in a sort of sick fashion that the thing had halted opposite to the door of the girl's bedroom. And then I was aware that Parsket was standing rocking in the doorway with his arms spread across, so as to fill the doorway with his body. Parsket was extraordinarily pale and the blood was running down his face from the wound in his forehead; and then I noticed that he seemed to be looking at something in the passage with a peculiar, desperate, fixed, incredibly masterful gaze. But there was really nothing to be seen. And suddenly the clungk, clunk—clungk, clunk recommenced and passed onward down the passage. In the same moment Parsket pitched forward out of the doorway on to his face.

'There were shouts from the huddle of men down the passage and the two footmen and the butler simply ran, carrying their lanterns, but the Captain went against the side-wall with his back and put the lamp he was carrying over his head. The dull tread of the Horse went past him, and left him unharmed and I heard the monstrous hoof-falls going away and away through the quiet house and after that a dead silence.

'Then the Captain moved and came towards us, very slow and shaky and with an extraordinarily grey face.

'I crept towards Parsket and the Captain came to help me. We turned him over and, you know, I knew in a moment that he was dead; but you can imagine what a feeling it sent through me.

'I looked at the Captain and suddenly he said:

'"That—That—That—" and I know that he was trying to tell me that Parsket had stood between his daughter and whatever it was that had gone down the passage. I stood up and steadied him, though I was not very steady myself. And suddenly his face began to work and he went down on to his knees by Parsket and cried like some shaken child. Then the women came out of the doorway of the bedroom and I turned away and left him to them, whilst I over to Beaumont.

'That is practically the whole story and the only thing that is left to me is to try to explain some of the puzzling parts, here and there.

'Perhaps you have seen that Parsket was in love with Miss Hisgins and this fact is the key to a good deal that was extraordinary. He was doubtless responsible for some portions of the "haunting"; in fact I think for nearly everything, but, you know, I can prove nothing and what I have to tell you is chiefly the result of deduction.

'In the first place, it is obvious that Parsket's intention was to frighten Beaumont away and when he found that he could not do this, I think he grew so desperate that he really intended to kill him. I hate to say this, but the facts force me to think so.

'I am quite certain that it was Parsket who broke Beaumont's arm. He knew all the details of the so-called "Horse Legend", and got the idea to work upon the old story for his own end. He evidently had some method of slipping in and out of the house, probably through one of the many French windows, or possibly he had a key to one or two of the garden doors, and when he was supposed to be away, he was really coming down on the quiet and hiding somewhere in the neighbourhood.

'The incident of the kiss in the dark hall I put down to sheer nervous imaginings on the part of Beaumont and Miss Hisgins, yet I must say that the sound of the horse outside of the front door is a little difficult to explain away. But I am still inclined to keep to my first idea on this point, that there was nothing really unnatural about it.

'The hoof sounds in the billiard-room and down the passage were done by Parsket from the floor below by bumping up against the panelled ceiling with a block of wood tied to one of the window-hooks. I proved this by an examination which showed the dents in the woodwork.

'The sounds of the horse galloping round the house were possibly made also by Parsket, who must have had a horse tied up in the plantation near by, unless, indeed, he made the sounds himself, but I do not see how he could have gone fast enough to produce the illusion. In any case, I don't feel perfect certainty on this point. I failed to find any hoof marks, as you remember.

'The gobbling neighing in the park was a ventriloquial achievement on the part of Parsket and the attack out there on Beaumont was also by him, so that when I thought he was in his bedroom, he must have been outside all the time and joined me after I ran out of the front door. This is almost probable. I mean that Parsket was the cause, for if it had been something more serious he would certainly have given up his foolishness, knowing that there was no longer any need for it. I cannot imagine how he escaped being shot, both then and in the last mad action of which I have just told you. He was enormously without fear of any kind for himself as you can see.

'The time when Parsket was with us, when we thought we heard the Horse galloping round the house, we must have been deceived. No one was very sure, except, of course, Parsket, who would naturally encourage the belief.

'The neighing in the cellar is where I consider there came the first suspicion into Parsket's mind that there was something more at work than his sham-haunting. The neighing was done by him in the same way that he did it in the park; but when I remember how ghastly he looked I feel sure that the sounds must have had some infernal quality added to them which frightened the man himself. Yet, later, he would persuade himself that he had been getting fanciful. Of course, I must not forget that the effect upon Miss Hisgins must have made him feel pretty miserable.

'Then, about the clergyman being called away, we found afterwards that it was a bogus errand, or, rather, call and it is apparent that Parsket was at the bottom of this, so as to get a few more hours in which to achieve his end and what that was, a very little imagination will show you; for he had found that Beaumont would not be frightened away. I hate to think this, but I'm bound to. Anyway, it is obvious that the man was temporarily a bit off his normal balance. Love's a queer disease!

'Then, there is no doubt at all but that Parsket left the cord to the butler's bell hitched somewhere so as to give him an excuse to slip away naturally to clear it. This also gave him the opportunity to remove one of the passage lamps. Then he had only to smash the other and the passage was in utter darkness for him to make the attempt on Beaumont.

'In the same way, it was he who locked the door of the bedroom and took the key (it was in his pocket). This prevented the Captain from bringing a light and coming to the rescue. But Captain Hisgins broke-down the door with the heavy fender-curb and it was his smashing the door that sounded so confusing and frightening in the darkness of the passage.

'The photograph of the monstrous hoof above Miss Hisgins in the cellar is one of the things that I am less sure about. It might have been faked by Parsket, whilst I was out of the room, and this would have been easy enough, to anyone who knew how. But, you know, it does not look like a fake. Yet, there is as much evidence of probability that it was faked, as against; and the thing is too vague for an examination to help to a definite decision so that I will express no opinion, one way or the other. It is certainly a horrible photograph.

'And now I come to that last, dreadful thing. There has been no further manifestation of anything abnormal so that there is an extraordinary uncertainty in my conclusions. If we had not heard those last sounds and if Parsket had not shown that enormous sense of fear the whole of this case could be explained in the way in which I have shown. And, in fact, as you have seen, I am of the opinion that almost all of it can be cleared up, but I see no way of going past the thing we heard at the last and the fear that Parsket showed.

'His death—no, that proves nothing. At the inquest it was described somewhat untechnically as due to heartspasm. That is normal enough and leaves us quite in the dark as to whether he died because he stood between the girl and some incredible thing of monstrosity.

'The look on Parsket's face and the thing he called out when he heard the great hoof-sounds coming down the passage seem to show that he had the sudden realization of what before then may have been nothing more than a horrible suspicion. And his fear and appreciation of some tremendous danger approaching was probably more keenly real even than mine. And then he did the one fine, great thing!'

'And the cause?' I said. 'What caused it?'

Carnacki shook his head.

'God knows,' he answered, with a peculiar, sincere reverence. 'If that thing was what it seemed to be one might suggest an explanation which would not offend one's reason, but which may be utterly wrong. Yet I have thought, though it would take a long lecture on Thought Induction to get you to appreciate my reasons, that Parsket had produced what I might term a kind of "induced haunting", a kind of induced simulation of his mental conceptions to his desperate thoughts and broodings. It is impossible to make it clearer in a few words.'

'But the old story!' I said. 'Why may not there have been something in THAT?'

'There may have been something in it,' said Carnacki. 'But I do not think it had anything to do with this. I have not clearly thought out my reasons, yet; but later I may be able to tell you why I think so.'

'And the marriage? And the cellar—was there anything found there?' asked Taylor.

'Yes, the marriage was performed that day in spite of the tragedy,' Carnacki told us. 'It was the wisest thing to do considering the things that I cannot explain. Yes, I had the floor of that big cellar up, for I had a feeling I might find something there to give me some light. But there was nothing.

'You know, the whole thing is tremendous and extraordinary. I shall never forget the look on Parsket's face. And afterwards the disgusting sounds of those great hoofs going away through the quiet house.'

Carnacki stood up:

'Out you go!' he said in friendly fashion, using the recognized formula.

And we went presently out into the quiet of the Embankment, and so to our homes.

CASE OF THE
VEIL OF ISIS

Sax Rohmer

Sax Rohmer (1883–1959) was the pen name of Arthur Henry Ward, born in Birmingham, England, to Irish immigrant parents. He is most renowned—or notorious—as the creator of the fictional character, master criminal Dr. Fu Manchu. Fu Manchu was incredibly popular, featuring in stories, novels, comic strips, television, and movies for decades, but also drew condemnation for stereotyping and racism toward the Chinese and East Asians, in general.

Ward worked as a poet, songwriter, and a comedy sketch writer for music hall performers before becoming an author of weird fiction and assuming the name Sax Rohmer. His short story "The Mysterious Mummy" was published in Pearson's Weekly *in 1903. The first Fu Manchu novel,* The Mystery of Dr. Fu Manchu, *appeared in installments starting in October 1912. An immediate success, it made Rohmer one of the world's highest paid authors during the 1920s and 1930s.*

In the manner of Sir Arthur Conan Doyle's frustration with Sherlock Holmes, Rohmer tired of Fu Manchu and attempted to end the series, only to be convinced by public demand to revive the villain. Rohmer authored other books, too, such as the supernatural horror novels The Green Eyes of Bast *and* Brood of the Witch Queen. *His* Romance of Sorcery, *published in 1914, an exploration of occult history, was praised by Rohmer's friend Harry Houdini. However, all his other books and characters, like Moris Klaw, his occult detective, would inevitably be overshadowed by the great fame of Fu Manchu.*

Klaw is a dream detective—he solves mysteries by dreaming. Klaw investigates both criminal and supernatural mysteries. His stories are narrated by Mr. Searles, who is fascinated by Klaw. Isis Klaw, the detective's stylish daughter, appears in almost all the Dream Detective stories, although not in "Case of the Veil of Isis." Isis Klaw assists her father with his detecting, as does Searles.

Moris Klaw stars in ten stories, which first ran in New Monthly Magazine, *beginning in 1913. "Case of the Veil of Isis," the last of the stories, was first published in the January 1914 issue. The stories were later collected and published in the 1920 compilation* The Dream Detective: Being Some Account of the Methods of Moris Klaw.

Case of the Veil of Isis

I

I HAVE MADE NO ATTEMPT, in these chronicles, to arrange the cases of my remarkable friend, Moris Klaw, in sections. Yet, as has recently been pointed out to me, they seem naturally to fall into two orders. There were those in which he appeared in the role of criminal investigator, and in which he was usually associated with Inspector Grimsby. There was another class of inquiry in which the criminal element was lacking; mysteries which never came under the notice of New Scotland Yard.

Since Moris Klaw's methods were, if not supernatural, at any rate supernormal, I have been asked if he ever, to my knowledge, inquired into a case which proved insusceptible of a natural explanation—which fell strictly within the providence of the occult.

To that I answer that I am aware of several; but I have refrained from including them because readers of these papers would be unlikely to appreciate the nature of Klaw's investigations outside the sphere of ordinary laws. Those who are curious upon the point cannot do better than consult the remarkable work by Moris Klaw entitled *Psychic Angels*.

But there was one case with which I found myself concerned that I am disposed to include, for it fell between the provinces of the natural and supernatural in such a way that it might, with equal legitimacy, be included under either head. On the whole, I am disposed to bracket it with the case of the headless mummies.

I will take leave to introduce you, then, to the company which met at Otter Brearley's house one night in August.

"This is most truly amazing," Moris Klaw was saying; "and I am indebted to my good friend Searles"—he inclined his sparsely covered head in my direction—"for the opportunity to be one of you. Is it a séance? Yes and no. But there is a mummy in it—and those mummies are so instructive!"

He extracted the scent-spray from his pocket and refreshed his yellow brow with verbena.

"How to be regretted that my daughter is in Paris," he continued, his rumbling voice echoing queerly about the room. "She loves them like a mother—those mummies! Ah, Mr. Brearley, this will cement your great reputation!"

Otter Brearley shook his head.

"I am not yet prepared to make it public property," he declared, slowly. "No one, outside the present circle, knows of my discovery. I do not wish it to go further—at present."

He glanced around the table, his prominent blue eyes passing from myself to Moris Klaw and from Klaw to the clean-cut, dark face of Dr. Fairbank. The latter, scarce heeding his host's last words, sat watching how the shaded light played, tenderly, amid the soft billows of Ailsa Brearley's wonderful hair.

"Shall you make it the subject of a paper?" he asked suddenly.

"My dear Dr. Fairbank!" rumbled Moris Klaw, solemnly, "if you had been paying attention to our good friend you would have heard him say that he was not prepared, at present, to make public his wonderful discovery."

"Sorry!" said Fairbank, turning to Brearley. "But if it is not to be made public I don't altogether follow the idea. What *do* you intend, Brearley?"

"In what way?" I asked.

"In every way possible!"

Dr. Fairbank sat back in his chair and looked thoughtful.

"Rather a comprehensive scheme?"

Brearley toyed with a bundle of notes under his hand.

"I have already," he said, "exhaustively examined seven of the possibilities; the eighth, and—I believe, the last—remains to be considered."

"Listen to me now, Mr. Brearley," said Moris Klaw, wagging a long finger. "I am here, the old curious, and find myself in delightful company. But until this evening I know nothing of your work except that I have read all your books. For me you will be so good as to outline all the points—yes?"

Otter Brearley mutely sought permission of the company, and turned the leaves of his manuscript. All men have an innate love of "talking shop," but few can make such talk of general interest. Brearley was an exception in this respect. He loved to talk of Egypt, of the Pharaohs, of the temples, of the priesthood and the mysteries; but others loved to hear him. That made all the difference.

"The discovery," he now began, "upon which I have blundered—for pure accident, alone, led me to it—assumes its great importance by reason of the absolute mystery surrounding certain phase of Egyptian worship. In the old days, Fairbank, you will recall that it was my supreme ambition to learn the secrets of Isis-worship as practised in early Egyptian times. Save for impostors, and legitimate imaginative writers, no one has yet lifted the veil of Isis. That mystical ceremony by which a priest was consecrated to the goddess, or made an arch adept, was thought to be hopelessly lost, or, by others, to be a myth devised by the priesthood to awe the ignorant masses. In fact, we know little of the entire religion but its outward form. Of that occult lore so widely attributed to its votaries we know nothing—absolutely nothing! By we, I mean students in general. I, individually, have made a step, if not a stride, into that holy of holies!"

"Mind you don't lose yourself!" said Fairbank, lightly.

But, professionally, he was displeased with Brearley's drawn face and with the feverish brightness of his eyes. So much was plain for all to see. In the eyes of Ailsa Brearley, so like, yet so unlike, her brother's, he read understanding of his displeasure, I think, together with a pathetic appeal.

Brearley waved his long, white hand carelessly.

"Rest assured of that, doctor!" he replied. "The labyrinth in which I find myself is intricate, I readily admit; but all my steps have been well considered. To return, Mr. Klaw"—addressing the latter—"I have secured the mummy of one of those arch adepts! That he was one is proved by the papyrus, presumably in his own writing, which lay upon his breast! I unwrapped the mummy in Egypt, where it now reposes; but the writing I brought back with me, and have recently deciphered. A glance had showed me that it was not the usual excerpts from the Book of the Dead. Six months' labour has proved it to be a detailed account of his initiation into the inner mysteries!"

"Is such a papyrus unique?" I asked.

"Unique!" cried Moris Klaw. "Name of a little blue man! It is priceless!"

"But why," I pursued, "should this priest, alone amongst the many who must have been so initiated, have left an account of the ceremony?"

"It was forbidden to divulge any part, any word, of it, Searles!" said Brearley. "Departure from this law was visited with fearful punishments in this world and dire penalties in the next. Khamus, for so this priest was named, well knew this. But some reason which, I fear, can never be known, prompted him to write the papyrus. It is probable, if not certain, that no eye but his, and mine, has read what is written there."

A silence of seconds followed his words.

"Yes," rumbled Klaw presently; "it is undoubtedly a discovery of extraordinary importance, this. You agree, my friend?"

I nodded.

"That's evident," I replied. "But I cannot altogether get the hang of the ceremony itself, Brearley. That is the point of upon which I am particularly hazy."

"To read you the entire account in detail," Brearley resumed, "would occupy too long, and would almost certainly confuse you. But the singular thing is this: Khamus distinctly asserts that the goddess appeared to him. His writing is eminently sane and reserved, and his account of the ceremony, up to that point, highly interesting. Now, I have tested the papyrus itself—though no possibility of fraud is really admissible, and I have been able to confirm many of the statements made therein. There is only one point, it seems to me, remaining to be settled."

"What is that?" I asked.

"Whether, as a result of the ceremony described, Khamus did see Isis, or whether he merely imagined he did!"

No one spoke for a moment. Then—

"My friend," said Moris Klaw, "I have a daughter whom I have named Isis. Why did I name her Isis? Mr. Brearley, you must know that that name has a mystic and beautiful significance. But I will say something—I am glad that my daughter is not here! Mr. Brearley—beware! Beware, I say: you play with burning fires; my friend—beware!"

His words impressed us all immensely; for there was something underlying them more portentous than appeared upon the surface.

Fairbank stared at Brearley, hard.

"Do I understand," he began, quietly, "that you admit the first possibility?"

"Certainly!" replied Brearley, with conviction.

"You are prepared to admit the existence, as an entity, of Isis?"

"I am prepared to admit the existence of *anything* until it can be proved not to exist!"

"Then, admitting the existence of Isis, what should you assume it, or her, to be?"

"That is not a matter for presumption; it is a matter for inquiry!"

The doctor glanced quickly towards Ailsa Brearley, and her beautiful face was troubled.

"And this inquiry—how should you propose to conduct it?"

"In surroundings as nearly as possible identical with those described in the papyrus," replied Brearley, with growing excitement. "I should follow the ceremony, word by word, as Khamus did!"

His eyes gleamed with pent-up enthusiasm. We four listeners, again struck silent, watched him; and again it was the doctor who broke the silence.

"Is the ceremony spoken?"

"In the first half there is a long prayer, which is chanted."

"But Egyptian, as a *spoken* language, is lost, surely?"

"The exact pronunciation, or accent, is lost, of course; but there are many who can speak it. I can, for instance."

"And I," rumbled Moris Klaw, gloomily. "But these special surroundings? Eh, my friend?"

"I have spent a year in searching for the necessary things, as specified in the writing. At last, my collection is complete. Some of the things I have had made, in the proper materials mentioned. These materials, in some cases, have been exceedingly difficult to procure. But now I have a complete shrine of Isis fitted up! Khamus' initiation took place in a small chamber of which he gives concise and detailed account. It is because my duplicate of this chamber is ready that I have asked you to meet me here to-night."

"How long have you been at work upon this inquiry?" asked Fairbank.

He put the question as he might have put one relating to a patient's symptoms; and this Brearley detected in his tone, with sudden resentment.

"Fairbank," he said, huskily. "I believe you think me insane."

With his pale, drawn face and long, fair hair, he certainly looked anything but normal, as he sat with bright, staring eyes fixed upon the other across the table.

"My dear chap," replied the doctor, soothingly, "what a strange idea! My question was prompted by a professional spirit, I will admit, for I thought you had been sticking to this business too closely. You are the last man in the world I should expect to go mad, Brearley, but I should not care to answer for your nerves if you don't give this Isis affair a rest."

Brearley smiled, and waved his hand characteristically. "Excuse me, Fairbank," he said, "but to the average person my ideas do seem fantastic, I know. That is what makes me so touchy on the point, I suppose."

"You are hoping for too much from what is at most only a wild conjecture, Brearley. Your translation of the manuscript, alone, is a sufficiently notable achievement. If I were in your place, I should leave the occult business to the psychical societies. 'Let the cobbler,' you know."

"It has gone too far for that," returned Brearley, "and I must see it through, now."

"You are putting too much into it," said the doctor, severely. "I want you to promise me that if nothing results from your final experiment, you will drop the whole inquiry."

Brearley frowned thoughtfully.

"Do you really think I'm overdoing it?" he asked.

"Sure," was the answer. "Drop the whole thing for a month or two."

"That is impossible."

"Why?"

"Because the ceremony must take place upon the first night of *Panoi*, the tenth month of the Sacred Sothic year. This we take to correspond to the April of the Julian year."

"Yes," rumbled Moris Klaw, "it is to-night!"

"Why!" I cried, "of course it is! Do you mean, Brearley, that you are going to conduct your experiment *now*?"

"Exactly," was the calm reply; "and I have asked you all—Mr. Moris Klaw in particular—in order that it may take place in the presence of competent witnesses!"

Moris Klaw shook his massive head and pulled at his scanty, toneless beard, in a very significant manner. All of us were vaguely startled, I think, and through my mind the idea flashed that the first of April was a date pathetically appropriate for such an undertaking. Frankly, I was beginning to entertain some serious doubts regarding Brearley's sanity.

"I have given the servants a holiday," said the latter. "They are at a theatre in town; so there is no possibility of the experiment being interrupted."

Something of his enthusiasm, unnatural though it seemed, strangely enough began to communicate itself to me.

"Come upstairs," he continued, "and I will explain what we all have to do."

Moris Klaw squirted verbena on his brow.

II

"Doctor Fairbank!"

Fairbank, startled by the touch on his arm, stopped. It was Ailsa Brearley who had dropped behind her brother and now stood confronting us. In the dense shadows of the corridor one could hardly distinguish her figure, but a stray beam of light touched one side of her pure oval face and burnished her fair hair.

She wanted help, guidance. I had read it in her eyes before. I was sorry that her sweet lips should have that pathetic little droop.

"Doctor Fairbank! I have wanted to ask you all night—do you think he—"

She could not speak the words, and stood biting her lips, with eyes averted.

"Miss Brearley," he replied, "I do, certainly, fear that your brother is liable to a nervous breakdown at any moment. He has applied his mind too closely to this inquiry, and has studiously surrounded himself with a morbid atmosphere."

Ailsa Brearley was now watching him, anxiously.

"Should we allow him to go on with it?"

"I fear any attempt to prevent him would prove most detrimental, in his present condition."

"But—" There was clearly something else which she wanted to say. "But, apart from that—" she suddenly turned to Moris Klaw, instinctively it almost seemed—"Mr. Klaw—is this—ceremony *right*?"

He peered at her through his pince-nez.

"In what way, my dear Miss Brearley—how right?"

"Well—what I mean is—it amounts to idolatry, does it not!"

I startled. It was a point of view which had not, hitherto, occurred to me.

"You probably understand the nature of the thing better than we do, Miss Brearley," said Fairbank. "Do you mean that it involves worship of Isis?"

"He has always avoided a direct answer when I have asked him that," she said. "But it is only reasonable to suppose that it does. His translation of the writing I have never seen. But he has been dieting in a most extraordinary manner for nearly a year! Since the workmen completed it, no one but himself has been inside the chamber which he has had constructed at the end of his study; and he spends hours and hours there every day—and every night!"

Her anxiety became more evident with each word.

"You saw that he ate nothing at dinner," she continued, "and taxed him with faddism. But it is something more than that. Why has he sent the servants away to-night? Oh, Dr. Fairbank! I have a dreadful foreboding! I am so afraid!"

The light in her eyes, suddenly upturned to him in the vague half-light, the tone in her voice, the appeal in her attitude—were unmistakable. Fairbank had been abroad for three years, and I could see that between these two was an undeclared love, and almost I felt that I intruded. Moris Klaw looked away for a moment, too. Then—

"My dear young lady," he rumbled, paternally, "do not be afraid. I, the old know-all, so fortunately am here! Perhaps there is danger—yes, I admit it; there may be danger. But it is such danger as dwells here"—he tapped his yellow brow—"it is a danger of the mind. For thoughts are things, Miss Brearley—that is where it lies, the peril—and thought-things can kill!"

"Ailsa! Fairbank! Mr. Klaw!" came Brearley's voice. "We have none too much time!"

"Proceed, my friends," rumbled Moris Klaw; "I am with you." And, oddly enough, I was comforted by his presence; so, it was evident, were the girl and the doctor; for Moris Klaw, beneath that shabby, ramshackle exterior, Moris Klaw, the Wapping curio-dealer was a man of power—and intellectual ark of refuge.

In the Egyptologist's study all appeared much the same as when last I had set foot there. The cases filled with vases, scarabs, tablets, weapons, and the hundred-and-one relics of the great, dead age with which the student had surrounded himself; the sarcophagi; the frames of papyri: all seemed familiar.

"We must begin immediately!" he said, as we entered.

A danger-spot burned lividly upon either pale cheek. His eyes gleamed brilliantly. The prolonged excitement of his strange experiment was burning the man up. His nerve-centres must be taxed abnormally I knew.

Brearley glanced at his watch.

"I must be very brief," he explained hurriedly, "as it is vitally important that I commence in time. Beyond the book-case, there, you will see that a part of the room has been walled off."

We looked in the direction indicated. Although it was not noticeable at first glance I now saw that the apartment was, indeed, smaller than formerly. The usual books covered the new wall, giving it much the same aspect as the old; but, where hitherto there had been nothing but shelves, a small, narrow door of black wood now broke the imposing expanse of faded volumes.

"In there," Brearley resumed, "is the Secret Place described by Khamus!"

He placed his long, thin hand upon a yellow roll that lay partly opened on the table.

"No one but myself may enter there—until after to-night, at any rate!" with a glance at Moris Klaw. "To the most minute particular"—patting the papyrus—"it is equipped as Khamus describes. For many months I have prepared myself, by fasting and meditation, as *he* prepared! There was, as no doubt you know, a wide-spread belief in ancient times that for any but the chosen to look upon the goddess was death. As I admit the possibility of Isis existing I must also admit the possibility of this belief being true—the more so as it is confirmed by Khamus! Therefore none may enter with me."

"One moment, Mr. Brearley," interrupted Klaw; "in what form does Khamus relate that the goddess appeared?"

A cloud crossed Brearley's face.

"It is the one point upon which he is not clear," was the reply. "I do not know, in the least, *what* to expect!"

"Go on!" I said, quickly. Although I seriously doubted my poor friend's sanity, I began to find the affair weirdly, uncannily fascinating.

Brearley continued—

"The ritual opens with a chant, which I may broadly translate as 'The Hymn of Dedication.' Its exact purport is not very clear to me. This hymn is the only part of the ceremony in which I am assisted. It is to be 'sung by a virgin beyond the door.' That is, directly I have entered yonder it must be sung out here. Ailsa has composed a sort of chant of the words, which, I think, is the proper kind of setting. Have you not, Ailsa?"

She bowed her graceful head, glancing, under her lashes, towards Fairbank.

"She has learned the words—for, of course, it must be sung in Egyptian—"

"But have no idea of their meaning," said his sister, softly.

"That is unnecessary," he went on, quickly. "After this, I want you all just to remain here in this room. I am afraid you will have to sit in the dark! Any sounds which you detect, please note. I will not tell you what to expect, then imagination cannot deceive you. I will be back in a moment."

With another hasty glance at his watch, he went out in excitement.

"Please," began Ailsa Brearley, the moment he was gone, "do not think that because I assist him I approve of this attempt! I think it is horrible! But what am I to do? He is wrapped up in it! I *dare* not try to check him!"

"We understand that," said Fairbank; "all of us. Do as he desires. When he has made the attempt, and failed—as, of course, he must do—the folly of the whole thing will become apparent to him. Do not let it worry you, Miss Brearley. Your brother is not the first man to succumb, temporarily, to the glamour of the Unknown."

She shook her head sadly.

"It is an unpleasant farce," she said. "But there is something more in it than that."

Her blue eyes were full of trouble.

"What do you mean, Miss Brearley?" asked Moris Klaw.

"I hardly know, myself!" was the reply; "but for the past two months an indefinable horror of some kind has been growing upon me."

With a deep sigh, she turned to a tall case and took from it a kind of slender harp. The instrument, of which the frame, at any rate, was evidently ancient Egyptian work, rested upon a claw-shaped pedestal.

"Do you play this? Yes? No?" inquired Moris Klaw, with interest.

"Yes," she said, wearily. "It comes from the tomb of a priestess of Isis and was played by her in the temple. It is scaled differently from the modern harp, but any one with a slight knowledge of the ordinary harp, or even of the piano, can perform upon it with ease. It is sweet-toned, but—creepy!"

She smiled slightly at her own expression, and I was glad to see it. Brearley returned.

He wore a single, loose garment of white linen, and thin sandals were upon his feet. Save for his long, fair hair, he looked a true pagan priest, his eyes bright with the fire of research that consumed him, his features gaunt, ascetic.

Some ghost of his old humorous expression played, momentarily, about his lips as he observed the astonishment depicted upon our faces. But it was gone almost in the moment of its coming.

"You wonder at me, no doubt," he said; "and at times I have wondered at myself! Do not think me fanatic. I scarcely hope for any result. But remembering that the writing is authentic and that there prevails, to this day, a wide-spread belief in the occult wisdom of the Egyptians, *why* should not this problem in psychics receive the same attention from me that one in physics would receive from you, Fairbank?"

There was reason in his argument and his manner of advancing it. Fairbank glanced from Brearley, to the girl sitting her with her white hands listlessly caressing the harp-strings. The silence of the great, empty house grew oppressive. Suppose the ancients indeed possessed the strange lore attributed to them? Suppose in those Dark Continents, the Past and the Future, somewhere in the vast unknown, there existed a power, a being, a spirit, named by the Egyptians, Isis?

Those were my thoughts, when Moris Klaw said suddenly—

"Mr. Brearley, it is not yet too late to turn back! This sensitive plate"—he tapped his forehead—"warns me that some evil thought-thing hovers above us! You are about to give form to that thought-thing. Be wise, Mr. Brearley—abandon your experiment."

His tone surprised every one. Otter Brearley looked at him, with an odd expression, and then glanced at the watch upon the writing table.

"Mr. Klaw," he said, quietly, "I had hoped for a different attitude in you; but if you really disapprove of what I am about to attempt, I can only ask you to withdraw; it is too late for further arguments—"

"I remain, my friend! I spoke not for myself—my life has been passed in this coping with evil things; I spoke for others."

None of us entirely understood his words, but Brearley went on, impatiently—

"Listen, please. I rely upon your co-operation. From onward I require absolute silence. Whatever happens make no noise."

"I shall not be noisy, my friend!" rumbled Moris Klaw. "I am the old silent; I watch and wait—until I am wanted."

He shrugged his shoulders and nodded, significantly.

"Good!" said Brearley and his voice quivered with excitement; "then the experiment, the final experiment, has begun!"

III

He suddenly extinguished the light.

Passing to a window, he looked up to the moon, and, a moment later, lowered the blind. Dimly visible, in his white garment, he crossed the room. He might be heard unfastening the door of the inner chamber, and a faint, church-like smell crept to our nostrils. The door closed.

Immediately the harp sounded.

Its tone was peculiar—uncomfortable. The strain which Ailsa played was a mere repetition of three notes. Then she began to sing.

Our eyes becoming more accustomed to the gloom, we could vaguely discern her, now; the soft outlines of her figure; the white, ghost-like fingers straying over the strings of the instrument. The music of the chant was very monotonous, and weird to a marked degree. The sound of that ancient tongue, dead for many ages, chanted softly by Ailsa Brearley's beautiful voice, was almost incredibly eerie. I found myself gripped hard by a powerful sense of the uncanny.

No other sound was audible. Throughout the rambling old house intense silence prevailed. A slight breeze stirred the cedars, outside. Every now and again it came—like a series of broken sighs.

How long the chant lasted, I cannot pretend to state. It seemed interminable. I became aware of a curious sense of physical loss. I found myself drawn to high tension, as though the continuance of the chant demanded a vast effort on my part. Though I told myself that imagination was tricking me, the music seemed to be draining my nerve force!

Ailsa's voice grew louder and clearer, until the queer words, of unknown purport, rang out passionately, imperatively.

She ceased.

In the ensuing silence, I could hear distinctly Moris Klaw's heavy breathing. A compelling atmosphere of mystery had grown up about us. Repel it how we might, it was there—commanding acknowledgement.

Fairbank, who sat nearest, was the first to see Ailsa Brearley rise, unsteadily, and move in the direction of the study door.

·   Something in her manner alarmed us all, and the doctor quietly left his seat and followed her. As she quitted the room, he came out behind her; and in the better light on the landing, as he told us later, saw that she was deathly pale.

"Miss Brearley!" he said.

She turned

"*Shh!*" she whispered, anxiously, "it is nothing—Dr. Fairbank. The excitement has made me rather faint, that is all. I shall go to my room and lie down. Believe me, I am quite well!"

"But there is no servant in the house," he whispered, "if you should become worse—"

"If I need anything I shall not hesitate to ring," she answered. "It is so still, you will hear the bell. Please go back! He has hoped so much from this."

Fairbank was nonplussed. But the appeal was so obviously sincere, and the situation so difficult, that he saw no alternative. Ailsa Brearley passed along the corridor. Fairbank slipped back into the study, where Moris Klaw and I anxiously awaited him.

From the inner room came Brearley's voice, muffled.

The long vigil began.

I found myself claimed by the all-pervading spirit of mystery. For some little time I listened in the expectation of hearing Ailsa Brearley returning. But soon the strange business of the night claimed my mind, to the exclusion of every other idea. I found myself listening only for Brearley's muffled voice. Although the half-audible words were meaningless, their sound assumed, as time wore on, a curious significance. They seemed potent with a strange power proceeding not *from* them, but *to* them.

Then I heard a new sound.

Fairbank heard it—for I saw him start, and Moris Klaw muttered something.

It did not come from the trees outside, nor from the inner room. It was somewhere in the house.

A faint rattling it was, bell-like but toneless.

Brearley's voice had ceased.

Again the sound arose—nearer.

I turned my head toward Fairbank, and seemed to perceive him more clearly. I had less difficulty in distinguishing the objects about.

Again it came—the shivering, bell-like sound.

Even the strings of the harp were visible, now.

"Curse me!" came Moris Klaw's hoarse whisper; "it seems to grow light! That is a delusion of the mind, my friends—repel it—repel it!"

Fairbank drew a quick, sibilant breath. A half-suppressed exclamation from Klaw followed; for the high-pitched rattle was close at hand! The sense of the supernatural had grown unbearable. Fairbank's science, and my own semi-scepticism, were but weapons of sand against it.

The door opened silently, admitting a flood of the soft moon-like radiance. And Ailsa Brearley entered!

Her slim figure was bathed in light; her fair hair, unbound, swept like a gleaming torrent about her shoulders. She looked magnificently, unnaturally beautiful. A diaphanous veil was draped over her face. From her radiant figure I turned away my head in sudden, stark *fear!*

Fairbank, clutching the arms of his chair, seemed to strive to look away, too.

Her widely opened eyes, visible even through the veil, were awful in their supernormal, significant beauty. *Was* it Ailsa Brearley? I clenched my fists convulsively; I felt my reason tottering. As the luminous figure, so terrible in its perfect loveliness, moved slowly towards the inner door, with set gaze that was not for any about her, Dr. Fairbank wrenched himself from his chair and leapt forward.

"Ailsa!"

His voice came in a hoarse shriek. But it was drowned out by a rumbling roar from Moris Klaw.

"Look away! look away!" he shouted. "The good God! do not look at her! *Look away!*"

The warning came too late. Fairbank had all but reached her side, when she turned her eyes upon him—looking fully in his face.

With no sound or cry he went down as though felled by with a mighty blow!

She passed to the door of the inner room. It swung open noiselessly. A stifling cloud of some pungent perfume swept into the study; and the door reclosed.

"Fairbank!" I whispered, huskily, "My God! he's dead!"

Moris Klaw sprang forward to where Fairbank, clearly visible in the soft light, lay huddled upon the floor.

"Lift him!" he hissed. "We must get him out—before she returns—you understand?—before she returns!"

Bending together, we raised the doctor's inanimate body and half dragged, half carried him down, and stood panting. A voice, clear and sweet, was speaking. I recognised neither the language nor the voice. But each liquid syllable thrilled me like any icy shock. I met Moris Klaw's gaze, set upon me through the pince-nez.

"Do not listen, my friend!" he said.

Raising Fairbank, we dragged him into the first room we came to—and Klaw locked the door.

"Here we remain," he rumbled, "until something has gone back where it came from!"

Fairbank lay motionless at our feet.

Presently came the rattling.

"It is the *sistrum*," whispered Moris Klaw, "the sacred instrument of the Isis temples."

The sound passed—and faded.

"Searles! Fairbank!" It was Brearley's voice, sobbingly intense— "do not *touch* her! Do not *look* at her!"

The study door crashed open and I heard his sandals pattering on the landing.

"Fairbank! Mr. Klaw! Good God! answer me! Tell me you are safe!"

Moris Klaw unlocked the door.

Brearley, his face white as death and bathed in perspiration, stood outside. As Klaw appeared, he leapt forward, wild eyed.

"Quick! Did any one—"

"Fairbank," I said huskily.

Brearley pushed into the room and turned on the light. Fairbank, very pale, lay propped up against an armchair. Moris Klaw immediately dropped on his knee beside him and felt his heart.

"Ah, the good God! he is alive!" he whispered. "Get some water—no brandy, my friend—water. Then look to your sister."

Brearley plunged his trembling hands into his hair, and tugged at it distractedly.

"How was I to know!" he moaned, "how was I to know! There is water in the bottle, Mr. Klaw. Searles will come with me. I must look for Ailsa."

A bizarre figure, in his linen robe, he ran off. Moris Klaw waved at me to follow him.

The door of his sister's room was closed.

He knocked, but there was no reply. He turned the knob and went in, whilst I waited in the corridor.

"Ailsa!" I heard him call, and again: "Ailsa!" then, following an interval, "Are you all right, dear?" he whispered.

"Oh, thank Heaven it is finished!" came a murmur in Ailsa Brearley's soft voice. "It *is* finished, is it not?"

"Quite finished," he answered.

"Just look at my hair!" she went on, with returning animation. "My head was so bad—I think that was why I took it down. Then I must have dropped off to sleep."

"All right, dear," said Brearley. "I want you to come downstairs; be as quick as you can."

He rejoined me in the corridor.

She was lying with her hair strewn all over the pillow!" he whispered, "and she had been burning something—ashes in the hearth—"

Ailsa came out. She seemed suddenly to observe her brother's haggard face.

"Is something the matter?" she said, quickly. "Oh! has something dreadful happened?"

"No, dear," he answered, reassuringly. "Only Dr. Fairbank was overcome—"

She turned very pale.

"He is not ill?"

"No. He became faint. You can come and see for yourself."

Very quickly, we all hurried downstairs. Moris Klaw, on his knees beside the doctor, was trying to force something between his clenched teeth. Ailsa, with a little cry, ran forward and knelt upon the other side of him.

"Ralph!" she whispered; "Ralph!"—and smoothed the hair back from his forehead.

He sighed deeply, and with an effort swallowed the draught which Klaw held to his lips. A moment later he opened his eyes, glaring wildly into Ailsa's face.

"Ralph!" she said, brokenly.

Then, realising how tenderly she had spoken—using his Christian name—she hung her graceful head in hot confusion. But he had heard her. And the wild light died from his eyes. He took both her hands in his own and held them fast; then, rather unsteadily, he stood up.

As his features came more fully into the light, we all saw that a small bruise discoloured his forehead, squarely between the brows.

Then Brearley, who had been back into the study, came running, crying—

"The papyrus! And my translation! Gone!"

I thought of the ashes in Ailsa Brearley's room.

IV

"My friends," rumbled Moris Klaw, impressively, "we are fortunate. We have passed through scorching fires unscathed!"

He applied himself with vigour to the operating of the scent-spray.

"God forgive me!" said Brearley. "What did I do?"

"I will tell you, my friend," replied Klaw; "you clothed a thought in the beautiful form which you knew as your sister! Ah! you stare! Ritual, my friends, is the soul of what the ignorant call magic. With the sacred incense, *kyphi* (yes, I detected it!), you invoked secret powers. Those powers, Mr. Brearley, were but *thoughts*. All such forces are thoughts.

"Thoughts are things—and you gathered together in this house, by that ancient formula, a thought-thing created by generations of worshippers who have worshipped the moon!

"The light that we saw was only the moonlight, the sounds that we heard were thought-sounds. But so powerful was this mighty thought-force, this centuries-old power which you loosed upon us, that it drove out Miss Ailsa's own thoughts from her mind, bringing what she mistook for sleep; and it implanted itself there!

"She was transformed by that mighty power which for a time dwelled within her. She was as powerful, as awful, as a goddess! None might look upon her and be sane. Hypnotism has similarities with the ancient science of thought—yes! *Suggestion* is the secret of all so-called occult phenomena!"

With his eyes gleaming oddly, he stepped forward, resting his long white hands upon Fairbank's shoulders.

"Doctor," he rumbled, "you have a bruise on your forehead."

"Have I!" said Fairbank, in surprise. "I hadn't noticed it."

"Because it is not a physical bruise; it is a mental bruise, physically reflected! Nearly were you slain, my friend—oh, so nearly! But another force—as great as the force of ancient thought—weakened the blow. Dr. Fairbank, it is fortunate that Miss Ailsa loves you!"

His frank words startled us all.

"Look well at the shape of this little bruise, my friends," continued Moris Klaw. "Mr. Brearley—it is a shape that will be familiar to you. See! it is thus:" (He drew an imaginary outline with his long forefinger)—

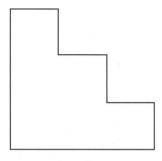

"And that is the sign of Isis!"

THE VAMPIRE

Alice and Claude Askew

Both Alice Jane de Courcy Leake (1874–1917) and Claude Askew (1865–1917) had already been published independently when they married in London on July 10, 1900. After their marriage, they became a successful writing team. The British couple was extremely prolific and versatile—it's estimated that they wrote more than ninety novels, plus assorted serials and short fiction in various literary genres. Their first published work, the 1904 novel The Shulamite, *became the basis for the 1921 silent film,* Under the Lash, *starring Gloria Swanson.*

Their Aylmer Vance stories are an anomaly—the Askews were not known for writing supernatural fiction. It is unknown whether the Askews studied occult lore in any fashion, although it's tempting to wonder, as the character of Zaida the witch, who appears in "The Vampire," bears such a strong resemblance to the witch–demon–vampire–spirit, Lilith. Was this intentional on the part of the Askews, or did Lilith herself somehow insinuate herself into the tale?

The couple traveled to Serbia in 1915 to help with the relief efforts of a British field hospital and to serve as special correspondents for the newspaper, the Daily Express. *They spent six months there—Alice working as a nurse, while Claude was given an honorary commission as a major in the Serbian Army. They described their experiences in what remains their most famous work,* The Stricken Land: Serbia as We Saw It *(1916).*

In early October 1917, a torpedo from a German submarine hit the steamer on which the Askews were returning to Serbia from leave in Italy. Claude's body was not recovered, but the body of a woman discovered on October 29 on the shore at Korcula, now in modern Croatia, was identified as Alice. Her grave in Karbunia on the isle of Korcula may be visited.

Aylmer Vance, their occult detective, appears in eight stories that were first published in July and August 1914 in consecutive issues of the Weekly Tale-Teller. *Vance is identified as a ghost seer and a ghost hunter. In addition to presenting supernatural mysteries and their solutions, the stories chronicle the relationship of Vance and his friend and student, Dexter, who narrates the tales. Dexter, who is fascinated by Vance, takes lodgings in the building where Vance lives and soon graduates from being merely an observer to being an active participant in the cases, especially after Vance recognizes and helps to develop Dexter's latent clairvoyance.*

The Vampire

AYLMER VANCE HAD ROOMS in Dover Street, Piccadilly, and now that I had decided to follow in his footsteps and to accept him as my instructor in matters psychic, I found it convenient to lodge in the same house. Aylmer and I quickly became close friends, and he showed me how to develop that faculty of clairvoyance which I had possessed without being aware of it. And I may say at once that this particular faculty of mine proved of service on several important occasions.

At the same time I made myself useful to Vance in other ways, not the least of which was that of acting as recorder of his many strange adventures. For himself, he never cared much about publicity, and it was some time before I could persuade him, in the interests of science, to allow me to give any detailed account of his experiences to the world.

The incidents which I will now narrate occurred very soon after we had taken up our residence together, and while I was still, so to speak, a novice.

It was about ten o'clock in the morning that a visitor was announced. He sent up a card which bore upon it the name of Paul Davenant.

The name was familiar to me, and I wondered if this could be the same Mr Davenant who was so well known for his polo playing and for his success as an amateur rider, especially over the hurdles? He was a young man of wealth and position, and I recollected that he had married, about a year ago, a girl who was reckoned the greatest beauty of the season. All the illustrated papers had given their portraits at the time, and I remember thinking what a remarkably handsome couple they made.

Mr Davenant was ushered in, and at first I was uncertain as to whether this could be the individual whom I had in mind, so wan and pale and ill did he appear. A finely-built, upstanding man at the time of his marriage, he had now acquired a languid droop of the shoulders and a shuffling gait, while his face, especially about the lips, was bloodless to an alarming degree.

And yet it was the same man, for behind all this I could recognize the shadow of the good looks that had once distinguished Paul Davenant.

He took the chair which Aylmer offered him—after the usual preliminary civilities had been exchanged—and then glanced doubtfully in my direction. 'I wish to consult you privately, Mr Vance,' he said. 'The matter is of considerable importance to myself, and, if I may say so, of a somewhat delicate nature.'

Of course I rose immediately to withdraw from the room, but Vance laid his hand upon my arm.

'If the matter is connected with research in my particular line, Mr Davenant,' he said, 'if there is any investigation you wish me to take up on your behalf, I shall be glad if you will include Mr Dexter in your confidence. Mr Dexter assists me in my work. But, of course—'

'Oh, no,' interrupted the other, 'if that is the case, pray let Mr Dexter remain. I think,' he added, glancing at me with a friendly smile, 'that you are an Oxford man, are you not, Mr Dexter? It was before my time, but I have heard of your name in connection with the river. You rowed at Henley, unless I am very much mistaken.'

I admitted the fact, with a pleasurable sensation of pride. I was very keen upon rowing in those days, and a man's prowess at school and college always remain dear to his heart.

After this we quickly became on friendly terms, and Paul Davenant proceeded to take Aylmer and myself into his confidence.

He began by calling attention to his personal appearance. 'You would hardly recognize me for the same man! was a year ago,' he said. 'I've been losing flesh steadily for the last six months. I came up from Scotland about a week ago, to consult a London doctor. I've seen two—in fact, they've held a sort of consultation over me—but the result, I may say, is far from satisfactory. They don't seem to know what is really the matter with me.'

'Anaemia—heart' suggested Vance. He was scrutinizing his visitor keenly, and yet without any particular appearance of doing so. 'I believe it not infrequently happens that you athletes overdo yourselves—put too much strain upon the heart—'

'My heart is quite sound,' responded Davenant. 'Physically it is in perfect condition. The trouble seems to be that it hasn't enough blood to pump into my veins. The doctors wanted to know if I had met with an accident involving a great loss of blood—but I haven't. I've had no accident at all, and as for anaemia, well, I don't seem to show the ordinary symptoms of it. The inexplicable thing is that I've lost blood without knowing it, and apparently this has been going on for some time, for I've been getting steadily worse. It was almost imperceptible at first—not a sudden collapse, you understand, but a gradual failure of health.'

'I wonder,' remarked Vance slowly, 'what induced you to consult me? For you know, of course, the direction in which I pursue my investigations. May I ask if you have reason to consider that your state of health is due to some cause which we may describe as super-physical?'

A slight colour came to Davenant's white cheeks.

'There are curious circumstances,' he said in a low and earnest tone of voice. 'I've been turning them over in my mind, trying to see light through them. I daresay it's all the sheerest folly—and I must tell you that I'm not in the least a superstitious sort of man. I don't mean to say that I'm absolutely incredulous, but I've never given thought to such things—I've led too active a life. But, as I have said, there are curious circumstances about my case, and that is why I decided upon consulting you.'

'Will you tell me everything without reserve?' said Vance. I could see that he was interested. He was sitting up in his chair, his feet supported on a stool, his elbows on his knees, his chin in his hands—a favourite attitude of his. 'Have you,' he suggested, slowly, 'any mark upon your body, anything that you might associate, however remotely, with your present weakness and ill-health?'

'It's a curious thing that you should ask me that question,' returned Davenant, 'because I have got a curious mark, a sort of scar, that I can't account for. But I showed it to the doctors, and they assured me that it could have nothing whatever to do with my condition. In any case, if it had, it was something altogether outside their experience. I think they imagined it to be nothing more than a birthmark, a sort of mole, for they asked me if I'd had it all my life. But that I can swear I haven't. I only noticed it for the first time about six months ago, when my health began to fail. But you can see for yourself.'

He loosened his collar and bared his throat. Vance rose and made a careful scrutiny of the suspicious mark. It was situated a very little to the left of the central line, just above the clavicle, and, as Vance pointed out, directly over the big vessels of the throat. My friend called to me so that I might examine it, too. Whatever the opinion of the doctors may have been, Aylmer was obviously deeply interested.

And yet there was very little to show. The skin was quite intact, and there was no sign of inflammation. There were two red marks, about an inch apart, each of which was inclined to be crescent in shape. They were more visible than they might otherwise have been owing to the peculiar whiteness of Davenant's skin.

'It can't be anything of importance,' said Davenant, with a slightly uneasy laugh. 'I'm inclined to think the marks are dying away.'

'Have you ever noticed them more inflamed than they are at present?' inquired Vance. 'If so, was it at any special time?'

Davenant reflected. 'Yes,' he replied slowly, 'there have been times, usually, I think perhaps invariably, when I wake up in the morning, that I've noticed them larger and more angry looking. And I've felt a slight sensation of pain—a tingling—oh, very slight, and I've never worried about it. Only now you suggest it to my mind, I believe that those same mornings I have felt particularly tired and done up—a sensation of lassitude absolutely unusual to me. And once, Mr Vance, I remember quite distinctly that there was a stain of blood close to the mark. I didn't think anything of it at the time, and just wiped it away.'

'I see.' Aylmer Vance resumed his seat and invited his visitor to do the same. 'And now,' he resumed, 'you said, Mr Davenant, that there are certain peculiar circumstances you wish to acquaint me with. Will you do so?'

And so Davenant readjusted his collar and proceeded to tell his story. I will tell it as far as I can, without any reference to the occasional interruptions of Vance and myself.

Paul Davenant, as I have said, was a man of wealth and position, and so, in every sense of the word, he was a suitable husband for Miss Jessica MacThane, the young lady who eventually became his wife. Before coming to the incidents attending his loss of health, he had a great deal to recount about Miss MacThane and her family history.

She was of Scottish descent, and although she had certain characteristic features of her race, she was not really Scotch in appearance. Hers was the beauty of the far South rather than that of the Highlands from which she had her origin. Names are not always suited to their owners, and Miss MacThane's was peculiarly inappropriate. She had, in fact, been christened Jessica in a sort of pathetic effort to counteract her obvious departure from normal type. There was a reason for this which we were soon to learn.

Miss MacThane was especially remarkable for her wonderful red hair, hair such as one hardly ever sees outside of Italy—not the Celtic red—and it was so long that it reached to her feet, and it had an extraordinary gloss upon it so that it seemed almost to have individual life of its own. Then she had just the complexion that one would expect with such hair, the purest ivory white, and not in the least marred by freckles, as is so often the case with red-haired girls. Her beauty was derived from an ancestress who had been brought to Scotland from some foreign shore—no one knew exactly whence.

Davenant fell in love with her almost at once and he had every reason to believe, in spite of her many admirers, that his love was returned. At this time he knew very little about her personal history. He was aware only that she was very wealthy in her own right, an orphan, and the last representative of a race that had once been famous in the annals of history—or rather infamous, for the Mac-Thanes had distinguished themselves more by cruelty and lust of blood than by deeds of chivalry. A clan of turbulent robbers in the past, they had helped to add many a blood-stained page to the history of their country.

Jessica had lived with her father, who owned a house in London, until his death when she was about fifteen years of age. Her mother had died in Scotland when Jessica was still a tiny child. Mr MacThane had been so affected by his wife's death that, with his little daughter, he had abandoned his Scotch estate altogether—or so it was believed—leaving it to the management of a bailiff—though, indeed, there was but little work for the bailiff to do, since there were practically no tenants left. Blackwick Castle had borne for many years a most unenviable reputation.

After the death of her father, Miss MacThane had gone to live with a certain Mrs Meredith, who was a connection of her mother's—on her father's side she had not a single relation left. Jessica was absolutely the last of a clan once so extensive that inter-marriage had been a tradition of the family, but for which the last two hundred years had been gradually dwindling to extinction.

Mrs Meredith took Jessica into Society—which would never have been her privilege had Mr MacThane lived, for he was a moody, self-absorbed man, and prematurely old—one who seemed worn down by the weight of a great grief.

Well, I have said that Paul Davenant quickly fell in love with Jessica, and it was not long before he proposed for her hand. To his great surprise, for he had good reason to believe that she cared for him, he met with a refusal; nor would she give any explanation, though she burst into a flood of pitiful tears.

Bewildered and bitterly disappointed, he consulted Mrs Meredith, with whom he happened to be on friendly terms, and from her he learnt that Jessica had already had several proposals, all from quite desirable men, but that one after another had been rejected.

Paul consoled himself with the reflection that perhaps Jessica did not love them, whereas he was quite sure that she cared for himself. Under these circumstances he determined to try again.

He did so, and with better result. Jessica admitted her love, but at the same time she repeated that she would not marry him. Love and marriage were not for her. Then, to his utter amazement, she declared that she had been born under a curse—a curse which, sooner or later was bound to show itself in her, and which, more-over, must react cruelly, perhaps fatally, upon anyone with whom she linked her life. How could she allow a man she loved to take such a risk? Above all, since the evil was hereditary, there was one point upon which she had quite made up her mind: no child should ever call her mother—she must be the last of her race indeed.

Of course, Davenant was amazed and inclined to think that Jessica had got some absurd idea into her head which a little reasoning on his part would dispel. There was only one other possible explanation. Was it lunacy she was afraid of?

But Jessica shook her head. She did not know of any lunacy in her family. The ill was deeper, more subtle than that. And then she told him all that she knew.

The curse—she made use of that word for want of a better—was attached to the ancient race from which she had her origin. Her father had suffered from it, and his father and grandfather before him. All three had taken to themselves young wives who had died mysteriously, of some wasting disease, within a few years. Had they observed the ancient family tradition of intermarriage this might possibly not have happened, but in their case, since the family was so near extinction, this had not been possible.

For the curse—or whatever it was—did not kill those who bore the name of MacThane. It only rendered them a danger to others. It was as if they absorbed from the blood-soaked walls of their fatal castle a deadly taint which reacted terribly upon those with whom they were brought into contact, especially their nearest and dearest.

'Do you know what my father said we have it in us to become?' said Jessica with a shudder. 'He used the word vampires. Paul, think of it—vampires—preying upon the life blood of others.'

And then, when Davenant was inclined to laugh, she checked him. 'No,' she cried out, 'it is not impossible. Think. We are a decadent race. From the earliest times our history has been marked by bloodshed and cruelty. The walls of Blackwick Castle are impregnated with evil—every stone could tell its tale, of violence, pain, lust, and murder. What can one expect of those who have spent their lifetime between its walls?'

'But you have not done so,' exclaimed Paul. 'You have been spared that, Jessica. You were taken away after your mother died, and you have no recollection of Blackwick Castle, none at all. And you need never set foot in it again.'

'I'm afraid the evil is in my blood,' she replied sadly, 'although I am unconscious of it now. And as for not returning to Blackwick—I'm not sure I can help myself. At least, that is what my father warned me of. He said there is something there, some compelling force, that will call me to it in spite of myself. But, oh, I don't know—I don't know, and that is what makes it so difficult. If I could only believe that all this is nothing but an idle superstition, I might be happy again, for I have it in me to enjoy life, and I'm young, very young, but my father told me these things when he was on his death-bed.' She added the last words in a low, awe-stricken tone.

Paul pressed her to tell him all that she knew, and eventually she revealed another fragment of family history which seemed to have some bearing upon the case. It dealt with her own astonishing likeness to that ancestress of a couple of hundred years ago, whose existence seemed to have presaged the gradual downfall of the clan of the MacThanes.

A certain Robert MacThane, departing from the traditions of his family, which demanded that he should not marry outside his clan, brought home a wife from foreign shores, a woman of wonderful beauty, who was possessed of glowing masses of red hair and a complexion of ivory whiteness—such as had more or less distinguished since then every female of the race born in the direct line.

It was not long before this woman came to be regarded in the neighbourhood as a witch. Queer stories were circulated abroad as to her doings, and the reputation of Blackwick Castle became worse than ever before.

And then one day she disappeared. Robert MacThane had been absent upon some business for twenty-four hours, and it was upon his return that he found her gone. The neighbourhood was searched, but without avail, and then Robert, who was a violent man and who had adored his foreign wife, called together certain of his tenants whom he suspected, rightly or wrongly, of foul play, and had them murdered in cold blood. Murder was easy in those days, yet such an outcry was raised that Robert had to take to flight, leaving his two children in the care of their nurse, and for a long while Blackwick Castle was without a master.

But its evil reputation persisted. It was said that Zaida, the witch, though dead, still made her presence felt. Many children of the tenantry and young people of the neighbourhood sickened and died—possibly of quite natural causes; but this did not prevent a mantle of terror settling upon the countryside, for it was said that Zaida had been seen—a pale woman clad in white—flitting about the cottages at night, and where she passed sickness and death were sure to supervene.

And from that time the fortune of the family gradually declined. Heir succeeded heir, but no sooner was he installed at Blackwick Castle than his nature, whatever it may previously have been, seemed to undergo a change. It was as if he absorbed into himself all the weight of evil that had stained his family name—as if he did, indeed, become a vampire, bringing blight upon any not directly connected with his own house.

And so, by degrees, Blackwick was deserted of its tenantry. The land around it was left uncultivated—the farms stood empty. This had persisted to the present day, for the superstitious peasantry still told their tales of the mysterious white woman who hovered about the neighbourhood, and whose appearance betokened death—and possibly worse than death.

And yet it seemed that the last representatives of the MacThanes could not desert their ancestral home. Riches they had, sufficient to live happily upon elsewhere, but, drawn by some power they could not contend against, they had preferred to spend their lives in the solitude of the now half-ruined castle, shunned by their neighbours, feared and execrated by the few tenants that still clung to their soil.

So it had been with Jessica's grandfather and great-grandfather. Each of them had married a young wife, and in each case their love story had been all too brief. The vampire spirit was still abroad, expressing itself—or so it seemed—through the living represen- tatives of bygone generations of evil, and young blood had been demanded as the sacrifice.

And to them had succeeded Jessica's father. He had not profited by their example, but had followed directly in their footsteps. And the same fate had befallen the wife whom he passionately adored. She had died of pernicious anaemia—so the doctors said—but he had regarded himself as her murderer.

But, unlike his predecessors, he had torn himself away from Blackwick—and this for the sake of his child. Unknown to her, however, he had returned year after year, for there were times when the passionate longing for the gloomy, mysterious halls and corri- dors of the old castle, for the wild stretches of moorland, and the dark pinewoods, would come upon him too strongly to be resisted. And so he knew that for his daughter, as for himself, there was no escape, and he warned her, when the relief of death was at last granted to him, of what her fate must be.

This was the tale that Jessica told the man who wished to make her his wife, and he made light of it, as such a man would, regarding it all as foolish superstition, the delusion of a mind overwrought. And at last—perhaps it was not very difficult, for she loved him with all her heart and soul—he succeeded in inducing Jessica to think as he did, to banish morbid ideas, as he called them from her brain, and to consent to marry him at an early date.

'I'll take any risk you like,' he declared. 'I'll even go and live at Blackwick if you should desire it. To think of you, my lovely Jessica, a vampire! Why, I never heard such nonsense in my life.'

'Father said I'm very like Zaida, the witch,' she protested, but he silenced her with a kiss.

And so they were married and spent their honeymoon abroad, and in the autumn Paul accepted an invitation to a house party in Scotland for the grouse shooting, a sport to which he was absolutely devoted, and Jessica agreed with him that there was no reason why he should forgo his pleasure.

Perhaps it was an unwise thing to do, to venture to Scotland, but by this time the young couple, more deeply in love with each other than ever, had got quite over their fears. Jessica was redolent with health and spirits, and more than once she declared that if they should be anywhere in the neighbourhood of Blackwick she would like to see the old castle out of curiosity, and just to show how absolutely she had got over the foolish terrors that used to assail her.

This seemed to Paul to be quite a wise plan, and so one day, since they were actually staying at no great distance, they motored over to Blackwick, and finding the bailiff, got him to show them over the castle.

It was a great castellated pile, grey with age, and in places falling into ruin. It stood on a steep hillside, with the rock of which it seemed to form part, and on one side of it there was a precipitous drop to a mountain stream a hundred feet below. The robber MacThanes of the old days could not have desired a better stronghold.

At the back, climbing up the mountainside were dark pinewoods, from which, here and there, rugged crags protruded, and these were fantastically shaped, some like gigantic and misshapen human forms, which stood up as if they mounted guard over the castle and the narrow gorge, by which alone it could be approached.

This gorge was always full of weird, uncanny sounds. It might have been a storehouse for the wind, which, even on calm days, rushed up and down as if seeking an escape, and it moaned among the pines and whistled in the crags and shouted derisive laughter as it was tossed from side to side of the rocky heights. It was like the plaint of lost souls—that is the expression Davenant made use of—the plaint of lost souls.

The road, little more than a track now, passed through this gorge, and then, after skirting a small but deep lake, which hardly knew the light of the sun so shut in was it by overhanging trees, climbed the hill to the castle.

And the castle! Davenant used but a few words to describe it, yet somehow I could see the gloomy edifice in my mind's eye, and something of the lurking horror that it contained communicated itself to my brain. Perhaps my clairvoyant sense assisted me, for when he spoke of them I seemed already acquainted with the great stone halls, the long corridors, gloomy and cold even on the brightest and warmest of days, the dark, oak-panelled rooms, and the broad central staircase up which one of the early MacThanes had once led a dozen men on horseback in pursuit of a stag which had taken refuge within the precincts of the castle. There was the keep, too, its walls so thick that the ravages of time had made no impression upon them, and beneath the keep were dungeons which could tell terrible tales of ancient wrong and lingering pain.

Well, Mr and Mrs Davenant visited as much as the bailiff could show them of this ill-omened edifice, and Paul, for his part, thought pleasantly of his own Derbyshire home, the fine Georgian mansion, replete with every modern comfort, where he proposed to settle with his wife. And so he received something of a shock when, as they drove away, she slipped her hand into his and whispered:

'Paul, you promised, didn't you, that you would refuse me nothing?'

She had been strangely silent till she spoke those words. Paul, slightly apprehensive, assured her that she only had to ask—but the speech did not come from his heart, for he guessed vaguely what she desired.

She wanted to go and live at the castle—oh, only for a little while, for she was sure she would soon tire of it. But the bailiff had told her that there were papers, documents, which she ought to examine, since the property was now hers—and, besides, she was interested in this home of her ancestors, and wanted to explore it more thoroughly. Oh, no, she wasn't in the least influenced by the old superstition—that wasn't the attraction—she had quite got over those silly ideas. Paul had cured her, and since he himself was so convinced that they were without foundation he ought not to mind granting her her whim.

This was a plausible argument, not easy to controvert. In the end Paul yielded, though it was not without a struggle. He suggested amendments. Let him at least have the place done up for her—that would take time; or let them postpone their visit till next year—in the summer—not move in just as the winter was upon them.

But Jessica did not want to delay longer than she could help, and she hated the idea of redecoration. Why, it would spoil the illusion of the old place, and, besides, it would be a waste of money since she only wished to remain there for a week or two. The Derbyshire house was not quite ready yet; they must allow time for the paper to dry on the walls.

And so, a week later, when their stay with their friends was concluded, they went to Blackwick, the bailiff having engaged a few raw servants and generally made things as comfortable for them as possible. Paul was worried and apprehensive, but he could not admit this to his wife after having so loudly proclaimed his theories on the subject of superstition.

They had been married three months at this time—nine had passed since then, and they had never left Blackwick for more than a few hours—till now Paul had come to London—alone.

'Over and over again,' he declared, 'my wife has begged me to go. With tears in her eyes, almost upon her knees, she has entreated me to leave her, but I have steadily refused unless she will accompany me. But that is the trouble, Mr Vance, she cannot; there is something, some mysterious horror, that holds her there as surely as if she were bound with fetters. It holds her more strongly even than it held her father—we found out that he used to spend six months at least of every year at Blackwick—months when he pretended that he was travelling abroad. You see the spell—or whatever the accursed thing may be—never really relaxed its grip of him.'

'Did you never attempt to take your wife away?' asked Vance.

'Yes, several times; but it was hopeless. She would become so ill as soon as we were beyond the limit of the estate that I invariably had to take her back. Once we got as far as Dorekirk—that is the nearest town, you know—and I thought I should be successful if only I could get through the night. But she escaped me; she climbed out of a window—she meant to go back on foot, at night, all those long miles. Then I have had doctors down; but it is I who wanted the doctors, not she. They have ordered me away, but I have refused to obey them till now.'

'Is your wife changed at all—physically?' interrupted Vance.

Davenant reflected. 'Changed,' he said, 'yes, but so subtly that I hardly know how to describe it. She is more beautiful than ever—and yet it isn't the same beauty, if you can understand me. I have spoken of her white complexion, well, one is more than ever conscious of it now, because her lips have become so red—they are almost like a splash of blood upon her face. And the upper one has a peculiar curve that I don't think it had before, and when she laughs she doesn't smile—do you know what I mean? Then her hair—it has lost its wonderful gloss. Of course, I know she is fretting about me; but that is so peculiar, too, for at times, as I have told you, she will implore me to go and leave her, and then perhaps only a few minutes later, she will wreathe her arms round my neck and say she cannot live without me. And I feel that there is a struggle going on within her, that she is only yielding slowly to the horrible influence—whatever it is—that she is herself when she begs me to go, but when she entreats me to stay—and it is then that her fascination is most intense—oh, I can't help remembering what she told me before we were married, and that word'—he lowered his voice—'the word "vampire"—'

He passed his hand over his brow that was wet with perspiration. 'But that's absurd, ridiculous,' he muttered; 'these fantastic beliefs have been exploded years ago. We live in the twentieth century.'

A pause ensued, then Vance said quietly, 'Mr Davenant, since you have taken me into your confidence, since you have found doctors of no avail, will you let me try to help you? I think I may be of some use—if it is not already too late. Should you agree, Mr Dexter and I will accompany you, as you have suggested, to Blackwick Castle as early as possible—by tonight's mail North. Under ordinary circumstances I should tell you as you value your life, not to return—'

Davenant shook his head. 'That is advice which I should never take,' he declared. 'I had already decided, under any circumstances, to travel North tonight. I am glad that you both will accompany me.'

And so it was decided. We settled to meet at the station, and presently Paul Davenant took his departure. Any other details that remained to be told he would put us in possession of during the course of the journey.

'A curious and most interesting case,' remarked Vance when we were alone. 'What do you make of it, Dexter?'

'I suppose,' I replied cautiously, 'that there is such a thing as vampirism even in these days of advanced civilization? I can understand the evil influence that a very old person may have upon a young one if they happen to be in constant intercourse—the worn-out tissue sapping healthy vitality for their own support. And there are certain people—I could think of several myself—who seem to depress one and undermine one's energies, quite unconsciously, of course, but one feels somehow that vitality has passed from oneself to them. And in this case, when the force is centuries old, expressing itself, in some mysterious way, through Davenant's wife, is it not feasible to believe that he may be physically affected by it, even though the whole thing is sheerly mental?'

'You think, then,' demanded Vance, 'that it is sheerly mental? Tell me, if that is so, how do you account for the marks on Davenant's throat?'

This was a question to which I found no reply, and though I pressed him for his views, Vance would not commit himself further just then.

Of our long journey to Scotland I need say nothing. We did not reach Blackwick Castle till late in the afternoon of the following day. The place was just as I had conceived it—as I have already described it. And a sense of gloom settled upon me as our car jolted us over the rough road that led through the Gorge of the Winds—a gloom that deepened when we penetrated into the vast cold hall of the castle.

Mrs Davenant, who had been informed by telegram of our arrival, received us cordially. She knew nothing of our actual mission, regarding us merely as friends of her husband's. She was most solicitous on his behalf, but there was something strained about her tone, and it made me feel vaguely uneasy. The impression that I got was that the woman was impelled to everything that she said or did by some force outside herself—but, of course, this was a conclusion that the circumstances I was aware of might easily have conduced to. In every other aspect she was charming, and she had an extraordinary fascination of appearance and manner that made me readily understand the force of a remark made by Davenant during our journey.

'I want to live for Jessica's sake. Get her away from Blackwick, Vance, and I feel that all will be well. I'd go through hell to have her restored to me—as she was.'

And now that I had seen Mrs Davenant I realized what he meant by those last words. Her fascination was stronger than ever, but it was not a natural fascination—not that of a normal woman, such as she had been. It was the fascination of a Circe, of a witch, of an enchantress—and as such was irresistible.

We had a strong proof of the evil within her soon after our arrival. It was a test that Vance had quietly prepared. Davenant had mentioned that no flowers grew at Blackwick, and Vance declared that we must take some with us as a present for the lady of the house. He purchased a bouquet of pure white roses at the little town where we left the train, for the motorcar has been sent to meet us.

Soon after our arrival he presented these to Mrs Davenant. She took them it seemed to me nervously, and hardly had her hand touched them before they fell to pieces, in a shower of crumpled petals, to the floor.

'We must act at once,' said Vance to me when we were descending to dinner that night. 'There must be no delay.'

'What are you afraid of?' I whispered.

'Davenant has been absent a week,' he replied grimly. 'He is stronger than when he went away, but not strong enough to survive the loss of more blood. He must be protected. There is danger tonight.'

'You mean from his wife?' I shuddered at the ghastliness of the suggestion.

'That is what time will show.' Vance turned to me and added a few words with intense earnestness. 'Mrs Davenant, Dexter, is at present hovering between two conditions. The evil thing has not yet completely mastered her—you remember what Davenant said, how she would beg him to go away and the next moment entreat him to stay? She has made a struggle, but she is gradually succumbing, and this last week, spent here alone, has strengthened the evil. And that is what I have got to fight, Dexter—it is to be a contest of will, a contest that will go on silently till one or the other obtains the mastery. If you watch, you may see. Should a change show itself in Mrs Davenant you will know that I have won.'

Thus I knew the direction in which my friend proposed to act. It was to be a war of his will against the mysterious power that had laid its curse upon the house of MacThane. Mrs Davenant must be released from the fatal charm that held her.

And I, knowing what was going on, was able to watch and understand. I realized that the silent contest had begun even while we ate dinner. Mrs Davenant ate practically nothing and seemed ill at ease; she fidgeted in her chair, talked a great deal, and laughed—it was the laugh without a smile, as Davenant had described it. And as soon as she was able to she withdrew.

Later, as we sat in the drawing-room, I could feel the clash of wills. The air in the room felt electric and heavy, charged with tremendous but invisible forces. And outside, round the castle, the wind whistled and shrieked and moaned—it was as if all the dead and gone MacThanes, a grim army, had collected to fight the battle of their race.

And all this while we four in the drawing-room were sitting and talking the ordinary commonplaces of after—dinner conversation! That was the extraordinary part of it—Paul Davenant suspected nothing, and I, who knew, had to play my part. But I hardly took my eyes from Jessica's face. When would the change come, or was it, indeed, too late!

At last Davenant rose and remarked that he was tired and would go to bed. There was no need for Jessica to hurry. He would sleep that night in his dressing-room and did not want to be disturbed.

And it was at that moment, as his lips met hers in a goodnight kiss, as she wreathed her enchantress arms about him, careless of our presence, her eyes gleaming hungrily, that the change came.

It came with a fierce and threatening shriek of wind, and a rattling of the casement, as if the horde of ghosts without was about to break in upon us. A long, quivering sigh escaped from Jessica's lips, her arms fell from her husband's shoulders, and she drew back, swaying a little from side to side.

'Paul,' she cried, and somehow the whole timbre of her voice was changed, 'what a wretch I've been to bring you back to Blackwick, ill as you are! But we'll go away, dear; yes, I'll go, too. Oh, will you take me away—take me away tomorrow?' She spoke with an intense earnestness—unconscious all the time of what had been happening to her. Long shudders were convulsing her frame. 'I don't know why I've wanted to stay here,' she kept repeating. 'I hate the place, really—it's evil—evil.'

Having heard these words I exulted, for surely Vance's success was assured. But I was to learn that the danger was not yet past.

Husband and wife separated, each going to their own room. I noticed the grateful, if mystified glance that Davenant threw at Vance, vaguely aware, as he must have been, that my friend was somehow responsible for what had happened. It was settled that plans for departure were to be discussed on the morrow.

'I have succeeded,' Vance said hurriedly, when we were alone, 'but the change may be a transitory. I must keep watch tonight. Go you to bed, Dexter, there is nothing that you can do.'

I obeyed—though I would sooner have kept watch, too—watch against a danger of which I had no understanding. I went to my room, a gloomy and sparsely furnished apartment, but I knew that it was quite impossible for me to think of sleeping. And so, dressed as I was, I went and sat by the open window, for now the wind that had raged round the castle had died down to a low moaning in the pine trees—a whimpering of time-worn agony.

And it was as I sat thus that I became aware of a white figure that stole out from the castle by a door that I could not see, and, with hands clasped, ran swiftly across the terrace to the wood. I had but a momentary glance, but I felt convinced that the figure was that of Jessica Davenant.

And instinctively I knew that some great danger was imminent. It was, I think, the suggestion of despair conveyed by those clasped hands. At any rate, I did not hesitate. My window was some height from the ground, but the wall below was ivy-clad and afforded good foothold. The descent was quite easy. I achieved it, and was just in time to take up the pursuit in the right direction, which was into the thickness of the wood that clung to the slope of the hill.

I shall never forget that wild chase. There was just sufficient room to enable me to follow the rough path, which, luckily, since I had now lost sight of my quarry, was the only possible way that she could have taken; there were no intersecting tracks, and the wood was too thick on either side to permit of deviation.

And the wood seemed full of dreadful sounds—moaning and wailing and hideous laughter. The wind, of course, and the screaming of night birds—once I felt the fluttering of wings in close proximity to my face. But I could not rid myself of the thought that I, in my turn, was being pursued, that the forces of hell were combined against me.

The path came to an abrupt end on the border of the sombre lake that I have already mentioned. And now I realized that I was indeed only just in time, for before me, plunging knee deep in the water, I recognized the white-clad figure of the woman I had been pursuing. Hearing my footsteps, she turned her head, and then threw up her arms and screamed. Her red hair fell in heavy masses about her shoulders, and her face, as I saw it in that moment, was hardly human for the agony of remorse that it depicted.

'Go!' she screamed. 'For God's sake let me die!'

But I was by her side almost as she spoke. She struggled with me—sought vainly to tear herself from my clasp—implored me, with panting breath, to let her drown.

'It's the only way to save him!' she gasped. 'Don't you understand that I am a thing accursed? For it is I—I—who have sapped his life blood! I know it now, the truth has been revealed to me tonight! I am a vampire, without hope in this world or the next, so for his sake—for the sake of his unborn child—let me die—let me die!'

Was ever so terrible an appeal made? Yet I—what could I do? Gently I overcame her resistance and drew her back to shore. By the time I reached it she was lying a dead weight upon my arm. I laid her down upon a mossy bank, and, kneeling by her side, gazed intently into her face.

And then I knew that I had done well. For the face I looked upon was not that of Jessica the vampire, as I had seen it that afternoon, it was the face of Jessica, the woman whom Paul Davenant had loved.

<hr />

And later Aylmer Vance had his tale to tell.

'I waited', he said, 'until I knew that Davenant was asleep, and then I stole into his room to watch by his bedside. And presently she came, as I guessed she would, the vampire, the accursed thing that has preyed upon the souls of her kin, making them like to herself when they too have passed into Shadowland, and gathering sustenance for her horrid task from the blood of those who are alien to her race. Paul's body and Jessica's soul—it is for one and the other, Dexter, that we have fought.'

'You mean,' I hesitated, 'Zaida the witch?'

'Even so,' he agreed. 'Hers is the evil spirit that has fallen like a blight upon the house of MacThane. But now I think she may be exorcized for ever.'

'Tell me.'

'She came to Paul Davenant last night, as she must have done before, in the guise of his wife. You know that Jessica bears a strong resemblance to her ancestress. He opened his arms, but she was foiled of her prey, for I had taken my precautions; I had placed That upon Davenant's breast while he slept which robbed the vampire of her power of ill. She sped wailing from the room—a shadow—she who a minute before had looked at him with Jessica's eyes and spoken to him with Jessica's voice. Her red lips were Jessica's lips, and they were close to his when his eyes were opened and he saw her as she was—a hideous phantom of the corruption of the ages. And so the spell was removed, and she fled away to the place whence she had come—'

He paused. 'And now?' I inquired.

'Blackwick Castle must be razed to the ground,' he replied. 'That is the only way. Every stone of it, every brick, must be ground to powder and burnt with fire, for therein is the cause of all the evil. Davenant has consented.'

'And Mrs Davenant?'

'I think,' Vance answered cautiously, 'that all may be well with her. The curse will be removed with the destruction of the castle. She has not—thanks to you—perished under its influence. She was less guilty than she imagined—herself preyed upon rather than preying. But can't you understand her remorse when she realized, as she was bound to realize, the part she had played? And the knowledge of the child to come—its fatal inheritance—'

'I understand,' I muttered with a shudder. And then, under my breath, I whispered, 'Thank God!'

A VICTIM OF
HIGHER SPACE

Algernon Blackwood

H. P. Lovecraft ranked Algernon Blackwood (1869–1951) among the four modern masters of horror literature. Blackwood, an extremely prolific author, was born in Shooter's Hill, now part of London. Like his character, occult detective Dr. John Silence, Blackwood traveled extensively and immersed himself in studies of the occult and mysticism. He was also a member of the Ghost Club, believed to be the oldest paranormal research and investigation society in the world, having been founded in London in 1862. Blackwood joined the esoteric organization Order of the Golden Dawn in 1900.

Dr. John Silence is a man of independent means who devotes himself to healing the afflictions of others. A true free agent, Dr. Silence only serves those without resources to pay for good medical care, especially artists and creative people, as well as those whose cases interest him, especially those in a paranormal vein.

Although Silence dislikes the word "occult," he spent five years traveling the world seeking and studying its mysteries. He is a master of psychic empowerment and demonstrates his own clairvoyant abilities. Silence first appeared in 1908 in Blackwood's book John Silence, Physician Extraordinary *(London, Eveleigh Nash), which featured five stories. "A Victim of Higher Space," the sixth John Silence tale, was first published in the December 1914 issue of the* Occult Review.

A Victim of Higher Space

"THERE'S A HEXTRAORDINARY GENTLEMAN to see you, sir," said the new man.

"Why 'extraordinary'?" asked Dr. Silence, drawing the tips of his thin fingers through his brown beard. His eyes twinkled pleasantly. "Why 'extraordinary,' Barker?" he repeated encouragingly, noticing the perplexed expression in the man's eyes.

"He's so—so thin, sir. I could hardly see 'im at all—at first. He was inside the house before I could ask the name," he added, remembering strict orders.

"And who brought him here?"

"He come alone, sir, in a closed cab. He pushed by me before I could say a word—making no noise not what I could hear. He seemed to move so soft like—"

The man stopped short with obvious embarrassment, as though he had already said enough to jeopardise his new situation, but trying hard to show that he remembered the instructions and warnings he had received with regard to the admission of strangers not properly accredited.

"And where is the gentleman now?" asked Dr. Silence, turning away to conceal his amusement.

"I really couldn't exactly say, sir. I left him standing in the 'all—"

The doctor looked up sharply. "But why in the hall, Barker? Why not in the waiting-room?" He fixed his piercing though kindly eyes on the man's face. "Did he frighten you?" he asked quickly.

"I think he did, sir, if I may say so. I seemed to lose sight of him, as it were—" The man stammered, evidently convinced by now that he had earned his dismissal. "He come in so funny, just like a cold wind," he added boldly, setting his heels at attention and looking his master full in the face.

The doctor made an internal note of the man's halting description; he was pleased that the slight signs of psychic intuition which had induced him to engage Barker had not entirely failed at the first trial. Dr. Silence sought for this qualification in all his assistants, from secretary to serving man, and if it surrounded him with a somewhat singular crew, the drawbacks were more than compensated for on the whole by their occasional flashes of insight.

"So the gentleman made you feel queer, did he?"

"That was it, I think, sir," repeated the man stolidly.

"And he brings no kind of introduction to me—no letter or anything?" asked the doctor, with feigned surprise, as though he knew what was coming.

The man fumbled, both in mind and pockets, and finally produced an envelope.

"I beg pardon, sir," he said, greatly flustered; "the gentleman handed me this for you."

It was a note from a discerning friend, who had never yet sent him a case that was not vitally interesting from one point or another.

"Please see the bearer of this note," the brief message ran, "though I doubt if even you can do much to help him."

John Silence paused a moment, so as to gather from the mind of the writer all that lay behind the brief words of the letter. Then he looked up at his servant with a graver expression than he had yet worn.

"Go back and find this gentleman," he said, "and show him into the green study. Do not reply to his question, or speak more than actually necessary; but think kind, helpful, sympathetic thoughts as strongly as you can, Barker. You remember what I told you about the importance of *thinking*, when I engaged you. Put curiosity out of your mind, and think gently, sympathetically, affectionately, if you can."

He smiled, and Barker, who had recovered his composure in the doctor's presence, bowed silently and went out.

There were two different reception-rooms in Dr. Silence's house. One (intended for persons who imagined they needed spiritual assistance when really they were only candidates for the asylum) had padded walls, and was well supplied with various concealed contrivances by means of which sudden violence could be instantly met and overcome. It was, however, rarely used. The other, intended for the reception of genuine cases of spiritual distress and out-of-the-way afflictions of a psychic nature, was entirely draped and furnished in a soothing deep green, calculated to induce calmness and repose of mind. And this room was the one in which Dr. Silence interviewed the majority of his "queer" cases, and the one into which he had directed Barker to show his present caller.

To begin with, the arm-chair in which the patient was always directed to sit, was nailed to the floor, since its immovability tended to impart this same excellent characteristic to the occupant. Patients invariably grew excited when talking about themselves, and their excitement tended to confuse their thoughts and to exaggerate their language. The inflexibility of the chair helped to counteract this. After repeated endeavours to drag it forward, or push it back, they ended by resigning themselves to sitting quietly. And with the futility of fidgeting there followed a calmer state of mind.

Upon the floor, and at intervals in the wall immediately behind, were certain tiny green buttons, practically unnoticeable, which on being pressed permitted a soothing and persuasive narcotic to rise invisibly about the occupant of the chair. The effect upon the excitable patient was rapid, admirable, and harmless. The green study was further provided with a secret spy-hole; for John Silence liked when possible to observe his patient's face before it had assumed that mask the features of the human countenance invariably wear in the presence of another person. A man sitting alone wears a psychic expression; and this expression is the man himself. It disappears the moment another person joins him. And Dr. Silence often learned more from a few moments' secret observation of a face than from hours of conversation with its owner afterwards.

A very light, almost a dancing, step followed Barker's heavy tread towards the green room, and a moment afterwards the man came in and announced that the gentleman was waiting. He was still pale and his manner nervous.

"Never mind, Barker" the doctor said kindly; "if you were not psychic the man would have had no effect upon you at all. You only need training and development. And when you have learned to interpret these feelings and sensations better, you will feel no fear, but only a great sympathy."

"Yes, sir; thank you, sir!" And Barker bowed and made his escape, while Dr. Silence, an amused smile lurking about the corners of his mouth, made his way noiselessly down the passage and put his eye to the spy-hole in the door of the green study.

This spy-hole was so placed that it commanded a view of almost the entire room, and, looking through it, the doctor saw a hat, gloves, and umbrella lying on a chair by the table, but searched at first in vain for their owner.

The windows were both closed and a brisk fire burned in the grate. There were various signs—signs intelligible at least to a keenly intuitive soul—that the room was occupied, yet so far as human beings were concerned, it was empty, utterly empty. No one sat in the chairs; no one stood on the mat before the fire; there was no sign even that a patient was anywhere close against the wall, examining the Bocklin reproductions—as patients so often did when they thought they were alone—and therefore rather difficult to see from the spy-hole. Ordinarily speaking, there was no one in the room. It was undeniable.

Yet Dr. Silence was quite well aware that a human being *was* in the room. His psychic apparatus never failed in letting him know the proximity of an incarnate or discarnate being. Even in the dark he could tell that. And he now knew positively that his patient—the patient who had alarmed Barker, and had then tripped down the corridor with that dancing footstep—was somewhere concealed within the four walls commanded by his spy-hole. He also realised—and this was most unusual—that this individual whom he desired to watch knew that he was being watched. And, further, that the stranger himself was also watching! In fact, that it was he, the doctor, who was being observed—and by an observer as keen and trained as himself.

An inkling of the true state of the case began to dawn upon him, and he was on the verge of entering—indeed, his hand already touched the door-knob—when his eye, still glued to the spy-hole, detected a slight movement. Directly opposite, between him and the fireplace, something stirred. He watched very attentively and made certain that he was not mistaken. An object on the mantelpiece—it was a blue vase—disappeared from view. It passed out of sight together with the portion of the marble mantelpiece on which it rested. Next, that part of the fire and grate and brass fender immediately below it vanished entirely, as though a slice had been taken clean out of them.

Dr. Silence then understood that something between him and these objects was slowly coming into being, something that concealed them and obstructed his vision by inserting itself in the line of sight between them and himself.

He quietly awaited further results before going in.

First he saw a thin perpendicular line tracing itself from just above the height of the clock and continuing downwards till it reached the woolly fire-mat. This line grew wider, broadened, grew solid. It was no shadow; it was something substantial. It defined itself more and more. Then suddenly, at the top of the line, and about on a level with the face of the clock, he saw a round luminous disc gazing steadily at him. It was a human eye, looking straight into his own, pressed there against the spy-hole. And it was bright with intelligence. Dr. Silence held his breath for a moment—and stared back at it.

Then, like some one moving out of deep shadow into light, he saw the figure of a man come sliding sideways into view, a whitish face following the eye, and the perpendicular line he had first observed broadening out and developing into the complete figure of a human being. It was the patient. He had apparently been standing there in front of the fire all the time. A second eye had followed the first, and both of them stared steadily at the spy-hole, sharply concentrated, yet with a sly twinkle of humour and amusement that made it impossible for the doctor to maintain his position any longer.

He opened the door and went in quickly. As he did so he noticed for the first time the sound of a German band coming in gaily through the open ventilators. In some intuitive, unaccountable fashion the music connected itself with the patient he was about to interview. This sort of prevision was not unfamiliar to him. It always explained itself later.

The man, he saw, was of middle age and of very ordinary appearance; so ordinary, in fact, that he was difficult to describe—his only peculiarity being his extreme thinness. Pleasant—that is, good—vibrations issued from his atmosphere and met Dr. Silence as he advanced to greet him, yet vibrations alive with currents and discharges betraying the perturbed and disordered condition of his mind and brain. There was evidently something wholly out of the usual in the state of his thoughts. Yet, though strange, it was not altogether distressing; it was not the impression that the broken and violent atmosphere of the insane produces upon the mind. Dr. Silence realised in a flash that here was a case of absorbing interest that might require all his powers to handle properly.

"I was watching you through my little peep-hole—as you saw," he began, with a pleasant smile, advancing to shake hands. "I find it of the greatest assistance sometimes—"

But the patient interrupted him at once. His voice was hurried and had odd, shrill changes in it, breaking from high to low in unexpected fashion. One moment it thundered, the next it almost squeaked.

"I understand without explanation," he broke in rapidly. "You get the true note of a man in this way—when he thinks himself unobserved. I quite agree. Only, in my case, I fear, you saw very little. My case, as you of course grasp, Dr. Silence, is extremely peculiar, uncomfortably peculiar. Indeed, unless Sir William had positively assured me—"

"My friend has sent you to me," the doctor interrupted gravely, with a gentle note of authority, "and that is quite sufficient. Pray, be seated, Mr.—"

"Mudge—Racine Mudge," returned the other.

"Take this comfortable one, Mr. Mudge," leading him to the fixed chair, "and tell me your condition in your own way and at your own pace. My whole day is at your service if you require it."

Mr. Mudge moved towards the chair in question and then hesitated.

"You will promise me not to use the narcotic buttons," he said, before sitting down. "I do not need them. Also I ought to mention that anything you think of vividly will reach my mind. That is apparently part of my peculiar case." He sat down with a sigh and arranged his thin legs and body into a position of comfort. Evidently he was very sensitive to the thoughts of others, for the picture of the green buttons had only entered the doctor's mind for a second, yet the other had instantly snapped it up. Dr. Silence noticed, too, that Mr. Mudge held on tightly with both hands to the arms of the chair.

"I'm rather glad the chair is nailed to the floor," he remarked, as he settled himself more comfortably. "It suits me admirably. The fact is—and this is my case in a nutshell—which is all that a doctor of your marvellous development requires—the fact is, Dr. Silence, I am a victim of Higher Space. That's what's the matter with me— Higher Space!"

The two looked at each other for a space in silence, the little patient holding tightly to the arms of the chair which "suited him admirably," and looking up with staring eyes, his atmosphere positively trembling with the waves of some unknown activity; while the doctor smiled kindly and sympathetically, and put his whole person as far as possible into the mental condition of the other.

"Higher Space," repeated Mr. Mudge, "that's what it is. Now, do you think you can help me with *that*?"

There was a pause during which the men's eyes steadily searched down below the surface of their respective personalities. Then Dr. Silence spoke.

"I am quite sure I can help," he answered quietly; "sympathy must always help, and suffering always owns my sympathy. I see you have suffered cruelly. You must tell me all about your case, and when I hear the gradual steps by which you reached this strange condition, I have no doubt I can be of assistance to you."

He drew a chair up beside his interlocutor and laid a hand on his shoulder for a moment. His whole being radiated kindness, intelligence, desire to help.

"For instance," he went on, "I feel sure it was the result of no mere chance that you became familiar with the terrors of what you term Higher Space; for Higher Space is no mere external measurement. It is, of course, a spiritual state, a spiritual condition, an inner development, and one that we must recognise as abnormal, since it is beyond the reach of the world at the present stage of evolution. Higher Space is a mythical state."

"Oh!" cried the other, rubbing his birdlike hands with pleasure, "the relief it is to be able to talk to some one who can understand! Of course what you say is the utter truth. And you are right that no mere chance led me to my present condition, but, on the other hand, prolonged and deliberate study. Yet chance in a sense now governs it. I mean, my entering the condition of Higher Space seems to depend upon the chance of this and that circumstance. For instance, the mere sound of that German band sent me off. Not that all music will do so, but certain sounds, certain vibrations, at once key me up to the requisite pitch, and off I go. Wagner's music always does it, and that band must have been playing a stray bit of Wagner. But I'll come to all that later. Only first, I must ask you to send away your man from the spy-hole."

John Silence looked up with a start, for Mr. Mudge's back was to the door, and there was no mirror. He saw the brown eye of Barker glued to the little circle of glass, and he crossed the room without a word and snapped down the black shutter provided for the purpose, and then heard Barker snuffle away along the passage.

"Now," continued the little man in the chair, "I can begin. You have managed to put me completely at my ease, and I feel I may tell you my whole case without shame or reserve. You will understand. But you must be patient with me if I go into details that are already familiar to you—details of Higher Space, I mean—and if I seem stupid when I have to describe things that transcend the power of language and are really therefore indescribable."

"My dear friend," put in the other calmly, "that goes without saying. To know Higher Space is an experience that defies description, and one is obliged to make use of more or less intelligible symbols. But, pray, proceed. Your vivid thoughts will tell me more than your halting words."

An immense sigh of relief proceeded from the little figure half lost in the depths of the chair. Such intelligent sympathy meeting him half-way was a new experience to him, and it touched his heart at once. He leaned back, relaxing his tight hold of the arms, and began in his thin, scale-like voice.

"My mother was a Frenchwoman, and my father an Essex bargeman," he said abruptly. "Hence my name—Racine and Mudge. My father died before I ever saw him. My mother inherited money from her Bordeaux relations, and when she died soon after, I was left alone with wealth and a strange freedom. I had no guardian, trustees, sisters, brothers, or any connection in the world to look after me. I grew up, therefore, utterly without education. This much was to my advantage; I learned none of that deceitful rubbish taught in schools, and so had nothing to unlearn when I awakened to my true love—mathematics, higher mathematics and higher geometry. These, however, I seemed to know instinctively. It was like the memory of what I had deeply studied before; the principles were in my blood, and I simply raced through the ordinary stages, and beyond, and then did the same with geometry. Afterwards, when I read the books on these subjects, I understood how swift and undeviating the knowledge had come back to me. It was simply memory. It was simply *re-collecting* the memories of what I had known before in a previous existence and required no books to teach me."

In his growing excitement, Mr. Mudge attempted to drag the chair forward a little nearer to his listener, and then smiled faintly as he resigned himself instantly again to its immovability, and plunged anew into the recital of his singular "disease."

"The audacious speculations of Bolyai, the amazing theories of Gauss—that through a point more than one line could be drawn parallel to a given line; the possibility that the angles of a triangle are together *greater* than two right angles, if drawn upon immense curvatures—the breathless intuitions of Beltrami and Lobatchewsky—all these I hurried through, and emerged, panting but unsatisfied, upon the verge of my—my new world, my Higher Space possibilities—in a word, my disease!

"How I got there," he resumed after a brief pause, during which he appeared to be listening intently for an approaching sound, "is more than I can put intelligibly into words. I can only hope to leave your mind with an intuitive comprehension of the possibility of what I say.

"Here, however, came a change. At this point I was no longer absorbing the fruits of studies I had made before; it was the beginning of new efforts to learn for the first time, and I had to go slowly and laboriously through terrible work. Here I sought for the theories and speculations of others. But books were few and far between, and with the exception of one man—a 'dreamer,' the world called him—whose audacity and piercing intuition amazed and delighted me beyond description, I found no one to guide or help.

"You, of course, Dr. Silence, understand something of what I am driving at with these stammering words, though you cannot perhaps yet guess what depths of pain my new knowledge brought me to, nor why an acquaintance with a new development of space should prove a source of misery and terror."

Mr. Racine Mudge, remembering that the chair would not move, did the next best thing he could in his desire to draw nearer to the attentive man facing him, and sat forward upon the very edge of the cushions, crossing his legs and gesticulating with both hands as though he saw into this region of new space he was attempting to describe, and might any moment tumble into it bodily from the edge of the chair and disappear from view. John Silence, separated from him by three paces, sat with his eyes fixed upon the thin white face opposite, noting every word and every gesture with deep attention.

"This room we now sit in, Dr. Silence, has one side open to space—to Higher Space. A closed box only *seems* closed. There is a way in and out of a soap bubble without breaking the skin."

"You tell me no new thing," the doctor interposed gently.

"Hence, if Higher Space exists and our world borders upon it and lies partially in it, it follows necessarily that we see only portions of all objects. We never see their true and complete shape. We see their three measurements, but not their fourth. The new direction is concealed from us, and when I hold this book and move my hand all round it I have not really made a complete circuit. We only perceive those portions of any object which exist in our three dimensions; the rest escapes us. But, once we learn to see in Higher Space, objects will appear as they actually are. Only they will thus be hardly recognisable!

"Now, you may begin to grasp something of what I am coming to."

"I am beginning to understand something of what you must have suffered," observed the doctor soothingly, "for I have made similar experiments myself, and only stopped just in time—"

"You are the one man in all the world who can hear and understand, *and* sympathise," exclaimed Mr. Mudge, grasping his hand and holding it tightly while he spoke. The nailed chair prevented further excitability.

"Well," he resumed, after a moment's pause, "I procured the implements and the coloured blocks for practical experiment, and I followed the instructions carefully till I had arrived at a working conception of four-dimensional space. The tessaract, the figure whose boundaries are cubes, I knew by heart. That is to say, I knew it and saw it mentally, for my eye, of course, could never take in a new measurement, or my hands and feet handle it.

"So, at least, I thought," he added, making a wry face. "I had reached the stage, you see, when I could imagine in a new dimension. I was able to conceive the shape of that new figure which is intrinsically different to all we know—the shape of the tessaract. I could perceive in four dimensions. When, therefore, I looked at a cube I could see all its sides at once. Its top was not foreshortened, nor its farther side and base invisible. I saw the whole thing out flat, so to speak. And this tessaract was bounded by cubes! Moreover, I also saw its content—its insides."

"You were not yourself able to enter this new world," interrupted Dr. Silence.

"Not then. I was only able to conceive intuitively what it was like and how exactly it must look. Later, when I slipped in there and saw objects in their entirety, unlimited by the paucity of our poor three measurements, I very nearly lost my life. For, you see, space does not stop at a single new dimension, a fourth. It extends in all possible new ones, and we must conceive it as containing any number of new dimensions. In other words, there is no space at all, but only a spiritual condition. But, meanwhile, I had come to grasp the strange fact that the objects in our normal world appear to us only partially."

Mr. Mudge moved farther forward till he was balanced dangerously on the very edge of the chair. "From this starting point," he resumed, "I began my studies and experiments, and continued them for years. I had money, and I was without friends. I lived in solitude and experimented. My intellect, of course, had little part in the work, for intellectually it was all unthinkable. Never was the limitation of mere reason more plainly demonstrated. It was mystically, intuitively, spiritually that I began to advance. And what I learnt, and knew, and did is all impossible to put into language, since it all describes experiences transcending the experiences of men. It is only some of the results—what you would call the symptoms of my disease—that I can give you, and even these must often appear absurd contradictions and impossible paradoxes.

"I can only tell you, Dr. Silence"—his manner became exceedingly impressive—"that I reached sometimes a point of view whence all the great puzzle of the world became plain to me, and I understood what they call in the Yoga books 'The Great Heresy of Separateness'; why all great teachers have urged the necessity of man loving his neighbour as himself; how men are all really one; and why the utter loss of self is necessary to salvation and the discovery of the true life of the soul."

He paused a moment and drew breath.

"Your speculations have been my own long ago," the doctor said quietly. "I fully realise the force of your words. Men are doubtless not separate at all—in the sense they imagine—"

"All this about the very much Higher Space I only dimly, very dimly, conceived, of course," the other went on, raising his voice again by jerks; "but what did happen to me was the humbler accident of—the simpler disaster—oh, dear, how shall I put it—?"

He stammered and showed visible signs of distress.

"It was simply this," he resumed with a sudden rush of words, "that, accidentally, as the result of my years of experiment, I one day slipped bodily into the next world, the world of four dimensions, yet without knowing precisely how I got there, or how I could get back again. I discovered, that is, that my ordinary three-dimensional body was but an expression—a projection—of my higher four-dimensional body!

"Now you understand what I meant much earlier in our talk when I spoke of chance. I cannot control my entrance or exit. Certain people, certain human atmospheres, certain wandering forces, thoughts, desires even—the radiations of certain combinations of colour, and above all, the vibrations of certain kinds of music, will suddenly throw me into a state of what I can only describe as an intense and terrific inner vibration—and behold I am off! Off in the direction at right angles to all our known directions! Off in the direction the cube takes when it begins to trace the outlines of the new figure! Off into my breathless and semi-divine Higher Space! Off, *inside myself*, into the world of four dimensions!"

He gasped and dropped back into the depths of the immovable chair.

"And there," he whispered, his voice issuing from among the cushions, "there I have to stay until these vibrations subside, or until they do something which I cannot find words to describe properly or intelligibly to you—and then, behold, I am back again. First, that is, I disappear. Then I reappear."

"Just so," exclaimed Dr. Silence, "and that is why a few—"

"Why a few moments ago," interrupted Mr. Mudge, taking the words out of his mouth, "you found me gone, and then saw me return. The music of that wretched German band sent me off. Your intense thinking about me brought me back—when the band had stopped its Wagner. I saw you approach the peep-hole and I saw Barker's intention of doing so later. For me no interiors are hidden. I see inside. When in that state the content of your mind, as of your body, is open to me as the day. Oh, dear, oh, dear, oh, dear!"

Mr. Mudge stopped and again mopped his brow. A light trembling ran over the surface of his small body like wind over grass. He still held tightly to the arms of the chair.

"At first," he presently resumed, "my new experiences were so vividly interesting that I felt no alarm. There was no room for it. The alarm came a little later."

"Then you actually penetrated far enough into that state to experience yourself as a normal portion of it?" asked the doctor, leaning forward, deeply interested.

Mr. Mudge nodded a perspiring face in reply.

"I did," he whispered, "undoubtedly I did. I am coming to all that. It began first at night, when I realised that sleep brought no loss of consciousness—"

"The spirit, of course, can never sleep. Only the body becomes unconscious," interposed John Silence.

"Yes, we know that—theoretically. At night, of course, the spirit is active elsewhere, and we have no memory of where and how, simply because the brain stays behind and receives no record. But I found that, while remaining conscious, I also retained memory. I had attained to the state of continuous consciousness, for at night I regularly, with the first approaches of drowsiness, entered *nolens volens* the four-dimensional world.

"For a time this happened regularly, and I could not control it; though later I found a way to regulate it better. Apparently sleep is unnecessary in the higher—the four-dimensional—body. Yes, perhaps. But I should infinitely have preferred dull sleep to the knowledge. For, unable to control my movements, I wandered to and fro, attracted, owing to my partial development and premature arrival, to parts of this new world that alarmed me more and more. It was the awful waste and drift of a monstrous world, so utterly different to all we know and see that I cannot even hint at the nature of the sights and objects and beings in it. More than that, I cannot even remember them. I cannot now picture them to myself even, but can recall only the *memory of the impression* they made upon me, the horror and devastating terror of it all. To be in several places at once, for instance—"

"Perfectly," interrupted John Silence, noticing the increase of the other's excitement, "I understand exactly. But now, please, tell me a little more of this alarm you experienced, and how it affected you."

"It's not the disappearing and reappearing *per se* that I mind," continued Mr. Mudge, "so much as certain other things. It's seeing people and objects in their weird entirety, in their true and complete shapes, that is so distressing. It introduces me to a world of monsters. Horses, dogs, cats, all of which I loved; people, trees, children; all that I have considered beautiful in life—everything, from a human face to a cathedral—appear to me in a different shape and aspect to all I have known before. I cannot perhaps convince you why this should be terrible, but I assure you that it is so. To hear the human voice proceeding from this novel appearance which I scarcely recognise as a human body is ghastly, simply ghastly. To see inside everything and everybody is a form of insight peculiarly distressing. To be so confused in geography as to find myself one moment at the North Pole, and the next at Clapham Junction—or possibly at both places simultaneously—is absurdly terrifying. Your imagination will readily furnish other details without my multiplying my experiences now. But you have no idea what it all means, and how I suffer."

Mr. Mudge paused in his panting account and lay back in his chair. He still held tightly to the arms as though they could keep him in the world of sanity and three measurements, and only now and again released his left hand in order to mop his face. He looked very thin and white and oddly unsubstantial, and he stared about him as though he saw into this other space he had been talking about.

John Silence, too, felt warm. He had listened to every word and had made many notes. The presence of this man had an exhilarating effect upon him. It seemed as if Mr. Racine Mudge still carried about with him something of that breathless Higher–Space condition he had been describing. At any rate, Dr. Silence had himself advanced sufficiently far along the legitimate paths of spiritual and psychic transformations to realise that the visions of this extraordinary little person had a basis of truth for their origin.

After a pause that prolonged itself into minutes, he crossed the room and unlocked a drawer in a bookcase, taking out a small book with a red cover. It had a lock to it, and he produced a key out of his pocket and proceeded to open the covers. The bright eyes of Mr. Mudge never left him for a single second.

"It almost seems a pity," he said at length, "to cure you, Mr. Mudge. You are on the way to discovery of great things. Though you may lose your life in the process—that is, your life here in the world of three dimensions—you would lose thereby nothing of great value—you will pardon my apparent rudeness, I know—and you might gain what is infinitely greater. Your suffering, of course, lies in the fact that you alternate between the two worlds and are never wholly in one or the other. Also, I rather imagine, though I cannot be certain of this from any personal experiments, that you have here and there penetrated even into space of more than four dimensions, and have hence experienced the terror you speak of."

The perspiring son of the Essex bargeman and the woman of Normandy bent his head several times in assent, but uttered no word in reply.

"Some strange psychic predisposition, dating no doubt from one of your former lives, has favoured the development of your 'disease'; and the fact that you had no normal training at school or college, no leading by the poor intellect into the culs-de-sac falsely called knowledge, has further caused your exceedingly rapid movement along the lines of direct inner experience. None of the knowledge you have foreshadowed has come to you through the senses, of course."

Mr. Mudge, sitting in his immovable chair, began to tremble slightly. A wind again seemed to pass over his surface and again to set it curiously in motion like a field of grass.

"You are merely talking to gain time," he said hurriedly, in a shaking voice. "This thinking aloud delays us. I see ahead what you are coming to, only please be quick, for something is going to happen. A band is again coming down the street, and if it plays—if it plays Wagner—I shall be off in a twinkling."

"Precisely. I will be quick. I was leading up to the point of how to effect your cure. The way is this: You must simply learn to *block the entrances*."

"True, true, utterly true!" exclaimed the little man, dodging about nervously in the depths of the chair. "But how, in the name of space, is that to be done?"

"By concentration. They are all within you, these entrances, although outer cases such as colour, music and other things lead you towards them. These external things you cannot hope to destroy, but once the entrances are blocked, they will lead you only to bricked walls and closed channels. You will no longer be able to find the way."

"Quick, quick!" cried the bobbing figure in the chair. "How is this concentration to be effected?"

"This little book," continued Dr. Silence calmly, "will explain to you the way." He tapped the cover. "Let me now read out to you certain simple instructions, composed, as I see you divine, entirely from my own personal experiences in the same direction. Follow these instructions and you will no longer enter the state of Higher Space. The entrances will be blocked effectively."

Mr. Mudge sat bolt upright in his chair to listen, and John Silence cleared his throat and began to read slowly in a very distinct voice.

But before he had uttered a dozen words, something happened. A sound of street music entered the room through the open ventilators, for a band had begun to play in the stable mews at the back of the house—the March from *Tannhäuser*. Odd as it may seem that a German band should twice within the space of an hour enter the same mews and play Wagner, it was nevertheless the fact.

Mr. Racine Mudge heard it. He uttered a sharp, squeaking cry and twisted his arms with nervous energy round the chair. A piteous look that was not far from tears spread over his white face. Grey shadows followed it—the grey of fear. He began to struggle convulsively.

"Hold me fast! Catch me! For God's sake, keep me here! I'm on the rush already. Oh, it's frightful!" he cried in tones of anguish, his voice as thin as a reed.

Dr. Silence made a plunge forward to seize him, but in a flash, before he could cover the space between them, Mr. Racine Mudge, screaming and struggling, seemed to shoot past him into invisibility. He disappeared like an arrow from a bow propelled at infinite speed, and his voice no longer sounded in the external air, but seemed in some curious way to make itself heard somewhere within the depths of the doctor's own being. It was almost like a faint singing cry in his head, like a voice of dream, a voice of vision and unreality.

"Alcohol, alcohol!" it cried, "give me alcohol! It's the quickest way. Alcohol, before I'm out of reach!"

The doctor, accustomed to rapid decisions and even more rapid action, remembered that a brandy flask stood upon the mantelpiece, and in less than a second he had seized it and was holding it out towards the space above the chair recently occupied by the visible Mudge. Then, before his very eyes, and long ere he could unscrew the metal stopper, he saw the contents of the closed glass phial sink and lessen as though some one were drinking violently and greedily of the liquor within.

"Thanks! Enough! It deadens the vibrations!" cried the faint voice in his interior, as he withdrew the flask and set it back upon the mantelpiece. He understood that in Mudge's present condition one side of the flask was open to space and he could drink without removing the stopper. He could hardly have had a more interesting proof of what he had been hearing described at such length.

But the next moment—the very same moment it almost seemed—the German band stopped midway in its tune—and there was Mr. Mudge back in his chair again, gasping and panting!

"Quick!" he shrieked, "stop that band! Send it away! Catch hold of me! Block the entrances! Block the entrances! Give me the red book! Oh, oh, oh-h-h-h!!!"

The music had begun again. It was merely a temporary interruption. The *Tannhäuser* March started again, this time at a tremendous pace that made it sound like a rapid two-step as though the instruments played against time.

But the brief interruption gave Dr. Silence a moment in which to collect his scattering thoughts, and before the band had got through half a bar, he had flung forward upon the chair and held Mr. Racine Mudge, the struggling little victim of Higher Space, in a grip of iron. His arms went all round his diminutive person, taking in a good part of the chair at the same time. He was not a big man, yet he seemed to smother Mudge completely.

Yet, even as he did so, and felt the wriggling form underneath him, it began to melt and slip away like air or water. The wood of the arm-chair somehow disentangled itself from between his own arms and those of Mudge. The phenomenon known as the passage of matter through matter took place. The little man seemed actually to get mixed up in his own being. Dr. Silence could just see his face beneath him. It puckered and grew dark as though from some great internal effort. He heard the thin, reedy voice cry in his ear to "Block the entrances, block the entrances!" and then—but how in the world describe what is indescribable?

John Silence half rose up to watch. Racine Mudge, his face distorted beyond all recognition, was making a marvellous inward movement, as though doubling back upon himself. He turned funnel-wise like water in a whirling vortex, and then appeared to break up somewhat as a reflection breaks up and divides in a distorting convex mirror. He went neither forward nor backwards, neither to the right nor the left, neither up nor down. But he went. He went utterly. He simply flashed away out of sight like a vanishing projectile.

All but one leg! Dr. Silence just had the time and the presence of mind to seize upon the left ankle and boot as it disappeared, and to this he held on for several seconds like grim death. Yet all the time he knew it was a foolish and useless thing to do.

The foot was in his grasp one moment, and the next it seemed—this was the only way he could describe it—inside his own skin and bones, and at the same time outside his hand and all round it. It seemed mixed up in some amazing way with his own flesh and blood. Then it was gone, and he was tightly grasping a draught of heated air.

"Gone! gone! gone!" cried a thick, whispering voice, somewhere deep within his own consciousness. "Lost! lost! lost!" it repeated, growing fainter and fainter till at length it vanished into nothing and the last signs of Mr. Racine Mudge vanished with it.

John Silence locked his red book and replaced it in the cabinet, which he fastened with a click, and when Barker answered the bell he inquired if Mr. Mudge had left a card upon the table. It appeared that he had, and when the servant returned with it, Dr. Silence read the address and made a note of it. It was in North London.

"Mr. Mudge has gone," he said quietly to Barker, noticing his expression of alarm.

"He's not taken his 'at with him, sir."

"Mr. Mudge requires no hat where he is now," continued the doctor, stooping to poke the fire. "But he may return for it—"

"And the humbrella, sir."

"And the umbrella."

"He didn't go out *my* way, sir, if you please," stuttered the amazed servant, his curiosity overcoming his nervousness.

"Mr. Mudge has his own way of coming and going, and prefers it. If he returns by the door at any time remember to bring him instantly to me, and be kind and gentle with him and ask no questions. Also, remember, Barker, to think pleasantly, sympathetically, affectionately of him while he is away. Mr. Mudge is a very suffering gentleman."

Barker bowed and went out of the room backwards, gasping and feeling round the inside of his collar with three very hot fingers of one hand.

It was two days later when he brought in a telegram to the study. Dr. Silence opened it, and read as follows:

"Bombay. Just slipped out again. All safe. Have blocked entrances. Thousand thanks. Address Cooks, London.—MUDGE."

Dr. Silence looked up and saw Barker staring at him bewilderingly. It occurred to him that somehow he knew the contents of the telegram.

"Make a parcel of Mr. Mudge's things," he said briefly, "and address them Thomas Cook & Sons, Ludgate Circus. And send them there exactly a month from to-day and marked 'To be called for.'"

"Yes, sir," said Barker, leaving the room with a deep sigh and a hurried glance at the waste-paper basket where his master had dropped the pink paper.

THE WITNESS IN
THE WOOD

Rose Champion de Crespigny

Rose Champion de Crespigny, née Annie Rose Charlotte Cooper-Key (c. 1859–1935) was an artist who specialized in watercolors, mainly of marine subjects, and the prolific author of more than twenty novels. Rose was also a devout Spiritualist and knowledgeable esotericist, which is reflected in her stories featuring occult detective Norton Vyse and also in several of her other works, such as The Mark *(published in 1912), which includes a reincarnation theme, and* The New Forest: Its Traditions, Inhabitants, and Customs *(1895), about the forest in Hampshire, England, that has deep historical associations with witchcraft and with English witches such as Gerald Gardner and Sybil Leek. Rose also wrote historical romances and regular—not occult—detective stories, such as* The Riddle of the Emeralds, *published in 1929.*

Following the death of her husband, Philip de Crespigny, in 1912, Rose's interest in Spiritualism increased. Rose consulted Etta Wriedt, the Detroit-born direct voice medium, and through Wriedt believed that she had obtained evidence of survival after death. Rose held high office in various psychical societies—she was the president of the Leeds Psychic Research Society and the honorary principal of the British College of Psychic Science. She wrote Spiritualist pamphlets and lectured on esoteric topics.

Rose Champion de Crespigny's occult detective, Norton Vyse, is a psychometrist— meaning that he obtains information from objects by touching them. Vyse uses his powers of psychometry to solve mysteries and crimes. He appears in a series of six stories, all first published in 1919 in Premier Magazine.

The Norton Vyse stories appeared before the 1951 repeal of the Witchcraft Act of 1604. Before the repeal, it was illegal to publish books in the United Kingdom that advocated the practice of witchcraft—or anything that might be defined as witchcraft. And so, to circumnavigate this law, Rose cloaked the knowledge she wished to share as fiction, in the same manner as Gerald Gardner, credited as the founder of modern Wicca, and Dion Fortune, whose story "The Return of the Ritual" may be found on page 269 of this book. Thus, if one reads the Norton Vyse series of stories, in addition to enjoying a good story, you can learn about telepathy, automatic writing, mediumship, and theories of possession.

The Witness in the Wood

VYSE STEPPED FROM the train on to the inadequately illuminated platform of Lesser Hamberdene Station and peered about him.

The letter inviting him—if a pressing appeal for his immediate presence could be called an invitation—had promised he should be met and driven to Hamberdene Grange, but in the dusk and welter of fine drizzling rain it was some moments before he descried the expectant chauffeur, who, seizing the modest impedimenta for a twenty-four hours' visit, preceded him through the exit gate to the softly purring car outside the station.

Norton Vyse's fame as a psychic of unusual powers had spread even to the out-of-the-way village of Lesser Hamberdene. That morning he had received the urgent appeal from the mistress of the Grange, and 'sensing' that there was a case in which his powers might be of practical use, it had induced him to give up some of the time of which he had so little to spare, and brought him down by an afternoon train, in spite of several engagements in London.

So far he knew but little of the case he was called upon to investigate, and as the car ran through the tortuous and narrow lanes bordered by dripping hedges, that lay between the station and the Grange, he gave himself over to thought. His eyes—grey, and of a particular transparency, usually the index of an inner peace shining with steady radiance upon a restless world—looked tired; the lean, clean-shaven face, with its squarish chin, and lines that told of practised asceticism, was slightly drawn with an unwonted fatigue. There had been unusual drains on his vitality during the previous weeks, on the life energy he expended so freely in the cause of others, and he was not altogether sorry for the few hours' run into the fresh country air.

His mind ran idly over some of the problems it had been his lot to solve during the immediate past. To one whose finer senses had reached so advanced a state of development it was difficult to realise the coarseness of the fibre of which the nervous tissues of the general run of humanity is composed. To 'sense' surrounding conditions, to see, to hear, with senses still awakened in the man in the street, but in himself developed to a high pitch of responsiveness, had become so much a part of his life, of himself, that the want of the faculties in others was often a matter of surprise to him.

He was accustomed to ridicule, but met it with a quiet smile that seemed to transmute it into something very cheap and negligible. He had been called 'swindler' by more than a few—who had never seen him; no honest man could look into Norton Vyse's clear grey eyes, or note the steadfast set of the firm, straight lips, and fail to recognize a soul honest as his own. But in a world at last realizing its own limitations, Vyse was steadily coming into his own, the shaft of the old type of hidebound scoffer was falling short of the mark, and there was a growing tendency among people of intellect and standing, when confronted by any of the mysterious problems outside the range of ordinary dealings, problems which have arisen from time immemorial, to call for Norton Vyse.

The letter had been vague, the main gist of it an appeal for help. A dark pool in a wood, unaccountable tragedies in its neighborhood, giving the spot an evil name for miles round, and the gardener's daughter found dead without any apparent cause, was the sum total of any direct information he could father from it.

But Mrs Deane was evidently in distress over what had occurred, and a word or two, written without definite intention but into which Vyse thought he could read a special meaning, had aroused his own interest in the case. A few hours' personal investigation on the spot would be more valuable than any letters exchanged between himself and Mrs Deane, who with the best intentions was a little incoherent, and Hamberdene Grange was less than two hours from King's Cross Station.

The owner of the Grange received him with great cordiality and evident relief. It was a large, rambling old house, built on to and restored at different periods of its history, standing in a pretty wooded country half a mile from the river Hamber. In the autumn dusk Vyse, from the drawing-room windows, could see a large, well-laid out garden stretching away to high woods on every side, and after dinner, at which the party had been himself, his hostess, her niece, Alice Crayton, and a young man named Ronald Bargrave to whom she was apparently engaged, he plunged into the business before him, asking Mrs Deane for a detailed account of the events resulting in her appeal for his assistance.

'The last tragedy, although sufficiently sad in itself, had nothing about it that would have justified me in making demands upon your time,' she began, leading him to where a couple of chairs stood invitingly beside an open window. 'Alice and Ronald have vanished as usual into the smoking-room,' she interpolated with a smile. 'They are to be married next month. After coffee has been brought in we shan't be interrupted, and the story is a long one,' she added as the door opened to admit the butler with the tray.

Vyse noticed his hand shook slightly as he handed the coffee.

'Yes,' Mrs Deane remarked as he left the room, 'we are all a good bit shaken, and not the least old Milsom, who has known the poor girl since she was baby—as, indeed, we all have. A dear, sweet child, just fifteen, and as pretty as a picture. She was my gardener's daughter'—she put down the empty cup and faced Vyse earnestly—'and she was found dead in the wood about half a mile from here yesterday morning.'

'What was the cause of death?' Vyse asked.

'Apparently, just heart failure. But there was nothing what-ever to account for it, beyond a curiously fixed expression of acute fear in the eyes, which were open. She was found lying against a large stone close to the pool by one of the keepers, and his story is confirmed by the local policeman. Exactly the same description was given me by both of them. The girl had never had anything wrong with her heart. The doctor said a terrible fright or shock might have caused it. But no one knows what the shock could have been—at least—'

She hesitated.

'Please be quite frank, Mrs Deane,' Vyse urged. 'You said some-thing about the pool in your letter.'

'I was coming to that. She was found close what they call here the dark pool. Tradition says it's haunted—but Alice laughs at me so if I mention it that I am rather shy of doing so. Certainly enough tragedies have taken place on the edge of it to account for any num-ber of stories. No one will go near it after dark, and no one knows what took Amy Trevor there—or ever will, I suppose. It may have been curiosity, or she may have lost her way in the dusk.'

'Had she fallen into the pool? Were her clothes wet?' Vyse asked. 'That might have accounted for the fright.'

'No. Her clothes were quite dry. As a matter of fact, she was not actually by the water's edge, but had fallen across the big stone close by it.'

'Tell me about the history of the place.' Vyse rose to put his empty cup on a table. 'Is the pool in the wood over there?' he asked, pointing to some high trees on the left of the gardens.

'Yes, in the very centre. In summer the sunshine never pen-etrates the heavy leafage and undergrowth. I only went there once, out of pure curiosity, and I never wish to go again. It's a dismal-looking place—just a huge, moss-grown stone and the horrid, dark pool.'

She shivered slightly.

'And its past history?' Vyse reminded her, still standing at the window.

'The last event was even more sensational but less inexplicable,' Mrs Deane went on. 'A man murdered his sweetheart about two years ago. Stabbed her with a knife, left her there lying dead, and went straight into the village and gave himself up. He seemed half distracted at what he had done. That mystery was never solved; he managed to do away with himself before the trial came on. Then, before that, a woman was found there—heart failure from fright—just the same as poor Amy Trevor. What is it they see, Mr Vyse, that frightens them so?'

She broke off, staring at him curiously.

'That is what I am here to find out,' he replied with a smile, looking out over the woods. 'There is nothing to prove, so far, they saw anything. Perhaps—but I can tell you more after I have seen the place myself.'

'We have a history of the property—*Hamberdene and Its Traditions* it is called; the place is mentioned in the Domesday Book. I'll look it out for you, if you like. It was published about forty years ago.'

'Thank you; it may be of use. I will take it up to my room with me and study it tonight, if you don't mind,' Vyse replied, turning away from the window. 'Its past history might prove very elucidating in unraveling the present.'

Alice Crayton and young Bargrave coming into the room at this moment, the conversation drifted into desultory discussion of the possible explanation of the tragedies. Miss Crayton being of the placid, complacent type that is quite content with the limited range of vision that is its heritage, did not believe in 'ghosts', and ruled out anything that could not be confirmed by her own five senses. She was careful to be quite nice about it, to say nothing likely to hurt their guest's susceptibility—Vyse knew the type, unimaginative and without a suspicion that at times her own opinion might be wrong. She was evidently satisfied that a verdict of heart failure left further investigation unnecessary.

'Brought on by a vivid imagination and possibly something indigestible for dinner,' she explained gently.

'I don't see how something indigestible for dinner explains the murders,' Mrs Deane retorted a little sharply. 'If so, when a man commits murder you have better hang his cook.'

Alice Crayton smiled.

'That is rather overstating the question, isn't it? After all, most people die of heart failure in some form or other, don't they?'

'So I have been told,' her aunt replied drily, 'but everybody doesn't die of a stab in the back, which is another form of the tragedies in the pool. Mr Vyse,' she went on, turning to her guest, and disregarding Alice, who shook her head with a smile, gently indulgent of her aunt's folly, 'you will wish to visit the spot first thing in the morning. I will tell Binks, the under-gardener, to show you the way; he is the only man on the place at this moment who would go near the pool, and even he would jib at it after dark.'

But Vyse had other plans in view. He bid his hostess and Miss Crayton good night, and watched them mount the stairs, the latter babbling complacently of village superstitions to her aunt, who apparently paid no attention, before following Bargrave into the smoking-room.

'Do you know the way to this place in the wood?' he asked, closing the door behind him, 'and are you game to take me there now? I don't want to lose time, and I may just as well begin investigations now as wait till tomorrow.'

'Right you are,' was the cheerful assent; 'there's a lantern in the hall. I'm game enough but,' he laughed, and Vyse rather liked the frank, open look of him, 'to tell the square-toed truth, I don't much believe in the ghost idea. It's better to be honest,' he added deprecatingly, 'but I'll come with you like a shot. Perhaps there is something in it after all—the occult, or whatever you call it, and all that.'

Vyse assented to this somewhat vague premise, and a few minutes later, their evening clothes exchanged for tweeds, armed with sticks and the lantern, they crept through the smoking-room window on to the upper terrace of the garden and started for the woods.

The fates were with them. The rain had stopped and, as they slipped through a gate leading from the gardens into the wood, the moon emerged from the drifting mist overhead in full glory, and Bargrave remarked the lantern would hardly be required after all.

'Though it's dark enough at the pool in broad daylight, so it's just as well we've got it. I don't mind confessing to you,' he lowered his voice confidentially, 'that, although I don't believe in spooks and that sort of thing, I get an awful eerie feeling sometimes—a sort of feeling there's someone else in the room—when there isn't. You know?'

'Yes, I know,' Vyse assented, 'you are more sensitive than you realise, sensitive to the unseen influences around you. We are all so more or less. Every action, every vivid thought leaves its mark behind it in the ether—its special vibration, and some of us are quicker to respond to them than others.'

'I wrote a letter once,' Bargrave went on, 'that I didn't mean to a bit. I was just playing about with a pencil, and somehow a lot of words got written on the paper—it seemed a sort of message. I said I had done it without knowing, but Alice said it was absurd; everybody did, and no one would believe I wasn't taking them in. But I swear I don't know how those words came on the paper. But, of course, that's different to spooks,' he added hurriedly.

'These vibrations left on the ether,' Vyse went on, 'attract entities good or evil, as the case may be, who have attuned themselves on this plane to that particular rate, and who add the urge of their own desires to the vibrating ether, resulting in a strong wake of influence either for good or evil to those among us who are sensitive enough to be aware of them.'

'That sounds all right,' the other assented, 'but it's a bit deep.'

'It is not really difficult to understand when you analyse it. What is the influence we undoubtedly exert upon one another on this physical plane caused by? Surely by the impingement of vibrations generated by chemical changes in the brain tissues, set in action by an effort of the will? Why should it be more difficult to believe that such influences can be exercised through vibrations set in action on more subtle planes, and reaching us through that link between mind and matter, the nervous centres of the brain?'

Bargrave laughed.

'Well, I am willing to take your word for it, and certainly one is sometimes conscious of influences that one doesn't know how to account for. Such as when I wrote that message, you know.'

'Don't give in to them blindly,' the other remarked seriously. 'Be always master of yourself. Use them intelligently, but be master of them—not their slave. That is how bad habits are formed, allowing them to master you. Some people deliberately train themselves to respond to these vibrations bombarding us from the super-physical world; when they succeed—in olden days they used to be called magicians; now they are called swindlers,' he finished gravely.

Bargrave looked at him quickly; then, responding to the look of quiet amusement on Vyse's face, laughed.

'Well, I can't quite swallow it all myself. But here we are. Gruesome sort of hole, isn't it?'

Vyse looked round, his interest concentrated on the matter in hand.

It certainly was an uninviting spot. Tall trees interlaced their branches overhead so densely that, although autumn was already thinning the heavy leafage, only here and there a shaft of pale moonlight straggled through, making mottled patterns on the moss and rank undergrowth. Where a beech stem with ghostly gleam stood guard beside a crooked thorn-brush, a sullen glint of water drew Vyse's attention to the pool of ill repute, still, dark, lifeless; a few yards beyond it a stone six or seven feet long, by three or four wide, oblong in shape, caught a wandering ray of moonlight, that lit up the grey, lichen-grown surface with a faint gleam, one end of it disappearing in the tangle and scrub of the wood's undergrowth.

Vyse made his way carefully round the pool, avoiding the treacherous edge of it hidden by moss and reeds, and seating himself on the stone, gazed thoughtfully at the dark blot of stagnant water that had earned for itself so undesirable a reputation. Bargrave stood where he was, watching, ready to light the lantern if required, but Vyse was apparently lost in thought, his hand moving restlessly over the moss-stained surface of the grey boulder, his eyes fixed on the dark splash of water that lay between them. After a few moments, the silence, the mottled moonlight, the remembrance of the scenes of death and terror enacted on the spot got on the other's nerves; he moved restlessly, then cried:

'I say, do you want the lantern? I'll light it, if you like. Let's get out of this beastly hold as we can—it's—it's—well, the place is enough to get on a chap's nerves, let alone spooks—which, of course, are all rot!' he added irritably.

To his surprise, Vyse rose at once.

'I am quite ready,' he assented cheerfully, picking his way back round the pool. 'I know all I want to know, so we'll get back. I think we ought to apologise to the pool,' he laughed; 'it has been much maligned.'

Bargrave turned with obvious relief.

'Of course, it's all rubbish. Alice has always said so, and she has a lot of common sense. The murders and things were just accidents. I am very glad you agree with me.'

'I didn't say I think it all rubbish,' Vyse protested; but as his companion seemed disinclined to continue the conversation, he let it drop.

To Mrs Deane's astonishment her visitor refused the offer of Binks as guide the following morning, announcing his intention at breakfast of returning to London by an early train. He explained how he and Ronald Bargrave had visited the scene of the tragedies overnight by moonlight, that he had learnt quite as much of the mysteries of the pool as he was likely to learn, and that, if he might take the history of Hamberdene away with him for careful perusal, he would communicate with her in a day or two.

With this she was forced to be content, for neither pointed inquiry nor judicious probing could extract any hint of further discovery, and Vyse left the room to put his things together.

Alice Crayton smiled cryptically.

'We don't seem much further on, do we?' she observed to no one in particular. 'What happened last night, Ronald? Incantations and all the rest of it, dark mutterings, and the exorcising of demons?' she laughed lightly. 'Tell us what interesting ceremonies took place by the light of the moon.'

'Vyse sat on the stone for about five minutes and looked at the pool, and never said a word,' Bargrave answered shortly, rising from the table to open the door for Mrs Deane. 'Then we came away.'

'Very impressive,' Alice retorted, with gentle sarcasm; 'and you never saw a spook at all? Not even the ghost of a spook?'

Mrs Deane turned at the door.

'You think you know all there is to know, Alice, and that your opinion is worth a lot,' she said slowly; 'and you look upon Mr Vyse with a sort of indulgent contempt. You are hedged round in a narrow complacency of your own making. Some day you will realise, perhaps, you are as a man born blind is to those who can see. If he doesn't choose to believe them, they can never prove to him that the sky is blue or a rose red. He is entirely content with his own limitations. But they *know*."

'Quite a long sentence for Aunt Jean,' Alice observed, as Mrs Deane closed the door behind her. 'I think this pool business is getting on her nerves.'

Four days later Vyse sat in his rooms in the pleasant London suburb, with the history of Hamberdene on the table, and pen and paper before him. The window stood open, in spite of a chill already creeping into the autumn sunshine. Across the lawn, the peacock trailed the glory of his shining feathers.

'Dear Mrs Deane,' he began, 'I hasten to give the conclusions I have to after a careful study of that part of the history relating to the pool, and my visit to it on Monday last. It is extremely interesting, and, to anyone acquainted with the working of the less obvious laws of Nature, very illuminating.

'To begin with, you will notice the series of tragedies associated with the spot recur in two forms, with hardly any variation—the victim succumbs either from heart failure, due, it would seem, from the expression of the eyes, to terror, or to a stab with a knife or other sharp instrument. In the most recent case—that of Amy Trevor—the cause was fear, as no sign of violence was present. I notice there have been in all eight known occurrences of the sort on the spot mentioned in the history, and two at dates since the history was written, at intervals varying from a few months to long stretches of years. A bad record indeed, and one to give the most casual observer pause; hardly to be attributed to either accident or coincidence. Among them all one only was the case of suicide— William Angerson, in 1785, took his own life. In 1822, Robert Jephson, it would seem, was hung for stabbing his cousin, John Ablin, at the pool, for apparently no motive; he gave none himself, nor could any likely one be discovered. Otherwise the victims seem to have been women. The earliest record I see carries the tradition of the pool tragedies back as far as 1369; beyond that date the history is silent on the subject. What the tale would be if complete, who can tell?

'From my observations on the spot, I feel sure the mischief neither lies in, nor emanates from, the pool; also that there is a remedy, but I must give you my reasons—'

The opening of the door, to admit a maid with the second post, made an interruption at this moment, and Vyse laid down his pen. The letters were three in number, and he noticed the last was in Mrs Deane's handwriting. He rose, and stepped over the low sill of the window to read his correspondence in the sunshine. The peacock, with a swish of bronze and blue feathers, ran forward, strutting across the graveled path with spasmodic dart and twist of its head in greeting. Vyse stopped mechanically, offering a hand for the bird to peck at, and retire disappointed in the absence of the usual dainty morsel; then he opened the letter and read.

It was only an appeal for news. What conclusion had Mr Vyse come to? Did he think another visit to the spot would be advisable? If so, Mrs Deane would be only too glad to see him. Had his wonderful intuition made any sort of discovery, or was the mystery of the pool beyond his power of solution? Must it for ever remain unsolved?

But there was a postscript.

'Robert Bargrave and my niece Alice have determined to do a little investigation on their own account. They are planning to go to the pool tomorrow at dusk, and await this terrible something that frightens people to death. Alice, of course, doesn't believe in it; she considers it her duty to show an example to the village— though I don't quite understand what of—but Ronald has promised me to take his revolver.'

Vyse stood rigidly still for a few seconds, his brows drawn together.

Tomorrow—that was today. The clear transparency of his clear grey eyes was suddenly clouded, and when he looked up from the written page the whole aspect of him had changed into the alertness of the man of action. He stepped back into the room, looked out a train for Lesser Hamberdene—there was a slow one which he could catch if he hastened, dusk would begin to fall about 5.30, even earlier should the evening be dull—and seizing his hat and stick went out in search of a taxi to take him at racing speed to King's Cross. It might be a journey thrown away, but Vyse knew enough not to take any chances.

A few hours later he was standing among the brushwood surrounding the dark, over-shadowed pool in Hamberdene Wood. On the long, grey stone, scarred and stained with age, Alice Crayton was seated, half turned from her companion, Robert Bargrave; the latter stood, facing Vyse, but so utterly absorbed in the working of his own mind as to be unconscious of the intruder.

As Vyse came upon the scene, Miss Crayton was saying in her exasperatingly even voice:

'It's no use trying to frighten me, Ronald, by talking about blood and the rest of it. I dare say my skull would, as you say, smash with a soft thud like an eggshell, but it doesn't sound attractive to me at all.' She laughed quietly. 'If you mean it for a joke, I don't think it the least funny. I told you nothing would happen, and of course, nothing has, and as for the poor fools who died of fright, they were probably the sort who were afraid to say "Boo" to their own shadows. I have no patience with these silly superstitions. Aunt Jean has got it into her head this Mr Vyse is endowed with all sort of powers, which perhaps he himself may imagine he has—I don't mean to say the man is a conscious fraud—but which anyone with two ideas in their head knows to be utter nonsense!'

But Vyse was not listening to Alice Crayton's complacent babblings. He was watching Bargrave warily, prepared for what he felt was coming. Bargrave, too, paid no attention to the placid flow of words beside him; his face was working curiously, his eyes gleaming uncannily in the twilight of the wood. He was putting out a cautious hand to grasp something lying on the lichen-stained surface of the long oblong stone.

But Vyse was too quick for him. With a sudden spring he seized the revolver before the other could touch it, and opening the breach drew out the cartridges and slipped the empty weapon into his pocket.

The two men faced each other. Then Bargrave stammered:

'Good lord! What I was—you—Vyse!' and again he muttered, 'Good lord! It's incredible—I—I—'

He disappeared among the shadows of the tree stems, and Vyse turned to Miss Crayton, who seemed quite unperturbed at the sudden intrusion.

'You, Mr Vyse? Where has Ronald gone? How did you get here?'

'I came by train,' Vyse answered cheerfully. 'You see, I still fancy I may be of use in unravelling the riddle, and another visit to the spot seemed unnecessary. Bargrave has left this little plaything behind, perhaps you will give it back to him if I don't see him myself.'

And he laid the revolver beside her.

'Ronald and I thought we would do a little detecting on our own account,' she said, rising; 'but nothing has happened; no apparition has terrified us into heart failure. But it's growing cold, and I have kept vigil long enough. Won't you come up to the house, Mr Vyse? I am sure my aunt will be very pleased to see you.'

'Thank you, but I must get back. I shouldn't keep any more vigils here if I were you, Miss Crayton, it's a very unhealthy spot.'

'It's a very unattractive one—even if one doesn't altogether believe in supernatural occurrences,' she said gently. 'Do you really and truly believe in them?'

'In what?' he asked shortly.

'In the supernatural?'

'In the *supernatural*? Not for a moment,' he replied, to her astonishment; and lifting his hat disappeared in the direction of the station, muttering with a smile, 'And she doesn't even know the elements of what she is talking about!'

After breakfast on the following morning, and a stroll round the lawn with the peacock in attendance, Vyse finished his letter for Mrs Deane:

'To sensitives whose inner faculties are sufficiently developed to respond to the finer reactions of matter, it is a well-known fact that thought and action can so impress themselves upon the other as to react perceptibly on organisms capable of receiving these delicate impressions. Clear, sharply defined thought resulting in vibratory emanations from the brain cells will crystallise into form perceptible to those who can "see". The energy of strong thought will create strong thought-forms, imbued with the characteristics of and vibrating at the same rate as the emotional impulse that brought it into being. Just as an object can be impregnated with a certain rate of vibrations that will for ever convey to a sensitive "receiver" definite sensations, so can a place, a locality, be so affected through the conditions of the ether surrounding—the crystallised thought—as to affect in its turn the subtle bodies of man in certain circumstances.

'What these circumstances are remains a problem, but a problem, I have no doubt, time and careful investigation will solve. Some are born more susceptible to these hidden influences than others; some respond to them under great emotional stress—physical ill-health, or weakness, or a natural trend of disposition towards the state of mind or morals to which the vibrations are attuned. A man living an evil life will more readily respond to the temptations of evil, and so on. Some deliberately awaken their inner faculties by a method of training, and can respond at all times and at will to these unseen influences by the conscious readjustment of the centre of activity, the physical powers becoming for the moment latent, the more subtle the being brought into play.

'When I visited that extremely unpleasant spot in the wood, I realised at once the mischief did not lie in the pool. The peculiar shape and nature of the stone beyond it drew my attention, and passing my hand over its surface I found the runnel, circular in the centre and running off at the side, which is often to be found in the ancient altar-stones of heathen rites. Taking the tragic associations connected with its history, and the undoubted age of the Hamberdene property, I felt sure that not only had the altar-stone served for the purpose of animal sacrifice, but that human sacrifices had also been perpetrated on the grey, moss-grown slab over and over again. Here you would have two elements continually pouring the stream of their vibratory influence into the recording ether—the thirst for blood and paralysing terror; the former on the part of the operator, the latter of the victim. Think this out, dear Mrs Deane, and you will see the history of the spot bears out every detail of this theory.

'Get rid of the stone. Have it removed at once and dropped into the river. This is my urgent advice, and I think you will find that, although the dark pool may retain its evil character through force of tradition, the bad influences that have undoubtedly haunted the spot will gradually die away in the absence of the focus through which they were concentrated. I can only repeat that, were the property mine, this course should be adopted without delay.'

Vyse said no more, but Mrs Deane was sufficiently impressed by his explanation of the repeated tragedies by the pool to carry out his instructions to the letter. Alice Crayton brought all the force of her common sense to bear against such absurd obedience to superstitious tyranny, not to mention the unnecessary expense. She proved to her own satisfaction that Vyse was the more or less willing victim of mental hallucination, and deplored that so apparently normal a member of society should not make a greater effort to subdue the vagaries of a vivid imagination. She will never know that she probably owed her life to him that evening in the dusk of the wood.

But Ronald Bargrave knows.

THE EYES
OF DOOM

Ella M. Scrymsour

Ella Mary Scrymsour-Nichol, actress and author, was born Ella Mary Campbell-Robertson in Battersea, London, on December 25, 1888. She died in East Sussex in 1962. Very little information exists regarding Scrymsour. She wrote numerous novels, beginning with The Perfect World: A Romance of Strange People and Strange Places *(London, 1922).*

"The Eyes of Doom" is the first of six stories starring Shiela Crerar, who finding herself to be newly penniless, is forced to make her living. She discovers that her gift of second sight—her innate psychic talent—is a gift, indeed. The stories were first published in the Blue Magazine *in 1920, but the magazine folded shortly afterward. Shiela was more or less forgotten until the publication of* Shiela Crerar: Psychic Investigator *(Ash-Tree Press, 2006), which collects all six stories into one volume. If not for her psychic powers, young Shiela would bear some resemblance to such "girl detectives" as Nancy Drew and Kay Tracey, who also sometimes investigate mysteries with a supernatural tinge—although, unlike Shiela's, their mysteries inevitably have a nonsupernatural solution.*

The Eyes of Doom

SHIELA CRERAR FELT VERY LONELY as she sat in her tiny sitting-room in her dreary lodgings. She was tired, too, mentally as well as physically, and she tried to forget the misery of the past six months.

An orphan, she had been brought up by an uncle who idolised her. For twenty-two years she had lived in happiness in their home in the Highlands. She could visualise it now. A smallish house for a laird, built in the true Scottish baronial style, with turreted roof and pepper-box corners and a tiny courtyard. 'Kencraig' was built on the top of a high eminence overlooking Loch Lubnaig, and it had been one of her chief delights to sit among the heather and watch the rippling waters of the lake beneath. To her left was Ben Ledi, and she revelled in his rugged beauty. He stood for strength and chivalry in her young mind, and she always thought of him as a rough but courteous Bruce, with shaggy locks and tartan kilts flying in the wind. It was only a girlish fancy, but to her the Ben was a living personality—nature's gentleman—a Highland chief.

For twenty-two years she had bid him good morning and waved him a good night. For twenty-two years she had wandered among the heather, bathed in the Loch, and driven into Callender once a week to do her shopping. And now—she wondered why this sorrow should have come to her. Six months ago she had been out in the woods gathering rowan berries. She had gone home gay and bright, but there was no welcoming figure of Uncle John waiting at the door for her. She went into his study—and, oh, the horror of it! He was sitting at his desk, his eyes open wide, his mouth twisted sideways, his hands cold. He did not answer her call. She knew he was dead. 'Heart failure,' the doctor said, and Shiela felt that the light had gone out of her world.

The funeral over, she had gone into the library with Mr MacArthur, her uncle's attorney. At first Shiela did not understand what Mr MacArthur was trying to tell her. She couldn't realise that she had been left penniless, with only a heavily mortgaged estate as a legacy. Mr MacArthur advised her to sell Kencraig, pay off the mortgage, and with what little remained over fit herself to take her place among the workers of the great world. But Shiela refused to sell her home. Every stone was precious to her, every corner was a dear, living friend.

At last she agreed to let it on a five years' lease to a rich American widow.

'What do you intend doing now?' he asked.

'I shall have about a hundred pounds. I shall go to London, and try and get something to do there.'

She was obstinate. She procured cheap rooms in London in a road derisively called Air Street. Her hundred pounds did not go far. In vain she tried for work in the great Metropolis; no one wanted her. Depressed and silent, she sat in her little room, and wondered what would happen when her scanty money gave out. She was a petite maid, with nut-brown hair and grey eyes that looked all too trustingly at a cruel and heartless world.

She had no money to spend on amusements, and as she walked the streets of the great city she saw visions of the long ago. She wandered in Lincoln's Inn, and saw the passing of sedan chairs; watched gallants, with silken coat and jewelled sword, bend low before their lady loves. She sought out 'old London', and lived alone in the seventeenth century. Always psychic, her gift seemed trebled in her sorrow and loneliness, and her only friends now were the dim ghosts of the past.

She was sitting in the gardens of Lincoln's Inn one day, when she suddenly became aware of a quaint figure beside her—a wizened man of perhaps sixty years, in a dark, claret-coloured suit, with a black three-cornered hat upon his knee. And as she looked, he took a pinch of snuff from a beautifully enamelled box, and applied it to his nostrils, his little finger delicately poised like a bird on the wing.

'You are sad and lonely, little lady,' he said suddenly. 'Why not help those that are sad and lonely too? You have a gift—a most wonderful gift of sight. Use that sight for your own benefit and the benefit of mankind. I promise you, you will not fail.'

'But how?' she began, but the quaint little figure had gone; and there was only a fat old woman, with an untidy dress and a rusty black bonnet, watching her curiously from the further corner of the seat.

Shiela felt dazed. She rose and looked round. No, she was still in the bustling world of taxis and motor-buses. The picturesque past had vanished. She smiled a little, and went home, but her brain was working hard. She slept well that night, and when morning came her mind was made up.

For the next three days an advertisement appeared in the agony column of *The Times*:

Lady of gentle birth, Scottish, young, penniless, possessing strong psychic powers, will devote her services to the solving of uncanny mysteries or the 'laying of ghosts'. Offer quite genuine. Reply, with particulars and remuneration offered, to S. C. c/o Mrs Barker, 14b Air Street, Regent's Park, London.

And now she was waiting—waiting. Two days had passed since her advertisement had first appeared. A double knock sounded. The postman! A footstep sounded outside, and Mrs Barker appeared.

'A registered letter for you, my dear,' she remarked cheerily. 'I'll be bringing yer supper in 'alf a tick. See, it's a bloater tonight, ain't it? A poor man's steak, I calls it.'

And Shiela shuddered slightly. The well-meant vulgarity repelled her; the stench of cooking fish nauseated her. She felt nervy, restless, ill. The Highlands were calling her—she longed to feel the springy heather under her feet—to drink in the strong air. It was the call of the hills!

She looked at the thick, crested envelope curiously. It was certainly an answer to her advertisement, for it was addressed to her initials—S. C. Slowly she read it, and a flush of excitement crept into her cheeks.

Dunfunerie,
Loch Long, N.B.

If S. C.'s offer is really genuine, will she accept the enclosed £10 on account for immediate expenses, and wire Lady Kildrummie that she is prepared to try to solve, and perhaps lay for ever, the very unpleasant mystery known as the 'Kildrummie Weird'? If S. C. states the time she will arrive at Arrochar Station, Lady Kildrummie will see that there is a car sent to meet her.

Shiela's eyes glowed. Arrochar! Scotland! Her luck had turned at last. She was going back to her beloved Highlands. But would she succeed in her undertaking? Then she remembered the 'little old man' in Lincoln's Inn. 'You will not fail,' he had said. Of course, she had heard of the 'Kildrummie Weird'. Who had not? Was it not as much speculated upon as the hidden mystery of Glamis? Was it not even as mysterious? What was the story—did not some great calamity happen when the Weird appeared?

Next day she wired Lady Kildrummie that she would come at once, and she caught the night train to Glasgow where she changed for the West Highland line. At Arrochar Station, over which Ben Lomond towers, she looked round eagerly.

A tall man in the late thirties came towards her—a handsome man, rugged, strong, in a kilt of the Cameron tartan, his mother's clan.

'Miss Crerar?' he asked, raising his bonnet. 'I am Stavordale Hartland. My aunt, Lady Kildrummie, asked me to meet you.'

His voice was pleasantly tuneful, and the wholesome admiration in his eyes could do nought but please her. Instantly she compared him to rugged Ben Ledi, and, had the man at her side but known, it was the greatest compliment she could have paid him.

Dunfunerie was situate on the Argyllshire side of Loch Long, nestling under the great shoulder of 'The Cobbler' himself. Lady Kildrummie met her with outstretched hands. 'How good of you to come, my dear. Are you by any chance related to Crerar of Kencraig?'

'He was my uncle.'

'Then you are doubly welcome, for Kencraig was my late husband's greatest friend. Now, Stavordale, you can leave Miss Crerar and me to have tea together.'

It was not until they had finished their tea that her hostess commenced her story.

'My dear, I am in great trouble,' she said, by way of starting. 'Your advertisement interested me, and I wondered if you could "lay for ever" the Weird that haunts this place. Up to now the story has been kept absurdly secret—I think none of us wanted to believe in it. Since the time of Coinneach the Strong, in the latter part of the sixteenth century, Kildrummie has been cursed by this Weird. Every twenty-three years some terrible calamity has occurred in the family, preceded for about six months by "The Eyes".'

'The Eyes?'

'Yes, the "Eyes of Doom" they are called. The Kildrummie Weird takes the form of eyes that appear and disappear, and are mainly seen in the west wing. In recent years calamity has fallen on this house after the Eyes have been seen. In 1874, the year I was married, my husband's two elder brothers died—each by his own hand. One was found drowned in the Loch, the other was shot on the summit of the "Cobbler" yonder. At both inquests the verdict was "accidental death", but we all knew better. It was "the Eyes" that had driven them mad. My husband became heir to the title, and in 1897 my eldest son poisoned himself. Again it was put down to an accident. He was dabbling in photography, and it was supposed that he took some cyanide by mistake for his medicine. But it was no accident—twenty-three years had passed, and he had seen "The Eyes". This is 1920, Miss Crerar; it is twenty-three years since Diarmid died, and I am afraid. My son Duncan, the only one left to me, is now twenty-six years old. Lately he has complained of being kept awake at night by curious creakings. He has seen strange lights, and, oh, he is changed. I can't explain what I mean; you will see for yourself; he is all nerves. I am convinced he has seen "The Eyes of Doom". Will you try and solve the mystery for me, Miss Crerar? What the cause is I don't know, but the hideous waiting for some tragedy to fall is terrible.'

'I'll do my best, Lady Kildrummie. I can promise you no more.'

That evening Shiela met Duncan Kildrummie. Although young, he was a distinguished soldier—had won the D.S.O., and been mentioned several times in despatches, and had the reputation among his friends of being a regular dare-devil. But Shiela had a shock when she saw him. His hands were restless, the flesh under his eyes was puffy and dark, and if he was spoken to suddenly his whole body would respond with nervous twitchings.

'Lady Kildrummie,' she said after dinner, 'will you put your son into another room to sleep, and leave his empty for me to examine? I can see he is in a state of great mental distress. Can't you get him to go away for a change?'

'It's no use, Miss Crerar. I have begged him to go away, but nothing will induce him to leave.'

That night Shiela changed into a dark rest-gown, and when everyone had retired to bed she prowled up and down the long corridors armed only with a tiny flash-lamp. She unlocked the chapel door and went inside. Suddenly she felt an icy blast that seemed to pierce through her, and the heavy door closed silently behind her. She felt startled, and tried to open it, but the catch was down on the other side. She was locked in! The sudden gust of wind was not repeated, yet she found she was shivering with cold from head to foot. Always venturesome, the thought never entered her head to find a way of rousing the household. If she was unable to get out, then she would stay in the chapel till day came.

She sat down in one of the old-fashioned pews and looked about her. The moon was conveniently bright, and she could distinguish objects quite clearly by its light.

As she sat she became aware that someone was looking at her, and she turned sharply round.

A pair of eyes was gazing at her, eyes so mournful, so full of grief that Shiela felt her own fill with tears of sympathy.

And as she met the piteous gaze she became suddenly conscious of the fact that the eyes were not framed by a face! She rose with a startled exclamation of horror, and turned away, but to her right another pair of eyes appeared, eyes this time that were mad with hate; eyes so filled with loathing and malevolence that Shiela backed away from them in fear. But now the whole chapel seemed filled with the ghastly sight. Eyes with expression, eyes without! Eyes kind, eyes cruel! Eyes imbecile, eyes fanatical! Eyes with every expression in them that man could conceive.

Shiela put out her hands to beat the swelling mass away, but even as her arms were extended in front of her they were caught in a ghostly vice, and she was dragged to the vestry door.

She was drawn by unseen hands—hands that possessed an unseen body. All that she could see of her captor was two eyes, eyes that shone in the moonlight and that looked at her with cruel menace.

The vestry door swung silently open, and she was dragged through, followed by the eyes. She had no time to look round, for the door that communicated with the west wing, which was always doubly locked and barred, now stood open wide, and through it Shiela was taken.

The west wing was partly a ruin, and the wind whistled through glassless windows and roofless halls. Then the grip of iron relaxed, and she found she was in a small turret chamber, and around her were twenty-three pairs of eyes—all baleful and cruel, except one, and that one pair seemed as if they might belong to a wounded deer, so plaintive were they, so mournful and sad.

Shiela moved towards the door, but the eyes surrounded her. She tried to dodge them, tried to get away from them, but it was impossible. She was as keenly guarded as if by living bodies. Then she grew really frightened, terrified, her brain seemed to go numb, her teeth chattered, and she cried aloud in her agony of dread. But the eyes grew fiercer and more cruel—they seemed to menace her. With a cry she threw herself at the bodiless terrors, and all became dark.

For awhile she remembered nothing, then she was conscious that she was being carried down long corridors and up steep stairs. There was the sound of a click, and a voice said, 'Do you want anything, Miss Crerar? I heard you call out, so I came across to you.' It was Lady Kildrummie.

'I'm thirsty,' cried Shiela, 'and, oh, please, Lady Kildrummie, will you put the light on.'

But Lady Kildrummie stared in amazement, for she had switched on the electric light as she entered the room! She bent over the girl. Her eyes were open wide, but they met her gaze with a cold stare. The sight had gone!

'My dear, my dear,' she breathed, 'what has happened?'

'I—I hardly know. I—I was in the chapel—oh, do please put on the light. It is so dark here.'

Tenderly the elder woman put her arms about the girl.

'Tell me first what is the matter,' she said gently. 'The dark is so peaceful, and I am here with you.'

Incoherently Shiela spoke. 'I was in the chapel—through the turret room. There were twenty-three eyes—' The girl's voice trailed off. She seemed to be in a stupor, but her eyes were still wide open. Lady Kildrummie rang a bell.

'Tell Doctor Graeme to come here at once,' she said to the startled maid. 'Miss Crerar is ill.'

The genial doctor, a guest in the house, came hurriedly and examined the girl.

'She's had a shock,' he said.

'Her eyes! Her eyes!' cried Lady Kildrummie, distractedly.

'My God! Blind! But she was all right at dinner!' said the doctor.

That night a watchful vigil was kept over Shiela, and when the sun rose she awoke from her torpor and looked at Lady Kildrummie in amazement.

'What is the matter?' she asked, curiously. 'Why are you here?'

And her hostess realised that she had regained the power of sight. When the doctor saw her he stared at her in amazement.

'My dear young lady, why, I—I—bless my soul—there's nothing wrong with her!'

Shiela told Lady Kildrummie of her experience in the night, but her hostess smiled.

'You have certainly described the turret room, Miss Crerar, but you couldn't have got into it last night, as I hold the key.'

'But I did,' protested Shiela. 'The door was open wide.'

'Well, we will go and look at it as soon as you are up, but I assure you it would be quite impossible for anyone to open the door without my key.'

'Now,' said Lady Kildrummie later, 'you see this door is twice bolted and twice locked.'

The bolts were stiff and the key turned with great difficulty, but the nail-studded door swung open at last. Shiela gave a little cry of triumph. The floor, thickly coated with the dust of ages, was marked by freshly made footprints—footprints of long, pointed boots that crossed and recrossed each other—and among the old-fashioned prints were some made by a little, light modern shoe.

Shiela took hers off, and bent down to the mark nearest the door. It fitted exactly!

'I was here last night,' she whispered, hysterically.

But Lady Kildrummie was almost speechless, and terror shone in her eyes. 'The Eyes of Doom,' she muttered, hoarsely. 'God help us, for our troubles are beginning.'

That night as Shiela was preparing for bed again the melancholy eyes appeared. She looked at them fearfully. It was an awe-inspiring sight to watch those expressive eyes move about, propelled by an unseen force. They seemed to float in the air, and she knew their power of locomotion rested in the bodies that were hidden from her sight. And even as she waited the other eyes manifested themselves. She tried to resist, but the ghostly hands were too strong, and again she was taken to the turret room. A circle of eyes was around her— eyes on a level with her own, but only space above them and space below. But they seemed less malignant, less cruel, though terrifying nevertheless. They seemed to be trying to tell her something, but she was unable to read their message. She was nervous, she was on the defensive, and unconsciously she rendered herself out of tune with the Weird. She was not in a fit psychic state to understand them. She was in too material a condition. The eyes seemed to realise this, and they grew menacing again, fretful, impatient. Again there came to the girl a space of forgetfulness, and when she awoke to realities she was back in her room, and she realised she was blind!

She moved uncertainly about the room. Everything seemed unfamiliar to her, unreal. Her eyes hurt her, they seemed inflamed, they were sore. All night long the pain was unbearable, and she sat on a chair, helpless and miserable. But as the dawn came so a veil seemed to be lifted from her eyes, and she could see once more. It was a blindness that came with the darkness and went with the morning light.

During the day Shiela was trying to get into communion with the astral world. She was trying to fit herself to 'see' even deeper into the mysteries of the 'unknown'. It was her first trial alone, and she was gradually becoming fitted for the task she had set herself.

Daily Duncan Kildrummie grew more silent, more morose, more taciturn. The Kildrummie Weird was trying to claim him as its victim, and he realised it and knew he was too weak to hold out against it for long. Soon he, too, would die—and die 'accidentally', as so many members of his family had done.

The eyes grew more venturesome. One night a pair hovered over the dinner table, and gazed at Duncan intently. All saw them, and as Lady Kildrummie screamed in terror they disappeared. But Duncan rose, and stumbled blindly out of the room. Stavordale went quickly after him, and found his cousin staring at the cold waters of the Loch. He was staring, staring, and there was a look of madness in his eyes. The next night several pairs circled round him. He tried to beat them off, but they seemed always just out of his reach, and their expression mocked him.

Stavordale Hartland attached himself to Shiela, and she found his strong personality a great help to her in the nerve-racking time she was going through. Night after night when the eyes claimed her she found she was a helpless entity in their grasp. And in the turret room they supplicated, entreated, menaced her, and still she was unable to read their meaning.

And daily the eyes seemed to appear more often. They followed Duncan from room to room, they drove him out of the house, and he would disappear for hours at a time, and his mother's heart would ache with apprehension.

One night Shiela resolved not to go to bed, and Lady Kildrummie and Stavordale agreed to sit up all night with her in the library. For Shiela had come to dread the period of blindness that was forced upon her in so mysterious a way, and she wondered if in company she would be strong enough to resist the ghostly hands.

First one pair of eyes appeared, and then another, until all twenty-three pairs surrounded the trio. As if turned to stone, Lady Kildrummie and Stavordale Hartland watched Shiela forcibly dragged out of the room. They could neither move nor speak, and when Shiela returned to them she found that three helpless people would have to stay in the library until dawn, for this time they were all blind!

Next night Shiela and Stavordale were standing together watching Duncan walking restlessly up and down the terrace.

'Don't you think you had better give all this up, little girl?' said Stavordale Hartland, and his voice held a tender, caressing note.

'I can't,' she said, passionately. 'Look at him. He is all his mother has. Can't you see the Eyes are driving him mad? The Weird will claim another victim unless I can prevent it.' And even as she spoke the evil eyes appeared, phosphorescent in the darkness, and with a wild shriek Duncan Kildrummie fled into the blackness of the night. Until the morning he roamed the country at large, and when he appeared at breakfast he was haggard and worn, and the most inexperienced eye could tell that he was really ill.

Shiela alone seemed to have a soothing effect upon him, and when later in the day Dr Graeme administered a sleeping draught, he suggested that Shiela should sit by his bedside until it took effect. Lady Kildrummie left her for a moment, and immediately Shiela was conscious that the Eyes were watching her.

Before she realised it she was in the turret room, and she found she was numb from head to foot—she was powerless to move. As she watched, the eyes suddenly materialised into men. Gradually their bodies appeared until twenty-two men in doublet and hose stood before her. Their garments were of silk and velvet—rich, costly, gay. And the twenty-third of that ghostly company was a girl, almost a child of not more than fifteen years. Her hair was unbound and her face distorted with grief, and she clung piteously to a black-bearded man of middle age. A ghostly play began, and all the while Shiela watched with increasing horror. Others appeared on the scene— men in kilt and plaid, with dirks drawn, dirks red with blood. Roughly the girl was torn from the arms of her father and bound with hempen ropes.

The scenes that followed were hideous to behold, and Shiela knew that there was a power at work that compelled her to watch.

The captive girl writhed and tore at her bonds, but all to no purpose—they were too cunningly tied. Not a word was said aloud, but the agonised expressions, the black terror spoke louder than words.

Two ghostly figures in black carried in a red-hot brazier; the coal burned and seemed to splutter, yet made no sound. Two long irons were placed in the glowing coals. The prisoners made a desperate effort to overpower their captors; for a few moments the whole place was in confusion, but gradually their efforts were subdued, and one by one they were dragged to the fire. One by one the red-hot iron was plunged into their eyes, one by one they were blinded and flung aside to die.

Shiela watched twenty-two men done to death in this awful way. She watched their agonies of pain, their writhings, their torments, and the scene was all the more horrible because of the deathly silence that accompanied it.

There was but one more victim—the girl. Roughly she was dragged to the brazier, but a merciful Providence intervened, she stumbled and fell, and when a man roughly turned her over with his foot he found the gentle spirit had fled.

The assassins looked round the room at the dead, and even as they did so the scene changed, and Shiela found she was out in the chestnut avenue, standing before the giant tree, the pride of Dunfunerie. The rain poured down in torrents, the wind blew hard, her dress clung to her figure and chilled her, her shoes were covered with mud. A black-cowled monk approached, with beads and breviary. Horror came into his countenance as he stumbled over the still warm bodies. He touched the girl in gentle pity, but he was jostled away rudely. He opened his book, and Shiela could see that he was pleading to be allowed to say a prayer over the bodies. A huge man struck him, and as he picked himself up he silently cursed the murderers. He cursed them on the Holy Book, but they jeered in his face and continued their nefarious work.

There under the spreading chestnut tree a pit was dug, and, with neither prayer nor priest, into it the girl was flung. Then followed the other twenty-three. The hole was small—the bodies protruded above the sides. With a ribald smile on his cruel face, the menacing figure in black forced the ground to receive them. The pit was covered in with earth, the murdered ones were safely hidden away, and Shiela realised she had witnessed a scene that had taken place some three hundred years before, a scene that had been re-enacted for her benefit. At last she knew what 'the Eyes' had tried to tell her.

The figures died away, they seemed to be absorbed into the atmosphere itself, and once more only twenty-three pairs of eyes were left, but they were eyes that looked at her with gratitude. They knew she understood.

And as she watched them, too, fade away she was conscious that her limbs were once more warm. She looked round in bewilderment—there on the bed lay the sleeping form of Duncan Kildrummie. She was back in his room. She felt her dress—it was quite dry. Her shoes had no trace of mud upon them. Lady Kildrummie entered.

'My dear, I'm sorry,' she said, 'I am afraid I have been rather a long time. Why' she broke off, 'what's the matter?' For Shiela was gazing at the open door, and her expression was soft and pitiful. But Lady Kildrummie could not see the figure of a frail young girl, dressed in a soft homespun with a white kerchief round her shoulders, a girl who looked at Shiela with thanks in her soft brown eyes.

'I think I shall be able to help you lay your "Weird" successfully, Lady Kildrummie,' said Shiela. 'I'll tell you later, after I have had time to think.' Next day a small party gathered underneath the chestnut tree. The turf was smooth and velvety—it had grown undisturbed for many centuries, but now it was being removed.

'Ah!' said Shiela, suddenly, for as the spade dug deep into the rich brown earth a skeleton arm appeared. Reverently the mould was moved. Twenty-two skeletons were unearthed, twenty-two skeletons of full-grown men, but at the bottom of the pit was a tiny skeleton, a skeleton crushed and broken. And Shiela knew it was the last remains of the girl—the Weird with the mournful eyes!

Reverently the bones were placed in an empty stone sarcophagus in the little chapel, and reverently the minister spoke the prayers for the dead. And as the last amen was said, Shiela heard an unseen choir burst out in song. It was the 'Gloria in Excelsis Deo'.

Lady Kildrummie drew her cloak about her shoulders. 'Do you hear the wind whistling?' she asked. Shiela smiled. She knew.

Six weeks later Duncan Kildrummie was up for the first time, after a serious attack of brain fever, during which for some days his life had been in the balance. But now the nervous twitchings were entirely gone, and his eye was clear and steady.

'And you think we are free of the "Weird" at last?' asked Lady Kildrummie, as she was bidding Shiela goodbye.

'I hope so. I don't know the history of the turret room, but I should say the twenty-three were trapped there, and perhaps for religious reasons were foully murdered by some of your forebears. They were refused a Christian burial, and that accounted for their hatred and their hauntings. Their poor spirits were unable to rest in peace. Every twenty-three years—their number—they returned, but they could not make themselves understood.'

Stavordale accompanied Shiela to Glasgow. He was very silent during the journey, but as the train was drawing into the city he suddenly took one of her hands.

'Miss Crerar—Shiela—I—I—won't you give all this up?' he urged.

'I—I can't, Mr Hartland.'

'But why? Shiela, won't you be my wife?'

'I—I can't explain, but I have a mission to fulfil. I have set myself a task, and I must complete it.' She smiled at him. 'Won't you wait a little?'

'Then you do care,' he said, triumphantly, as he sought to draw her towards him, but the train had already stopped at the platform of the Glasgow terminus. Then all was bustle and rush, and it was not until he had said goodbye to her as she left for Edinburgh, where she had engaged rooms, that he realised she had not replied to his question!

Well, perhaps the time was not yet ripe for his love-making, but he realised whate'er might befall he had met his fate. And, like a knight in the 'days of long ago', the wish of his lady was his law. He would bide her time, impatient though he might be.

THE RETURN OF
THE RITUAL

Dion Fortune

Dion Fortune (1890–1946) is the nom de plume of Violet Mary Firth, among the most significant occultists of the first half of the 20th century. Her works continue to influence the Western Esoteric Tradition, as well as modern witchcraft, Wicca, and Neo-Paganism. She adapted her family's motto, "Deo, non Fortuna" ("God, not Fortune"), to serve as her magical name and her pen name. A prolific author, she published books and pamphlets on many topics, including magic, vegetarianism, contraception, and psychic self-defense, in addition to mystical fiction. Fortune was also a respected psychiatrist and a dedicated ceremonial magician—things shared in common with her occult detective, Dr. Taverner.

Born in Bryn-y-Bia, Llandudno, North Wales, Fortune began demonstrating mediumistic abilities from a very early age, reputedly having dreams and visions of Atlantis by age four and later claiming to have been a priestess there in a previous life. Fortune was briefly involved with Helena Blavatsky's Theosophical Society (see "The Cave of the Echoes" on page 65) and, in 1919, was initiated into the Hermetic Order of the Golden Dawn. However, Fortune disliked mingling Eastern and Western traditions, rendering both Theosophy and the Golden Dawn unsatisfying to her. She left the Golden Dawn in 1927 to found what is now the Society of the Inner Light. Her own philosophy was based on a foundation of mystical Christianity and British mythology, especially the Arthurian Grail mythos.

The fictional character Dr. John Richard Taverner was reputedly inspired by Dr. Theodore Moriarty, who trained Fortune when she was working as a lay Freudian analyst around the time of World War I and who specialized in what she called astro-etheric psychological conditions. Moriarty inspired her to pursue her interests in occultism. He died in 1921. The first Dr. Taverner stories appeared in

1922 in Royal Magazine. *"The Return of the Ritual" is the second story in the series. Dr. Rhodes, Taverner's assistant, narrates the stories and plays Watson to Taverner's Holmes. The stories were collected and published together in 1926 as* The Secrets of Dr. Taverner, *becoming the first of Fortune's six books of esoteric fiction.*

The Return of the Ritual

IT WAS TAVERNER'S CUSTOM, at certain times and seasons, to do what I should call hypnotize himself; he, however, called it 'going subconscious,' and declared that, by means of concentration, he shifted the focus of his attention from the external world to the world of thought. Of the different states of consciousness to which he thus obtained access, and of the work that could be performed in each one, he would talk by the hour, and I soon learnt to recognize the phases he passed through during this extraordinary process.

Night after night I have watched beside the unconscious body of my colleague as it lay twitching on the sofa while thoughts that were not derived from his mind influenced the passive nerves. Many people can communicate with each other by means of thought, but I had never realized the extent to which this power was employed until I heard Taverner use his body as the receiving instrument of such messages.

One night while he was drinking some hot coffee I had given him (for he was always chilled to the bone after these performances) he said to me: 'Rhodes, there is a very curious affair afoot.'

I inquired what he meant.

'I am not quite sure,' he replied. 'There is something going on which I do not understand, and I want you to help me to investigate it.'

I promised my assistance, and asked the nature of the problem.

'I told you when you joined me,' he said, 'that I was a member of an occult brotherhood, but I did not tell you anything about it, because I am pledged not to do so, but for the purpose of our work together I am going to use my discretion and explain certain things to you.

'You know, I daresay, that we make use of ritual in our work. This is not the nonsense you may think it to be, for ritual has a profound effect on the mind. Anyone who is sufficiently sensitive can feel vibrations radiating whenever an occult ceremonial is being performed. For instance, I have only got to listen mentally for a moment to tell whether one of the Lhassa Lodges is working its terrific ritual.

'When I was subconscious just now I heard one of the rituals of my own Order being worked, but worked as no Lodge I have ever sat in would perform it. It was like a rendering of Tschaikowsky picked out on the piano with one finger by a child, and unless I am very much mistaken, some unauthorized person has got hold of that ritual and is experimenting with it.'

'Someone has broken his oath and given away your secrets,' I said.

'Evidently,' said Taverner. 'It has not often been done, but instances have occurred, and if any of the Black Lodges, who would know how to make use of it, should get hold of the ritual the results might be serious, for there is great power in these old ceremonies, and while that power is safe in the hands of the carefully picked students whom we initiate, it would be a very different matter in those of unscrupulous men.'

'Shall you try to trace it?' I inquired.

'Yes,' said Taverner, 'but it is easier said than done. I have absolutely nothing to guide me. All I can do is to send round word among the Lodges to see whether a copy is missing from their archives; that will narrow our zone of search somewhat.'

Whether Taverner made use of the post or of his own peculiar methods of communication I do not know, but in a few days' time he had the information he required. None of the carefully guarded rituals was missing from any of the Lodges, but when search was made among the records at headquarters it was discovered that a ritual had been stolen from the Florentine Lodge during the middle ages by the custodian of the archives and sold (it was believed) to the Medici; at any rate, it was known to have been worked in Florence during the latter half of the fifteenth century. What became of it after the Medician manuscripts were dispersed at the plundering of Florence by the French was never known; it was lost sight of and was believed to have been destroyed. Now, however, after the lapse of so many centuries someone was waking its amazing power.

As we were passing down Harley Street a few days later, Taverner asked me if I would mind turning aside with him into the Marylebone Lane, where he wished to call at a second-hand bookshop. I was surprised that a man of the type of my colleague should patronize such a place, for it appeared to be stocked chiefly with tattered paper covered Ouidas and out-of-date piousness, and the alacrity with which the shopboy went to fetch the owner showed that my companion was a regular and esteemed customer.

The owner when he appeared was an even greater surprise than his shop; unbelievably dusty, his frock-coat, beard and face all appeared to be of a uniform grey-green, yet when he spoke his voice was that of a cultured man, and, though my companion addressed him as an equal, he answered as to a superior.

'Have you received any reply to the advertisement I asked you to insert for me?' asked Taverner of the snuff-coloured individual who confronted us.

'I have not; but I have got some information for you—you are not the only purchaser in the market for the manuscript.'

'My competitor being—?'

'A man named Williams.'

'That does not tell us very much.'

'The postmark was Chelsea,' said the old bookseller with a significant look.

'Ah!' said my employer. 'If that manuscript should come into the market I will not limit you as to price.'

'I think we are likely to have a little excitement,' observed Taverner as we left the shop, its dust-covered occupant bowing behind us. 'The Chelsea Black Lodges have evidently heard what I heard and are also making a bid for the ritual.'

'You do not suppose that it is one of the Chelsea Lodges that has got it at the present moment?' I inquired.

'I do not,' said Taverner, 'for they would have made a better job of it. Whatever may be said against their morals, they are not fools, and know what they are about. No, some person or group of persons who dabbles in the occult without any real knowledge has got hold of that manuscript. They know enough to recognize a ritual when they see it, and are playing about with it to see what will happen. Probably no one would be more astonished than they if anything *did* happen.

'Were the ritual confined to such hands as those I should not be worried about it; but it may get into the possession of people who will know how to use it and abuse its powers, and then the consequences will be much more serious than you can realize. I will even go so far as to say that the course of civilization would be affected if such a thing occurred.'

I saw that Taverner was profoundly moved. Regardless of traffic he plunged into the roadway, making a bee-line for his rooms.

'I would give any price for that manuscript if I could lay my hands on it, and if it were not for sale I would not hesitate to steal it; but how in the name of Heaven am I to trace the thing?'

We had regained the consulting-room, and Taverner was pacing up and down the floor with long strides. Presently he took up the telephone and rang up his Hindhead nursing home and told the matron that we should be spending the night in Town. As there was no sleeping accommodation at the house in Harley Street, where he had his London headquarters, I guessed that a night of vigil was in contemplation.

I was fairly used to these watch-nights now; I knew that my duty would be to guard Taverner's vacated body while his soul ranged through outer darkness on some strange quest of its own and talked to its peers—men who were also able to leave their bodies at will and walk the starry ways with him, or others who had died centuries ago, but were still concerned with the welfare of their fellow men whom they had lived to serve.

We dined at a little restaurant in a back street off Soho, where the head waiter argued metaphysics in Italian with Taverner between courses, and returned to our Harley Street quarters to wait until the great city about us should have gone to sleep and left the night quiet for the work we were about to embark upon. It was not till well after midnight that Taverner judged the time was suitable, and then he settled himself upon the broad consulting-room couch, with myself at his feet.

In a few minutes he was asleep, but as I watched him I saw his breathing alter, and sleep gave way to trance. A few muttered words, stray memories of his previous earthly lives, came from his lips; then a deep and sibilant breath marked a second change of level, and I saw that he was in the state of consciousness that occultists use when they communicate with each other by means of telepathy. It was exactly like 'listening in' with a wireless telephone; Lodge called to Lodge across the deeps of the night, and the passive brain picked up the vibrations and passed them on to the voice, and Taverner spoke.

The jangle of messages, however, was cut off in the middle of a sentence. This was not the level on which Taverner meant to work to-night. Another sibilant hiss announced that he had gone yet deeper into the hypnotic condition. There was a dead stillness in the room, and then a voice that was not Taverner's broke the silence.

'The level of the Records,' it said, and I guessed what Taverner meant to do; no brain but his could have hit upon the extraordinary scheme of tracing the manuscript by examining the subconscious mind of the human race. Taverner, in common with his fellow psychologists, held that every thought and every act have their images stored in the person's subconscious mind, but he also held that records of them are stored in the mind of Nature; and it was these records that he was seeking to read.

Broken fragments of sentences, figures, and names, fell from the lips of the unconscious man, and then he got his focus and steadied to his work.

'*Il cinquecento, Firenze, Italia, Pierro della Costa,*'[8] came a deep level voice; then followed a long-drawn-out vibrating sound halfway between a telephone bell and the note of a 'cello, and the voice changed.

'Two forty-five, November the fourteenth, 1898, London, England.'

For a time there was silence, but almost immediately Taverner's voice cut across it.

'I want Pierro della Costa, who was reborn November the fourteenth, 1898, at two-forty-five a.m.'

Silence. And then Taverner's voice again calling as if over a telephone: 'Hullo! Hullo! Hullo!' Apparently he received an answer, for his tone changed. 'Yes; it is the Senior of Seven who is speaking.'

Then his voice took on an extraordinary majesty and command.

'Brother, where is the ritual that was entrusted to thy care?'

What answer was given I could not divine; but after a pause Taverner's voice came again. 'Brother, redeem thy crime and return the ritual whence it was taken.' Then he rolled over on to his side, and the trance condition passed into natural sleep, and so to an awakening.

Dazed and shivering, he recovered consciousness, and I gave him hot coffee from a Thermos flask, such as we always kept handy

---

8 'The fifteenth century, Florence, Italy, Peter della Costa.'

for these midnight meals. I recounted to him what had passed, and he nodded his satisfaction between sips of the steaming liquid.

'I wonder how Pierro della Costa will effect his task,' he said. 'The present day personality will probably not have the faintest idea as to what is required of it, and will be blindly urged forward by the subconscious.'

'How will it locate the manuscript?' I inquired. 'Why should he succeed where you failed?'

'I failed because I could not at any point establish contact with the manuscript. I was not on earth at the time it was stolen, and I could not trace it in the racial memories for the same reason. One must have a jumping-off place, you know. Occult work is not performed by merely waving a wand.'

'How will the present day Pierro go to work?' I inquired.

'The present day Pierro won't do anything,' said Taverner, 'because he does not know how, but his subconscious mind is that of the trained occultist, and under the stimulus I have given it, will perform its work; it will probably go back to the time when the manuscript was handed over to the Medici, and then trace its subsequent history by means of the racial memories—the subconscious memory of Nature.'

'And how will he go to work to recover it?'

'As soon as the subconscious has located its quarry, it will send an impulse through into the conscious mind, bidding it take the body upon the quest, and a very puzzled modern young man may find himself in a difficult situation.'

'How will he know what to do with the manuscript when he has found it?'

'Once an Initiate, always an Initiate. In all moments of difficulty and danger the Initiate turns to his Master. Something in that boy's soul will reach out to make contact, and he will be brought back to his own Fraternity. Sooner or later he will come across one of the Brethren, who will know what to do with him.'

I was thankful enough to lie down on the sofa and get a couple of hours' sleep, until such time as the charwoman should disturb me; but Taverner, upon whom 'going subconscious' always seemed to have the effect of a tonic, announced his intention of seeing the sun rise from London Bridge, and left me to my own devices.

He returned in time to take me out to breakfast, and I discovered that he had given instructions for every morning paper and each successive edition of the evening ones to be sent in to us. All day long the stream of printed matter poured in, and had to be gone over, for Taverner was on the lookout for Pierro della Costa's effort to recover the ritual.

'His first attempt upon it is certain to be some blind lunatic outburst,' said Taverner, 'and it will probably land him in the hands of the police, whence it will be our duty as good Brethren, to rescue him; but it will have served its purpose, for he will, as it were, have "pointed" the manuscript after the fashion of a sporting dog.'

Next morning our vigilance was rewarded. An unusual case of attempted burglary was reported from St. John's Wood. A young bank clerk of hitherto exemplary character, had effected an entry into the house of a Mr. Joseph Coates by the simple expedient of climbing on to the dining room window-sill from the area steps, and, in full view of the entire street, kicking the glass out of the window. Mr. Coates, aroused by the din, came down armed with a stick, which, however, was not required, the would-be burglar (who could give no explanation of his conduct) meekly waiting to be taken to the police station by the policeman whom the commotion he made had also attracted to the spot.

Taverner immediately telephoned to find out what time the case would be coming on at the police court, and we forthwith set out upon our quest. We sat in the enclosure reserved for the general public while various cases of wife beaters and disorderly drunkards were disposed of, and I watched my neighbours.

Not far from us a girl of a different type from the rest of the sordid audience was seated; her pale oval face seemed to belong to another race from the irregular Cockney features about her. She looked like some mediaeval saint from an Italian fresco, and it only needed the stiff brocaded robes to complete the resemblance.

"'Look for the woman,'" said Taverner's voice in my ear. 'Now we know why Pierro della Costa fell to a bribe.'

The usual riff-raff having been dealt with, a prisoner of a different type was placed in the dock. A young fellow, refined, highly strung, looked round him in bewilderment at his unaccustomed surroundings, and then, catching sight of the olive-cheeked madonna in the gallery, took heart of grace.

He answered the magistrate's questions collectedly enough, giving his name as Peter Robson, and his profession as clerk. He listened attentively to the evidence of the policeman who had arrested him, and to Mr. Joseph Coates, and when asked for his explanation, said he had none to give. In answer to questions, he declared that he had never been in that part of London before; he had no motive for going there, and he did not know why he had attempted to enter the window.

The magistrate, who at first had seemed disposed to deal leniently with the case, appeared to think that this persistent refusal of all explanation must conceal some motive, and proceeded to press the prisoner somewhat sharply. It looked as if matters were going hard with him, when Taverner, who had been scribbling on the back of a visiting card, beckoned an usher and sent the message up to the magistrate. I saw him read it, and turn the card over. Taverner's degrees and the Harley Street address were enough for him.

'I understand,' said he to the prisoner, 'that you have a friend here who can offer an explanation of the affair, and is prepared to go surety for you.'

The prisoner's face was a study; he looked round, seeking some familiar faces, and when Taverner, well-dressed and of imposing appearance, entered the witness box, his perplexity was comical; and then, through all his bewilderment, a flash of light suddenly shot into the boy's eyes. Some gleam from the subconscious reached him, and he shut his mouth and awaited events.

My colleague, giving his name as John Richard Taverner, doctor of medicine, philosophy and science, master of arts and bachelor at law, said that he was a distant relation of the prisoner who was subject to that peculiar malady known as double personality. He was satisfied that this condition was quite sufficient to account for the attempt at burglary, some freak of the boy's other self having led to the crime.

Yes, Taverner was quite prepared to go surety for the boy, and the magistrate, evidently relieved at the turn affairs had taken, forthwith bound the prisoner over to come up for judgement if called upon, and within ten minutes of Taverner's entry upon the scene we were standing on the steps of the court, where the Florentine madonna joined us.

'I don't know who you are, sir,' the boy was saying, 'nor why you should help me, but I am very grateful to you. May I introduce my *fiancée*, Miss Fenner? She would like to thank you, too.'

Taverner shook hands with the girl.

'I don't suppose you two have eaten much breakfast with this affair hanging over your heads,' he said. They admitted that they had not.

'Then,' said he, 'you must be my guests for an early lunch.'

We all packed into a taxi, and drove to the restaurant where the metaphysical head waiter held sway. Here Peter Robson immediately tackled Taverner.

'Look here, sir,' he said, 'I am exceedingly grateful to you for what you have done for me, but I should very much like to know why you did it.'

'Do you ever weave daydreams?' inquired Taverner irrelevantly. Robson stared at him in perplexity, but the girl at his side suddenly exclaimed:

'I know what you mean. Do you remember, Peter, the stories we used to make up when we were children? How we belonged to a secret society that had its headquarters in the woodshed, and had only to make a certain sign and people would know we were members and be afraid of us? I remember once, when we had been locked in the scullery because we were naughty, you said that if you made this sign, the policeman would come in and tell your father he had got to let us out, because we belonged to a powerful Brotherhood that did not allow its members to be locked in sculleries. That is exactly what has happened; it is your daydream come true. But what is the meaning of it all?'

'Ah, what, indeed?' said Taverner. Then turning to the boy: 'Do you dream much?' he asked.

'Not as a rule,' he replied, 'but I had a most curious dream the night before last, which I can only regard as prophetic in light of subsequent events. I dreamt that someone was accusing me of a crime, and I woke up in a dreadful way about it.'

'Dreams are curious things,' said Taverner, 'both day dreams and night dreams. I don't know which are the stranger. Do you believe in the immortality of the soul, Mr. Robson?'

'Of course, I do.'

'Then has it ever struck you the eternal life must stretch both ways?'

'You mean,' said Robson under his breath, 'that it wasn't all imagination. It might be—memory?'

'Other people have had the same dream,' said Taverner, 'myself among them.' Then he leant across the narrow table and stared into the lad's eyes.

'Supposing I told you that just such an organization as you imagined exists; that if, as a boy even, you had gone out into the main street and made that Sign, someone would have been almost certain to answer it?

'Supposing I told you that the impulse which made you break that window was not a blind instinct, but an attempt to carry out an order from your Fraternity, would you believe me?'

'I think I should,' said the lad opposite him. 'At any rate, if it isn't true, I wish it were, for it appeals to me more than anything I have ever heard.'

'If you care to go deeper into the matter,' said Taverner, 'will you come this evening to my place in Harley Street, and then we can talk the matter over?'

Robson accepted with eagerness. What man would refuse to follow his daydreams when they began to materialize?

After we had parted from our new acquaintance, we took a taxi to St. John's Wood and stopped at a house whose front ground floor window was in process of being reglazed. Taverner sent in his card, and we were ushered into a room decorated with large bronze Buddhas, statuettes from Egyptian tombs, and pictures by Watts. In a few minutes Mr. Coates appeared.

'Ah, Dr. Taverner,' he said, 'I presume you have come about the extraordinary matter of your young relative who broke into my house last evening?'

'That is so, Mr. Coates,' replied my companion. 'I have come to offer you my sincere apologies on behalf of the family.'

'Don't mention it,' said our host, 'the poor lad was suffering from mental trouble, I take it?'

'A passing mania,' said Taverner, brushing it away with a wave of his hand. He glanced round the room. 'I see by your books that you are interested in a hobby of my own, the ancient mystery religions. I think I may claim to be something of an Egyptologist.'

Coates rose to the bait at once.

'I came across the most extraordinary document the other day,' said our new acquaintance. 'I should like to show it to you. I think you would be interested.'

He drew from his pocket a bunch of keys, and inserted one in the lock of a drawer in a bureau. To his astonishment the key pushed loosely through the hole, and he pulled the drawer open only to find that the lock had been forced off. He ran his hand to the back of the drawer, and withdrew it empty! Coates looked from Taverner to myself and back again in astonishment.

'That manuscript was there when I went to the police court this morning,' he said. 'What is the meaning of this extraordinary business? First of all a man breaks into my house and makes no attempt to steal anything, and then someone else breaks in and, neglecting many objects of value, takes a thing that can be of no interest to anyone but myself.'

'Then the manuscript which has been stolen is of no particular value?' said Taverner.

'I gave half-a-crown for it,' replied Coates.

'Then you should be thankful to have got off so light,' said Taverner.

'This is the devil, Rhodes,' he went on, as we re-entered the waiting taxi. 'Someone from a Chelsea Black Lodge, knowing Coates would be at the police court this morning, has taken that manuscript.'

'What is to be the next move?' I inquired.

'Get hold of Robson; we can only work through him.'

I asked him how he intended to deal with the situation that had arisen.

'Are you going to send Robson after the manuscript again?' I inquired.

'I shall have to,' said Taverner.

'I do not think there is the makings of a successful buccaneer in Robson.'

'Neither do I,' agreed Taverner; 'we shall have to fall back on Pierro della Costa.'

Robson met us at Harley Street, and Taverner took him out to dinner.

After dinner we returned to the consulting room, where Taverner handed round cigars, and set himself to be an agreeable host, a task in which he succeeded to perfection, for he was one of the most interesting talkers I have ever met.

Presently the talk led round to Italy during the Renaissance, and the great days of Florence and the Medici; and then he began to tell the story of one, Pierro della Costa, who had been a student of the occult arts in those days, and had brewed love philtres for the ladies of the Florentine court. He told the story with considerable vividness, and in great detail, and I was surprised to see that the attention of the lad was wandering, and that he was apparently pursuing a train of thought of his own, oblivious of his surroundings. Then I realized that he was sliding off into that trance condition with which my experience of my colleague had made me familiar.

Still Taverner talked on, telling the history of the old Florentine to the unconscious boy—how he rose to be custodian of the archives, was offered a bribe, and betrayed his trust in order that he might buy the favour of the Woman he loved. Then, as he came to the end of the story, his voice changed, and he addressed the unconscious lad by name.

'Pierro della Costa,' he said, 'why did you do it?'

'Because I was tempted,' came the answer, but not in the voice in which the boy had talked to us, it was a man's voice calm, deep, and dignified, vibrating with emotion.

'Do you regret it?' asked Taverner.

'I do,' returned the voice that was not the boy's voice. 'I have asked of the Great Ones that I may be permitted to restore that which I stole.'

'Thy request is granted,' said Taverner. 'Do that which thou hast to do, and the blessing of the Great Ones be upon thee.'

Slowly the boy rolled over and sat up, but I saw at a glance that it was not the same individual who confronted us; a man, mature, of strong character and determined purpose, looked out of the boy's blue eyes.

'I go,' he said, 'to restore that which I took. Give me the means.'

We went round, he and Taverner and I, to the garage, and got out the car. 'Which way do you want to go?' asked my colleague. The lad pointed to the south-west, and Taverner turned the car in the direction of the Marble Arch. Piloted by the man who was not Robson, we went south down Park Lane, and finally came out in the tangle of mean streets behind Victoria Station; thence we turned east. We pulled up behind the Tate Gallery, and the boy got out.

'From here,' he said, 'I go on alone,' and he disappeared down a side street.

Although we waited for a matter of half-an-hour, Taverner did not stop the engine. 'We may want to get out of here quick,' he said. Then, just as I was beginning to wonder if we were going to spend the night in the open, we heard running footsteps coming down the street, and Robson leapt into the car. That Taverner's precaution in not stopping the engine was justified was proved by the fact that close upon Robson's heels other footsteps sounded.

'Quick, Rhodes,' cried Taverner. 'Hang the rug over the back.' I did as I was bid, and succeeded in obscuring the number plate, and as the first of our pursuers rounded the corner, the big car leapt into its stride, and we drew clear.

No one spoke on the journey to Hindhead.

We entered the sleeping house as quietly as might be, and as Taverner turned on the office lights, I saw that Robson carried a curious looking volume bound in vellum. We did not tarry in the office, however, for Taverner led us through the sleeping house to a door which I knew led down to the cellar stairs.

'Come too, Rhodes,' said Taverner. 'You have seen the beginning of this matter, and you shall see the end, for you have shared in the risk, and although you are not one of Us, I know that I can rely on your discretion.'

We passed down the spiral stone stairs and along a flagged passage. Taverner unlocked a door, and admitted us to a wine cellar. He crossed this, and unlocked a further door. A dim point of flame illumined the darkness ahead of us, swaying uneasily in the draught. Taverner turned on a light, and to my intense surprise I found myself in a chapel. High carved stalls were built into the walls on three sides, and on the fourth was an altar. The flickering light I had seen in the darkness came from the floating wick of a lamp hung above our heads as the centre point of a great Symbol.

Taverner lit the incense in a bronze thurible, and set it swinging. He handed Robson the black robe of an Inquisitor, and he himself assumed another one; then these two cowled figures faced one another across the floor of the empty chapel. Taverner began what was evidently a prayer. I could not gather its substance, for I am unable to follow spoken Latin. Then came a Litany of question and response, Robson, the London clerk, answering in the deep resonant voice of a man accustomed to intone across great buildings. Then he rose to his feet, and with the stately steps of a processional advanced to the altar, and laid thereon the ragged and mildewed manuscript he held in his hands. He knelt, and what absolution the sombre figure that stood over him pronounced, I cannot tell, but he rose to his feet like a man from whose shoulders a great burden has been rolled.

Then for the first time, Taverner spoke in his native tongue. 'In all moments of difficulty and danger'—the booming of his deep voice filled the room with echoes—'make this Sign.' And I knew that the man who had betrayed his trust had made good and been received back into his old Fraternity.

We returned to the upper world, and the man who was not Robson bade us farewell. 'It is necessary that I should go,' he said.

'It is indeed,' said Taverner. 'You had better be out of England till this matter has blown over. Rhodes, will you undertake to drive him down to Southampton? I have other work to do.'

As we dropped down the long slope that leads to Liphook, I studied the man at my side. By some strange alchemy Taverner had woken the long dead soul of Pierro della Costa and imposed it upon the present day personality of Peter Robson. Power radiated from him as light from a lamp; even the features seemed changed. Deep lines about the corners of the mouth lent a firmness to the hitherto indefinite chin, and the light blue eyes, now sunken in the head, had taken on the glitter of steel and were as steady as those of a swordsman.

It was just after six in the morning when we crossed the floating bridge into Southampton. The place was already astir, for, a dock town never sleeps, and we inquired our way to the little-known inn where Taverner had directed us to go for breakfast. We discovered it to be an unpretentious public house near the dock gates, and the potman was just drawing the bright curtains of turkey twill as we entered.

It was evident that strangers were not very welcome in the little tavern, and no one offered to take our order. As we stood there irresolute, heavy footsteps thundered down creaking wooden stairs, and a strongly built man wearing the four lines of gold braid denoting the rank of Captain entered the bar parlour. He glanced at us as he came in, and indeed we were sufficiently incongruous to be notable in such a place.

His eyes attracted my attention; he had the keen, outlooking gaze so characteristic of a seaman, but in addition to this he had a curious trick of looking at one without appearing to see one; the focus of the eyes met about a yard behind one's back. It was a thing I had often seen Taverner do when he wished to see the colours of an aura, that curious emanation which, for those who can see it, radiates from every living thing and is so clear an indication of the condition within.

Grey eyes looked into blue as the newcomer took in my companion, and then an almost imperceptible sign passed between them, and the sailor joined us.

'I believe you know my mother,' he remarked by way of introduction. Robson admitted the acquaintanceship, though I am prepared to swear he had never seen the man before and we all three adjourned to an inner room for breakfast, which appeared in response to the bellowed orders of our new acquaintance.

Without any preamble he inquired our business, and Robson was equally ready to communicate it.

'I want to get out of the country as quietly as possible,' he said. Our new friend seemed to think that it was quite in the ordinary course of events that a man without luggage should be departing in this manner.

'I am sailing at nine this morning, going down the Gold Coast as far as Loango. We aren't exactly the Cunard, but if you care to come you will be welcome. You can't wear that rig, however; you would only draw a crowd, which I take is what you don't want to do.'

He put his head through a half-door which separated the parlour from the back premises, and in response to his vociferations a little fat man with white chin whiskers appeared. A consultation took place between the two, the newcomer being equally ready to lend his assistance. Very shortly a suit of cheap serge reach-me-downs and a peaked cap were forthcoming, these being, the sailor assured us, the correct costume for a steward, in which capacity it was designed that Peter Robson should go to sea.

Leaving the inn that the mysterious Fellowship had made so hospitable to us, we took our way to the docks, and passing through the wilderness of railway lines, cranes, and yawning gulfs that constitute their scenery, we arrived at our companion's ship, a rusty-side tramp, her upper works painted a dirty white.

We accompanied her captain to his cabin, a striking contrast to the raffle outside: a solid desk bearing a student's shaded lamp, a copy of Albrecht Durer's study of the *Praying Hands*, a considerable shelf of books, and, perceptible beneath the all-pervading odour of strong tobacco, the faint spicy smell that clings to a place where incense is regularly burnt. I studied the titles of the books, for they tell one more of a man than anything else; *Isis Unveiled* stood cheek by jowl with *Creative Evolution* and two fat tomes of Eliphas Levi's *History of Magic*.

On the drive back to Hindhead I thought much of the strange side of life with which I had come in contact.

Yet another example was afforded me of the widespread ramifications of the Society. At Taverner's request I looked up the sea captain on his return from the voyage and asked him for news of Robson. This he was unable to give me, however; he had put the lad ashore at some mudhole on the West Coast. Standing on the quay stewing in the sunshine he had made the Sign. A half-caste Portuguese had touched him on the shoulder, and the two had vanished in the crowd. I expressed some anxiety as to the fate of an inexperienced lad in a strange land.

'You needn't worry,' said the sailor. 'That Sign would take him right across Africa and back again.'

When I was talking the matter over with Taverner, I said to him: 'What made you and the captain claim relationship with Robson? It seemed to me a perfectly gratuitous lie.'

'It was no lie, but the truth,' said Taverner. 'Who is my Mother, and who are my Brethren but the Lodge and the initiates thereof?'

ABOUT THE AUTHOR

PHOTO BY RACHEL NAGENGAST

JUDIKA ILLES is a leading authority on magic, mysticism, and the occult as well as a lover of mysteries and detective stories. She is the editor of *The Weiser Book of the Fantastic and Forgotten* and the author of numerous books devoted to the magical arts including *Encyclopedia of 5000 Spells, Encyclopedia of Witchcraft,* and *Encyclopedia of Spirits*. Judika lectures and leads workshops throughout the United States and internationally. Visit her at *www.judikailles.com*.

TO OUR READERS

Weiser Books, an imprint of Red Wheel/Weiser, publishes books across the entire spectrum of occult, esoteric, speculative, and New Age subjects. Our mission is to publish quality books that will make a difference in people's lives without advocating any one particular path or field of study. We value the integrity, originality, and depth of knowledge of our authors.

Our readers are our most important resource, and we appreciate your input, suggestions, and ideas about what you would like to see published.

Visit our website at *www.redwheelweiser.com* to learn about our upcoming books and free downloads, and be sure to go to *www.redwheelweiser.com/newsletter* to sign up for newsletters and exclusive offers.

You can also contact us at *info@rwwbooks.com* or at

Red Wheel/Weiser, LLC
65 Parker Street, Suite 7
Newburyport, MA 01950